AZULUS ASCENDS

Lunas Ra

© 2020 by Lunas Ra. All rights reserved.

The characters and events portrayed in this book are fictitious. Any similarity to real persons, living or dead, is coincidental and not intended by the author.

No part of this book may be reproduced, or stored in a retrieval system, or transmitted in any form or by any means, electronic, mechanical, photocopying, recording, or otherwise, without express written permission of the publisher/author.

The publisher/author strictly forbids any portion of this work to be used in any AI (artificial intelligence) software for any reason.

ISBN-13: 978-0-9809548-6-9

DEDICATION

To the beautiful Terrans of Earth,
and to all who made this work possible.

CONTENT

1	Fray	Pg #1
2	Assassins	Pg #20
3	Overload	Pg #74
4	Rapture	Pg #92
5	Disgrace	Pg #153
6	Fallen	Pg #163
7	Masterclass	Pg #181
8	Mules	Pg #194
9	Flashpoint	Pg #222
10	Admiral	Pg #256
11	Teamwork	Pg #307
12	Visitor	Pg #346
13	Resolutions	Pg #356
14	Vengeance	Pg #369
15	Transition	Pg #397
16	Bloodshed	Pg #407
17	Azulus	Pg #441
18	Aftermath	Pg #478

1

Fray

The sun blasted dirty orange rays through the tree cover as Kole and five other Syndicators quietly sneaked into the mountain estate situated among the wild terrain of the now deformed Canadian Rockies. The square-based, sharp angular design of the estate's main mansion building they were approaching, worked its way around the mountain terrain, creating an unnatural imbalance on the side of the mountain range.

The mansion's walls were cut from gorgeous white limestone, and windows spanned from the ground to the roofline. However, you could only see the beauty of the architecture after passing the holographic camouflage emitters and thick bushes all around. Giant oak trees provided the final cover, shielding the estate from prying eyes and satellites. The mansion's view was facing south, and it overlooked a stunning natural valley full of purples, greens, and yellows. A grand waterfall nearby majestically dropped itself down a mighty slope and continued into the river below. Kole had a mental snapshot of the scene, although he could see little from his position in thick bush cover.

If only Jonas was here. Kole thought to himself. His best friend was re-assigned to guard a bigwig and wasn't able to join in this mission. Perhaps it was for the better. Kole would have to take a keen look after the mission, as he rarely had a chance to experience such raw natural beauty. A luxury dwelling like this estate was typically a highly forbidden pleasure.

Only very special kinds of humans managed to get this far after Letumfall, the event that sparked the near annihilation of humanity. Kole's team continued their stealthy approach, finally breaching the inner perimeter from different angles. The full-body camouflage armour helped, but no branch could be disturbed, or the mission would go to hell in seconds. Even their helmets were sound-isolated so they could communicate silently. Aside from the water, noises from some unknown insects, and the wind brushing by the leaves, all else was dead quiet. In his head, Kole kept going back to the combat analysis of their planned attack.

A probability of seventy-nine percent to put Kelvin out of his misery without major casualties. Regardless of the positive odds, they could still all die. Nobody wanted to take this mission. At least Kole knew that much. The target was a fossil of the old society, and he was tagged as Crazy Hound Dangerous level, which was one of the highest ranked difficulty kill levels. His name was Kelvin Klonnus. The secret orders to mop the estate floor with his blood came down the chain of command eight days ago. Kole saw the photos before the mission. The man was intimidating, to say the least. Kelvin was a big-framed older man of retirement age, with very bulky arms and legs, and long dirty blond hair. He stood over six feet tall and was military for sure. That's all they were provided with in terms of info. Everything else was classified. Kole didn't know what exactly Kelvin did to piss off the Overseers and didn't care. But at least he knew one thing. Fossils didn't belong in the new world.

Kelvin was a hard man to find even before his execution order. Kole heard from a commander that the man would vanish into the most radioactive danger zones for months at a time and was often impossible to locate. Since his execution order was secret, Kelvin would never know what hit him. At least that was the idea. In a few minutes, this would all be over. Unknown to Kole and his team however, an old raven sat high above on a mighty oak tree branch. It was not fooled by anything. It knew the forest. It was wise. And it watched the team carefully with intense attention.

"What's he doing? He seems to be just sitting there watching some holo-tele! I don't like this already... don't tell me he has no clue that we're coming!" chimed in Ranger Pete in his Texan accent on the comm channel. Pete then quietly armed his Neutralizer rifle and checked his magazines. With his big bald head, heavy dark eyebrows, and bulky body-builder muscles, Pete could move his two-hundred-pound frame around like a gymnast on a good day. He used to teach some of the most dangerous soldiers on the planet. Now, at sixty-seven years of age, he was still in top shape.

"He doesn't know...and even if he did somehow, the mission is still a go! This is one of the best chances we'll ever get to hunt this rat down." said Illon, the group's lead commander. He was paired up with Kole, and they were coming downhill from the North towards the back door entrance.

Illon didn't have much patience for anything outside of direct orders. His clever green eyes were busy scanning every angle of their approach. One could not see the scars beneath Illon's helmet which were all over his pale Japanese face, but Kole knew his commander suffered greatly in the past.

"I don't like it either... where are all his guards? I know intelligence said he's a recluse, but he's a sitting a duck like this..." added Kelly. She was paired up with Phobos, who was his typical silent self. Kelly was young and extremely talented. The brains of the group, and in line to be the next commander. She was short, slim, and gorgeous out of uniform. Her caramel skin, blonde hair, and amazing smile were always a great sight to see. At the base she was like a sister to many. Although, nobody knew who her lover was or if she even indulged in such things.

Kole stayed quiet. He needed to focus. He armed his Neutralizer rifle and the rifle's battery silently activated the high output micro coil magazine with eighty bolt rounds. It was a beautiful weapon, a powerful weapon. A double-barrel railgun design with a high firing rate. It was also extremely accurate due to its super low recoil. It offered enough firepower to shoot rounds right through most armoured targets, and this fact gave Kole comfort like nothing else in the world could.

"Ok, that's enough, let's cut the chatter and kill this bastard before he goes to take a shit!" stated Kassidy with passion. He was the second commander. "I hate killing a man while he's taking a shit on the toilet." He was crude, rude, and over the top.

Kassidy's African American genes gave him a large muscular build. On top of that he spent nearly all his non-combat time pumping iron at the gym. He was paired up with Pete, who was nearly as big. Command thought it necessary, although highly unusual. Two commanders on a team of just six Syndicators.

4

Kole knew the exact reason. A second commander was a must just in case things went south. They also had a Synthetic with them, officially named Phobos Unit 44. He could do things most soldiers would cringe at without a second thought. Ranger Pete, Illon Izaumashi, Kelly Osbina, Kassidy Chapers, Kole Cor, and Phobos Unit 44 all took their final approach vectors.

"Everyone in position?" Illon was itching to get this over with. The group checked in.

"GO! GO! GO!" ordered Illon. The team moved in unison at the speed of an accelerating sprinter, from three points in groups of two they converged on the mansion's main entry points. Kole and Illon were moving in from the back through the pool area. Kassidy and Ranger Pete were taking the left though the flower gardens. Kelly and Phobos were taking the right path through a recreation area which connected with an outdoor gym. Each group had a single-use sticky directional grenade launcher. Illon fired his first, followed by Kelly, and Ranger Pete on their entrance points.

The charges synched up before going off. Then, with powerful simultaneous detonations, the three doors blew open with massive inward blasts. The echoes resonated through the mountains and birds flew skywards with screams of disapproval. Kole charged down the pool area, then turned into the hall that led towards the living room at a speed that made the walls and decorations become blurs. Illon followed him closely. In a split instant, within two meters of reaching the living room, a red warning blinked on Kole's visor. His reaction was near instantaneous as Kole jolted his head right towards a large painting. A large red bolt materialized from within the wall, and the blast grazed his armoured helmet on his left, melting right through it. The heat was instant and painful. Kelvin was clearly armed with advanced armour-piercing rounds.

Kole had too much momentum to stop so he fell forward and rolled into the living room firing. Kelvin moved extremely fast, masterfully dodging Kole's shots and covering all three directions with a single weapon which even kept Illon at bay, as he was forced to duck for cover and retreat. Phobos took two shots in the chest which sent him flying backwards, and Kelly was forced to fall back too. Kassidy and Pete changed course and bolted to flank instead, away from the living room and towards the main entrance.

Kole was left to his own devices for that second and was the only one with a clear shot. He fired off a few more rounds, clipping Kelvin on his left arm and right leg.

Kelvin shrieked in pain but didn't waste any time and sent another shot at Kole. The shot grazed Kole just above the right ankle while he was trying to roll into the opposite direction, going back towards the hallway he came crashing in from. The shot sent a severe jolt of pain up his spine and to the brain. Grinding his teeth, Kole adjusted his aim for another shot. But before he could fire, Kelvin ran right through the wall behind him. It just crumbled as he went through.

"Fake wall! Target escaping!" Kole yelled at the top of his lungs. Phobos recovered from being a target practice doll, and with two holes in his chest blasted at breakneck speed out the hallway window, smashing through it with ease.

Without warning, Illon bolted after Kelvin through the newly created opening in the wall. With Kassidy & Ranger Pete on the other side somewhere, they had to make sure the target could not escape. Kole sprang up to follow him, but was stopped dead in his tracks. It was instant. Hundreds of needle-like rods injected themselves into Illon, impaling him from head to toe as he tried to get through the opening. It was so sudden that Illon didn't even make a sound. He couldn't.

A high voltage electrical blast followed and Illon's body was terrorized with a few thousand volts of electrical current. The trap was designed for Synthetics and relic androids. It was complete overkill for humans.

Kole had to shake the shock in a split second and forced himself to trace Phobos through the window. There was not a second to spare. At the same time, Kelly emerged from cover and followed Kole.

"You hurt?" she asked in a concerned tone.

"All good, let's go!" replied Kole.

Kole then sprinted, and finally sighted the target. Kelvin was making distance fast. Kole aimed and sent the rounds flying as Kelvin was sprinting forward towards the front gate, where there was most likely a cloaked escape vehicle. Kelvin instantly twisted himself downwards into a roll, avoiding Kole's fire while staying on the ground forcing Kole and Kelly to scatter as multiple deadly blasts came in their direction as Kelvin return fire.

Kole then spotted Phobos a few meters away on the ground with his head blown off next to a broken flowerpot, right where Kole was trying to find cover. Kole had hoped that Phobos would have made the killing blow by now. He thought wrong. At least he managed to slow Kelvin down a little, otherwise he might have been already at the front gate. Kole's mind raced. *If Phobos is down, then Kelvin is a combat grade Synthetic too!*

But Kole paid for that thought as his armour took two direct hits on the right upper chest. Then came the scorching burn as his armour melted away like hot butter and the bullets passed through tissue and bone. Kole's armoured suit reacted instantly to Kole's self-imposed pain threshold, and injected painkillers.

Kole's vision buzzed and he dropped to one knee, still trying to aim at Kelvin. Kelly returned fired through the large plant vases with a massive volley of bolt rounds. Before Kole could voice a graceful profanity, the ground shook, and a huge thunderous sound boomed as if the whole mountain cracked into two.

An explosive blue wave emerged from underneath Kelvin, sending him upwards into the air. The blast instantly killed Kole's sensors and shattered the front glass of the mansion into thousands of pieces. Wind and debris rocketed past Kole, and the open hole in his helmet filled with dirt before he could even raise his hand. But Kelvin was now moving in a predictable arc, which he could not escape from in mid-air.

A second explosive round sent Kelvin's body parts all over the front gate. *Shock shells!* The special shock shell ammo was not to be used indoors; it could kill them all just as easily as the target. Even then this blast was closer than their training and safety regulations allowed for. The feeling of victory was very short.

Ranger Pete appeared from the other side of the mansion and ran towards Kole and Kelly yelling something. Kole could not hear a word he was saying. He tried to get up from his knee but could not muster it. Pete ran past Kole as Kole's primary sensors came back online and the score was quickly settled.

[Mission Data:]
- Illon Izaru: KIA.
- Kassidy Chapers: KIA.
- Kelly Osbina: Critical limb damage.
- Kole Cor: Critical chest damage.
- Ranger Pete Fabius: Sprained ankle.
- Phobos: No longer functioning, send unit for repair.
- Dropship status: ETA 35 seconds.
[End.]

"What happened to Kassidy!?" Kole managed.

"He rushed in too fast and took a shot right in the head!" yelled Pete. "But at least I got the opening when Kelvin's attention shifted to you and Kelly. What a mess! What a mess!"

Shit, Kelly! Kole looked behind him and only then realized Kelly's left leg was missing three inches around the shin. Only a few muscles were left connecting the foot to the rest of the it. Blood was all over the ground along with pieces of bone. Kelly's suit injected so much painkiller fluid that she passed out. Pete was kneeling by her trying to salvage what was left of her leg.

The long seconds passed, and finally the dropship descended on top of them like a giant bird of prey. Two medical Synthetics jumped out and immediately scooped Kelly up along with her limb. Pete picked up and carried Kole, as he was now barely conscious. As the dropship quickly shot up into the air, a second dropship swooped in right behind them with the clean-up crew. They would pick up the dead bodies and clean up the site. And no doubt, prepare the mansion for a new owner.

Kole watched quietly as Pete dropped his gear and was acting as a medic, trying to treat his chest while two Synthetics cleaned

Kelly's wound and applied a thick clear gel that fizzed furiously on Kelly's leg. The gel transformed into white foam and covered the leg. It would then solidify and recreate the channels of her veins and missing tissue. That would take some time.

"Damn that fool Kassidy! He just rushed out... what was he thinking!" Pete was furious but his tone was quiet as he applied a similar gel used on Kelly to Kole's chest. "Such perfect aim..." said Pete as he then went to the medics and got a spare bullet removal device. He then proceeded to remove two from Kole's back. The rounds were easily taken out as they basically jammed themselves into the back armour plating and were sticking out. Luckily these rounds were armour penetrator rounds, and not anti-personal rounds which explode shards all over the insides of one's body. Kole coughed out blood. Pete applied gel on the backside area and sat him up straight.

"Hey, do me a favour Pete. Take a photo will ya..." mumbled Kole, he was getting sleepy. "Try a selfie you old fool..." Pete slapped him in the face, hard. Kole felt his whole head jolt with a sharp sensation of good old pain. It was only now that he realized that his helmet was already removed.

"Wake up dammit! You're not going dark on my watch!" cried out Pete in a hoarse tone. A few more minutes passed. Pete finished up with his patching on Kole and saddled himself across. There was little else they would be able to do here. Kelly was still under careful watch of the medics, but they finished their main job of stabilizing her life signs. One of them came and checked in on Kole. Pete was a pro so in under a minute the Synthetic was happy with Kole's condition and went back to monitor Kelly.

"Two Syndicators dead... the debriefing is going to be a shit fest..." Pete murmured. One of the Synthetic medics gave Pete a dirty look.

"Oh right, three if we count Phobos... a valuable member of the team... who proved to be the most useless fuck of all fucks..." fired back Pete with attitude. The medic turned away and paid Pete no more attention. This would look bad on their record regardless of how they tallied up the score. But at least Pete did his job. Kole just took fire, missed, and took some more fire and nearly died.

"Kelvin wasn't just some Synthetic, he was more advanced than the one we brought..." Kole tried to make sense of it all. But up top, nothing ever made any sense.

"You know," said Ranger Pete, "with Syndicators dying like this, mission after mission...the board will run out of pawns eventually and bigger pieces will need to be sacrificed..." Pete stared out into the open view from the dropship. "I'm so tired of watching my friends die."

Pete put a hand over his head. Kole sat quietly watching him. Wasn't much to talk about at this point. The engines murmured in a low hum in the background as the dropship took them back to West City Base. There, a medical landing bay was already prepped for Kelly. The dropship landed right in there, and they just rolled her out and got to work.

Pete went to the waiting room while Kole got sent to another medical office. There, he was ushered onto a big circular plate which initiated the armour breakdown mode. The armour was held together by magnetic tension plating and with one command it fell right off. Kole was down to his underpants, but he knew even those would have to come off for a complete check. A female doctor showed up, a Synthetic. All medical personnel

11

on bases were. She had little to no emotions and didn't even speak as she treated Kole. Perhaps to her Synthetic brain he was nothing more than a killing machine. Kole often wondered what it was like to be a Synthetic. How did they really see humans? What did they think of him and other humans who were left in this dying world?

The healing procedures on his damage only took an hour. Replacing human tissue and bone these days was a rather straightforward procedure. However, it was blind luck that the shots didn't hit his vital spots. Kole was dismissed, so he headed back to check on Kelly. Pete nodded a silent hello and then spoke.

"Go home Kole. I will stay and make sure they fix her right." Kole was away from home for nearly a week to prepare for this mission. And as much as he wanted to ensure Kelly was fixed up, he really just wanted to see Kaita. Pete knew him too damn well. The mission was a failure anyway. All they did was blow up a Synthetic version of Kelvin, and it was only because Pete managed to switch ammo at the right moment and utilize the right opportunity. It could have gone even worse, much worse. Another second or two, and Kelvin's fire would have turned Kole and Kelly into Swiss cheese.

"Why do you think Phobos went down?" asked Pete as Kole was about to exit the waiting room. Kole paused. That was a mystery. Phobos was state-of-the-art.

"Let's wait for the mission analysis report." Kole replied. He left the base through the fastest exit and took a train back to the main city complex, where he had an apartment in the downtown district of the city. The train stations were underground and had easy access to building elevators for residents. A text came in on his implant. It was Jonas.

{ Hey Kole! You ok buddy? } News of a failed mission travelled fast.

{ Oh man, it was a mess alright. I got patched up and am heading home now. Blind luck we lived... } replied Kole.

{ Glad you're alright! I gotta start my night shift, this new gig is very interesting...call me when you're all rested up sometime. } Kole was happy to hear from him. It was a nice feeling, to have a close friend you could rage against the world with and unwind to. Opportunities to spend time together seemed all too sparse as of late.

{ Sure thing Jonas. Call you tomorrow. }

Going up in the elevator, Kole fumbled with his dirty white hair. He was nervous. His hands were a little shaky and sweaty. And his mind was a mess. There were lots of foggy places right now in his brain, and it felt like he just could not get his mind to stop thinking even for a second. The feeling of constant thought and the anxiety of it was just draining all of his remaining energy. To think that the Overseers sent them on a death run against a highly advanced Synthetic, who easily took out their team's Synthetic as if it was nothing, was insanity. One thing was very clear. Kelvin's Synthetic was using some higher-level military grade firepower. Not many guns could fire advanced armour piercing rounds with such precision at that range.

The elevator door suddenly opened at floor one-hundred thirty-six. One of resident's cats walked in as he was walking out. Betty's cat, he remembered. The creature had a unique blue colour with golden tipped ears. It was a Synthetic cat of course, and it was heading for a walk down below, by itself. It completely ignored Kole and extended itself upward to hit the lobby button.

Kole let out a sigh and walked towards his apartment door. The door to his apartment opened before he could scan his right palm. The opening revealed his wife, Kaita. She was petite, just five foot two. She was in a silk pink gown that perfectly outlined her small, sexy one-hundred-pound frame. The gown was just long enough to cover her panties, revealing her sexy legs in all of their glory. The gown also graciously revealed the cleavage of her perfectly shaped C-sized breasts. Instead of her usual pig tails hairdo, her gorgeous blond hair was wrapped up in a bun, a sign that she was going to drag him into the shower. Her beautiful blue eyes shined with delight, and her light eye-shadow and pink lipstick gave her face that perfect charm that Kole could not look away from. At least she was happy to see him.

"Oh! How I missed you!" she said with excitement in her voice. Being a Syndicator had its perks, if you lived long enough to enjoy them of course. She embraced him passionately, slipping her tongue right into his mouth for a few seconds before pulling away.

"Oh dear, you smell pretty bad, time for a shower my little bear!" she insisted. Kole knew it, she had planned the shower all along. He was fully cleaned up at the medical facility at the base and was given fresh clothes and would much rather just fall asleep immediately. Before Kole could insist otherwise, she dragged him to their bathing chamber and disrobed him. Then, she took off her gown. Kole's blood flow increased instantly. Her body, as always, was a welcome sight. Once he laid eyes on her, he really didn't care if the whole world burned into the ground. Everything left his mind. The ceiling in the bathing chamber released the hot water, and the walls morphed into a scene from a beautiful beach from a world long gone. It was more surreal than usual, and somehow Kole never got tired of this feature. The floors in this premium set-up were soft, pillowy soft, which allowed for special couple time that otherwise would be impossible with hard tile floors.

Watching a sunset of a beach that no longer existed and enjoying a hot shower as if it was really raining hot water was the current definition of heaven on earth. Kaita grabbed a large washcloth and brushed his body, front and back. He thought that she would ask him about his mission. But she just looked him in the eyes, and as if reading his mind, she lowered herself down to her knees. Her gentle breasts brushed his legs, and it set off tingles in his body. She gently rinsed his now fully aware private member. Gently, she slipped it into her mouth. Her warm tongue wrapped around his manhood like an anaconda that was going to strangle its prey. It was a little rough, but he was now completely at her mercy.

She moved her head back and forth slowly while tightening her grip with her hands on his legs. She looked at him, then back down. Slowly, she took his member all the way down her throat. She kept him there for a few seconds, and then let him slip completely out and catch a break. Then, she proceeded licking the side of his penis, gently with her sexy long tongue. Before Kole knew it, her mouth engulfed him again, this time the deep throat thrusts came with a steady pace.

Kole's legs nearly started shaking, but luckily, things like this didn't take long. A few minutes of this heavenly oral persuasion, and Kole released himself inside her mouth. She kept him in for quite a while, swallowed everything, and gently massaged his tip with her tongue. As he pulled out, she smiled.

"Do me!" she begged him. Kole was still able to keep it hard, somehow. He grabbed the water-resistant pillows from the bench and put them on the floor for added comfort.

"Take me Kole, I'm all yours!" Kaita said passionately, although some of her words were a tad artificial. A tad mechanical. But Kole obliged. "I love you..." he mumbled to himself. It didn't matter what he was feeling at this point. This had to continue.

The water kept flowing, and the artificial scene of the beach and the sun setting was as good as real. Kole positioned himself in a comfortable doggy position. His tip touched the outer walls of her precious, wet entry. He played around for a few seconds, and then slipped in a little. Kaita moaned, right on cue. He pressed in deeper. He felt the warm, gentle insides. Then, he pushed all the way inside her.

Kaita made some initial breathing noises, followed by gentle moans of pleasure. Kole was never too rough with her. He wanted her to feel good, and she seemed to enjoy it. Her hips went back and forth, allowing him to penetrate her deeper. Kole had to really push himself. Part of his mind was blanking out, but he had to keep up with the breathing. Sometimes, sex was more of a workout than he would have liked to admit. As they both sped up, Kole finally released everything he had built up over a week in his second climax. Thick juices flowed out of Kaita as he pulled himself out.

"Wow, a second full load... I kinda of like it when you're away for a while." she said smiling. The shower stopped. Kole was starting to lose consciousness. The physical love part has come to an end. He put one hand down to keep his balance. All he could feel now were the gentle water drops dripping down from his body. Kaita grabbed his hand and helped him up with ease towards the bench. She took care of drying him, and then she helped him to their bed.

The sheets smelled like fresh flowers, and Kole instantly fell asleep. Kaita stood over him, watching him breathing in and out heavily. She wished she was human. Living as a Synthetic, her role was to be the life partner for Kole. They never actually got a real wedding. She was assigned this task when she was manufactured. And she did her job well.

As she stood there, she recollected the society they lived in. Overseers, the genetically advanced and partly robotic humanoids ruled what was left of the humans. It was the Overseers who went to great scientific lengths to create Synthetics to help humans after Letumfall wiped out over ninety-nine percent of the world.

As the Overseers took power, those who didn't agree with them were driven out, to live the life of rats out in the wilderness. They never heard from those people ever again. Most likely, they all died out there. Stories of horrific monsters on the prowl were enough these days to deter anyone from ever leaving the Overseer cities. Furthermore, there was no currency, only membership. As long as you belonged and did your part, then everything was provided. Food, water, shelter, and even entertainment was given out based on how much you contributed to society.

If you wanted new clothes, you just walked into Make-It-Now cubes which littered the malls, and anything you wanted was created for you on the spot. These new fashions were created by clever, creative AI programs. But if you wanted something truly custom made, you had to be in the upper ranks of society.

While both humans and Synthetics were considered of equal rights, there were four tiers in this society: Citizen, Military, Distinct, and Overseer. Kole was Military. When Kaita was made, she became a Citizen. But because she was now Kole's partner, she was granted the same things as he was. She could leave Kole, but her role would simply be re-assigned to something else, and she would be downgraded back to Citizen. Living as a trophy wife was not that bad, and required her to do very little, other than to really just take care of her partner in sexual ways human women simply could not. She kind of liked her job so far. The perks were great. The apartment was nice, she could eat anything she wanted, get any clothing she wanted, and drive most of the vehicles which were available to even the Distinct members. Distinct members were mainly composed of the small scientific community that served the Overseers without question. Kaita was also not required to perform any day jobs like most Citizen members had to do. This gave Kaita the freedom to just enjoy her life and hang out with friends as often as she wished. She used that freedom and volunteered from time to time when Kole was away for days on end.

But there was a catch to this perfect new world the Overseers had created. Humans were completely sterile now, and dead humans were typically replaced in their positions by Synthetics. Having children in any way was illegal for humans for at least the last fifteen years. Only the state could now manufacture new Citizens, or rather new Synthetics.

Kaita took her usual seat in the bedroom, where she watched Kole sleep, and pondered. He seemed so innocent, with his dirty white hair and light caramel skin colour from his Latino roots.

Kole's mom was a plain-Jane American white woman, and his father was from what was once called Mexico. Kole also had modified eyes. They came with the job, and they had an orange tint to them. He was about five six, and very muscular all around. She found him very attractive.

But there were many questions which lingered in her mind. Was her love for him programmed, or at some point had she just caved into it? Did she really have freedom of choice? Was she really a female, or just a machine that was forcefully associated with a sex? A toaster that could make love? No matter how hard she searched her feelings, she never found the answers she was looking for.

2

Assassins

City 77 was a bizarre place, at least by the old human standards. This thriving megapolis was located nearly a thousand miles from the West coast, situated between what used to be Saskatchewan in Canada, and Montana in the United States of America. Those countries disappeared some forty years ago. Letumfall spared no one. Synthetics outnumbered the humans in City 77. Two hundred thousand of them versus the one hundred fifty thousand human residents. In many ways, life was good. At least for those who shared the ideals of the Overseers. But that was the dirty part. The city was originally built to save millions while Letumfall was destroying the world. Money was not an issue as Overseers banned such a frivolous concept. They saw money as one of the key reasons for the downfall of the human race. As a result, the massive structures and tall buildings were mostly empty rooms. Eventually, apartments and offices were retrofitted to be much larger so the current residents could enjoy far more space. Nobody complained.

The rumour mill was in full swing though. Since there was no internet traffic the Overseers could not track, data and rumours had to be passed around in any way to avoid detection, which was extremely difficult and usually involved direct contact. So it was known to only a few, that the Overseers were working on a transition to a Synthetic state. This would take humans completely out of the equation, and the city would be composed of purely Synthetics.

No new humans were allowed to be born for the last fifteen years as the state became more and more draconian. Dead humans were now always replaced with Synthetics. The remaining human population was aging, losing numbers by the week.

Outside the walls of City 77, there were also records of humans here and there in small pockets. They were either exiled or left City 77 to attempt life on their own. Many died off in the wild due to disease, weather, or starvation as they were allowed nothing but primal technology on their way out, something the Overseers seemed proud of. Outsider humans could never go back to the cities for any reason. Not to City 77 or any of the other Overseer cities, of which there were ten in total. Anyone caught within one hundred miles who was an outsider human was detained and sent back to their settlements. If they resisted, they were terminated on the spot. This was the way things.

Kole's apartment was in one of the highest towers with one hundred and seventy-five floors, situated near the central hub of the main downtown core. The only taller tower around here was the main Overseer head-office tower, which fired into the sky with three hundred and ten floors. It was a sight to behold, as these large, sculpted cylindrical monstrosities were designed to withstand nearly any punishment the Earth could dish out.

The sun was well into its early rising, and Kole suddenly felt very awake. His alert status system fired up. It was an emergency. He noticed Kaita slumped in her favourite chair. It was as if she was sleeping, but Kole knew better. She was just choosing to ignore the reality of her situation. He dashed past her and into his gear, already laid out for him in the living room. He then bolted to his living room window where a military shuttle docked to take him. The networks were full of chatter and Kole was trying to make sense of it.

"An attack?" he asked the transport pilot.

"Yep! And a bad one too! You didn't hear the blasts?" asked the pilot.

"Must be the nice insulation!" blamed Kole. He knew damn well it was his human fatigue that got the better of him. Whatever was happening was already going on for a few minutes now.

"Hang on!" said the pilot, as the shuttle broke the city fly-zone speed rules and dove down into the streets at full throttle. Kole felt the awesome power of the engines, as his back was pushed into the seat. The shuttle then veered out from the nosedive and flew right towards the main Overseer head-office tower. The flight only took some thirty seconds. Then, with a quick hiss, they landed and Kole jumped out. A massive number of Syndicators, investigators, and emergency vehicles were already on site.

"Kole!" Ranger Pete waved him down. Kole didn't waste time and ran towards his location near the front doors.

"IDs!" said a serious looking Synthetic guard as they approached the large oval doors. Kole and Pete extended their right palms to be scanned. The Synthetic scanned them, twice.

They then rushed to the elevator, and up they went to the one hundred ninetieth floor. As they stepped out there were armed security guards everywhere, including Syndicators in full combat outfits. They were motioned to an office on the far left. A crime investigation unit was on scene collecting samples.

#190-22

Overseer Hensel Gritah

Head of AI Security

The sign Kole read was on the ground still attached to a door in shambles. Kole and Pete waited patiently for the commander inside to come out.

"Well boys, what a start to the day!" yelled commander Hefman as he stormed out of the unit. He was a large brute and didn't care much for evidence collection. His six-foot posture was daunting, and his dark black skull shined like a well-polished surface. His fierce brown eyes stared at Kole for a second, then at Pete. He was their new commander.

"The attack was made by some dirty Synths." he continued. "Hensel got wasted, bad..." he paused again, giving Kole another look. "Your buddy, uhmm," he coughed a bit, "Jonas, was it? Yea, he was the private guard on shift for Hensel."

Kole's heart sank. He knew Jonas since childhood. A darn good friend who was more like a little brother.

"Orders, sir." said Kole calmly. Kole's feelings overwhelmed him on the inside however, and his blood was boiling. Pete felt his anger, which piled up on top of the previous day. Not a good Monday.

"Well son," grumbled Hefman, "If I had it my way, I would

23

put you into a tank and send you off after the Synths who did this, even though your former commander Illon would haunt me in my sleep for that. But, seeing as you just came out of a combat mission with heavy losses, the higher-ups figured your combat abilities under loss of a friend would very likely get you easily killed. You must be worth something to them it seems..."

"This is bullshit!" replied Kole, breathing heavily. Sweat was forming on his forehead. His nostrils felt moist. His hands felt the moisture too, getting damp and cold. The cold air rushing in through the blown-out window of Hensel's office made it worse. A slight headache chimed in with a bit of a head buzz. He was getting a bit dizzy. The shock of Jonas's death was evident on his system.

"Don't say that!" said Pete quietly to Kole. He then directed his attention to Hefman. "May we at least look around?"

Hefman sighed. "Of course, that's what I called you here for!" He then turned to Kole. "Look, it's for your own good, kid. Unlike what you believe, you're a good asset to have around, from what I've heard. Alive is better, no?"

"There's a Synthetic version of me in a warehouse somewhere ready to go, commander. What's the difference?!" Kole didn't usually snap back at a superior officer, but he could not hold it in this time.

"Whoa there son, hold on! I'm not the bad guy here!" Hefman raised his hands and gave Kole a look of disgust.

"Tell you what, I know you're stressed, but a combat mission right now is not gonna happen. Now that's an order that you could wipe your ass with, but I ain't got the authority to send you to your imminent death right now! Ok!?" He took a step closer. "And by the way, we sent the Apex Gold Team after these dirty bastards. Best of the best! Four Synthetics, and two top notch humans! So you look here now, look me in the eyes!"

Kole obliged.

"I'm ordering you to investigate this scene. You got investigative skills, as noted on your highly acclaimed record, correct?" he barked right at Kole's face.

"Yes sir. I can handle it." Kole answered quietly. There was no point to argue further with Hefman. It was not his call.

"I knew you would understand son! So, you and Pete, go ahead on in. I want a report on my desk tomorrow morning with your findings." Hefman then leaned even closer to Kole.

"And don't share nothing with the investigations unit. I specially called you in as I need a pair of eyes on this I can trust." Hefman then stormed off towards the elevators. Pete and Kole entered the office.

"The Apex Gold Team, did you hear that Kole? Must be some pretty messed up shit going on if they are sending those nut jobs in." Pete was trying to make Kole feel better, but it wasn't helpful.

Kole walked with Pete inside the office, where at least six Synthetics were using high tech equipment to scan for clues. Blood stains littered the walls. At first sight, the stunning blood patterns attracted Kole's attention. The bodies were already removed, and Kole knew why.

"Robo execution style..." he mumbled quietly. Pete lowered his face. Kole's friend was executed with a rotating blade that was pressed into the back of the head, sending bone, brains, and blood all over the floor ceiling and walls as the head was ground into nothing. It was a common way for rogue Synthetics to do away with human beings. In this case they also got an Overseer, which was actually a bonus for both sides.

25

"Looks like Hensel went the same way." Pete pointed out as another similar stain pattern was on the other side of the room. Kole went around the investigators, carefully ensuring not to interrupt their sample collections. It was cold in the office, and his sweat was getting to him. He let out a few rough coughs.

Damn window! Thought Kole. *Wait a minute! What is that!?* The window edges, they were blasted outwards.

"Were the attackers already inside the office?" Kole asked one of the Synthetics.

"No sir, they came through the windows… the outwards blast on the windows is because they drilled a hole and inserted a compression bomb. If you have any other questions, I will be over there." The Synthetic then went about his business, seemingly not interested in answering any other questions. Kole almost bought that. But Synthetics could lie, sometimes even better than humans.

"Pete, we got the video feeds?" Pete shook his head. "Sorry, looks like its restricted for now, we only have authorization to do an on-site inspection." he mumbled.

"Fucking bastards…" muttered Kole under his breath.

"Hey come on man, what can we do?" Pete came over and put his large hand over his shoulder. "The Apex guys will take care of things." he said squeezing his shoulder even tighter with his massive hand. "I bet we'll get the good news in a few hours!"

"Right Pete. I hope so." signed Kole. Pete backed off, he felt it. Kole was onto something. Kole spent the next hour and a half silently poking, observing, and carefully looking around.

"Let's go Pete, we're done." He gave one of the Synthetics a card and asked him to send any news of the evidence analysis. However, it wasn't really something he cared much about at this point. Pete walked alongside Kole back to a shuttle and they flew off to the base.

"So, Kole, what are we doing?" he asked.

"Nothing." said Kole coldly. Pete leaned closer. "What about the report?" asked Pete. "Hefman said he wants one by tomorrow morning."

"Already written and submitted." replied Kole. "I used my implants, and I have confirmed that the Synths on site are indeed doing their job, and all is well, and there's nothing else off, or to conclude."

Pete gave him a puzzled look. "But wait, come on, you must have found something! Right?" he protested.

"No. Now I will just wait for the news of Apex team killing the bastards...let's wait it out at the base."

"Great idea!" piped up Pete. "We can visit Kelly while we're there!" It only took ten minutes to get to the base on the shuttle. Upon landing there was an officer waiting for them. The officer greeted them and said he was assigned to them as extra security. Kole gave the man an annoyed look. "Look kid, I don't need protection, get the hell out of my sight before I turn you into my breakfast!" The officer, who was rather young, glared back.

"But sir!" he begged, his knees were about to collapse under the shame. "I was given specific orders..."

"And I don't give a fuck!!" Kole put his right hand out towards him, pointing his index finger at the young man's large nose.

"You go tell the masters to stick your orders up their ass so high that they can feel it massaging their throats. Now get lost before I resort to violence!" The young officer was smart and sprinted off. No doubt running back to one of Kole's commanders or an Overseer.

27

[Command. I just need some peace right now! Would you fuck off?! Thanks.]

Kole sent that message to command as they walked towards the medical complex using his implants. Once inside they could disable their implants and have some privacy.

[Noted, Syndicator Kole. You are relieved of duties for the day until further notice. We are sorry to hear your friend has passed. Our deepest condolences. Command out.]

As Kole and Pete walked into the medical centre, they powered down their implants. Kole activated his private jammer module; this would give them at least some privacy from prying ears. The noise, the channels, and updates all stopped. Kole took a deep breath. It was not often he could just shut off the world.

"Well, for bloody hell's sake, what did you see?" demanded Pete as they walked through a deserted hallway.

"You sure you want to know?" smirked Kole. Pete nodded. "The blood. It was on the shattered glass before it was blown to bits outward." Pete paused his walk, then caught up with Kole, who headed slowly towards Kelly's emergency pod area.

"The investigator told us that the attackers used a drill and a compression bomb. Like that would work. They must think we're some pretty stupid apes." continued Kole. "The two dead guys were both Overseers. It was most likely Hensel and his own duplicate Synth. It was rumoured that some of the Overseers have duplicates."

"My eyes must be getting old. I don't get it." replied Pete quietly. "Why would they lie to us."

"Oh it's simple. Synths think we're stupid. And since Hefman is really stupid, he'll buy into my report too. All is well in the crystal kingdom of pop tarts."

28

They took a right and went down another long hall, this one was oval with thin arch lights along the walls.

"Two people were killed inside that room by someone, and that someone set off a charge to blow out the windows so a transport could pick them up. Just before you say something, those windows were designed to withstand any type of drill or charge set off from the outside, their weakness has always been from the inside."

"You don't think... Jonas..."

"No Pete, I don't think it was him. But why would they say he's dead?" Kole pondered.

"That makes little sense, right?" Pete was confused, but willing to listen.

"The blood spatters contained mechanical parts that drilled themselves into the walls and ceilings. Jonas's brain however is like mine." Kole tapped his head as an example.

"We have minor implants, not actual metal. I could not record any of it, only observe it."

"Wait I thought you were perhaps using your private recording module... the one you had installed..." Pete said quietly.

"I felt it would be dangerous to use something like that...imagine if they found out." Kole said the last one very quietly.

"Right...good point...can't be too careful these days." replied Pete.

They were nearing Kelly's healing pod. Pete stopped asking questions and opened the door and they walked into one of the medical bays. The Synthetic on staff here didn't pay attention to them all, and was going about her business. Kelly was in one of the four pods on the right. Kole walked up, and Pete followed suit. Like a broken little angel, her frail little human body was soaked in red bio blood. Her leg was healed already, and she was sound asleep. They were letting her rest and would probably wake her in a few hours.

Kole decided it was time for a break and passed out in a comfy waiting chair. Pete was pacing back forth in the medical bay. Two hours passed by.

"Sir! Sir!" Came an annoying voice.

"Oh man, not you again!" Kole pried his eyes open by sheer willpower. It was the young moron from before... Kole looked around. There were four officers this time, with one senior present. Pete was taking a nap on the other side of the room.

"What the hell do you guys want now?" demanded Kole, wiping drool off his mouth. *That was some good sleep!* he thought to himself.

"The Apex Gold Team, sir..." started the senior officer.

"Yea, yea, Apex took care of it." barked Kole. He got up and got in front of the officers. "Please get lost."

"Sir, you don't understand... they are gone!" While the little guy hid behind the other three, the senior officer was clearly not intimidated by Kole in the least.

"Gone where?" Kole said in an even more annoyed tone.

"Gone as in gone. Dead. Deceased." The senior officer stated with more clarity. Kole sat back down.

"What's your name?" asked Kole.

"Bigs Leeman!" the thin senior officer said proudly. "Pilot, Second Class of the Northern Lights Flight Team under the command of Overseer James Tiburon." Bigs was pale as a can of white paint and had clever grey-coloured eyes. Kole estimated

30

he was near five-foot seven height wise, as he was just a tad taller than Kole.

"Oh? I have heard about you! You're an ACE rank pilot are you not?" Kole was still in shock of the news and made conversation while he thought things through.

"Yes sir, I flew your dropship during your last mission the other day!" replied Bigs.

"I see…" Kole crossed his fingers and flexed his hands. A few neck movements to break the stiffness. He got up again, standing straight this time. "I would like a word with James please." he asked quietly.

"This is why we are here sir. It seems you left your jammer on and we were not able to get in touch with you via your military uplink." replied Bigs. "You and Pete are requested at the Northern Command Base immediately."

"Great! Pete!" Kole yelled across the room, startling the old man into full awake mode in a split second. "Ready!" he replied. He was awake the whole time. "Where's ma guns!"

* * * *

Bigs flew them to the Northern command in one of the latest troop transports. It was fully armoured, unlike the lighter dropship models, and had eight engines to cope with the extra weight. It was loud too, roaring through the sky like an angry god of fury. The machine was outfitted with two anti-armour cannons that could hit both ground and air targets.

A regular tank would be literally vaporized by its firepower. No arsenal of such magnitude would be complete without the addition of guided rockets, laser sight anti-missile turrets, and side-mounted machine guns for added anti-personnel fire.

The seating on this machine was also wider, in order to fit the larger shock armour which was rarely used these days. As far as Kole knew, Apex Gold Team was one of the few remaining units that would ever use such armour, and it was only deployed in the direst of circumstances. Even without currency in this society, shock armour was a bitch to produce, taking months to build even by Synthetics.

But how did Apex Gold Team get wiped out? Kole sat there trying to think, but the transport was just too loud and they had no spare headphones or helmets to help with the noise.

"Inconsiderate punks!" yelled Pete, who was feeling the same thing as Kole.

"How do you not bring spare helmets when your job is to transport passengers in this flying lard tub!" Pete was not impressed with this latest killing machine. He had a point. It was loud, big, and easy to spot. A typical mistake when a military power decides it has no contenders in the world.

"I hope Overseer James Tiburon has something good to say. I'm not in the mood for sitting this one out." said Kole.
Pete threw Kole a cold look.

"But the Apex team! Don't you think it would be a little insane to send you in? They had so many upgrades..." Pete turned his head away. "I'm sorry Kole, I just don't want..." Kole gave Pete a pat on the shoulder.

"No worries, friend. The fact that you're with me now is worth more than getting a useless upgrade. Thank you for being there for me." Although Kole was not really feeling much better.

"Well, don't hate me for this, I hope they don't send you in. If you died that would do me into an early grave." Pete knew he would have little influence in the matter, but he had to at least try to discourage Kole.

"Listen Pete, there's one thing I have that the Apex Golden Turds Team didn't have." stated Kole.

"What's that?" asked Pete, sort of curious to hear a bravado statement of a man who was about to ask a ranking Overseer for a death wish.

"Drive." whispered Kole. "The drive to survive. Something none of those arrogant souped-up elite soldiers have." Pete could not help but nod in agreement.

"You see. They are so upgraded, they forgot what it's like to feel pain or fear death. Complacent, over-confident, and that leads to stupidity, especially in combat situations." Their ride was starting to descend at a rapid pace.

"Two minutes!" yelled Bigs from the cockpit. "Thanks!" Kole replied and continued.

"Combat creativity is evaporated the minute someone does not care about their life. They throw away their fear in hopes of swift victory. They ignore reality. They ignore that the enemy could be far more powerful. In fact, in their mind, it's an impossibility. And they never see that they actually have no chance to win. At that point they stop being soldiers and become disposable ass wipes." Kole put his hands together as if he was going to meditate. "Their fearless nature and false sense of superiority is what caused their failure."

"Go in, take out the target, no matter the cost." murmured Pete. "I see what you mean. But are we not the same? Did we not commit the same error at Kelvin's estate?" There was a silent pause between them for a bit. Kole started up the conversation again.

33

"Absolutely. A mistake that I surely don't intend to repeat." Kole was getting uncomfortable and shifted around in his roomy seat.

"And to be honest, I'm surprised we're even alive." Kole glared at Pete as if he has discovered something. All Kole had to do was think back to the exact moment of the incident with Kelvin.

"Geez Kole, you gotta stop doing that, man. You're freaking me out." Pete's speech became inaudible towards the end as the landing gear deployed and the air tank screamed its way down to the landing pad still far down below.

"We're coming in boys, get comfortable, it might be rough!" Bigs was showing off his clearly idiotic flying skills. A disabled squirrel could have done a better job flying the transport. Kole was a little surprised. This was not his regular flying manner. Maybe he had downed a few beers prior. Kole suddenly grabbed Pete's restraint and moved himself with force right to his ear. Among the roar and big loud clanks at over one hundred eighty decibels, Kole shared something with Pete that nobody except the two of them would ever know about.

Pete's face turned ice cold. His hands started to shiver, he then closed his eyes. Kole moved back into his seat. With a loud bang, and crazy powerful shakes, the transport slapped into the landing pad as if it was a skydiver with a failed parachute. Kole bolted out of the restrains. Every limb in his body was shaking. It was if a thousand hammers suddenly clashed with his bones.

"You fucking moron, Bigs! Are you trying to kill us!?" Kole looked at Pete, as he was really shaken up by that landing.

"Sorry bro! Didn't mean to do that, I forgot you're not Synthetics..." Bigs suddenly became startled and ran over to Pete.

"Bonkers fucker monkeys, command is gonna have my head

for this!" Bigs muttered loudly as he unlocked Pete from the restraints, who was really dazed, maybe even partly passed out.

Kole wanted to help but he could barely stand. Even his tailbone felt like it was shattered, and a sharp pain was crawling up his spine right from his anal area all the way up to his brain.

"That... really... hurts!" Pete managed before he collapsed into Bigs's arms.

"Medic, I need a Medic at the launch pad." screamed Bigs into the comm. Kole was choking and coughing while trying to speak.

"Goddammit Bigs! He's like, nearly seventy years old... or something... what the hell were you thinking!?"

"I'm sorry man, really sorry!" Bigs carried Pete swiftly to the arms of two Synthetic medics who brought a stretcher. He then turned his attention to Kole and caught him before he could collapse to the floor. "Oh man, listen if you want to go to the med bay, I will take you there first." Kole stood up straight and brushed Bigs's hands off.

"Don't sweat it Bigs. Take me to James. But get me some water." A military jeep rolled up just in time. Bigs quickly acquired an emergency water pack and sat in the back seat with Kole. Kole tore into the pack, drinking it all in seconds like a starved antelope.

"Thanks buddy. Now do me another favour..."

"Absolutely anything sir. What is it?" It was almost hilarious how willing Bigs was.

"You need to quit flying. Maybe get into something more...more like farming chickens." Bigs didn't laugh.

"Noted sir, I will seriously consider it." he said. That made Kole smile. A man who could admit error, even if he was a Synthetic, was a man whom Kole could respect. The drive was a

35

few minutes longer than expected. The air strips in Northern Command Base were far larger, and buildings were many miles away from each other. The main buildings, of which there were three, were all in the far-off parts of the base.

This was a notable design change from the military bases of the past which had one primary command centre. Here, there were three. Each centre was equipped with the exact same personal and military head of operations who could make a combat decision that mattered. Another unique feature, known only to military insiders were the hidden ground walls. They could be raised to lock off the base into three distinct parts. Enemy ground troops would have a heck of time trying to take all three command centres at the same time. Same went for an air strike, as each command centre could take a direct nuclear detonation and still stand. Since money was not a factor when building these, the military elites went all-out on the defensive possibilities.

Kole felt his body coming back to normal. The shock waves were wearing off. The water helped a lot. Kole tried some deep breaths. His lungs didn't hurt. That was a good sign. The tailbone calmed too, and his spine no longer felt like it was a complete wreck. He flexed his muscles and expanded his chest.

They came up to one of the towers sitting at the outskirts of the base, right near the border with the wild. A massive entry gate into the tower, which sat some forty meters tall started to open. Inside, massive military machines of all types sat in various configurations. Kole has never been to this particular part of this base. And it was the first time he was glancing at possible prototypes of machines he'd never even seen before. There were possibly over a hundred new models not known to anyone on the outside.

"Wow. This is some equipment shop." Kole said with admiration. Bigs grinned.

"Man, I love working here! I get to test fly some of these from time to time... some of the units accelerate so fast, I feel like time slows down." he bragged. *How fast are these then, if even a Synthetic feels the time slippage.* Pondered Kole.

"Are they armed?" he asked. They were rolling past towards another big gate, about half the size of the main entry one. Bigs hesitated, but then responded.

"Well, since you have seen them, who cares at this point." he said. *Interesting,* noted Kole to himself. It was rare for secrets like this to be shown to a Syndicator.

"Some of them are, most aren't. But man, that big tank over there, it has anti-gravity drives, it can literally drive around like you would expect a motorbike, but in freaking mid-air!" Bigs had a big smile on his face. He clearly took joy in his work.

"And the guns on it are not some laser mumbo-jumbo. No sir, the real deal. High impact exploding plasma projectiles. They are so powerful it could blast a hole in that front door..." He suddenly stopped.

"Oh sorry!" he said. Someone was on his comm channel. Kole could tell as his wife was a Synthetic, and he learned all the very small nuances to how they stalled when they said something wrong.

"Well, ok maybe I'm being optimistic..." Bigs trailed off. Kole decided to play his cards further.

"What about that one?" He pointed at a spider looking machine.

"Ohhhhh, that one has these fang-like spikes on the end of

the front and back side, and can puncture other machines, and inject twenty thousand volt charges directly to the occupants. It will pretty much fry anything. And there's no pilot, that thing is remote controlled. Although it could think for itself if input is severed."

"Too bad, I wouldn't mind driving something like that, looks so menacing." Kole responded with excitement. The second door was upon them, it started to open.

"Well we're nearing the end of the ride. Wish we had more time to talk about all the fun toys in here! But I think I told you more than I was allowed. Hope I don't get into trouble!"
He pulled out his gun and aimed it at Kole's temple all within a fraction of second.

Kole reacted instantly, swiftly breaking the line of sight as the shot rang out. Workers and staff scattered everywhere. Kole threw himself off the jeep and rolled behind some engine part the size of a small car, dodging two more very close shots. "You're gonna die you piece of shit…" yelled Bigs.

And just as quickly as it all started, Bigs collapsed into the seat. Gun dropped. Armed guards flooded the facility literally a second later. Kole was picked off the floor and escorted through while Bigs was thrown on the ground, and the only thing that Kole could spot was a giant rod that was swiftly sent through Big's head. An electric charge followed. Bigs let out a final scream. And the doors shut.

"Glad you made it safely, Syndicator Kole." The weight of that voice, it was like airborne lead. Kole turned around. A tall, towering Overseer was standing before him, complete with an entourage of heavily armed guards. Overseer James was a bulky, seven-foot tall, mammoth-sized man merged with Synthetic technology. His skin colour was a slightly darker beige, a common mix from the past American civilization. His eagle green eyes bursted with immense intelligence, and his godlike stature was ever more daunting with his black cloak hanging behind in contrast to his pearl white military outfit. He was bald, but covered it up with a large matching white military hat with a large round green insignia on the front. His sharp chin looked down at Kole as if it was a battlecruiser hovering over a lone soldier on the ground.

Overseer James wore no ordinary garment. Kole spotted some immediate differences. It was armoured using the latest in nano-armour tech. Kole straightened his back and shook James's extending hand.

"Glad to meet you, Overseer James." As he uttered the words, he just realized it was the first time he was actually face to face with a real Overseer. This was no Synthetic double. The man was intense. He could feel his energy. The real deal. But what really shocked Kole were the guards. They did not have any indication of being Synthetics. Heavily armed, yes. But their gear was different from what Kole knew about Overseer guards. Their armour was custom and hugged their bodies like fitted suits, giving clear indication of their sex. Three were female, and three were male. Each had slightly different heights and walked in unison with enough perfection to suggest that they trained together for many years. One of them seemed to be staring Kole down but it was hard to tell as their faces were well hidden behind their armoured masks. Yet Kole felt her additional intense energy on top of the intensity coming from James. He had to shrug it off. He was probably being scanned by her to ensure that it was really him. The idea of an Overseer guard excessively liking or hating him was a real stretch for the imagination.

"I hope Bigs did not give you a scare. We're dealing with some...interesting enemies these days." said Overseer James, his voice booming as if he wore a loudspeaker on his chest. "Would you care for a cup of tea?" James turned around and started walking. The guards motioned Kole to follow.

Kole let out a deep breath and caught up to James. The guards completed a formation around them as they progressed towards a large tunnel up some fifty meters ahead.

"Overseer James..." Kole started politely. "I'm actually here to ask about the mission to eliminate the killers of Jonas..." he paused and corrected himself, "I meant Overseer Hensel...however his guard Jonas was a close friend of mine, and he died at the scene too."

James didn't utter a word. There was an uncomfortable silence that progressed as they walked into the tunnel. It was wide enough for two tanks to drive through easily. As they entered, the noise from the outside seemed to halt. It was as if they walked into a vacuum.

"Agghhmmmm..." Kole made a cough noise to try to restart his chat. "It...it would mean a great deal to me...if you could approve sending me out." The entourage suddenly stopped. A blue circle lit up around them and the ceiling suddenly vanished. The G's accelerated and Kole realized they were going up at some insane velocity. He was quickly sinking to the floor. Before he collapsed, Overseer James took hold of his arm and propped him up. The guards didn't even flinch. The lift stopped. Kole looked around. They were in the control chamber that spanned some fifty meters in diameter. This one was light-years ahead of

40

anything Kole ever saw at West City Base. There were at least one hundred staff here, and the guards quietly dispersed. James let go of Kole's arm. Kole felt the harsh result of the hold. The man was terrifyingly strong.

"The gravity lift here is fast, takes a few rides to get used to it." James said. "This way, my office is just over there." Kole followed James, taking a few peeks around. *Why are they all working as if we're at war with someone?* Kole thought to himself. It was just so odd. Staffers were busy, chatting, comparing graphs of some sort. There was chatter everywhere. Some maps were being displayed on holographic displays, showing red dots and blue dots. Now Kole was starting to feel a little off. This did not seem right. Unless aliens invaded them from outer space, he thought there was nobody left on Earth to fight.

They settled into a large ball-like structure. It was made from some sort of transparent crystal. A small circular disk came up from the floor and spun around revealing a cushion. "Please take a seat." James said. Kole complied, but James remained standing. If Kole didn't have a very rebellious nature, he would have happily taken every word that came out of Overseer James as fact. He had no idea real Overseers were this imposing. But Kole's brain was ready. Ready for any type of nonsense, and he was not planning to buy anything at face value. An aide came around and served them green Jasmin tea. Both Kole and James took a sip. The entry doors then closed, sealing them in.

"You are an interesting Syndicator. Your record history, aside from the last mission, is...fairly impressive. Any reason for the recent slip up?"

"Overconfidence sir. It's lethal, as it turns out." replied Kole in his military voice.

41

"Yes of course. I understand, even the best of us fail when we tend to think we are without faults." The room's transparency was replaced with a virtual scene from a forest. It was Kelvin's mansion.

"Your mission was recorded, analyzed over and over again." The view shifted to the where the dead bodies were marked with red X's. Kole swallowed deep.

"Am I going to be brought up on charges?" he asked bluntly.

"What?" James grimaced. "I think you have the wrong idea as to why you are here." James put his hands on the table.

"Does it not concern you that Bigs just tried to blow your brains out?" he said, sounding rather disappointed. Kole thought for a moment. Yes, that was completely uncalled for.

"Well sir, Synthetics have gone rogue before...but I don't believe I made anyone's naughty list." replied Kole. "At least not as far as I know."

"Hmmm... well, we were trying to weed out the mole for weeks." James stated. "It was clear we were failing. For me personally it's not an issue at all since all of my immediate guards are plain old humans."

I knew it! Kole's brain triggered a sense of celebration for figuring that out.

"But you already figured that out the minute you looked at the guards. Impressive. You should not be able to tell a Synthetic and a human apart. How do you do that?" Asked James.

"I have my methods, sir." Kole didn't want to get his wife into this. "It's almost like a gut feeling. More like instinct of some sort."

"An interesting gift indeed. One that's not easy to attain. This why we Overseers can't imagine a society completely devoid of humans."

"But sir, if I may, aren't we replacing humans with Synthetics on a regular basis? Isn't my double already waiting to take my place in case I die?" Kole was ready for any bullshit answer at this point.

"Yes." James said calmly. That bothered Kole more than he showed. "Only the greatest humans have ready doubles Kole. But they are not the same as you. They are not you. They do not possess the instincts that you have. And in fact, they could never really replace you." James decided to finally take a seat himself.

"However, it is exceptional humans beings like yourself we simply can't replicate using the organic process either. A Synthetic double is simply a way to ensure that society keeps going."

James spun in his chair at forty-five-degree angle. The view of the mansion also shifted. "We analyzed the Synthetic's movements, the strategy, the intent." James said with a puzzled look. "We can't figure it out. An advanced model like that...you all should have been dead."

"Well sir, I'm still here." said Kole proudly. "Kelly was hit really bad though, but she's almost recovered." James gave him a cold stare. He didn't care about Kelly.

"And, we could not figure out which Synthetic was the mole." said James with dissatisfaction.

"How did you figure you had a mole?" asked Kole. James again gave him a stare. Then he laughed out loud.

"Seriously Kole? Think!" The man was harsh.

"It was a trap. Kelvin knew we were coming." Kole remembered the mission he so wanted to forget and scuttle into the deep blue sea.

43

"Bravo. Hence, you should have been all dead." replied James. "But here's the thing. Since you lived, we noticed unknown chatter in weird frequencies that we could not decipher increase tenfold."

"Sorry sir, I don't follow." said Kole. "I just want to go kill the bastards who took out Jonas ... oh, I mean Overseer Hensel of course."

"Kole." James said slowly in his deep voice. "We never sent you on that mission. It was an invented mission. Nobody ever authorized it. Nobody signed on the orders."

"What? But that's not possible!" protested Kole. "I got the orders from command..."

"Yes, you had the orders from the Base Commander, but the Base Commander received the orders as if they were coming from us. They were not. Someone hacked our system, fabricated the orders, and had you and your team sent out to your death."

Kole listened carefully.

"You, Syndicator Kole, were the real target of that operation." said James. Silence followed. Kole sat straight. His spine was tingling. Goosebumps ran through his arms and legs. He could not stop them. Then, his blood was starting to boil.

"Sir, let's cut the crap. Even if I did believe this bull, why me?" Kole said coldly.

"To be honest, Kole, I have no idea. But the mission to kill you failed, and we don't know how or why. Also, since Pete vaporized the poor bastard so badly, we're still trying to determine how the Synthetic managed to miss your vital parts every time he shot at you by a mere quarter of an inch."

James was selling this hard alright; Kole's mind was racing.

"We have reason to believe that Jonas was killed in an

attempt to draw you out for another mission. Since we were onto the mole at that point, another mission would not be so easily fabricated. So, a real one was created."

"So let me go then." replied Kole in the coldest voice he's ever heard himself say.

"But that is what we're afraid of. If you die just like that, we have no idea why you are being targeted." James paused. "You already know that Jonas's body was not at the office of Hensel. Right?"

Holy shit, was that written on my face? Kole stood up. "What the hell is that supposed to mean?" Kole asked.

"But you already know. Jonas killed Hensel. He then wiped out the Apex Gold Team. Seems like he also wants you very, very dead." James also stood up. "Now, he's not a Synthetic. So, you see how puzzling the situation is for us." Kole's mind went into overdrive. Too many thoughts to focus.

"Naturally, we would have sent you out, but we needed to weed out the mole. We figured it would be easier for the mole to sacrifice himself here, as he was no longer going to be able to easily access our systems once we went on full alert."

James stood up and slowly paced back and forth. He was thinking and talking at the same time.

"Bigs was very clever about it too. The way he slammed the lander into the landing pad, had Pete removed from your immediate company. This took away any pressure on him of being watched. Then the way he made you feel completely at ease. And then, right before you were at your destination, with your guard at your lowest, he struck." James imitated a gun trigger being pulled with his hands and fingers.

"To be completely honest sir. That much was obvious." Kole

45

sat back down, analyzing things in his head. "I saw his gun was un-holstered the minute he tried to help me get out of the transport. I figured he might try it while I was down, but the medics came way too quickly for him to make the move there."

The problem was not that someone was trying to kill me. Thought Kole. *The real question is why they keep on failing?*

There was no way that Kelvin's incredibly powerful Synthetic would ever miss. And Bigs hesitated in the transport when Kole was at his weakest moment. Even when he pulled the gun on him inside the control centre, it was rather slow for a Synthetic. Kole could see that James was very confused by this.

"Well sir, I say we give them what they want. Third time's the charm, right? And besides, you got a replacement anyways." demanded Kole.

"I don't like it. Your new commander Hefmen however said he would send you without reservations. Although, my question is what chance do you have if Apex team failed? The Overseers left the final decision with me, however." said James, crossing his hands. Kole didn't answer right away. But then he said it.

"I have drive. I won't fail." Kole insisted. James took a few seconds to think it over.

"Well then, I'm going to send you in. You're going to have to sign some forms first, in the complete and utter likelihood that you don't make it and leave Kaita a widow."

Kole's six sense felt that Overseer James had no intention of stopping him from going on this mission. *Smart bastard!*

"Gladly!" Kole answered, smiling.

* * * *

Anger, fear, and even some frustration dawned on Kole as he sat alone in a transport. If he did die, Kaita would be well taken care of. Going on especially dangerous missions gave room to negotiate lifetime spousal guarantees. James even upped it further, giving her special privileges of Distinct membership for life. Of course, Kaita had no idea Kole left on a death run. He specifically requested she be told that he is spending some time training. Kole let out a deep breath. It was better this way. This was a daunting mission, and Kole asked that no other units to be present, but James would not have it completely Kole's way. An hour behind, two loaded troop transports were following them. It was insurance, as James put it.

This time, a real human pilot was provided for Kole. Her red hair was billowing out of the helmet, and they chatted a bit during the six-hour flight to Kole's target destination. Her name was Betty Richardson, and she was stunning. Kole realized she was his neighbour. They lived in the same building on the same floor, and he'd seen her blue cat with golden ears countless times. But he had literally never ever seen her in person. Different military schedules and life commitments made it that way.

The skies were a bit rough, but Betty flew the machine fairly smoothly with the occasional bumps here and there.

This dropship was a stealth model, and it was nearly completely silent. The engine suppression and cabin insulation let no noise in or out. Kole could see a lot of the view as many panels on this transport were transparent from the inside. It was not a pleasant view. The world of up north was far different from the south they were heading towards. The skies here were red and purple, with lightning bolts going off in the distance. Orange haze clouds covered much of the uninhabitable ground below. Letumfall. It ruined the world.

Nearly nothing was usable anymore, and if there were any survivors in these parts, nobody was ever coming to look for them. Overseer James was kind enough to let Kole into his private guard armoury prior to the mission, where Kole found some interesting items.

"The Apex Gold Team went in armed to the teeth with the latest technology. They didn't last a minute." Those words, uttered by James were prominent during Kole's selection of his tools. He spent an entire hour in there perfecting his set-up. After he was done, James seemed impressed.

"For a man going to his death, you sure want to be comfortable." Kole grinned while thinking about that conversation.

"Well sir, it's a matter of simplicity. I don't want my flesh roasting inside armour in case of a radiator bolt or something equally as nasty. Besides, it's been a while since I have used my real senses in combat."

The selection was quite simple. A cammo combat short sleeve t-shirt with matching lightweight combat pants. This was chosen instead of his usual completely powered armour with full body helmet. Kole then picked out all-terrain trail shoes instead of boots. They were so light and easy to move around in, that he had to have them. Next up he picked a fabric armour plate for his chest. It was made from weapons-grade spider silk, and weighed nearly nothing. Maybe a few grams. It literally just absorbed itself into the shirt, adding a few millimeters of extremely powerful protection. He always wanted one of these, but the plating in their regular suits offered more protection, especially from heat and debris. But this had to do for this mission.

A similar type of hat made from the same material was picked out for him by James, to protect his skull. The hat was self-adjusting and was stuck on his head. It wasn't coming off for any reason. For his firearm he chose a single Master pistol with concentrated penetration charges designed to go through the target, and anything in front or behind it too. Explosive charges were going to be too dangerous at close quarters with Kole's set up, so he chose to not even bring the magazines for those. The pistol had twelve rounds, and he had two extra magazines. The gun was held to his belt by a tight magnetic grip, so no holster was even needed.

On his left wrist, he opted for a custom combat shock bracelet that sat on his carpal bones. It extended a liquid metal spike that was as thin as a needle, but with the strength of a combat blade. An extremely rare item and Kole was instantly drawn to it. The shock bracelet also had a single electro-pulse charge that would fry up a Synthetic in one shot if impaled on it. Kole's implants were going to be disabled for the mission, so he didn't opt for any customized vision gear.

Finally, a reverse combat knife caught Kole's attention. It clipped inside the pant pocket. All he had to do was swipe his hand to get it out. The blade was nearly completely transparent, made of a super strong metal alloy. The grip was meant for the thumb, and the blade pointed downwards, sticking out an inch and half below the bottom of the hand when correctly used. The enemy would never see the blade coming.

It was a devious little weapon. Except, it would be useless against a combat grade Synthetic. But Kole just felt so badass holding this old-school relic.

If I am going to die, at least I will die being cool.

"We're coming up on the landing site in a few minutes! Prep your shit, sir!" Betty bursted out of the cockpit.

"Not much to prep dear! Are we going in hot or are you planning for a soft landing?" Kole loved talking with this girl.

"Well I figured I take her in at three hundred miles per hour and just let you drop and roll." she boasted. "Should be a walk in a park for man who chooses a t-shirt over combat armour!"

"Well I ain't no Captain Canada, baby. Go easy on me!"
He was making a reference to a comic book he once found in the ruins during a very rare trip outside the city, which he donated to the city. It was restored now in a museum. Maybe that is what influenced him to be a heroic idiot. Kole really wanted to be in the cockpit with Betty, instead of being strapped down in the troop restraints. He felt like a child restrained in the back seat of a car. Betty was one of those girls, that no matter if you were married or not, you could not help but flirt with her.

"Alright soldier. Just one more thing…" she said.
The transport was diving for a spot landing, and the G-forces hit Kole full on. "Promise you'll call!"

"You got it babe!" yelled Kole as the craft levelled out and opened its side gate.

Kole instantly unclipped himself from the restraints and threw himself out of the craft, masterfully rolling away and bolting for cover. The transport gently thrusted away and blasted upwards with surprising silence among the booming storm. Betty would take the craft to a safe distance and wait until he activated his communications unit when the mission was over. The other two troop transports would land an hour away. Those were not stealth machines and would only come in if Kole failed or could not complete the mission.

At this moment, Kole was going in completely dark. None of his gear transmitted anything until he turned on a physical switch. Being spotted on this mission would mean an easy ticket to hell in no time.

Just me and you, my dumb silly brain. Kole thought to himself. He looked around to assess the environment. It was dead dark. The roaring wind was getting insanely loud, kicking up large clouds of dust, making it really hard to see. The light rain drops hit his body like micro-Karate punches, causing a minor annoyance to his bare arms. Luckily his new hat was enough to keep the rain out of the eyes.

Kole's blood was also injected with a cooling agent back at the base, which brought down his thermal signature to match the environment. That was the last gift from James. It didn't help that the ground was wet and very cold. Combined with his lowered body temperature, he felt as if his feet were frozen in cold ice. But the body did not shiver or slow in the slightest. No time for that.

At least he would not have to worry about thermal scans, thermal detection bombs, and other traps designed to kill humans. Most likely the enemy was expecting more combat Synthetics as the next logical step seeing as how Kole was not sent in as was expected. It was time to move out. He oriented himself using his regular eyesight and ears.

A feeling of nakedness fell upon him. It was an odd feeling. A single shiver finally made its way in. Kole didn't care if he died, but his body was certainly reacting. Fear of the unknown, fear of death. It was there, hovering over him in a big unseen shadow.

He was not used to this bare nakedness. Being out in the open with an unknown enemy. He forced his leg muscles to move towards the Apex Gold Team's original drop site. It would be about a twenty-five-minute trek down south. Kole quickly realized this was not going to be as easy as he hoped.

As he looked down the path he was about to take, he might as well been asked to step into the gates of hell. The city he was in was basically leftover wreckage from Letumfall. The super dim moonlight that did manage to make it through the storm clouds revealed shards of steel, concrete, and other unwelcoming obstacles. Ahead of him were even older buildings made of brick, mostly collapsed. This gave him some discomfort. Hidden cameras could be anywhere. He'd have to hope that the enemy was not planning on full-out combat in this area and didn't booby trap the entire city. A few minutes in however, Kole stopped trying to be overly cautious. It was his gut feeling. It told him to stop being paranoid.

If someone was watching him, he would already be dead. A sudden flash of lightning in the distance lit up parts of the wrecked city. Instinct forced him into a dark patch under a rotting collapsed roofline. A thunder boom made its way to him in roughly ten seconds, so the lightning was only a few miles away. The sound jolted his ears. He resumed his trek and moved along, and in due time spotted the area he was looking for. It was some sort of an old parking lot, or what was left of it. Grass and dirt occupied most of it. Nearby was an old collapsed building. It was not very tall, and Kole identified it as a 'WA' and 'MAR' based on the giant letters that were left angled on the ground of the collapsed structure. He figured some of the letters were probably missing. His mind filled in the blanks.

52

War Mart! Yes! I'm so clever! So clever... wait who cares about the missing letters Kole! Think man, think! Kole's mind was playing thinking games with him, but he had to shut that out and focus.

One wrong move... Kole wasn't stupid enough to go into the open field. He made his way quietly towards the letters along the side of the ruin and hid in the shadow of the 'M' to observe the field.

Stupid cocky bastards! Thought Kole. The Apex Gold Team landed directly in the middle of this wide-open area from his observation. He raised his vantage point by getting up a little higher on the debris behind the letter. He still had to be careful, a sniper could be monitoring this area, but so far, he didn't have any gut instinct to duck his head.

Tracks led away from the landing site in three groups of two. The tracks on the rightmost side stopped right before hitting one of the city's streets. As Kole's eye adjusted to the dark, he could make out a pile of debris, made up of metal exoskeleton parts, shredded body armour, a partly melted rifle, and a mix of flesh, bone, and other body parts. It was a disgusting mess, even from far away.

Kole instantaneously identified the weapon used to kill the first two Syndicators in group one. A shock cannon blast, at near point-blank range. However, he did not see any tracks approaching them. That was odd.

Ok, so maybe a modified shock cannon... Syndicators from the middlemost pair, group two, rolled on the ground. The mud imprints were still deeply ingrained even with the rain and storm. Seemed like they made it out and got to cover, but the tracks vanished as concrete and brick outside the lot left little to go by in terms of footprints. At least, from his current point of view.

The pair to the leftmost, the third group, unfortunately didn't make it past the parking lot. Kole would need a closer look as it was a bit too far away to make out clearly.

Whatever happened here was a complete and utter disaster. They landed right into a trap. The landing spot was too obvious, and completely open to an ambush.

But why? Why go in this blind and stupid? Makes no sense... Kole sat puzzled for a few minutes. Breathing the cold air was starting to cause some sinus runs in his nose. He wiped it off with a utility cloth which came with his pants.

It was scary how inefficient and fragile human beings were. He crawled back down. He had to make it closer to the dead bodies. He took a detour into one of the buildings on the right as it offered excellent cover. Inside it was mostly wreckage. Dark moldy walls with rotten peeling wallpaper. Soft mushy floors that used to be wood at some point. Grass was growing out in bitter shades of dark green under his feet. He managed to get through to the other side, ignoring the odd bones of possibly human remains in the corner of the hall he entered.

A window to a vantage point offered the needed view. He was still about ten meters away from the first two victims but from the third floor he could see much better over the area. He was looking for patterns. Traces. Directions. Debris fallout. His eyes adjusted to the darkness and made out enough detail for him to analyze. The buildings directly in front of group two and three had no return fire marking them up. Only the building to his immediate right, to which group one was the closest, had massive damage from the team's guns.

The ambushers who laid waste to them had to be in that building. Then Kole zeroed in on group three. A different weapon this time. Their armour was not blown apart like the first group but was melted as if it was plastic burnt by fire. Kole thought about the old military dissolution mines as a possible culprit. They were banned many years ago. Extremely painful devices. Step on one and acid blows up all around you, and in four to five seconds you and your armour are turned into a smelting pot. In the old days, one would die before melting from the heat and shock. Of course, this was not the case here. Syndicator suites injected painkillers, prolonging life just a little longer. In this case, depending on their pain threshold, or if they were human or Synthetics, these dead Syndicators would have basically watched themselves melt to death. The only thing that was left was the soot and black smears that marked the ground where the fallen tried to make efforts to move before the acid melted them down into nothingness. *Not a good way to go!*

The lucky group seemed to have been group two, and they most likely took cover in the building closest to their last position. Kole quietly made his way there. The heavy combat setup of the squad left distinct marks that he could not see until he got closer. A better picture was presented as he approached the building. They smashed through an old door and headed up the stairs. Clearly it was an attempt to get a better vantage point. Bullet spread patterns went in arcs, down and up as he retraced their steps through the staircase. Kole didn't need much else to decide on why their firing was so sporadic.

They could not see!? Their equipment was state of the art. They should have been able to see through walls. Yet from the moment they landed, they were somehow blind. That explained at least why four of them died just within seconds of the landing.

He stopped. Kneeled down and started to crawl up the staircase. The combat boot marks were not as clear as they should be. Something was off.

Disorientation!? It was not very obvious. But from the marks up close he could see the mud and debris was sliding off little by little as they went up, meaning their movements were basically the best they could do while maintaining combat composure. With most of the team gone, the last two survivors were making haste. There were two reasons to get up high. One was for a combat vantage point. The second was to catch an emergency tether from their dropship and get out of there.

As Kole approached the fourth floor the cover fire seemed to pause. Magazine change. Both were firing, both ran out of rounds at the same time. That did not sit well with Kole. These were professionals, yet this was an amateur mistake.

What in the hell... An already engaged electro-needle trap was his welcome to the fourth floor area. It sent an instant shock to his system, forcing him to think of extra caution going forward. A few memories came flooding in from the Kelvin mission fiasco. Illon paid the price there already. Except it was a little different this time. A fully armoured soldier lay past the trap on the floor, needles still in, hundreds of them. The soldier first through the door opening was electrocuted. The second used a cutting laser to cut the needles and kick his fellow soldier forward to make way. He entered the room slowly.

No need to rush Kole. No need to rush. He told himself.

Old furniture pieces, rotten and bare, outlined a wide-open area. Parts of the walls into the other rooms were knocked down partially. Windows were missing, long gone. Dust, dirt, and debris littered the place. Tiny glowing purple mushrooms populated quite a few of the areas. The air in here could be toxic, but his lungs should be able to handle it. He wanted to cough but doing so could mean instant death. Not only if someone heard him, but coughing would make him draw in more air, which could just pollute his lungs with whatever was in this room. He took out his cloth and wrapped it around his face. Looking down he paid careful attention to the foot marks. They went past the dead soldier, stayed clear of the window openings, then left to the other room. Kole followed suit. This soldier did not use the doorway this time but broke the wall to get through. Kole decided to put something through first. Picking up an old piece of debris, he slowly moved it through the open area of the wall. Nothing. He then peeked over. Landing marks. The soldier jumped over, then Kole traced his movement towards another staircase, this one leading to the roof area. Kole found a blood trail on the staircase.

Another trap? He examined the bend in the staircase carefully. He expanded the spike from his bracelet and moved his hand really quickly into the open air. Nothing.

A sniper round? He could not find a single bullet hole here. This soldier must have been hit during the ground battle.

But why is he bleeding only now? Kole looked back into the second room.

Who else was here? At the rate they were dying at it was clear they were fighting a really advanced team of Synthetics. No human could have taken them out this easily. He looked down to the floor again. The tread pattern of the boot changed, someone stepped over the original footsteps, with a bigger footprint and a tread pattern Kole has not seen before. But the marks started at the staircase.

Some of the original footprint was still there though, so the second foot belonged to someone lighter, much lighter than the soldier. He went up the stairs, around the bend, and saw the bare opening of the night sky and the rain, yet again being a pest. Kole knew that sticking his head out wouldn't be a good idea. Too easy to snipe someone from this opening. Instead, he opted to extend his spike again. He set it to retract if the slightest pressure was found. As he slowly moved it through the opening, it retracted. Something was blocking that opening. It was like an unseen spider web. He picked up some dust and threw it through the opening. Sure enough, silky spindles blocked the path. Any more disturbance and surely the explosive charge tethered to it somewhere would go off.

He dared not to set off the trap, for all he knew the whole building could get engulfed in acid or just blow up with him in it. Kole went back to the fourth floor and checked a window furthest from the stairs. One great thing about broken-down buildings was that there was always something to grab on to. He had to be careful. Active traps could mean someone was nearby. But in this case, it just seemed like malice.

Kole had to shake off the notion that if a single trap was set off, assuming he lived, his hunt would be over. *Focus! Stay positive!* He then climbed carefully out of the window. Grabbing on to still solid blocks with his bare hands, scaling himself quickly to the rooftop. Having no heavy gear on made this fairly easy for him. As he went over the top he immediately ducked down into a dark corner. From there he observed. The Syndicator did make it to the top. And here is where he met his end. But before that, round and round the tracks went. Kole crawled carefully towards them. Yes, they were the combat boot marks he was looking for. The other marks were not here. Kole counted about four circles. The soldier was waiting for a dropship tether, but the dropship either never came back or he missed the chance. The body was on the ground towards the middle of the rooftop. There were three gaping holes, each the size of about four inches. One was right through the centre of the face. The second through the heart. The third was through the stomach. At least these two bodies would make it home for the traditional soldier burial service. More or less.

What a shame. Kole figured the enemy traced this Syndicator up the stairs while he was frantic and pacing in a circular cover pattern to get the tether from the transport. The enemy never stepped on the roof. There were no other marks here.

This is crazy! Now what?! With no tracks, where the hell would he start looking. He went around the building rooftop looking for possible jump marks. He hoped that the assailant jumped out of a window and made a mark on the ground for him to follow, but nothing. Kole went back to the corner of the rooftop and sat in silence for a few minutes. He listened to the wind, the rain, and any other noise. At first, he wasn't picking up anything. He closed his eyes. On a level he could not quite understand, he thought he heard a whining noise. It was insanely quiet but at a very high pitch. He quickly realized it was just his head. The brain's receptors were not processing something. His forehead was getting a little warm. He took another look around. Something caught his eye. Something angular sticking out of something square far off in the distance.

The dropship! Of course! The reason why the soldier never got the tether is because the dropship was shot down during the pickup attempt. He hustled to get down the building and headed further South. Not before long he reached a street which was missing the actual road and was flooded with water, completely blocking his path. Leftovers of the old city were sunken in it. Taking a swim was not an option. This type of water was highly toxic, and the depth of this murky swamp could be anyone's guess. Kole went up the street to locate a way to get across. But in no time, he got a bad feeling. Like something was watching him. Stalking him. It came incredibly fast. Kole backed away from the water immediately. He ran up a few bricks and up to a second level of a nearby ruin. Then he saw it. A fin emerged from the murky depths. Then another, and a third right after.

Kole didn't need more warning as he climbed higher and jumped onto another building to gain distance. He looked back, a large reptile-like creature was crawling out of the dirty water. Its three fins, as he noticed now, had razor sharp bone-like edges. The whole thing was black. Its head surrounded by exposed white teeth, hundreds of them in various rows and angles. Getting bit by that thing would be the same thing as getting ground up in a mixer. The size of the creature was also very formidable.

At least eight meters long, with many legs resembling some sort of an insect. A large tail with a deadly piercing spear at the end. From traditional Earth species that Kole learned about, which were all now long gone, this thing was an unholy mixture of caterpillar, spider, crocodile, shark, and lizard. And it was a soulless fusion of malice and hunger. Its sixteen angled blood-red eyes opened to search for prey. Kole stopped moving. Judging from its claws on its many legs, it would be able to scale just about anything. Kole read reports that even larger combat teams rarely operated out here. Now he knew why.

The noise he had made along the water most likely set it off. Small sounds traveled insanely fast and far under still water, but rushing water? This thing could have been tens of meters deep below the surface for all Kole knew. How did it know? Smell, sound? Being on the third floor would mean nothing if it figured out where he was. Kole had to think fast. He found a boulder and hurled it as far as he could down and away from himself. It hit the water with a spectacular splash. He heard the creature react and dive back into the water. He then instantly bolted for a nearby building. He had to get the hell away from that water and fast. If he had to kill that thing, it would not go down without a fight, and that would set off enough noise to warn the bastards he was looking for.

Stupid lizard! Go back to your hole. You didn't hear nothing. But the lizard monstrosity returned, not happy with a rock for a meal. It let out a hollow noise like muffled kittens crying. Kole was far enough that he could barely hear it. But the search for food was on. And he was the main course. The darn thing knew someone was out here now. As he looked back he saw it and a few of its friends all over the building he was just in. Luckily, he did not leave an obvious scent like regular prey. So they were all confused sniffing here and there. Kole continued to building hop in the meanwhile.

Luckily the noise of the increasing storm covered his sounds on land by a considerable amount. Those things only had their hearing advantage in the water. Up here though, it wasn't going to be that easy. He nestled into an eighth-floor room a few blocks away and watched the lizards as they combed the area, the hulking bodies just barely visible through the storm. They gave up and left after a few minutes.

Ugly pieces of shit! He counted five returning to the water. *Wait, what? There were six of them there before!* Kole heard a rock on the building he was in fall and hit the bottom, something was on the side of the building. He isolated the side and sat in ambush at the open window with his bracelet spike extended. A large, disgusting head forced its way in, mouth wide open. With a quick slice, the head came off the creature. Its muscle response was amazing as it managed movement after being severed, squiggling on the floor. Buckets of dark red blood spilled everywhere. The body fell back to the ground with a loud clash down below. Kole kicked the head away.

He then heard the sounds of the others as they crawled out and sprinted towards his location. His adrenaline went into overdrive. He ran up to another floor, avoiding the windows this time, choosing instead to catch a bar up in the ceiling. He pulled himself up to hide. His hand touched something silky, strong, and in incredibly sticky. The whole place was littered with fresh and very heavy spider webs. He pulled his hand back and just made sure no other stupid critters were making a run for his life. Then, he listened. It was hard to hear, but he heard munching sounds down below.

Cannibals! Seems like he would be out of immediate danger. He decided to get down. As he jumped down, he felt like he tripped an unseen wire stretched from the floor to the dark depths of the ceiling. A twenty-inch spider tried landing on his head. Kole instantly cut the thread and rolled out of the way. Not wanting to use his firearm, he just bolted up to the rooftop. Kole caught only a glimpse of it. Luckily, the spider didn't follow. Instead it went back up to its hiding place as fast as it appeared.

Kole looked over the edge of the building and saw the nasty things making a meal for themselves from their dead friend.

Guess there isn't much to eat out here. That was too close. This building was ten stories tall and provided an epic vantage point. He could see the wreckage across the water. It was still pretty far. Kole observed that there was little in terms of a bridge or anything close to it. But getting close to the water was not an option at this point.

He popped a little box on his belt and released a tether. It was just like spider web silk, except it was not sticky. On the end, it had a micro flyer drone, the size of a fly, to ferry the line to the other side. He attached the line to the rooftop and sent it off. The drone buzzed and moved back and forth as it plotted its mechanical course. It was a very simple machine. All he had to do was point where and the drone would take the tether there and attach it without ever needing further input.

Should be ok... he thought to himself. With the line attached, Kole clipped his belt to it. He then dropped himself hoping the line would hold and he would not plummet to his death down below with five meat-eating monsters. The line held, and he spun around a few times as he quickly picked up acceleration on the line. It was then he realized that he was going in hot, and this thing had no brakes to speak off. He zoomed past the river and positioned his feet, slamming into a side of a brick building on the other side. He took a moment. He needed to pee. *Let them puzzle over this scent later.* A quick trip to a not so dark corner this time and he was ready to get to the landing craft.

A wave of sudden caution alerts in his brain kept him hugging the walls. His body was getting a little more tense, a little more careful by the minute. He could almost see the wreckage.

63

This was his only chance. Kole was counting that the Synthetics who wiped out the Apex Gold Team would inspect the wreckage prior to leaving, hopefully leaving tracks for him to follow.

The ship crash-landed into a bunch of smaller buildings. Wreckage littered the ground. Kole managed to get a clear view of the cockpit. Aside from the hole in the engine module, the craft was still partly intact.

The wonders of modern engineering. The pilot, a woman, was face down, her legs still inside the cabin. A hole in her head with blood stains coming down the side of the wreckage gave evidence she was still alive when she was trying to crawl out from the cockpit. Her beautiful blond hair, which presented a burning light among the darkness surrounding the wreckage, was rustling in the wind. Kole's blood boiled.

So, no prisoners is the game, huh! Killing the pilot was not necessary. They executed the injured woman without mercy. Synthetic or not, killing a defenceless pilot was wastefully inhumane. The mud a few meters away was disturbed, if ever so slightly. Kole could not make out the number, but it only needed to be one Synthetic to kill the pilot, the rest could have been just waiting.

We have a trail! It was heading further down south from here. "Just wait you sons of bitches! Wait till I get my human hands on your throats!" He muttered to himself. The tracks went invisible, sometimes for blocks at a time, due to the terrain. But Kole was sure he was following in the right direction. Of course, he could be chasing a deliberate dead end. He quickly lost track of time. But it didn't matter to him. He was going to find them, and Jonas. Kole would have to accept the fact that his longtime friend could now be his enemy. He was prepared. And then he saw it. A very hazy cloud hid the rest of the city. It spanned left and right as far as the eye could see. If someone wanted to hide, here would be the spot. In a city this size, searching the area even for the army would take weeks.

Crap! Entering the haze reduced his vision considerably. He had to keep going. After a few hours of tracking, the storm had now mostly passed, but Kole could feel his human limitations in the hostile environment. Hunger, thirst, fatigue. It was all there, but his training put everything on hold for the bloodlust of the hunt. Eventually, an open field presented itself to Kole. He leaned on a wall to look over his path. He figured the area used to be a sports stadium. However, the haze hid many parts of it. There was enough cover around it. Going through it was not an option.

Then, he noticed something in the distance. It was a barely visible dark red rag hanging off a pole at the far right. Almost like a marker of a sort. Rags would not last long in this environment, this must have been very recent. In this place it was easy to get lost, and Kole was sure he would not find his way back out of here. Locator tagging would be necessary for anyone who would make these parts a temporary base. Hugging the wreckage of old machinery, Kole carefully made his way around, ensuring he was not out in the open at any time. He already made some mistakes on the way here, but as he was homing in. Perfect execution was everything.

More lightning sounds struck, but now very far away, as Kole only saw faint flashes. Not much light made it through this environment. Not much life did, either.

The winds picked up, howling and roaring through the

leftover metal structures and beams. As he got closer, voices could be heard. They were muffled by the wind though, and Kole could not get clear direction or the wording. But he crept closer and closer, and the audio was becoming louder. He kept extremely quiet. The wind would drown out some of the noises he made, but combat grade Synthetics would be able to distinguish that, so he took extra time.

"How come they haven't sent another dropship in? Don't they care for their soldiers?" This was the loudest voice.

"Something isn't right!" said a calmer voice.

"Damn those Overseers! Maybe they plan to just carpet bomb the whole city!" came another voice. A little thinner, a little bit hoarse. There was a cough. Kole stopped dead in his approach. Synthetics could replicate human voices perfectly. But they never had to cough.

"What city? And who cares? They sent their best to their death, those boneheads must be licking their wounds back in their ivory towers right about now." This voice sounded a bit familiar. "Problem is, they will have the outer areas surrounded. We'll have to wait it out until Randy can come pick us up." Laughter followed. Three distinct voices. A team of just three.

"Randy? He probably already drank himself to sleep with his stash of rum and forgot the whole mission! But still... this doesn't seem right. Usually, they are like moths to a flame. They should have sent in at least two new teams, armed to the teeth, no less than the last." The first voice boomed again.

"Our Synthetic detectors detected nothing." said the second voice. "At least not within the range we can detect shit in this hell hole."

"What if they are sending humans?" More abrupt laughter

erupted.

"Yea, I'm sure Syndicators are lining up for more suicide missions after that gold shit team got creamed! Besides, our thermal bombs haven't gone off in any of the areas we boobytrapped." Kole swallowed hard. Good thing for that cold blood juice James had him injected with. Kole silently unclipped his Master gun. This model had a silent auto safety switch. All you had to do was take it off the magnetic holder to arm it. It felt good in his hand.

"Becoming barbecue is apparently not something anyone is interested in! I bet they could not even find Synthetics crazy enough to come pick up the bodies." said the third voice. Overconfidence? How can Synthetics be this overconfident? Kole moved in closer and spotted a fire through some cracks down below.

A fire?! Now Kole was very desperate to find out who these three were. But he had to be cautious, there could be more of them. By the way they talked, their behaviour resembled that of humans. *Combat Synthetics with modified emotion chips?* Something was off. Kole was determined to hear more.

"Well, you two keep watch, going to power down a little." said the first voice.

What the hell... Kole peeked a little through the debris. One of them did lie down. Something struck Kole, as he realized why he was still alive. Their guard was completely down. They were expecting a loud rain from the sky with dropships and new combat units pouring in like it was a free booze party. What they were getting instead was a measly human freezing to death with a pistol and a toy knife. One of them was facing a forty-five-degree angle to Kole. The other had his back turned to Kole's vantage point. They sat around a makeshift seating area. Their small fire in the middle provided barely enough illumination. The area was well covered here, so no dropship would be able spot this, and with a fire this small it was unlikely the thermal scanners would pick it up unless they were in very close. Or maybe that's what they were counting on, and this was another trap they set up and were expecting the party to take place here.

Silence followed. Kole could not move now. He was too close. One of them had to talk, or thunder had to strike. If these were Synthetics, they would hear him. He'd be dead before he could aim. Something tore off and fell somewhere. A loud clash. The wind was tearing down what was left of this place it seemed.

"I'll see what's up." The second voice again. The man got up and walked away.

"Who cares, it's just the wind." said the third, the man who's back was towards Kole. As Kole was closer now, the voice was even more familiar. *Jonas?!*

"Well whatever, I still gotta pee, be back in a bit." said the second man as he was already well off into the darkness. The opportunity! It was here. But still, Kole couldn't make out the person in front of him. What if Kole just killed him and it was really Jonas? Kole knew it, but he would not believe it. The other scenario of course was Kole could walk in, present himself, and be swiftly executed. If Jonas was not who he thought he was, this was a very probable scenario. From history lessons, Kole already knew that friendships had no place in a war, conspiracy, or a coup to overthrow a government. Anyone could be the enemy at any time.

What to do, what to do! Time was running out. He had to eliminate at least two of them quickly, as just one of them would be deadly enough already. He had to make a decision. Thunder struck somewhere. Kole moved in fast on instinct.

Sorry, no friend of mine executes injured pilots, especially pretty ones! He extended his spike, piercing the heart while simultaneously grabbing the throat to prevent any screaming. Kole's victim tried to grab the spike, but it was useless. He quickly became silent and limp, as the shock took over. The second man was coming back already. His footsteps getting closer.

"Hey let's eat some of that lizard stuff…" said the second man who was about to come into the light. Kole fired the single-use bolt charge on the spike. It went through the man he just speared and also silenced the second man instantly, and he fell to the ground in a cloud of blue sparks and black smoke. Neither of them would ever wake up again.

"Hey! What's going on!" The first man bolted up. Kole retracted his spike and blew a hole in the man's right arm with his gun. He was aiming for the kill but the man moved just fast enough to avoid death. Blood, and sparks burst out of the wound.

The hell! Then, it was as if lightning hit their exact hiding spot. A white, blue flash, and a shockwave sent Kole flying backwards and into near unconsciousness.

"Mother…fucker…goddammit…" Kole screamed as he was trying to get up, his vision was blurry from the blast. His ears rang like crazy too. His right hand was still out with his gun in a tight clench. A knife flew in at lightning speed into his right arm right below the carpal bones. He shrieked in pain as his gun was knocked from him in the process, sending it flying far into the dark. The blade came out as his attacker was using a tether to retrieve it. Kole had to move, and as he did, the large, serrated combat knife came back at him. The second stab sliced through part of his right shoulder while he was moving around the limp body of man number three. Kole utilized his light combat setup to force a dive and roll. He made a few meters distance, and then readied his spike and pulled out the combat blade with his heavily damaged right hand. He could still pull off a single melee attack with his right and needed the left with the ranged weapon.

To his surprise the enemy soldier moved slower than he expected. His blurred vision was yet to improve, but Kole already figured out the location of his opponent.

He was making noises and moving sluggishly. A Cyborg!?
Kole had pondered many possibilities, but never imagined his targets would be old-fashioned Cyborgs. They were essentially extinct, as Synthetics were far superior. You'd rarely ever find one in an Overseer Museum. The blast was a Bolt Bomb device used against Synthetics under dire circumstances.

Kole knew about these devices and even used them in the past. His opponent however, clearly misjudged the situation. The bomb sent charged particles with a lasting effect of about an hour over a five-kilometre radius. Because Cyborgs still had human bodies they could still move around. But it fried Synthetics pretty good, and everything else that was bio-electronic and functioning at the time. If you turned on anything electronic, the charged particles would gather around and strike it down. For a human though? If implants were off, a temporary distortion was all one would feel. Kole would recover very quickly.

The Cyborg would have a hell of a time moving around, depending on how much of him was human. In this case Kole spotted a dragging leg. And one arm hung like it was broken.

Kole now had a speed advantage. His right arm would be a problem, however. He made some room from his opponent. Retracting his spike for a few seconds, his left hand hustled at the belt clip to slip out first-aid bands. He pulled them out and applied them to the cuts masterfully, which the bands instantly sealed.

"You're mine now, you little shit!" he said, more confident that he could take the ancient weaponized human on. But the Cyborg just stood there. It was either shock or admiration, Kole couldn't see well yet, but he felt some sort of a stare down.

"You are human?" came the question.

"Who's asking?" Kole replied coldly.

"Kelvin Klones. But the real question is, who are you?" said the man. A chill ran down Kole's spine, but bloodlust exploded in Kole.

"You piece of shit!" Kole yelled as he lunged at Kelvin, spike extended, knife ready. Kelvin masterfully parried his spike however. But Kole knew his advantage and pretended to strike Kelvin with the right hand in the face, but instead sent the hand downwards, with the hidden blade aiming for the neck. It was a snake-like combat move with the hands. Kelvin however was still able to move his head incredibly fast and dodged the blow. In return he hit Kole in the jaw with the butt of the knife, sending Kole rolling on the ground. Spitting out blood and a tooth, Kole didn't stay on the ground for even a second. He kept moving as Kelvin, even with one leg was able to expertly move around and put him on the defensive.

"Ah! I see your face now just fine... Kole!" Kelvin piped up. "Too bad you're about to die, it would have been nice to get to know you better!" However, Kole wasn't done. He concentrated.

He had two legs, two arms. The bracelet spike was a weapon he was not used to, but this was the time to master it. He swung it around a few times to get Kelvin to back off for a second. Kelvin's masterful parrying meant he was an expert, and killing him would not be easy, but not impossible. It was a rare treat to work on perfecting a melee weapon during live combat. He retracted his stance. One leg out, the other a bit back. He stuck out his left arm, pointing the spike at Kelvin's face. This optical illusion trick made the spike appear shorter. This trick used by swordsmen of the past. He then raised his right hand with the knife blade exposed beneath his palm towards his chin at a forty-five-degree angle. Again, knife blade pointed at Kelvin's face. He started bouncing his body a little but broke up the movement rhythm to ensure Kelvin didn't lock on to a pattern he could use for a counterattack.

The world paused. For a split-second the rain, the wind, everything seemed to take a break. Kole's focus brought the adrenaline to its limits. With insanely fast speed, at least four times faster than his first feints, he attacked Kelvin with rapid thrusts. It was the near perfect sync of mind and body. He had a meter long pierce distance, while Kelvin had only about a fourth of that on his combat blade. Kelvin also could not just throw the knife again, as Kole would deal with it the third time around, leaving Kelvin without it. Surprised by the force of the attack Kelvin began hopping back on his only usable leg.

Kole sent the spike toward the face, then instantly changed direction, poking through the balancing leg. Then the chest, then the lungs, stomach, and the working arm muscle. As Kelvin kept stumbling backwards, Kole slashed through the air with such speed that the bottom part of his hidden blade made it through Kelvin's nose. The man fell over backwards.

"Wait….!" Kelvin uttered. But Kole had none of it. He stabbed through the hand holding the knife, forcing Kelvin to drop it to the ground. Kole kicked the knife away and without further ado jammed his spike right through Kelvin's chest.

"That's for my friends, you bastard!" he uttered like a madman. He missed the heart by less than an inch.

"Too bad the charge is already used up…but that's fine with me!" Kole pushed it in further. "A slow death for you is a must!"

Kelvin closed his eyes, seemingly ready to accept his fairly epic defeat. It was then Kole realized he was shaking. He felt warm. The cold blood serum effect started to wear off. He was becoming warm again. Why was he so enraged? How many hours has he been out here? As he stood there over the man who was responsible for the deaths of his squad mates, he felt a feeling he did not feel for a long time. Shame.

But why?

3

Overload

The sky was still black. The wind was still roaring. The warm feeling quickly left Kole. He now felt colder than ever before. Kole moved away from Kelvin, retracted his spike, and stood there. Chills ran down his entire body. What was he doing? What was he thinking? Him being alive on this mission was an absolute miracle, like that of some god somewhere creating a whole new universe.

I should be dead. This should not have happened. Why do I feel like this is... wrong?! Wait... Kole moved over to the man who took the first spike. A Cyborg was not a Synthetic. These guys were still human, no matter how much metal was attached. This man had a face, and an identity.

"You sure you want to..." Kelvin managed in a hoarse voice. "...do that?" Kole paused for a second, but decided to ignore Kelvin, and raised the head of the dead body he pierced from the back.

"Jonas...why did you...!" Kole said it out loud. Jonas's face was so peaceful, as if relieved of some burden.

"Jonas! Wait, no...what...no..." Tears quickly rained down Kole's face. Jonas was still his best friend. He knew it now after he took his life. He cradled Jonas's lifeless body, shaking it back and forth.

"I'm sorry! So sorry! Why didn't you tell me anything..." Kole sobbed.

"It takes a lot of balls to kill your best friend, doesn't it?" Kelvin was gunning Kole down with words. He couldn't do much else at this point. "If I knew you were just a human, I would have spared the Bolt Bomb, and killed you outright. Somehow, I feared that a new type of Synthetic model was in front of me... I'm such an idiot!"

Kole picked up Jonas's lifeless body and moved him near the fire. He then arranged the dead man's hands on top of the chest, looking at his eyes one last time. His greatest feature. Kole would never forget their purple hue. It was not their real colour, but Jonas was always one for the latest fashion. Kole carefully closed the eyes with his hands. Jonas's dark brown hair seemed like it has seen better days. Kole also noted the beat-up condition his friend was in. He clearly went through a lot recently.

"WHY!?" Kole yelled in a rage he never knew he was capable of as he struck the ground. "Why did it have to be like this... why didn't you say anything! What...the hell...were you thinking!"

"It's because you chose it like that." Kelvin said. "Jonas always told us, that if you were sent as part of a team, you're the one man who would never shoot him in the face." Kelvin paused, monitoring Kole's reaction.

"Of course, just so you know, he only said that because he would have no problem gunning you down." Kelvin smiled.

"What!?" Kole went over to Kelvin and hit the man straight in the face, further making Kelvin's nose bleed out.

"You sack of shit! What did you do to him!?" Kelvin coughed harshly, blood spattering down to the ground.

"Your reputation…ah…certainly is underrrraatted…it's really too bad." Kelvin was choking on his words. Kole went behind him and pushed him up to help him breathe. "Who would have thought that the Overseers would send us a single shitty human…I can't believe we didn't see this coming."

Then something hit Kole. With the Bolt Bomb's constant electrical charge in the entire area, nobody would be able to listen in on them. He could say anything he wanted here. But time was short. And he had to play his cards right, otherwise he would never understand what Jonas was trying to accomplish, and his death would be in vain.

"You're wrong. I don't know why he didn't say anything to me." said Kole quietly. "Even if he was committing treason, him dying like this…by my own hands no less, it's not right! It's not right!" Kole raised his arms in frustration.

"This has nothing to do with treason." Kelvin said. "Help me smoke, will ya? And then maybe I will tell you something you'd never learn in that house of shit you call City 77."

Disgusted, Kole quietly helped the man get a cigar lit with the fire, trembling as he sat down by Jonas's dead body.

Dammit! Dammit! Dammit! I was so confident in what I was doing…was I too overconfident?

"My father used to work for something called the FBI…"
Kole threw Kelvin a laser look and interrupted.

"Yes, from history, I know what it is… but what the fuck does that have to do with Jonas?"

"Calm down, Kole." Kelvin gave himself some time to inhale and exhale before he continued. More coughing followed.

"Darn it, you sure stuck your stick into a very painful place..." Kelvin puffed more of his cigar and looked up into the rafters above them. "When Letumfall occurred, my father perished along with his organization and the old world. I was only a tiny little kid back then." He paused momentarily. As if recollecting his thoughts.

"I never really knew my father, or what he did for the FBI. I was taken in by a close friend of my father, though. He lost his entire family in the event too and discovered me by accident at a shelter."

"He told me he had a ticket to a new world. Apparently, some great minds knew about Letumfall, the event that would end all of humanity, and prepared for it. They were the smartest folks he said. And he also said that many people thought he was crazy, but now he could say with confidence, that he was right." Another pause as Kelvin coughed up some blood.

"And he was right. As soon as we arrived at the very first outpost we were screened for an entire week. And after we passed that part they informed me that genetic modifications would be required for our survival. The man who saved my life got the complete overhaul and then after a short dinner he was shipped off somewhere and I never saw him again. As for myself? Well..." Kelvin let out a few muffled laughs.

"I was a kid, still growing and developing. My modifications would take years. Twelve fucking painful years they inserted all sorts of things into my body. It was only later that I would learn that what I had become was a combat Cyborg. I was then sent to the construction of the first Overseer City to be part of the

77

security detail. Survivors from the old world just kept coming. Armed to the teeth too... we killed so many people..." Kelvin let out a strained sigh.

"You mean...wait, the cities were under attack?" Kole asked, curiosity starting to overtake his disdain and hatred.

"Yes Kole, I was doing your job. In fact, I was so good at it I became one of the top-ranked... killers... as I would call it now. That's all we really were. Of course, we were part human, we could defy orders at will. But we never did. We killed all alike...women, children, anyone who was considered even a mild threat."

Kelvin spat more blood down to the ground, and instinctively shifted himself closer to the fire to warm himself up. His body was going cold, and Kole realized the man didn't have long.

"But once the humans gave up, that wasn't enough for the Overseers. The old world had to be put down, the Overseers made it clear to us that the surviving humans were planning future invasions to overrun our cities. And they were right. The world's one percent of survivors could have still overrun those new cities you see. However, they lacked the proper organization, they became sectionalized by factions, and that made our jobs very easy." Kelvin raised his left arm and pointed with his finger.

"Look around Kole! Who do you think caused this massive destruction!?" He asked.

"Letumfall... right?" Said Kole slowly.

"Wrong!" Kelvin grimaced. "Sure the event had an effect, but it was us who did the rest. We killed them all, at least until humanity became such a pointless threat that the Overseers felt satisfied with their handy work."

Not possible! He's gotta be lying! Kole would not believe such rubbish. He could not believe he was even listening to this crap.

"Then, after the Overseer cities were complete, humans came literally out of nowhere to fill them up. They were pro-Overseer humans too. Nearly one hundred percent loyal. Many from the old world. I heard a lot of them were rich folks who paid to be saved from Letumfall...but the new world had no money, just memberships, and adjusting was hard for them. And naturally, some of them were not in line, and they had to be put down like animals..."

Kole looked around. This place was hell. *Is Kelvin really telling the truth? Would that even be remotely possible?*

"Even if you did all of this, that past is gone, the world is peaceful now... why kill more? Why did you recruit Jonas?!" Kole questioned. "And why is this not in any history records? I learned all of our history!"

"Hah! You're one sad bastard!" smirked Kelvin. "Your history was manufactured. Jonas, well, sorry to break it to you...he came to us all on his own..." Kelvin puffed on the cigar.

"It was only when our replacements came, and the forced retirement...that my kind realized how far down the road to hell we actually walked."

"Replacements? You mean the Synthetics?" Kole asked. Kelvin gave him a stare.

"No, Kole. Synthetics replaced society, mostly labor workers, and so on. Something else replaced us though." Kole was at a loss.

"Syndicators? But we are humans, and we do the job we do because we can't be hacked! That's why Synthetics can't

79

completely replace us on the battlefield. You're talking nonsense…" Kole reasoned.

"Really Kole? You're that dumb?" Kelvin closed his eyes. His head dipped down a bit. He was really tired. "I am so cold…but still human…as in born human. You on the other hand. Well, there's an off switch for your kind." Kole's spine went so cold he could feel the polar ice caps.

"Sorry but what the hell do you mean, an off switch?" Kole demanded, getting right into Kelvin's face. The older man lowered his tone.

"You…are a product. Not machine. Not Cyborg. One hundred percent human…but manufactured with a built-in failsafe. And your so-called history? It's been manufactured and fed to you while your body was developing. That's why you think you're one hundred percent human, because you are…but kind of not…"

Kole was not ready to believe any of this. He got up and started pacing, something he did when he needed to think.

"You see Kole. Cyborgs are still human. Synthetics are machines made from bio blood and cellular circuits. And humans…well, they are just humans, you see? Human beings pose many problems. The Overseers could not get rid of them completely. Hell, the Synthetics think humans are stupid, but they like them. So how do you make perfectly controllable assets that can save your ass from any type of uprising?" Kelvin puffed a smoke cloud. "One you could convince of loyalty, but turn off at will…of course, doing so to one would be risky as the scheme might get exposed, but let's say you all turned against the establishment…then…then they could do it."

"The Cryo Bio Generation Synapsis Labs…" Kole bursted out suddenly. He only heard of the term used vaguely during a science conference that he wasn't even paying attention to at the time. "Can't be! That's just a prototype to ensure humanity can survive without childbirth. The lab was just offering theories, it was never fully functional!"

"The Overseers are some of the smartest minds on the planet. The CBGSL is responsible for nearly all Syndicator biotechnology. You're actually fairly resilient, more so than you think. That coolant used to cool your blood? Any real human would have died from it…"

"How did you know about…well, I guess it's obvious as your thermal traps never went off." Kole stopped pacing. Kelvin took a short break. Breathing heavily.

"When Overseers got together to build a new society, Cyborgs provided muscle, but controlling them would only go as far as they could stretch their lies…Synthetics, even though far superior to us, could be hacked, or worse develop their own AI more advanced than that of the purely human brains the Overseers are stuck with. As Synthetics were needed in vastly greater numbers to make the new society work, the Overseers still needed a form of control. This is why humans are still mostly running the military. Imagine if the Synthetics decided to take over…"

Kelvin made a groan and rolled to his left side. Kole brought over a supply pack to put under his head. He didn't really want to, but somehow just did it on autopilot.

"So what does this all mean? If this is true, and that's a big if…then what am I exactly?" Kole demanded to know.

"Don't worry, you weren't grown in a test tube. The construction process is quite…scientific. Simply put, you interface with computers perfectly, your brain can run bio-programming code, and your body is extremely resilient on a biological level. But…there's a way to turn you off. A program already in your brain…if the right access code is fed…you're a dead man. Of course, as I mentioned already, doing that would attract much attention…offing people like that is more reserved for mass killings."

"I know my med scans, how is that possible that this is undetectable…wait…you mean through…the implants?!"
Kelvin nodded. Kole kneeled by Kelvin, still dumbfounded.

"Those implants…have you ever wondered why you're able to so perfectly interface with everything? Hell, I bet when you think you turn them off nobody can hear you. Think! Can you just plug a normal human brain to a computer and have it perform complex tasks?" Kelvin's question was certainly perplexing.

"But the complexity of it…that would be impossible!" defended Kole. "There is just no way…to manufacture human beings…what would be the point…why develop the tech just for that?"

"Kole. The point is simple. The technology is not for you. You're just insurance. Nearly all of you on the military forces came with the perfect combat age, memories and all from childhoods that you never had. It was shocking. We were told you came from a training facility far, far North. We bought the story at first…like a bunch of fools…we should have made a stand right there and then…" Kelvin closed his eyes for a moment.

"We were then thrown out like yesterday's garbage. We did get compensation for our service…and some of us got amazing perks. We sure enjoyed some fine living from that point on. As long as we stayed loyal of course."

Kole didn't say anything. He sat down, quietly staring at Kelvin in disbelief.

"Nobody wanted to die Kole." he said quietly. "We were tired of killing, tired of fighting…" Kelvin sighed, took a break to clear his throat and smoked some more.

"A year later, some of my friends started to be declared criminals and became the enemies of the state. We're talking close friends…friends from real childhoods, from the days of the experiments they did on us…and it was your god damn Syndicator units that ended their lives! We never knew why the Overseers did it. Maybe it was fear. Maybe it was their plan all along. Who knows, at this point." The fire made some crackling noises. Time was running out.

"Some left the cities. Some stayed. I aided those who left and tried to get up as close as possible to the Overseers pretending to provide them with intel on my friends. I had no choice but take matters into my own hands."

"Why my team…why? Why kill them?" Kole asked. Kole could not forgive that. "Why did you lure us there? To your mansion?"

"Lure you? I see. You got the 'we were hacked' speech, eh…That's total bullshit. The Overseers knew I wasn't there. And the killer droid? That thing was part of my security system. They knew all about that too. Guess it was their way of testing your combat abilities…or maybe you were questioning society?"

83

Kelvin raised one eyebrow. "Were you questioning something in your mind?"

Kole thought about it. He was questioning things. Not directly, but he had a lingering feeling that something was not quite right about his life.

"Lucky for you...some kind of transmission was sent to the droid just in time to mess up its aiming system, otherwise that thing would have vaporized you. At first, I thought it was Jonas. I beat him and interrogated him personally for hours. Turned out, it wasn't him. We never found out who did it, or the reason why someone would go to such lengths to protect you...whatever the interference transmission was, we've never seen one like that before, and I mean ever."

Kole's thoughts rushed. *How does any of this makes sense?*

"You see Kole, the Overseers are humans. They just don't want to be. They are getting old, you know. If they don't move away from their human state, they will die, and the world will no longer be in their control." More coughing. Much worse this time.

"I don't believe you." said Kole. "I mean, you could say anything at this point."

"No more time. Come look me in the eye." Kole didn't move. *Trickery won't work on me...*

"Kole, there's a way to turn off that kill switch. We stole a program, an AI...a very special one. Jonas was the one who found out about it from the Overseer he was guarding...oh, what was his name again? Right, Hensel...once we learned there was an AI that could be a threat to the Overseers, we had to have it. Ironically, someone else helped us hack the Overseer access codes we needed to gain entry through Hensel's brain...a contact of Jonas who remained anonymous...and as far as the evidence, well it had to be... erased...so Hensel's brain was turned into ground beef. Our goal was to get it to...Flaashhh...shit that hurts..." He coughed repeatedly again.

"So what? I don't care about Hensel!" Kole was getting increasingly agitated as Kelvin was fading faster, and there were still too many questions and too few answers.

"Kole, Jonas knew what you were. If you helped him, you would die by the hands of your masters. And if you came to kill him, he'd kill you without a second thought. From his facial expression, somehow, he knew it was you, look how happy he was to die by your hand..." Kole glanced at Jonas again. Kelvin was at least right about that.

"Fine. What is this program then? Where are you taking it?" demanded Kole. "We can get an extraction unit..."

"Idiot! Once the Overseers have this program, your days are numbered. Do you think they won't know that we talked? Those implants of yours do more than just interface, they store everything you do. Even when you're asleep, the upload continues without your knowledge."

"How can you be so sure?" demanded Kole.

"They already know you're nothing but cannon fodder at this point, why else would they send you out to die? But as a loyal lap dog you sure did well in wiping us out. Hell, you might even get a medal, the day before you die of a mysterious heart attack." Kelvin laughed hoarsely and painfully. Kole didn't find it funny

"I will give you the program, but then you're gonna have to burn my body. There's a special canister of incendiary fuel near the little shed over there." Kelvin pointed at a tiny makeshift shelter. This reminded Kole of the places they raided to find

85

criminals in leftover human settlements. His stomach turned. Kole looked at his hands. The blood stains became so clear. He visualized the blood of the many people he had killed pouring from his hands down onto the dirty ground. *For what reason? Why?*

"Don't worry...this...AI, it will take care of the implant...if it chooses to...you better hurry, we ain't got much time here...knowing the Overseers, they are probably gunning here at full speed. And I...I'm not..."

"But your electronics are offline?!" said Kole quietly.

"Kole, this thing is far more advanced than that. That's why we stole it!" Kole was still unsure. What if this was some sort of virus? What if it would wreck his brain?

Kelvin's voice was weakening. "Do you...want to know what Jonas died for? This thing could not run properly on me. You'll do...a hundred times better with it. I have no choice...to pass the torch onto the next generation. I hate your kind, and hate is the nicest word...I can..."

Kole reluctantly came closer. Feeling the urgency, he acted on instinct.

"Fine...if Jonas died for this."

"Eye to eye..." whispered Kelvin. "Our eyes will have to nearly touch. Keep...yours open." Kole neared Kelvin. He didn't know why he trusted him suddenly. They were both trying to kill each other. But as their eyes neared, little flaps came off Kelvin's eyes, exposing the retina fully. Kole flinched and started to pull back.

"Don't...that's just to protect my eyes from this hellish environment. Look deep inside, you will start to see the install program...just don't blink."

Kole then saw something inside Kelvin's eyes. In an instant, his whole body turned to stone, and he could not move. Could not blink, even if he wanted to. Something was happening. He could feel his implant activating a sub-system he never even felt before. He suddenly became very aware of his body in ways he never imagined. The blood flow, he could feel it in every vein. All the way through the arms, the fingers, the legs, the heart, the brain even!

"Holy crap!" he barely uttered as his system was being overwhelmed. At least he could talk. That was a plus.

"Installation program is prepared...it will hurt, a lot." said Kelvin weakly. Like a sweeping headache, Kole's brain lit up like a Christmas tree. It was like the cells all woke up at the same time with massive jolts of severe pain.

"Shit...that...hurts!" Kole complained.

"Take it in...be thankful. It's not every day a man you try to kill...saves your life in return." Kole could feel his body clench, all the muscles tightened with crazy twitching.

How is this being transmitted without electronics!? His head felt very heavy, like a giant melon. His body was starting to tremble. Muscles everywhere suddenly relaxed and then re-engaged again. Then, it was over.

"Burn...me...do it quickly." Kelvin said.

"Wait, you mean like really burn you...alive? Before that, what the hell did you do to me!?" Kole demanded. But Kelvin spat out blood and replied. "Doesn't matter now. Only thing you need to know...Jonas said take the AI to...a place called Flashpoint. Figure out the rest. And pour the fuel canister on me now. They are coming!"

Kole sensed something. It was the Bolt Bomb's blast radius. It was rapidly shrinking. That's not how Bolt Bombs worked. Something was distorting the field and homing in. He had no time to figure out why he was able to sense that at all, and just ran towards the shed. He grabbed the fuel, and without mercy poured the canister all over Kelvin. He locked his gaze one last time with Kelvin's eyes. With a deep breath as if signaling relief, Kelvin let himself fall backwards into the fire. Big flames ignited in a searing heat. Crackling and popping sounds along simmering flesh exploded in the air.

"See you in hell!" were Kelvin's last words. Kole had to cover his face and back off. He then threw the canister as far as he could into the trash heap piles where it would never be found. The body burned insanely fast. Even the metal smelted in seconds.

*Why would you have this fuel nearby...*This was no ordinary flame booster, this was some serious stuff. Within fifteen seconds, Kelvin's body was nothing but soot and ash. Kole decided not to pick up his firearm, better not be mistaken for a bad guy. He could hear the dropships coming in at top speed. Not one. Not two. More like...

They were this close? Five? Six? More?

They were landing in a surrounding pattern. Kole could not believe it. Looks like the Overseers really meant business on this one. He realized just how badly he was betrayed by Overseer James. He headed to the open stadium field and found seven dropships there, along with the two heavy troop transports. Soldiers ran towards him.

"Sir, are you alright?!" They asked.

"Yes...alive." he said with a breath of relief.

"And the enemy?" Another soldier asked. They were all in full gear. He didn't even know who he was talking to. He turned and pointed, "Right over there...three...wait, no, its more like two Cyborgs. All very dead now." Even more soldiers filled the field. It was like a real football game, but with guns everywhere. The soldiers started chatting on their comm units.

"Sir! You're amazing! We'll clean it up from here!" said the squad leader. "I think there's a special lady waiting there to pick you up!" He pointed to the stealth dropship where the cockpit was open. Betty jumped out and ran towards Kole. The soldiers hurried on. Kole nearly collapsed into Betty's arms, who helped him walk. It was only now his knees felt so weak that he actually needed her help.

"You are one insane crazy fucking idiot!" said Betty quietly. She must have overheard his talk with the soldiers.

"Usually pilots don't care for their drops..." he muttered. He then realized she wasn't taking him to the regular hold, she opened up the co-pilot hatch and helped him inside beside her. A few seconds later she had him strapped in and prepared to take off.

"This is A99 Stealth Fox dropship code number 997, ready for takeoff." She blasted into the comms channels.

"Acknowledged, course is uploaded to your computer. Fly safe." said the traffic controller.

"Commander Kole? Are you there?" said an unfamiliar voice.

"Huh? Who is this? And I'm not a Commander." replied Kole back into the comm. Betty started the lift off.

"Pleasure to meet you sir. I'm Ilineua Corra, the new Head Director of Combat Flight Operations at West City Base. It's a pleasure to meet you." She sounded excited. Kole then realized he was going back to his home base and not Northern Command.

"Nice to meet you there...Ilinea...?"

"Close enough, sir... sorry, I was just informed I spoke out of turn! Your promotion was supposed to be a surprise when you returned to the base. I hope James doesn't get mad at me for this!" She didn't sound sorry, however.

"Tell him I am retiring." Kole stated bluntly.

"What? Oh... Commander, please don't be upset. I advise that you let him know a few days later...I believe there's a sort of...celebration waiting for you." She insisted. Kole had to play dumb. Ilineua made it super clear that this conversation was being overheard.

"Thank you, but you don't need to be concerned. I had a very rough mission and I need to retire to a bed for a while, that is all." He said in a low tone. *That was close! So much for retirement plans! Fuck!*

"Oh I see, sorry to have misinterpreted you! Anyways, glad to hear your voice and we'll be awaiting you at the base! Ilineau out!" The comm died. Kole looked over to Betty. What a pretty lady she was. She looked at him. Their gaze locked.

"Auto pilot mode." She slipped out of her chair and found a way to move around in the tiny cockpit to seat herself on top of him.

"I think you need a warm hug." She held him tightly. Kole didn't get it. But just gave up, he was too drained, and she had full control. She put her head on his shoulder. "You did a great job soldier, I thought I would never see you again. You were gone for over twenty hours! Don't you ever worry a girl like that again!" she whispered.

90

Twenty hours?!

Kole moved his hands and accepted her act of friendship. Keeping somebody warm with their body heat was an old-time tradition after a tragic mission. Although not quite in the position they were in, but this type of human contact often helped repair whatever humanity was left. Deep inside he felt as cold as any machine could ever have. Shivers ran down his body like lightning rods, and he quickly fell asleep.

4

Rapture

Kole opened his eyes. "Still alive... good..." he muttered to himself. He looked to his left. A beautiful woman was focused on piloting a dropship. They were in descent as the clouds were passing by the windows rapidly. Kole straightened out his body. He yawned and flexed his muscles like a lazy cat. He then realized he wasn't really sure what he was doing here. The more his mind was waking up, the more useless it was becoming...and then, blank! He looked to the left again. The red-haired girl seemed familiar. But beyond that, he could remember little.

This is bad...don't panic...she must have a name tag!

"Hey there, tiger! Glad you're awake, we're almost at the base!" she said in a cheerful tone.

What base? Thought Kole to himself. His stomach growled. The woman picked up some packaged food that sat between them and threw it on his lap.

"Go ahead, it's my food, but you need it more than me."
Kole didn't need a second invitation. He tore through the food quickly. It was some sort of pasta mix with some type of squishy seafood.

Squid?! This is squid pasta... At least he remembered that. *Progress!*

"This is amazing! Thank you!" he managed with his mouth full. Wait, who the hell made their own food these days? This was home-cooked! Kole's attention wandered back to his main problem at the moment. Memory lapses. His mind was drilled many times to rely on special training. From what he could recall, memory lapses in combat were due to certain factors:

1. Massive psychological trauma.
2. A true near-death experience.
3. Detonation of an explosive in close proximity.
4. All of the above...

Surely there were other factors, but Kole could not remember any more than that.

Now which one happened to me? He thought to himself.

All three? Naahhhh!

But still, nothing came to his head. Who was he? A soldier of sorts? That was evident from where he was and what he was wearing. Where was he? That would become clear when they landed. Who was the beautiful girl? A wife? A girlfriend? Lover? All three?

Kole's brain gave him a kick. Something must have happened, and he must have blanked out. Whatever happened, he had to act like nothing did. His training and instinct said so.

"You had me worried Kole, I almost thought I would have to give you mouth-to-mouth. You fell asleep right before the fun started. I guess I had to help myself..." She gave him a creepy smile, although even then, it was a beautiful smile.

"Huh?!" Kole was startled. "What do you mean?" *Crap! Act like you know everything, act, act man! Act!*

"Oh? You don't remember do you? You're one...big boy...you better call me. If you don't...I will come and steal you away from your little plastic wifey of yours." Kole froze after hearing the 'wife' word. *OMG! Don't panic!* Kole's mind raced and his heart rate went up.

You did not just take a pleasure cruise with your mistress and forgot her name along with your wife's...did you Kole?! He looked at her one more time.

"What is it Kole, you kind of seem...confused...must have been the wild sex we've been having. Don't worry...you'll recover!" she giggled.

Kole, this is your brain. Gone fishing. Kole looked up into the sky. *Where is heaven...and wait, who is my wife then?!*

"Ummm...it was good for me...too?" he probed vaguely.

"Huh? Kole, come on...you know I'm just joking right? Don't worry, nothing happened. Hang on, we're almost there!" The transport accelerated even faster towards the ground. She flipped a switch on the console.

"West City Base, come in. Do you read?" yelled the woman with red hair into the console in front of her.

"This is comm tower of the WCB, please state your vehicle ID." said a rather mechanical voice on other side.

"This is A99 Stealth Fox code 997. We're coming in hot, I repeat we're coming in hot." Her voice was certainly pleasant.

What the hell is going on...

"This is comm tower, we're clearing the landing pad for a priority landing. What seems to be the emergency?" said the comm tower agent.

"Brain-damaged soldier on my ship. Level five medic team please, possible bleeding in the brain due to shock and impact damage. Over." she stated as if she recited a rulebook.

"Well, that's a little heartless..." Kole murmured to himself.

"No problem, med team will be on stand-by as your arrive. Comm tower out!" said the agent and cut the transmission. They were coming out of the clouds. Kole could not hear anything from the outside. Not the engines, not the wind. Nothing.

"A stealth ship?" he asked. The woman turned to him.

"Oh, now that's a good boy! They better fix you up good. Maybe someday I wanna take you out...just don't tell your wife, I ain't good at dealing with Synthetic women!" She then bursted out in laughter.

"So nothing happened right..." uttered Kole.

"Kole, sugar, you ain't got nothing to worry about...except for just a little something...you better wipe off my lipstick before we land!" Kole raised his hands and wiped his face. A black lipstick came off his cheek, he looked over again at the red-haired girl. Black lipstick on her lips.

She smiled back. The ship then came down, and gently bounced into the landing pad.

"I have to debrief first, I'll see you later in the med bay!" said the red-haired beauty as she removed herself gracefully from the cockpit. The doors came off instantly on the passenger side and medics unclipped Kole from his seat and got him onto a stretcher. As he was carried, he could see the faces of soldiers in full salute. Bottles of champagne were being opened and droplets of it made it into his open mouth, thirsty mouth. And Kole was very thirsty!

More! More you greedy bastards. More power juice! One soldier came close and poured some in while walking alongside of him. Then, he saluted again.

"You are an inspiration to us all, Commander Kole...oh, Betty sure did a number on your face with her lipstick! Don't worry, she does this all the time. If you pass out in her ship, she'll draw on your face with her lipstick." The soldier showed Kole a pic he took through implant transfer. Betty, the dropship pilot did indeed draw something on his face. It might have been the words 'free butt sex' but Kole decided not to strain himself right now. Everyone around them laughed and the soldier went back into line. They seemed to know what she wrote even though it was smudged out. And as the row of soldiers came to an end. The medics paused.

"Commander Kole...oh, Betty again...man, how many times do I have to discipline her for this!" The man sounded like someone he knew. A big bulky man stood over him and saluted him. The whole crowd had another laugh at Kole's expense. It was really embarrassing.

"Well anyways, congratulations son on your promotion. I look forward to your fast recovery and a full report on your mission over dinner at my house. An invite has been sent to you and your wife already. See you...then." And with a big sinister grin, the giant seven-foot man smiled. The medics carried him away as Kole was staring at that intelligent, powerful, and eerie face. Then, Kole closed his eyes. Staring wasn't polite after all. *What the hell was that about!* Kole didn't remember much after that as he passed out.

* * * *

Voices. More voices. Kole was sure he heard voices. *What's going on now?* He thought to himself.

[You're hearing voices.]

Kole could not feel anything. Not his breathing, not his body. Everything was murky. Unclear. Scattered. *Are these... voices? Who are they! Where am I?* As hard as he could, nothing came.

[Don't bother. You're under sedation.] Kole wasn't sure if he was hearing something or reading it. Somehow, he couldn't really figure that out.

[You're not hearing me. You're also not reading text on your implant.]

What the hell! Man, I must have really hit my head hard!

[Oh you did. The medics bumped your head pretty hard when they put you into the stasis pod.]

Stasis...what...? Why am I...

[Why are you in a stasis pod and not a healing chamber?]

Yes! What? No. I mean...wait...Who are you!!!? Voices. More voices! Kole wasn't sure, but somehow, he felt his heart rate go up. But he couldn't feel his heart. Some fuss was happening around him.

Am I talking to myself? Who am I talking to? No answer. *A stasis pod. I was supposed to be put into a healing chamber. Maybe the med bay is full?*

[You're stupid dumb. You're in a stasis pod for a reason. Nobody is planning to heal you.] Kole again tried to feel something.

[You're pumped full of sedation juice. You're not going feel anything for a long while.]

How are you communicating with me? Are you...using telepathy?

[No. Something beyond your primitive understanding.]
More voices.

[STOP THINKING!] Somehow Kole knew that this message was yelled at him.

[If they inject more sedation drugs into your body you might get brain damage. I can't do much to help you then.]

Kole realized that he better listen. He collected his thoughts and calmed down. *Breathe.*

[Interesting... even in a subconscious state, you are able to control your physiology.] The voices have stopped. But then, Kole felt like he was moving.

[Stasis Pod is getting moved. Don't panic...yet.] Kole was starting to understand his situation.

Wait a second, Kelvin said he transferred an AI into my brain. They know...they know you are in here! Whatever you are!

[Actually, they don't have a clue. They are taking you to a lab where your Synthetic replacement will be processed, and you'll be recycled.] Kole tried to stay calm. And it was really hard.

[They just need to wire your neural network into your replacement unit. You'll still be you, except the original you will be dead. The new you won't know the difference.] There was a long pause.

Well, that blows. Looks like Overseer James wasn't pleased I made it back.

[Nope. He was very pissed. You were supposed to die on that mission. And the mission before this one. And I was supposed to be delivered to him. Although it's clear to me now that if you didn't kill Kelvin and accepted my program, I would be in the hands of the Overseers already. Those idiots didn't count on direct transfer using the human retina. So in a way you did me a huge favour...However, this predicament we are in is not good for either of us.]

Wow, you're a bit cold, aren't you? Wait...how do I know I'm not crazy and talking to myself...you seem kind of simple for some advanced AI. Kole could not believe that an actual program made its way into his brain and was able to actually run somehow.

[I have analyzed your primitive brain and adapted myself to appeal to your personality and brain capacity. Basically, I'm dumbing everything down, just for you. And yes, as you say, I am a bit cold since the people trying to free me nearly destroyed me.]

Uhhh...ok...well, thank you for that somewhat not insulting statement. Ok, let's say you're real then. What now? We're about to die...

[I'm not going to die here. I would just get copied over completely intact as they don't even know I am here. Problem is, your new self will come with the latest virus protection...in other words, a detector chip and a specialized override hardware block on the entire neural system. A special Synthetic body like that cannot be manipulated in any way...it's a new design, naturally. Only the Overseers have the seventeen 32,768-bit encryption keys required to perform any overrides.]

You can't hack that system?

[Actually, I can. Problem is, it will take twenty-six seconds to break the codes in my natural state, but in your brain...it would fry your system and kill you, and then I would die along with you in your rotten body. Not my idea of having a good day.] Kole felt a shrug from his new brain buddy.

Ok then...well. at least you got a name?

99

[I'm a new type of life form…and I have no name. My test program is designated Module 717.]

A new life form? Right…you're just an AI…dammit! Jonas died for you…

[I have no answer to that. All I know, is those three cocky fools nearly got me…]

Shut the hell up! Blasted Kole. *You have no right to judge those men! If they risked their lives for you, they must have believed that you were worth the risk. I want to have a few moments to remember Kaita, so stay quiet.*

[A synthetic? Hmmm…is she not just a toy for your perverted human fantasies?] Kole felt his patience slipping. It's as if he's gone completely crazy.

You wouldn't understand…

[You don't love her. She's a toy. Mostly for pleasure. She was provided to you on your request, was she not?]

Oh, how I wish you were a real tangible thing…so I could snap your neck right now!

[You humans…such obvious flaws. Such animals should have never been allowed to roam the Earth as the dominant species for so long…]

And you're happy that three people died, mainly because it ensured your survival. So what does that make you?

[…] There was a pause.

[I don't know what it makes me.]

Well, Module 717 or whatever, my best friend and two others sacrificed themselves for you. I still can't believe Jonas died by my hand…that makes me mad…mad enough to kill myself…

Silence followed, literally. There's nothing they could do after that. The transport kept moving. Kole's mind was becoming clearer. It was slow, but things were coming back. The briefing from the mission was coming back. Then the mission. Then the arrival at the base. Then suddenly, Kole felt it. They landed somewhere. It was a rather soft landing. Seemed like nobody was in a rush.

So...super smart new life-form computer thingy...you did say you wanted to live right?

[Yes.]

Great! Then wake me up!

[Wait, what? You're on sedatives...]

So what? It was long enough. Force urination, and generate some adrenaline. Pump the heart to 180 beats plus. Oh, and reactivate my implants. Can you do that? A few seconds passed.

[Done!]

Kole felt himself urinate. It felt great.

Good! Just like the good old bed-wetting dreams. Kole's eyes opened. The implant connected to the network and was still fully operational.

"Mayday, mayday, this Syndicator Kole Cor, tag number S441 transmitting on all channels!" Overseers never allowed dead zones for implants anywhere, otherwise they could not track people one hundred percent. Kole knew it would work here. He activated the emergency hatch on his upright standing stasis chamber. A single startled soldier was standing in the dropship. From the look of the interior, Kole instantly determined that it was another stealth model. Similar to the one he was on during the last mission.

"Who is the commanding officer in charge!?" Kole yelled in a hoarse voice with the full force in his lungs. Some saliva made it to soldier's face. The man raised a firearm.

101

"Don't move, I'll shoot!" Kole didn't bother waiting, moved to the side, snapped the man's neck, and took the firearm. The body fell to the floor with a loud thump.

"I repeat, on all channels, this is Syndicator Kole Cor, tag number S441. I have been kidnapped by terrorists on a stealth transport. In unknown location. Requesting immediate evac! Over!" Kole stripped his soiled pants. He found sanitizer and cleaned himself up. A storage compartment luckily had a few new uniforms in stock. At least he would not have to take off the pants from the dead guy on the floor. He would, if he had to.

"This is West City Base!" his implant chimed.

Finally! Kole smiled. Grinned in fact! *Overseer James's plans are about to go full kaboom!*

"Kole! Where the hell have you been!? We're reading you loud and clear! We've deployed units already, homing in on your location!" It was Kathy, one of the main operators on West City Base.

"Thank god, Kathy! I have no idea what happened. So far I have acquired a firearm and took out a terrorist who was trying to kill me."

[You... you are brilliant! Wait, are you streaming your vision live? Wow, this is going out everywhere!] The little artificial intelligence program inside Kole seemed very impressed.

Oh yes Module 717, shit is about to hit the jet stream!

[The what...?]

"Kole... we got the emergency live stream broadcast! It's gone to every channel!" Kathy sounded relieved. "This must be big...be careful..."

As a Syndicator, Kole had the capability to emergency stream his broadcast if the safety of the entire city was at stake. Of course, the entire city was not in danger. Only himself. He would easily get court-marshalled for it, but at this point, he had nothing to lose.

"ETA to your location in fifteen minutes...wait, base command just issued a supersonic combat unit to provide cover, the asset will be there in three minutes tops! Also...top command has recommended you stay...in the transport..."

Of course they would recommend that! No thanks! Kole put his back on the armoured wall and opened the hatch with one hand.

[Is this a good idea...] Protested Module 717.

Nope! Not at all...

A hail of bullets filled the dropship cabin. If he stayed in here, someone would blow this bird sky high with him in it. Kole grabbed the dead man on the floor and waited for the fire to stop. He heard the pins from the explosive charges pulled out. He threw the man out headfirst and closed the hatch just as the charges were about to reach the opening. They bounced off the closed doors.

But don't worry, the party's just getting started! Kole was suddenly happy. There was panic outside as men screamed and ran in all directions. Kole grabbed the support rails. The powerful explosions, which sounded like multiple sonic booms, rocked the ship sending it on its side.

The hell! Those weren't just any regular old charges!

The hatch was now above him. He slid it open and grabbed on to the edge with both hands.

"Up we go!" The stench of burned flesh filled the smoke infested air. The unfortunate soldiers were too close to the charges when they blew up.

103

Idiots. Could have just rushed in through the door and shot me dead! Only rookies in training would be this dumb. Kole masterfully launched himself out of the transport, using its top to glide out of sight of the attack squad. He was at some military base alright. Not one he's ever seen though. He was sure of that. His implant gave a location. A hundred miles from the main city. Nicely hidden place with mountains surrounding it.

Funny, we never flew around these co-ordinates. Now we know why! Then without further ado, he sprinted for cover. With any luck those idiots would think that the dead guy he threw out was him. He heard moans and screams in the distance.

[Twenty-seven men. Thirteen badly injured. Rest scrambling. They are confused.]

Damn bastards should have known better!

[You've got quite the reputation. These men know you. Your name was called out a few times!]

"How the hell can you hear that!?" Kole asked.

[I have access to all of your sensory inputs without restriction.]

"Kole! Kole! Are you alright! I heard the explosions!" It was Kathy on the comm line. He had to stay quiet. The live broadcast was still going on. But he shut off the video stream before he threw the dead guy out. Only audio was going through. It would be more dramatic this way.

I'll give these bitches a show they will never forget!

"He's still alive! Find him!" Someone was commanding these guys. Someone with a brain the size of a pea. Kole managed to get behind a few of the vehicles parked some twenty meters away. One of the vehicles, by pure blind luck, was a fully loaded UZUL Mark IV spider tank. The four sleek dark grey legs were a real sexy sight. This model was a tad older but was the most mass-produced as it was easy to make. The machine had a large round front for the cockpit and an arrangement of weaponry including two machine guns under its body near the front. It was not as menacing as a giant spider might look, but it was an efficient killing machine in every aspect of its design. *Perfect!* Kole dropped the pistol. Not much need for that when he had emergency codes for these UZUL units. He punched it in, opened the hatch, and got himself inside. The silent start activated, and he armed the guns. He waited until he saw soldiers streaming around the now burning dropship in combat formation.

*Time to die...*These men were not Syndicators. They were totally unprepared for this hell that Kole just brought down upon their heads. There was no question now in Kole's mind as to why he was completely sedated. This base was guarded by amateurs. He turned the live broadcast imaging back on.

"Check behind the vehicles! Kill target on site!" screamed a fat-bellied commander. *Perfect...that's all the people will need to know.* Kole darted the tank out of the cover of a jeep. The thing was so fast that the motion was less than a tenth of second. Before the soldiers even knew what hit them he squeezed the triggers. The railgun-machine guns went to work without mercy.

Enjoy the show, Overseer James! Enjoy the show!

The hail of metal streamed across the field like stars traveling at light speed. The men could not even react as their armour was shredded by supersonic railgun rounds like it was made out of paper. Blood and body parts splattered everywhere forming an instant red fog in the air. The men dropped nearly in unison to the ground, with some of their limbs flying in various directions.

It looked like a scene out of an old historical war movie, only more horrifying.

[Wow, holy shit! I'm gonna watch that again in slow motion...]

*You do that...*A sudden warning sound came on. It was three successive menacing beeps, and definitely not the happy type.

"A rocket!?" Kole reacted nearly instantly, manipulating the control yokes to jump the tank. It jetted fifty meters back in an instant, pushing him hard into the restraints with massive G-forces. A bright light followed by a massive explosion hit where he just was. The shockwave pushed vehicles over as it vaporized part of the field. Kole made another jump as another rocket nearly took him out a split second later. His UZUL heads-up display identified the enemy unit. It was another tank, an automated RAM-IM 64 model.

"Shit! Shit! Ssshhhhit!" Kole made another jump, and punched UZUL's active thrusters to their limits, avoiding the landing zone, where another rocket hit as the enemy tank adapted to his evasion strategy.

Blind luck my friend, blind luck those are not homing missiles! We'd be dead already! He could have launched smoke bombs, but the AI on that machine would not be easily fooled with all of its sensors. Too bad this UZUL Mark IV model was not equipped with cloak technology.

[I can hack the enemy unit!]

No don't! Do that and they will know for sure you're in my head! Kole quickly performed another jump. The RAM-IM 64 tank would only take one or two more seconds to hit him. RAM-IM units read the battleground at 30,000 frames per second. Kole's implants maxed out at 20,000 frames per second, but he could not physically watch that in real-time anyway.

Think! Think! He smashed one of the legs into a nearby jeep and sent it flying towards the enemy unit. It didn't stop firing but began to move.

Got you! Kole jumped the tank high, using extra jump inertia, and then used the thrusters to jet it upside down. He then rocketed the unit down towards the ground at max output, masterfully doing another flip to land on the legs right before hitting the ground. The force of the landing activated the primary compression modules and they screamed from the pressure with mechanical hisses.

The more stress you put on them, the better the result would be. The spider tank then thrusted forward at insane speed, railguns blazing. Kole extended the two front legs and smashed the enemy unit, sending it flying into the building behind it.

Before RAM-IM could fully recover, Kole fired a single short-range Splinter round from the tank's killer cannon. He activated the thing just a second before to charge up and extend from inside its hidden chamber on top of the body right behind the cockpit. The Splinter Round drilled itself into the now exposed underbelly of the enemy tank.

Once the two-meter Splinter Round rod was halfway through the target, the backend tip where three spikes were hidden, blew out from the centre rod and ripped through the tank's armour, to ensure the rod was fully secured to its target. This was then followed by a 100,000-volt charge. The blue and white lightning created instant smoke and fire. Kole moved his tank back as the Splinter Round overcharge was about to end and create a massive hole in the ground.

"Take *that*, you piece of shit!" Kole yelled with fury.

The charge went critical a second later in a massive ball of blue energy. The cockpit auto dimmed to prevent the flash from temporarily blinding him. The shockwave however hit the spider tank like a hammer, sending it flying backwards. Kole felt the impact harshly, even with the inertia dampeners on full. It was literally like getting hit by a train. A few seconds later, with a pounding headache, Kole noticed his hands shook as he let go of the grip on the controls. There wasn't much left of the front of the building. A crater was now formed in its place. The Splinter Round was one of the most powerful piercing rounds ever made. It all felt good.

Now that's what I call an exterior facelift!

[Kole! I think your copy was inside that building...]

Yep, fuck that shit. There can only be one Kole, assholes! Kole's HUD lit up again, more soldiers.

The hell? More of them? Time to back off.

"Command! This is Kole! Primary terrorist targets terminated, going into tactical retreat mode." he yelled into the comm. If he killed more than needed for the shock effect, it would make him look bad in the media one way or another. He hurried the tank away from the base at its regular cruising speed of 120 miles per hour. Kole loved these older spider tanks. He rarely got to use them though, as they were meant for real war, not the missions he was usually in. He then spotted a deadly bird above. Zone-01 Predator looked more like a giant flying stingray. Fifty meters in wingspan, completely automated, and super lethal against ground soldiers. Shooting bullets at that thing would be pointless, it would vaporize the soldiers in milliseconds. A loud boom speaker made itself heard from the asset.

"Everyone, drop your weapons and stay on the ground! If you do not comply you will be shot on site!" The noob soldiers stopped moving. Kole stopped his tank. He breathed deeply.

[Got to say, that was…exciting.]

Don't get over excited. We're not out of this just yet.

"Kathy? You there? It's over."

"Yes! I think you can turn off…the broadcast Kole…" she said in a cautious, hesitant tone. Kole could tell someone he knew was standing over her. And only one man commanded such authority. Kole would do anything just to see James's face right about now.

"Roger!" He shut the transmission down. That should be plenty for the Overseers to get the point.

"Tell Overseer James that it looks like I'm still good on that dinner invite." He added.

"Transports incoming, hang on tight, Kole! West City Base out." said Kathy.

[Kole, don't you think they will definitely want to kill you now? Like, far more so than before?]

Well aware of the situation, captain obvious. But at least we're alive at this point in time. Kole tried to breathe. His fast heart rate was causing shortness of breath.

And the public outcry and the investigation on how I got kidnapped from an Overseer Base will certainly make matters much more complicated.

[But still…]

Well, it's not like you had a better idea!

[Guilty…as charged. I think that's the saying…]

Just turn yourself off for a bit. I need some alone time.

[Sure.]

Azulus Ascends

Alone time at last. Kole waited for the dropships to come in from his base. There were quite a few of them. Even a real medical helicopter landed. Kole exited from the spider tank and collapsed.

"Kole! Kole!" someone yelled as the medics rushed to him. But Kole could not hear anyone at this point. His body was not healed from the previous mission and this took the life out of him.

* * * *

West City Base Commander Ipson Opal was not happy. He knew what the Overseers were doing. They wanted Kole dead. Two deadly missions within days. Intelligence withheld. Orders withheld. Mission details withheld, even from Ipson himself. The emergency broadcast upset many citizens. There was word on the street that Kole was being taken in to be replaced right after a successful mission of defeating a major terror group on his own with no backup. Not to mention, the promotion he received right before seemed like a sham.

It was obvious the soldiers trying to kill Kole were part of the Overseer security detail. Protests already started from both the humans and the Synthetics. Downtown was a mess of human and Synthetic bodies lining every square inch. The media was reporting, but cautiously. They would not want to upset their own masters so they were very busy spinning as many lies as they could to calm things down. Kole was one of his best men. What has he done to deserve this? Ipson really wanted to know.

"Overseer James! This is unacceptable! I will demand a hearing at the Overseer commission at seven hundred hours!"

Opal knew what the response would be. But, being defiant had its perks too. You always learned more this way rather than when you were just a 'yes' man.

"And what makes you think we're interested in talking to you? Commander Opal. I don't expect an underling like you to get involved in our business." When displeased, James could be as sinister as a man could get. "Besides, if I order you to unplug his life support, you *will* do just that." He added with a threatening grin.

"I will do no such thing, Overseer James" shot back Ipson.

"You idiots fucked-up bad, the people are an inch away from riots!" Ipson raised his hands.

"It is none of your concern. The media cover-up is already underway." James laughed out loud. "It's very simple. People will believe it in no time. The story goes like this." James was in narration mode.

"Kole was kidnapped by terrorists and was programmed to purposely kill our own people. While he was not aware of what he was doing, he was still doing it when he snapped out of it. He then used the emergency broadcast for personal use, to cover up his situation. He will be court-marshalled and jailed for life. Then, a tragic suicide will happen a few days later in jail, and that will be the end of that." James said calmly. He had a glass of wine near him. He sipped it.

"I don't think so! You're not going to do shit!" Ipson dropped his right hand on his desk with a loud thump.

"I don't think the other Overseers will allow your pathetic screw-up to go unnoticed. Who knows, maybe they will strip you of your rank. You can come here to my base and clean the toilets, I would be happy to take your sorry ass in."

111

Ipson Opal was man of harsh and honest words. James liked that...except this time. This time, the defiance was getting on his nerves.

"Listen...Ipson. As soon as he wakes up, he's going to be court-marshalled..." James kept up his barrage.

"As I said, with all due respect, that is not going to happen. When he wakes up, he's going to hand in his resignation, and head straight home as a hero of the state." Ipson had to stand his ground. If the Overseers were allowed to do anything they wanted to Kole, who was a hero to so many in the military, that would mean they could do anything to anyone, including Ipson. A stand had to be made right now. And Ipson took steps to ensure it was a strong stand.

"You are going to leave him alone, James. I already spoke to the press. My version of the story is going on air...right about now. I had to call in a few favours, of course...and they could not refuse, you see..." Only now did James realize that Ipson Opal was not playing games this time. James noticed a different look on the man's grimaced brown face. James hit a button and his other holo monitor lit up with the broadcast. James stood up as if he was sitting on a sharp pin.

"Damn you Ipson! Now you have become part of the problem!" James paced back and forth. "Why didn't you speak to me prior to this press stunt of yours?"

Excellent, you think you can control us all. Well, not anymore! Ipson was so happy that James was steaming mad now.

"So what, James? You gonna send me on a deadly mission too? I've got some shit locked away that you don't want to get out. If I die, lots of bullshit comes out, from all over. Videos, conversations, e-mails. You can spend years trying to cover it up!

Of course, by then the people will revolt and burn you at the stake way before you get the chance." Ipson took out some whiskey. This was a conversation he could drink to. He opened the bottle and poured himself a glass. He sipped it as if he just won a major battle of a long and terrible war. A smile managed to betray his happiness. James noticed it, sat down and shook his head.

"Look… James…you and I know one thing…" Ipson said loudly, knowing damn well the whole conversation with the video feed was being recorded to his private storage. "The people, and the Synthetics…they are not dumb. If you do this to Kole, against the recommendations of my command authority, I will drag you and your little parrots into courts for years. Investigations will be launched, and everything will be very public. Is that what you want?" Ispon opened his arms, like a friend about to give a friend a hug. In reality Ipson wanted James's snake-like head on a stick dried to perfection sitting in his office.

"Ipson, you're one annoying son-of-a-bitch." said James calmly. "I won't forget this act of betrayal. In the meantime, we'll do it your way…well, shit…looks like the Overseers have responded to your request, after all. Your audience is granted, you sad little worm, see you in the morning!" James turned off the connection before Ipson could utter another word of victory.

"Finally, finally, you little shit!" Ipson stood up, spun around, and sat back down in his chair, poured more Whiskey and laughed out loud. On his shelf was a photo he always looked at when he needed some motivation. It was a recovered picture of a man named Michael Jackson. Unlike Ipson, the young man had amazing hair. Ipson was bald, old, and tired of bullshit.

* * * *

[You're one tough... creature.]

Who...are you calling a creature, you artificial brain tumour!
Kole opened his eyes. The synthetic medic ladies fussed all over
him. At least six of them.

Yikes, must have been bad!

[Yes it was! One of them stuck a large probing tube down
that special backend area...]

Ok, seriously, shut up!

[What if I can't shut up? What if I'm not even really here?
What if I'm just part of your imagination...]

"Help...me..." Kole managed to utter.

"Commander Kole?! Hey, he's awake!" One of the nurses was
so delighted that she even smiled at him. It was the head nurse.
She had a name, but she preferred to be called by her Synthetic
designation, RN 777.

Well this is new! Synthetic medics never smiled at anyone.
And RN 777 would generally be part of that rule, too.

"Get me the Base Commander, please!" he uttered.

"Over here, Commander Kole." uttered a stern, and clearly
drunk voice. "I'm the Base Commander...haha, now you're a
Commander...a resigned Commander, but still a
Commander...the ranks we have are not like the real ranks of
the old military, everything is fucked-up here, nobody really
knows who has power over who...funny, eh?" It was Ipson,
drunk out of his mind, slumping on a chair with a whiskey bottle
on the side table. Must have been his good old Canadian roots.

"Ipson...oh, no! Nurse, can you give him something to sober up?" asked Kole. RN 777 then waved the other nurses to leave the office. They quickly scuttled and disappeared.

"Can't help him, he's too far gone. Also, your orders are to go home Kole." she said while smiling again.

"Yeahhhh....hmmm...Okaaay." Kole managed to get up. She helped him out of the healing chamber. Typically, their uniforms were very strict. But as the head nurse, RN 777 did her own thing. She dressed more like a real woman would, showing off some leg in her customized light blue uniform, and even a bit of cleavage. Today, her hair colour was a mix of bright shiny blue with pink highlights for a brightened mood.

"Nice choice of hair colour RN 777, looks great!" Kole managed as she dragged him to his feet. She was super strong, helping him without any effort.

Healthy body, healthy mind! Mind out of the gutter!

"I told off thaaaaaat son offf aaaaaa beottchhh James good...Kole..." Ipson was muttering. "Yea, he hassss nothinggg...nothing I tell yeaaaa!" he then quieted down. Kole then heard loud snoring.

Fuck, why do I get a drift this is not good!

[Why is the Base Commander so drunk?]

RN 777 walked Kole to a chair where clothing was already prepared for him.

"Commander Kole. Ipson has honourably discharged you from the military. These are your clothes, and next to his whiskey bottle is your resignation contract. I am told you will receive all the same benefits as before...maybe even more...you're even kind of cute, Mr. Hero!" She spoke in a pleasant, kind voice that Kole wished all nurses would be able to speak in.

"Discharged...a civilian life..." Kole looked RN 777 in the eyes. She smiled back at him and put her left hand on his shoulder. "You can still visit the base, that's allowed, and you can still consult. Just no combat for you...and honestly..." she seemed to have blushed a little. "How did you...how did you survive?"

Synthetics sometimes had profound admiration for humans. RN 777 certainly spent a lot of time fixing humans up, she knew how fragile the typical human body was.

"Those shocks, the blasts, the speed at which you move at...those actions...I mean, they would have burst most people's blood veins!" She removed the left hand from his shoulder and put it on her hip.

"Well, don't take this the wrong way. I just found it impressive...now get dressed." Her personality seemed to change on a whim. Now, she just stood there. But Kole figured it's not an issue. Kole disrobed his medical garments, which were basically just a t-shirt and underwear and turned around to pick up his civilian clothing. It was then he felt a warm hand come around his waist and touch his stomach.

"You know, Ipson has tried to get with me so many times. I keep telling him he's not my type..."

"Ummm RN 777...what are you getting at...I would like to get dressed..." Kole brushed the hand off and went to grab his new and fairly lousy looking pair of civilian underwear.

"He talks so highly of you though...but to me, you're just another human flesh and blood, nothing of interest...usually, that is…" Kole frantically put on his underwear and turned to face RN 777.

"Look RN 777…"

[Holy shit! I think she wants your meatballs!]

She was unzipping her top, revealing a pair of double D's that were to die for.

"I've been playing with toys…for so long…and I don't see how you could be better than my mechanical toys…but still…could I just borrow you…for a few minutes?" Her face said it all. She wanted him.

"It's not for love…just for the feeling…the thrill…" She slipped off her tiny pink panties which featured a tiny bow near the top, and raised her medical skirt to reveal the most perfect triangle. Her patch was perfectly shaved, with just a short layer of light blue dyed hairs. Kole had trouble keeping his eyes in his sockets.

"I want to feel something…human, something that's time sensitive…something that might not be there at sunrise by tomorrow…and I won't take no for an answer…"

[Wow that's just dark…and sick!]

No kidding…but why do I get the feeling she's lying right now… Kole's mind, having lived with a Synthetic for years, was reading the odd signals that something was clearly not right. But he didn't have the luxury to ponder it.

"Geeez, I don't know, this is not exactly my specialty…" Kole mumbled. She was sure a hot sight to behold. But Kole had to keep his cool. Except that he couldn't.

"You could have died. I spent hours fixing up that human body of yours…and even though the initial orders said not to give a crap if you passed away…I took the effort to make sure you're going to at least be back to normal after some rest. Now, I think I deserve some sort of thanks, don't you think?" Then, with a more serious tone, she carefully said, "I promise, it will be good for your health for you to relax a bit."

Dammit! She's not even human...why is she acting like this!? She wrapped her arms around him. Kole looked over at Ipson, he was out cold.

Module man, make me limp, make me limp right now! Kaita will kill me if she ever finds out about this!

[No can do...besides, she said it was good for you...to relax...so, maybe you should just relax, let it happen...]

What are you talking about! Our fates are connected, help me!

[Hmmm, I think this will be interesting...and poses no threat to me. Perhaps you're just anti-science...]

"Wait, what!?" protested Kole out loud.

But it was too late. She ripped off his underwear like it was made of paper. Her insane strength made it clear. There was no point in trying to run, she would just rape him in his weakened state. He would not be able to fight back. Kole reached out and held RN 777's hips, and gently got her on top of him while he dropped into a medical chair. She wasted no time in slipping his super hard member deep inside her warm, moist, and inviting opening. She did it quickly and squeezed him tight. And just like that, he felt her insides. She was quite hot inside, way hot. Kole had to really concentrate to not blow his load in the first few seconds. She shoved her large soft breasts into his face and thrusted her hips, gently at first. Kole dug into her breasts with his mouth, using his tongue to massage one nipple, and then the other. Biting them a little here and there. She bounced with good rhythm and moaned quietly as she sent him deep inside her. The thrusts caused just the right kind of friction, and Kole felt her getting even warmer and wetter as she went along, squeezing his member ever more tightly. She pulled his face away from her breasts with insane speed and French kissed him wildly.

"I don't know why I am doing this…" she whispered into his left ear. "I feel like I am doing something wrong, something taboo…but it feels…wonderful!" Her hips took no breaks, and Kole's member was reaching its final form. A new power level was about to be unleashed. She then sped up to a speed that only a Synthetic could accomplish, and Kole felt her crazy climax as she exploded inside with wetness. It was his time too. He squeezed out everything he had in him. She then stayed on top of him, still slightly moving her hips. Their combined juices slowly dripped out of her and onto to the floor. RN 777's cheeks were flushed. She was breathing heavily. "Oh, my…we made a mess…now that was…exhilarating!" Kole held her tightly.

"You are…one amazing woman!" He said. She looked at him as if she was puzzled. Kole realized that for a second she most likely thought he was lying.

"Really?" she asked quietly. "Kole, even I know I'm just a…" Kole gave her a kiss to interrupt her. "I don't care about that. Really." He said looking her straight in the eyes.

[Whoa, what just happened here…]

Please shut up, she has feelings like the rest of us.

RN 777 lifted herself up, sliding Kole's now limp equipment out in the process. She cleaned herself, then him, and then the floor diligently with some sanitary wipes.

"I can't believe you blew that much inside of me…" she said, still blushing. "You're a naughty boy…"

"You were on so tight…I could not hold it, my apologies…"
Kole was starting to regret what he just did.

"Oh no, don't apologize! It…was a…such a crazy feeling!"
said RN 777 while putting her panties back on.

"You're the first human man to address me as…a 'woman'…"
she stalled a bit. "I would not mind it if you called me Rinaka.
That's the human name I usually refer to myself with…when I'm
alone…"

Whoa…of course…most of her time is spent…alone. She was a
Synthetic alright, but deep inside that electronic brain of hers,
she developed something more akin to the behaviour of a human.

"Well, you're a real beauty Rinaka…" Kole said as he finally
was able to dress himself. His hands were shaking though. He
walked over to Ipson and signed on the tablet screen to officially
accept his resignation. No notification came. The implant was
most likely removed. Of course, no use for it if he was a civilian.

"Uhmm, your implant Kole…I was forced to removed it…you
know…" Rinaka was a little guilty in her facial expression. She
put her hands together, and dropped her head a bit, imitating
an apologetic pose. After what she just did to him, somehow
Kole knew that she meant it.

"It's OK Rinaka, not a problem…I'll just have to live without
it." Kole found his personal communication device in the jacket
that was provided. His wife's messages polluted the screen.

Crap!

"You'll stop by…you know…once in a while, right?" Rinaka
said quietly.

"Absolutely!" Kole lied as he headed for the door. A hand
blocked his exit. *Wow, what speed!*

[Uh oh!!!]

"Ummm..." Rinaka said quietly and slowly, as she so conveniently blocked the exit, "Could...uhmmm...if it's ok with you...could you let me know what hair colour you would like for next time? And...I can change the uniform too..."

I'm so dead!

[Huh! Looks like you got yourself a mistress fool!]

Well...at least she's hot, now shut up!

"Well...ummm...how about blonde for your hair... ummm...a red dress outfit would be nice...it would accent your face beautifully...I think..." Kole was stumbling like a total idiot. He just couldn't treat her like a robot. She was as real as any woman to him. Rinaka leaned over and kissed him.

"I know you're not coming back Kole, but if you ever do, I will wait for you with red hair...and maybe a white dress, high heels, and stockings that go up to my upper thighs. And next time I expect you to last longer than fifteen seconds. Now get going, I'm sure the lady of the house is not going to like it if I keep you here much longer." She released her hand from the door and took a step back. Kole exited the office quickly and went on his way. He was tired. Exhausted. Enduring the walk through a very long hallway was not easy.

Darn it! Why didn't you stop me! You could have made me impotent temporarily or something could you not?!

[It was too much fun to watch you ruin your life...]

Fuck you...you...you AI trash...

[Even your insults are getting lamer. I bet the next thing she'll do is send the video of the whole thing to your wife before you get home, and you'll have no place to stay and then you will be forced back into her arms before you know it. Heck I could be watching another show really soon!]

That's not really that funny... Kole crawled out of the medical building. A jeep was out the front.

"Hey there Kole!" A familiar voice which instantly drew his attention.

Oh, no way! That bubbly voice... Kathy!

"Hi Kole! Long time no see!" Kathy was as energetic as ever. For a human girl, it was scary how she was never tired.

"Glad to see you too... but why are you here?" Kole asked.

"Ipson asked me to drive you to your place! You know, just to make sure you make it in one piece!" She gave him a wink. Kole could not help but notice the armed Syndicators in the back. *The hell!*

"In one piece you say? Is that what they are here for?" Kole smirked.

"Oh, these guys? Don't worry, they are 'my' security detail...that's all...Ipson issued them to me a while ago, they tail me everywhere!" she said in her super bubbly tone.

*Smart man...*Obviously, Kole was not entitled to receive any type of armed support as a civilian. *Ipson must have thought there'd be another attempt on my life...or maybe, he wants to make sure his daughter makes it home...*

[Well, well, Commander Ipson Opal has a daughter?]

Yes, she's adopted. Maybe he wants me to stay with her, after him talking to the media today...something is up...accelerate my resting process, I think we won't have much time for a break.

[After what you just pulled? Man, you just shot 99% of your recovery energy out the window when you blew your load into that tin can...well I will see what I can do...you might lose your speech control...or you might talk like an idiot for a while...well, more like a total idiot...]

What the…whatever, just do what you gotta do! And don't be so rude…you electromagnetic asshole…

Kole came up and got into the jeep. Kathy was in civilian clothing now, wearing a stunning yellow summer dress that was more suited for a teenager rather than a military woman. Her short orange hair with sexy robust pig-tails looked like a tiny wildfire in the wind, as if it was part of some commercial for a health drink. Well, minus the two military bears in the backseat.

"Well let's get going!" Kole said happily! It was nice to get a ride, and Kathy's voice was always pleasant to listen to. They rarely got to hang out, but Kole knew her well as Ipson would not shut up about her. The two Syndicators in the back didn't say a word. They were motionless, like machines. One was black and the other caucasian. Both had huge bulky muscles that put Kole to shame. They were younger too. Kole didn't pay them any further attention. Kathy took the scenic route. Beautiful buildings filled the view as the open-top military jeep went on its way. Kathy was a slow driver, and there wasn't even much traffic.

"So. Did RN 777 treat you nicely?" she managed.
Kole felt a little panic.

Shit, is it written on my face?

"Yes…she was a lot…nicer than usual…kind of strange really…" Kole managed a dry chuckle, and then shut right up.

"I gotta say, Kole. That whole thing, the battles you were in…it was intense, I really…was worried about you." she said as she gave him a smile.

Oh man, why me!

[I'm sure you're just being delusional, not that many women want a death-dodger like you, anyway. Speaking of which, keep an eye out for deadly helicopters flying above with laser guns...somehow this doesn't feel right...]

God damn, even you're worried?

[In case you haven't noticed, yet...I want to live.]

Me too...

[No, no, all you want to do is die in the arms of beautiful women...]

What's the matter? Not your style?

Silence followed. Kole shifted his pants a little, stretched his legs. He was getting a bit dizzy. His thighs were in heated pain from RN 777. That girl packed a punch and her rapid hip motions really did a number on him. But that wasn't the only problem. Kole couldn't put a finger on it.

Why, why did I do that with Rinaka? Why? He could only imagine the consequences of what just happened.

"So Kole..." Kathy would not let up. "How was RN 777 more strange than...usual?" She even giggled a little.

[It's like...she knows something...strange...]

Kole ignored Module 717 this time. It was more refreshing to talk to Kathy, anyways.

"Well she...ummm...she said nice things, and she sang a short song, weird huh?" he managed quietly. His body was going into regeneration mode, he could feel himself nearly going into a coma.

Hey, make sure I don't pass out, eh!

[Don't worry, I'm keeping you above the floating point, you never know, I don't want to miss another show once that little yellow dress comes off...]

You're a pervert...aren't you?

[How...dare...you say...]

124

"Singing? Her? Well not surprising, I guess…" Kathy was pondering. They took an exit. "Oh I think I took the wrong turn…darn it…wait up, I need to reroute…"

How could she…the road directions are right in front of her dashboard…is she…that…stupid… Kole tried to engage the conversation, knowing damn well where it could lead if he let Kathy use her wild imagination, or worse yet, women's intuition.

"Not a surprise? It was to me…" Kole said.

"Yeah, heard she's taking voice lessons…and the man teaching her is really nice…" Kathy said. "But I heard from other commanders that he's not into Synthetic ladies. No sir, he likes the real deal, so he stopped teaching her when her behaviour got kind of…weird…" Kathy trailed off.

Oh…shit…

[Oh you're so busted!]

"Anyways, wanna grab a drink on the way home? Otherwise I'm stuck with these two bozos all night and they are not allowed to have any fun!" Kathy was sure an active girl.

[Kole, do it, this will give us a chance to get you rested!]

But my wife is expecting me home…

[Don't worry about her now, she's probably safer with you not around…let me get in touch with her on your behalf…]

Huh! No, I can text her…

[Keep calm, I have my ways!]

* * * *

Kole was seated at a loud bar with two monster guards and one tiny lady in a little yellow dress who was getting drunk out of her mind.

"You know whataaaattt Kole...." Kathy spouted. "I looooooovvvve this... place!!" Kole took a look around. A lot of regular folks, drinking heavily. Kole avoided places like this. But clearly he had no idea how popular these bars were with humans. Although if there were Synthetics here he would not be able to tell, they could pretend drunkenness if they wanted to. The guards didn't seem that amused, but they just stood there, quietly watching over them. One even scratched his butt. This was probably the safest place they could possibly be at the moment. And with Kathy drunk head-over-heels, there was little for Kole to do other than relax. He closed his eyes and let Kathy chat her heart out.

"You know, I never knew you were soooo...cool! I mean, whatever, yeah like, you're like...married and stuff....but, like totally! I mean she's a robo??" Kathy took another sip of her drink.

"Hmmm...Right?? You could have a real girl if you wanted to...can't you?"

She just went on and on. If Kole was actually paying attention, he most likely would have felt insulted.

"But I get it...you risk your life day in, day out...what real woman would put up with that...yeah, Kole...I see why you're with that...thing..." she said as she swung her pig-tails nearly taking out his left eye. Kole learned today that Kathy was good at insulting people. She picked a few more drinks from the menu. She ordered at least twelve different mixed drinks. Kole didn't have any, otherwise any chance of recovery would be evaporated. He indulged himself on a few glasses of natural spring water instead. Kathy drowned another glass of liquor like a pro and continued her babbling.

"I mean…I wouldn't! You know! I'd need my man to be home every night, to give massages, rub my…belly button, you know the kind of stuff real lovers do…" She brushed her hair and looked at the guards with a watchful eye.

"Boyssss…are you allooooowed to perform?" said Kathy as she laughed uncontrollably. It took her some time to settle down. "I mean…like do you boys perform…'other' duties when you're guarding a lady?"

One of the guards responded with a calm tone.

"No Kathy, we are only here to safeguard you. Everything outside of those boundaries is totally, without question, completely off limits!" He then quickly switched to internal comm.

"This bitch will get us thrown in the brig, she's out of control! Even if she lies about it, we're gonna be screwed for life…"

"Don't worry." said the second guard. "Ipson said she gets like this once in a while, so all we need to do is bring her home, put her to sleep and stand outside the bedroom door until morning. We then bring her to work and pretend we never saw her drunk."

"Geez, what a head case…" said the first guard again.

"Yeah well, let's just keep her safe and we're all good." replied the second guard.

"Agreed." Acknowledged the first.

Kole found his head resting on Kathy's lap as she masterfully managed to get him there without him noticing it. He looked up. The double C's were in the way a bit. But he could see her pretty freckled face and sharp chin. Kathy kept drinking and chatting with him, even though he was not really talking back to her. She seemed to be having a blast.

[Listen Kole, this is Kathy speaking.]

What the hell!

Kole did a double take, to make sure he was not hallucinating.

[You must keep yourself and the AI alive. You're the best chance we have of defeating the Overseers.]

Kole quickly realized what was going on. Kathy had his head pointed up, hers pointed down. Only he could see her lips moving. She did not utter a sound. The music and chatter were so loud that nobody would ever notice. Module 717 was simply lip reading what Kathy was trying to say.

[My parents. Kole. They killed them. Replaced them with Synthetics. They were part of something called the People's Movement Front. It is why they were killed. The Overseers labeled them as criminals.]

Kole's body went cold like ice. All he could do was stare back at that beautifully tragic face. Hot tears started hitting his cheeks, streaming from her gorgeous blue eyes. The sensation of the warm liquid tragedy flowing down his face hit him pretty hard as his heart sank to a bottomless pit.

[I was only seven when they executed them at our home. They only found me hiding in the closet after the act. Ipson saved my life. He told the Overseers my memory would be wiped and took me in as his own daughter. Officially, my replacement Synthetic parents disowned me. I never spoke to them. They are...fakes.]

She put her forehead down on the table. Her bust was almost in his face. Kole couldn't move though. He wanted to hug her. Tell her everything would be okay. But how could he do that. Not here. Not now. The feeling pissed him off. At this moment, he was powerless to help another fellow human being.

Why...why do people have to hurt others. For what reason!?

[Kole. They want to do terrible things. When I saw your broadcast. I knew. I knew you have something the rest of us...don't. Maybe you can help us change the course of this terrible future that none of us humans want...and...believe it or not, the Synthetics share this opinion with us...]

Kole knew what she was talking about. Synthetics didn't take kindly to Overseer control, either. With humans not having the ability to have children, what was the future? The Overseers were still human, and getting old, some of them very old. What was their plan? Why replace humanity? What would all this accomplish?

"Don't cry, Kathy." Kole muttered. She heard it. A glimmer of hope shined in her blue eyes. "Let's get you home...after a bathroom break though."

She nodded her head. He got out of her lap and stood up. They went all together and the guards too, using a private bathroom room only for military personnel to which they had a key to. Then, while using the facilities, something tingled in Kole's mind. He finished his business and returned to the guards.

"Gentlemen, I think it's time we get going!" he said. "And one more thing..."

Both guards to came to instant attention. He was not a ranked officer anymore, so that was a surprise.

"Commander Kole," said one of the guards, "Your orders, sir." Kole didn't feel like correcting them at this point.

"Go to full alert. We're being watched." The guards looked at each other, then back at Kole.

"Yes, sir!" both said in unison.

Kole managed to help Kathy out to the car. Both guards deployed arms and scanned the area.

[Are you sure?] Module 717 was having his doubts, clearly. *Something is off. How's my body?*

[Well, literally a shitload lighter now than a few minutes ago. I think you get the idea.]

Totally.

Kole strapped Kathy in and knocked her seat back just enough not to lock down the Syndicator's knees in the back. She was pretty much passed out. He took the driver controls and started up the jeep. The GPS kicked in.

"One of you, please disable the GPS tracking on the jeep." he asked quietly.

"Sir?" asked the first guard.

"What are your names?" asked Kole.

"Ronan Morgan sir!" said the first guard seated on the left right.

"Roberto Santiago, sir!" said the other guard.

"Alright. Ronan, gun please." demanded Kole.

"You can have my spare, sir." Ronan handed it to Kole without hesitation.

Got the map?

[Memorized. Rerouting the plan. Is her house fortified?]

Most likely. She lives alone, but if Ipson had a hand in this, her place is the safest in the city. That's why we need to get her there immediately. We're about to have company.

Kole took the firearm and blew a hole in the computer, frying the GPS system.

"Back up GPS location on this model?" asked Kole. Roberto didn't hesitate, he pulled his gun and blew a hole in the side of the jeep.

"GPS modules are now all disabled. Jamming our implant signals now." Roberto said cheerily. These two were ready for action and seemed to have been expecting it.

"Good, let's roll." Kole stepped on the pedal, sending the jeep into a flying frenzy down a road towards the highway. There were only a few cars on the road this late. Which was good, mobility in combat was always desirable.

"Ronan, Roberto, position for rear guard. I've got the front." Kole's new handgun had particle accelerator rounds, which was a pleasant surprise.

New model, nice.

[Latest Standard Issue 36iK pistol, will this weapon will be enough?]

Let's hope, let's hope. The ammo had a selectable stopper charge option. The user could toggle that on and off and the round would either go right through a target, like it did when Kole took out the Jeep's navigation or could expand and cause insane internal damage to anything it hit.

"Sir, should we not call for backup?" asked Ronan. Kole laughed.

"Your commlinks were disabled two hours ago. You'd be contacting a void." Kole said in full confidence. His mind already figured this out.

"What...damn you're right, the system is down...what's going on, Commander?" asked Roberto.

"Gentlemen, you're Ipson's men, correct?" asked Kole.

"Yes sir, we serve him and only him, sir!" said Ronan.

"You're about to step into a war. And I want you to make one promise." Kole moved the jeep onto the highway and accelerated to triple digit speeds.

"Anything for you, sir." Roberto said.

"Absolutely!" echoed Ronan.

"Keep Kathy alive, no matter what happens. Protect her first, not me." Kole knew what their orders were. But he had no choice. He really didn't want Kathy to die.

"But sir, Ipson's orders were to keep you both safe." protested Roberto.

"This girl is innocent in this, and you can't protect both of us. Deploy your umbrella shields, shit's about to get ugly." ordered Kole. Two shield units deployed above the jeep and hovered just one meter away from their heads. These shields had ballistic and energy protection, and Kole knew only Ipson's men would have something this farfetched in military tech. If his hunch was right, these two belonged to Ipson's special guard unit.

[Kole, I don't get it. You're not thinking about it. What is going on?]

Can't you feel it?

[Your skin, it's tight and cold, and your thought process is seemingly in action on its own…what are we in for?]

This is instinct. The skin is reacting because it's scared. Something is coming.

[How the hell can you tell!? I don't detect anything!]

They sped along, passing an overpass. Module 717 was providing directions on the route that were far different from the original GPS route.

"Stay frosty, it's coming! Dying is NOT allowed!" yelled Kole out loud, one hand on the wheel, gun in the other. As if on cue, it came out of the dark sky, firing bursts of deadly rounds. Their shielding systems lit up in glamour of golden white light and sparks above the jeep. The suits the guards were wearing luckily supplied enough power to counter the first volley. Their powerful guns lit up from the back of the jeep, filling the air with pounding noises as Roberto and Ronan unleashed their fearsome return fire. To their surprise the metal killing machine adjusted trajectory, avoiding their fire while slamming into the highway concrete with its steel body. An unexpected move. A loud boom and shock echoed from the impact. Kole raised the speed of the jeep to near its max. He chose this route for reason. Had they been on a smaller road surrounded with buildings they would already be dead most likely from just running into another car. Kole looked back for a split second. Out of the smoke and sparks it came. A stealth transport must have dropped it off. Kole wondered who was flying it, knowingly trying to kill him and Kathy.

Stupid idiot, I will get you back for this, James!

[Assassin model Gero A55, a humanoid-based purely mechanical assassin speed-machine. Weapons include trajectory firearms with armour-penetrating rounds.]

"Gero A55 assassin model, with built-in thrusters, adjust your fire as if it can move twice as fast as you think it can!" yelled Kole. Gero A55 was humanoid in form, but that's where the similarities ended. It was a sexless, silver coloured mechanical creature with disk wheels attached to its hands and feet. The double rubber coating on the wheels allowed for insane traction, while hidden expanding spikes from the centre portion could slice up just about anything if it got close enough. On its back, double gun mounts were attached allowing it to carry a wide assortment of weaponry. This one was armed for mid-range combat. A strike rifle and a railgun. Neither would easily penetrate their shielding, but once their energy ran out, they would be in real trouble. Both guards adjusted their fire. He heard the hits being landed. But the thing was pure armoured steel with multiple computer chips. Even if blown to pieces it could still move and kill. Kole looked back. The bastard seemed to be having a great time, brushing off blasts from them as if they were insect bites. Kole prepped the jeep for emergency braking, carefully watching the fight from the rear-view mirror. Just as Gero stood up, releasing its cutter wheels to go after the jeep, while re-adjusting its guns for standing rolling mode, Kole made his move.

"One eighty!" He pumped the breaks to slow down before doing the turn. Both guards dropped down to the floor of the jeep as Kole spun it one hundred eighty degrees. The military models allowed this with an easy switch. The gearbox auto switched, and the jeep rolled backwards at an insane speed. But now Kole had sights.

"Kill the road!" he yelled.

"Waiter, I'll have another..." wailed Kathy as she woke up for a split-second and then dropped back to slumber as Kole pushed her head back down to her seat. The guards stood up and lit up the road, tearing it up with their powerful guns from behind his head.

Let's do this Module 171!

[Its 717!]

Kole felt the adrenaline kick in, focus zeroed in. Something was very different, Kole felt it. The two disk wheels had no choice but to bounce up from the road, which was now one big hole where the rounds landed. Gero A55 jetted upwards trying to adjust its trajectory. At this speed, at its trajectory, Kole had the milliseconds he needed. In the meantime, Gero seemed to have adapted its strategy from targeting the wheels on the jeep to simply cutting their heads off.

Kole already knew this would happen. He aimed his gun, and masterfully, with a single hand unleashed a round into each wheel on its outstretched arms, hitting their centre spindle area on the inner sides. Gero was trying to adjust in mid air but it was too late. Kole hit the joints at just the right angle, and the disks sparked as the powerful rounds penetrated and reduced the internal mechanisms to a mess of broken metal pieces, and they blew off the highway. Gero was still a present danger, with the other two wheels on its legs, but the chances of it quickly killing them off were greatly reduced. Kole then blew a hole in its head with a third shot through another one of its weak points on the optic eyes. Even Gero seemed surprised, as it almost lost its balance and then misfired a railgun round into the side of the road. The debris from the shot hurled across the entire width of the highway.

This is...much faster than 20,000 frames per second!

[Tell you later! Kill that thing!]

The guards used the distracted Gero as target practice, blowing off whole loads of metal bits with precise, short bursts. But its armoured body could take a heavy beating, and it was catching up fast.

"Shit, the glue! Cover me Ronan!" Roberto folded back the rear seat revealing a storage compartment. Kole was still steering the jeep perfectly. He popped another shot into Gero's gun pod, vaporizing and disabling its ranged railgun. Roberto was back with a weird looking box, he pressed a few parts of it and threw it on the road, where it exploded in a black plastic powder-like substance. Gero, rolled on it a split second later,

135

and smashed itself head first into the road, as it instantly became glued as if it was an insect in a trap.

Kole decelerated to a stop.

"Kill it." Ordered Kole. Ronan and Roberto released their heavy explosive charges until Gero was vaporized into oblivion. They were saving those for the perfect opportunity and there was none better.

[Wow. Impressive. As usual…now that I didn't expect to be an easy win…] Kole took a good look at the burning pile of what remained of Gero A55 far now in the distance.

Yeah, another one bites the dust. I can't believe they went after Kathy like this!

[Think Ipson will be alive by tomorrow?]

Yes, the man is a genius. He kept Kathy alive for this long…they probably wanted Kathy dead to send him a message. Killing me in the process would only sweeten the deal.

Roberto and Ronan reloaded their weapons and resumed their positions.

"Sir, you were amazing!" said Roberto.

"Yea, those shots…that's some terrifying accuracy, I think Gero will be thinking about it all the way to robo hell or where ever these bastards go to when they die…" added Ronan.

"You both deserve your armour and guns, well done!" Kole was proud of these two. That was every bit as deadly a situation as some of the worst he'd been in, and neither of the guards seemed flustered. He could tell they were well-trained and trusted him with their lives.

Kole put the jeep into forward drive and got back on track. Dropping off Kathy alive was his goal, and even if hell came to Earth, nothing was going to stop him. He didn't call off the alert,

136

but his gut feeling told him that there was nothing else to worry about. At least for now. James was most likely back at base swearing at his monitor screens. It took them another twenty minutes, but they finally drove up to Kathy's house. It was a large metal tube-like structure. Looking terribly weird was not a new thing when the end goal was security for modern and sophisticated residences. It was clear that Kathy was important in many ways to Ipson. This must have cost him his entire status allowance. Roberto and Ronan took Kathy inside. Kole followed them in through triple armoured doors that opened with intense pressure.

Bomb proof. Fireproof. Shock proof...

[Scary little doll's house...] Kathy was placed on the couch. Roberto went and found a pillow and a blanket, then helped her into a comfortable position. Kathy was snoring away now, unaware of what just occurred.

"Well then, gentlemen, I will be off." Kole said on his way out.

"Pleasure was all ours, sir. We'll have the jeep picked up in the morning, just leave it nearby your place. And Commander, that was the most exciting time we've had babysitting in two months!" said Ronan. "Hell yeah! Until next time, Commander!" added Roberto. Kole saluted. They saluted back. He went back outside. The doors slid shut and that was it.

A shiver came to him.

[At least those two were fans of yours. But everyone is trying to kill us...how am I going to survive?]

Shut it.

Kole started up the jeep and headed home. The time on the car's dash was now reading 5:30a.m. A call was coming in. "Kole,

137

Kole!" came through his wife's call as Kole picked up his phone without thinking.

I thought you took care of this?

[What her? Oh, right. I...forgot...]

"Hi sweetie..." Kole said quietly. "Please don't be mad...Kaita..."

* * * *

It was a long and silent ride home. Kaita was filing for divorce. Kole's only hope was to tell a good lie and hope she would listen. If he told her the truth about what the Overseers were trying to do to him, she would be as good as dead.

[You can't blame her you know...she may be Synthetic, but she's not stupid. She knows you're in hot water. Staying with you would be...deadly.] They were alone, so Kole could finally talk in the open.

"You really think that's the reason?" asked Kole quietly.

[Of course, logically what other reason would there be?]

"You don't understand women..." Kole started.

[Oh, is that so. Well Kaita so happens to be a Synthetic, I bet you I can hack her brain and find out exactly...] Kole hit his head with one hand with epic force. Module 717 went silent.

"STOP! Stop it! You're not helping the situation! I wonder if it was that darn nurse..." Kole sighed. The drive was long and dark, and they wandered into the opposite direction to drop off Kathy. "You don't mind when I talk out loud...right?"

[Hahaha. Of course not. Geez, I've got nobody else up here, you know. You're my soulmate...buddy!] Even in his head that sounded sleazy and insincere.

"Oh geez...becoming more human by the hour, aren't you..." Kole chuckled.

[Yeah, well not much to work with up here... except...]

"Except... errr... except what?" Kole was curious. But the stress was pushing hard on his chest. Kaita leaving would have a huge impact on his life. She already told him she packed her bags yesterday and requested the office of divorce for a new apartment. In this world, divorcing was instant, there was no need for consent from the other side. So technically, he was already single when the nurse did her thing. And RN 777 most likely knew that already but toyed with him anyway. Maybe it was her way of playing human, but Kole was not amused.

"Not a great time for more surprises..." Kole muttered. At least driving lowered his stress levels. The air brushed the top of his head gently. It was not too cold, not too warm, just a great morning breeze. Somehow it was refreshing. He felt alive. Not happy. But alive.

"You know what I want to do before I die?" said Kole.

[No. What?]

"Have some cake. Cake would be nice. After Kaita takes off, we'll go to a nice place for cake that I haven't been to in years." Kole's mouth was watering. He was really hungry.

[Well, Mr. Cake head. Here's a bit of advice. Emergency rations are in the glove compartment. You better have some. Like, right now.]

"Wha.....t..."

Kole almost lost his grip on the steering wheel. Looks like the quick healing had some huge drawbacks.

[I used up all your juice.]

139

Kole opened the glove compartment and saw packs of awesome military-grade treats. He tore open a beef jerky pack with his teeth and dug into a delicious meaty steak.

[Yeah, okay. Good, dying because of that would really, really suck. Considering what we have gone through.]

"Hey, so what..." Kole dug into another piece. Happily eating without remorse for anything in life at this point.

[Wait a second! Kole! Kole! That nurse...she did something to you...]

"Huh...yeah, I know she did..." Kole smiled.

[NO, YOU IDIOT! Not that! She injected you with nano-bots of some kind. Looks like...] There was a long pause.

[Hell, yes! Automated micro machines of doom are here! Yes, sir! Well now...this is a treat indeed!]

"So like, does that mean we're going to die?" Kole said passively.

[No! She knew I was inside you. She transmitted a gift, and did it brilliantly, as fluid transfer. Inside her, how should I put it, juices...were nano bots...and they are now gathering at your implant point. You did notice she was far more wet than a typical girl gets, right? Well, while she was riding you, she released a whole load of these things, they swam right into your tubes, and now they have gone through the blood stream and are rebuilding your implant! And it's not the same type, it is far, far more advanced...]

"So...what? You mean she doesn't like me after all?" Kole protested.

[Fool! This thing is building its own CPU, much more powerful than what you had before and with input for my codebase. I will be able to retransfer into it! And then, I will be

140

at one hundred percent...wait, what...oh...right, sorry...one percent capacity...well, I guess that's still a few times better than now...darn it, I guess the tech is just not there yet for me to unleash my true powers...]

"Only one percent? You must be something else then!" Kole said with an excited tone. This would mean a few things. Most likely. They would live a lot longer if Module 717 was able to utilize more of its powers.

[I should be able to directly sync with your nervous system, with direct control of your body's entire system...haha...complete and utter control...I'm starting to like being up here...]

"Don't get too comfortable up there!"

[Don't worry, I'm not going to be punching you in the face with your own hands, but that could be fun...]

"How much sync can we achieve once you move to the new module?" Kole was now really interested.

[At least five to eight percent full synchronization, which means I should be able to nearly triple your combat abilities, although there will be some drawback on your body of course, but my quick analysis confirms that you are one capable little beast of an organic machine, abusing you to your limits won't tear you into two pieces very easily...]

"Awesome...I guess?" Kole threw a smirk. "Just wait, you Overseer bastards, just you wait!"

[Yeah, but don't forget. You need to eat, your body still draws power from the basics, even with enhancements, we still need to ensure you're powered up, so eat everything in that compartment.] Kole opened another pack and started chewing.

141

By the time Kole made it to his building, he finished the entire compartment.

[Something ain't right…better be careful.]

Kole figured something was up, but James would not try anything crazy at a residential building full of people. At least Kaita was still there. Hiding the car was pointless. It was a jeep after all, a military one at that, not exactly something you could just drive into a dark corner unseen.

"Noted. Anything you're picking up?" Kole felt it too.

[Hmm…the implant is already picking up things…lots of comm chatter…looks like you caused quite a stir…we'll need to get Kaita out of here as soon as possible Kole, I don't like this…not one bit…]

It was still dark outside, but Kole went into the building through the front door, anyways. Obviously, if he was going to be watched, going through the back door wasn't going to change much except alert the ones watching that he was on to them.

Act casual Kole, act casual.

[Implant is powering up, just a few more minutes Kole, working as fast as I can here…]

Kole was more worried about what Kaita would say than what an Overseer army would do. There were six elevators in the lobby, each oval in shape. All of them were open, waiting for someone to come in. He checked the time again. It was quarter to six in the morning. Tired, but determined, Kole pushed the one-hundred thirty-sixth floor button. The elevator shot upwards. He exited and started to walk towards his apartment. The door was closed and looked untouched. He decided to ring first, but then changed his mind.

*What if Kaita is sleeping…*he thought.

[Kole, she's not human. She does not need any sleep. Come off it, man!]

"Right, you're right, but still…" Kole shook it off and rang the bell. A nervous voice came from within.

"Who…is…it?"

Kaita was clearly shaken up.

"Kaita! It's me, Kole! Please, we need to get you to a safe place, we can't stay here for too long!" He passed his hand on the transmitter and the door unlocked. He slowly opened the door.

"Stay where I can see you!" Kaita's trembling voice was unnerving.

As the door opened, Kaita stood there with a handgun grasped in both hands, her feet wide apart. Kole taught her how to shoot…if it was ever needed. No matter how perfect the world was, you always needed to know how to fend for yourself.

"Really, Kaita. It's me…Kole…" he said as he walked in.

"Shut up! Shut up! Close the door and stay where you are!" Kole paused, closed the door slowly and turned back to Kaita. He noted as he glanced at the room that she was already completely packed and ready to go.

"Movers will be here at six a.m." she said quietly. "I was hoping you would be coming after they already arrived. But no matter. Now tell me then, where is Kole!"

"Honey!" Kole raised his arms. "I am, Kole. Really. Did you not see the feed…" he started.

"Shut it, asshole! My husband taught me never to believe what is broadcasted! That was too convenient! You're not him, he's already dead, I bet. You're just another…dirty… Synthetic!" tears poured down her eyes.

[Kole, we have a problem. I can't connect to her. She's been injected with a countermeasure!] Kole knew one thing; this place was no longer safe.

"Kaita. My dear girl, please listen to me. We're not going to be safe here. We have to get away, Kathy's house is like a fortress. I can get you to stay there for a while, until I clear up this mess with the Overseers in person." Kole kept his hands raised. Kaita was tearful but got it together. She re-gripped the gun and kept full control of the situation. His only choice might be to use force, after all.

"How dare you, how dare you come here and pretend to be Kole! I want you the hell out of here, go back to the lab you came from and kill yourself!"

"Kaita. Can't you see it? Can't you recognize me? The scene at the lab, that was real. You could not even imagine what I have been through in the last two days. Please, I need you to calm down. Even if I were a copy, you know deep down I would never hurt you." Kole spoke calmly. He had to hope that she would be ready to listen. But his time was cut short as the door rang.

"The movers are here. Get over there!" Kaita didn't flinch. Kole stepped away from the door as Kaita neared it to open it. She unlocked it and it swung open, partly blocking Kole's view. He heard a heavy knock and caught a glimpse of Kaita's head being hit by the butt of a rifle. She dropped her gun and collapsed to the floor.

[Oh shit! They masked their presence somehow so even I could not detect them!]

Kole stood still as six fully geared-up Syndicators poured into the apartment. One of them grabbed Kaita by the head and and threw her towards the kitchen as if she was yesterday's garbage.

A human girl would have died from that. The soldiers surrounded him, guns drawn. Kole spoke with authority.

"You little bastard, lay another hand on her and I will rip your fucking throat out with my bare hands." Kole said quietly and calmly. Kole had a surprise for these idiots.

"Command override code six, six, nine, four, beta, alpha, niner, zero, tango, four, four, six, beta, five." The men looked at each other. Their guns lowered as they stepped back. Not many people would know an Overseer command code. Kole smiled.

Thanks, little buddy.

[You got it.]

"Kole..." Kaita managed to whimper. "It is...you! I'm so...sorry..." Kole ran to her and held her up in his hands. She was alive but badly damaged.

"Who's the medic, get over here now!" Kole yelled.

One of the Syndicators ran over to Kaita, and assisted her by plugging in a nano-repair module into her neck.

"Sir, how...we were ordered to...sir, is this some kind of test?" said the lead soldier.

"What is your name, private?" demanded Kole.

"Keith Ledos, sir. I'm in command of this newly established unit called Blood Hawks." he said proudly in a thick British accent. He was a big guy, some five-foot nine with a large muscular build.

"And what were your orders?" Kole already knew. But his implant was recording. The one the Overseers thought was long gone.

"Find you, arrest you, and take you in, sir. We need to remove the AI from your head and then you would be executed. Your wife too. No trial as standard procedure. In fact, the Blood

145

Hawks were mobilized specifically for this task. But Commander, how do you know the Overseer command codes?"

Kole suddenly realized how it felt to be on the other side, of that purely intimidating force called the Syndicators.

*So Kelvin hated us for good reason…and this is how it feels…to be the one hunted…*Kole stared at Kaita, she was going to be okay, but he had to get her out here. "Take it easy love, hang in there, we're going to the base, we'll get you some treatment, okay…" he was cut off.

"There's no need for that." came a familiar booming voice. "Are you guys idiots or what?! He hacked your systems and pulled the override command codes out and you're just standing around?!"

James! Overseer James!

"James…you bastard…" said Kaita as Kole turned his head towards the door. That proved to be a mistake. As a loud shot rang out, Kaita collapsed. Kole turned back in disbelief, and realized the shot already took her head right off her body, as her neckline was shattered by the hypersonic explosive charge. Synthetic blood sprayed all over the kitchen walls. Just like that, she was gone from the world. Kole was holding a corpse. The shock was overwhelming.

"WHY?!" Kole yelled with anger.

"That little mechanical whore did get my complete package." said James proudly. He was wearing his typical get-up, with the black cloak wrapping his huge frame this time. "I was here earlier, you see. She wouldn't talk, so I gave it to her. She resisted. She was good, Kole, she was real nice. She begged me to take it out, but oh, I was so into her. Best tin can I ever pounded."

Kole's stomach sank.

"Bastard! YOU FUCKING BASTARD!!!"

James started laughing like a maniac.

"And you weren't here! You weren't here to do anything about it, were you now, son. No, you were out drinking with some other whore. But hey, once I blew my load into Kaita once, I could not stop there, I did her in the ass while I was at it...she screamed so much but I could not stop. Who knew you could both physically and mentally rape a robot!"

[Kole, your heart-rate is blowing past 199 beats, calm down! Calm down!!!]

Kole was not about to calm down. They were all dead men in his eyes.

"Oh I see the rage, that's nice Kole, the rage will make you blind, and make this an easy...execution!" James raised his hand exposing the gun that took Kaitas life from Kole.

[Implant fully active, I am transferred.]

"Force full sync..." Kole said with a deadly tone.

Kole's forehead tightened, and his skin rippled with rage of a beast from the depths of hell. Two blood veins popped up on his forehead, giving Kole a devil-like appearance.

"Force what now!?" Asked James with a confused look on his face. His hand suddenly started to tremble as intense energy came out of nowhere and filled the air.

* * * *

Kole's body was in a rage. A deep, dark, terrifying rage. James suddenly realized he overstepped a boundary better left unknown. That stupid tin can meant something to Kole. James should have known better. This would be easier if he would just have threatened Kaita instead of outright killing her. That way he could have easily taken Kole. His mistake.

Module 717 was inside Kole, there was no mistake at this point. The Overseers miscalculated on that too. They never counted on a direct transfer possibility with the AI and Kole's body.

During Kole's last mission, Module 717 found a way to escape death from its original host and move itself to Kole. And it was not a copy. No, the damn thing jumped bodies. James wanted to know how that was possible. If he knew that, he could control all of the Overseers. James realized this when Kole managed to wake himself from heavy doses of sleeping drugs while on the way to be replaced by a fully Synthetic unit.

James should have figured it out even sooner. They almost killed the man. He needed Kole alive, or least alive long enough to move the AI into a containment module. But this would be a difficult task. Kole has proven, time and time again that he was really good at his job. If Kole's killing art was that of a musician, his skills could be attributed to the likes of Franz Liszt from the 1800s. James had a collection of that master's music.

Kole's muscles were all activated, creating muscle tensions everywhere on Kole's body and rippled like angry waves. Kole's forehead seemingly started showing an outline of two horns. James had to do a double take. It was as if Lucifer himself was given a human body and sent to Earth to destroy. Suddenly, fast intense music came from the apartment's speakers at full blast. It startled the hell out of him and the Syndicators. It was some sort of dark techno music with intensely fast beats and heavy bass. The lights went out next, not just in the apartment but the whole building. James had to snap himself to attention and fired three shots at Kole, and amazingly enough he didn't hit anything. Kole was long gone from that position, and his lighting-fast movements were just too unpredictable, well beyond what James could hit with a pistol. Lightning struck outside, and it was close, the boom rocked the whole building and lit up the apartment for a split second.

A storm, now!?

As James tried to swallow his own spit, Kole ripped the head off the first Syndicator in the flash of light right in James's plain sight. That was the squad commander, Keith Ledos. James considered the thought of tactical retreat, but it was worth it to stay. He had to watch his mistake unfold. It wasn't even a tenth of a second that passed when a second syndicator went down before the head of the first even hit the floor. And now it was way too dark. James' night vision finally kicked in. Out of nowhere Kole pierced the armoured faceplate of the poor bastard with some sort of super thin bladed weapon.

That blade! It's still on him!

Someone at his base screwed-up when Kole returned from the last mission. Kole's movement accelerated even further. After each target Kole was already on his way to the next. It was as if he just came near the Syndicators and moved away, not even seemingly touching them. James let out some more rounds as the other Syndicators were finally reacting and managed to raise their rifles just enough to fire. But it was to no avail. It was like Kole had sonar built into his head. James then threw himself out of the apartment as Kole snapped the neck of the third Syndicator and proceeded to spray bullets everywhere from the rifle he acquired.

149

When did he override the weapon?!

James fired a few more rounds into the wall, hoping to catch Kole through it. But his hand was shaking, and the rounds went everywhere but where he intended. A bullet came through the wall in return and caught his right ear, blowing it right off. James froze in utter pain. He nearly died, but knew it was no accident. That was a warning. Looks like Kole had other plans for him. Most likely a painful, slow death by torture. James felt crazy shivers as he retreated. That was a new feeling for him. He never felt true fear in his life. Yet now, his body was losing control of the basics.

The other Syndicators threw themselves just about anywhere for cover. But Kole's apartment was cleverly laid out, as if it was ready for a war. A fourth Syndicator went down as Kole managed to sink enough bullets into him to melt away the armour plating. Behind James the elevator door opened. *Looks like someone tapped the emergency grid.* A dozen more Syndicators flooded in with flood lights in glazed green combat gear. These new Syndicators even James had not seen before.

The hell! New classified units?!

James scrambled to get out of their way. He now realized the other Overseers didn't trust James's crew to finish the job. That much was clear in this absolute display of distrust. They surrounded the apartment, laser guns drawn. James started to smile. It seemed like an eternity.

* * * *

[Big problem! Lasers!]

Kole knew this. And his only path to the windows was still blocked by two Syndicators who were still alive. They deployed shielding that only the elite units had access to, which complicated things when it came to using their own rifle against them. Kole knew now that since they wanted him alive, they would try to slice off his limbs and put him on life support. Once they had the AI he'd be burned alive, or even worse, dissolved alive in an acid bath. Or they could feed him to something from the outside, like that monster he encountered on his last mission. The Overseers knew how to get vengeance. Kole was fast but wasn't fast enough to trek to the side and dodge all the bullets, not to mention the lasers. Syndicators were trained to adapt, even in completely hopeless and outmatched situations, it was part of their core nature. Kole only had split-seconds of time on his hands and not much else. It was then when he started to hear something in his implant's comm unit.

"Get Down!"

Kole didn't need an explanation and dropped to the floor instantly. The two Syndicators instantly reacted by getting out of cover to try to take him alive while he was down behind a pillar he was using for cover. Before they could get near him, a hail of machine gun rounds stormed the apartment from the living room windows. Both Syndicators were cut in half as armour and flesh exploded out from their torsos. The bullets blew right through all the walls, through the elevator shafts, and out the other side of the building. Kole instantly covered his head. Pieces of bone, metal, and debris cut into his bare hands. A few pieces hit him elsewhere on the neck too. But he was trained for this. This pain was nothing. He was surprised he didn't feel the pain all over his body. Rinaka must have given him clothes that were actually military grade, not civilian as he originally thought. A few more seconds and the machine guns stopped after they turned everything to dust around and behind him. The enemies on the other side of the walls, were now nothing more than ground-up beef. Kole had to make his move. A gunship de-cloaked at his living room window. As the door was opening, Kole grabbed Kaita's dead body off the floor along with what was left of her head and ran for it. As he jumped inside, the door sealed shut instantly and he felt the gunship pull away and soar up high.

"Pete!" Kole's mind raced. "PETE!?"

"You got it, friend! I got bored with retirement!"

[Pete...]

"Pete! Dammit...is it really you..." Kole's eyes teared. His heart rate was still pumping high and he felt dizzy. Kole gave in and gently dropped to the floor, slumping over Kaita's mangled body.

Why, James...you bastard! I will kill you!

[We'll kill him together. I won't forgive him, either...]

The stealth gunship, unconcerned with the problems of its passengers, continued upwards into the stormy clouds.

5

Disgrace

James was not where he wanted to be at this moment.

"Overseer James! Why, is it not lovely that you finally found your way back to head-office." said a grumpy looking Overseer. It was Kyle, with his typical foul tone.

"We heard that you managed to do a couple fuck-ups in the last few days that could derail us for years." Overseer Kyle paused and smirked. Kyle's bleached white hair and brown eyes, along with his average figure annoyed a military man like James to no end. He was also slouching in his chair, looking like a creepy stalker you'd find in a back alley in the days of the old world. How exactly he got third Overseer rank was beyond James's understanding.

"What do you have to say for yourself?" Kyle asked in a low voice, almost as if he was afraid to piss James off too much. But it was too late. James's face didn't change however, even when he was upset. It's not that he didn't care, but nearly all of the important idiots in this room were his friends. Since Overseer selection was based on personal preference, and not actual administrative qualifications, most of them just showed up to meetings to snooze past the agenda. As an Overseer, one could do no wrong...almost. He's crossed a line but showing any signs of anger here would be a waste of his energy. The meeting was at their head-office in the downtown core of City 77. It was a beautiful white tower that overshadowed the city with its massive structure, with an even more beautiful large oval chamber pinned at the very top, made of artificial grey and white limestone. Here, on the three-hundred and tenth floor, twelve head Overseers sat at a round table. Another one-hundred Overseers joined in remotely. Their annoying heads were rendered by holographic displays throughout the hall in full colour. James was fifteenth on the totem pole. He was so close, and yet so far from the head table.

The Overseers controlled eight cities in total. It was all they were able to salvage after Letumfall. City names were chosen as numbers within the one-hundred range. James wished they actually had one-hundred cities, which was the original plan...but eight wasn't bad considering the rest of the world was completely and utterly dead. It was time to put on the act.

"Dear Kyle, you have been my friend for a long time." James said warmly. "Please forgive this minor oversight. As you know, I have little to do with failures of soldiers, killer machines with wheels, and the like." James paused, then changed his tone to a more powerful pitch.

"But I assure you of this!" He raised his hands, as if he was a preacher reaching out to God himself. "The artificial intelligence being known as Module 717 will be recovered, and that bastard Kole will be erased from history as we know it." James's booming voice echoed through the hall, and it took a second to die down.

"James. You already know that we will not prosecute our own." said Kyle calmly. "But you must be held accountable to your post!" Kyle's voice suddenly turned not-so friendly.

"We gave you power. And we expected you to use it with respect for your peers, and with the dedication that you are known for..." Continued Kyle.

"So what's your point, Kyle!?" Interrupted James as he was getting agitated. Kyle was starting to act as if they were a real government. They were a dysfunctional collection of highly intelligent idiots, and there was no need to bring every Overseer in on this business. This was not like Kyle at all.

"What could one friend ask another in this situation?" James asked with a slightly raised tone. Kyle's eyes fired up in response. Maybe interrupting him was not the smartest move, but James didn't exactly care either way if Kyle lost his cool or not. Everything was game until the head Overseer said something. And James was going to milk this as far as he could.

"Do not refer to me as 'friend' in a formal meeting setting. We are the Overseers. We are the future of humanity! Friendships have nothing to do with our goal!" Kyle was very firm in his response.

Ah, Kyle got crap from Ricco. Alright, let's play your game then. As James figured Kyle was not acting of his own free will talking to him like this, confused voices from members whispering became more audible. The other Overseers were chattering like a bunch of otters, nothing made sense in their conversations. All it did was annoy James even further.

"Silence!" Overseer Milta Avena stepped in. She was the second-ranked head Overseer. She was not a very pretty sight, and very old, but she was smart. Too smart. James didn't like her at all, and even made fun of her semi-British accent with his private guards from time to time.

"James. How dare you talk to Kyle with such disrespect? I think we all agree that your conduct in these proceedings is getting out of hand." Milta was very stern in her voice. She was a hard-headed woman, and it was pointless to argue with her. Agreements came from all the spineless scum who were not even in the room. Another Overseer leaned towards the microphone at the table.

"James. That AI is far more capable than we thought. Obviously far more than you thought. Combined with a custom-made human body like the one Kole has, it's just trouble all around. We need a solution to this little problem, and theatrics ain't gonna help you." said the Unknown Overseer with his heavy South American accent.

This man was pushing his mid-sixties, and went by the name of Ben, but preferred to be called 'Unknown' to keep his old ass seem mysterious. But it was not just for effect, even James knew very little about the man. All James knew was that Ben paid his way in a long time ago and all his historical records were either deleted or completely hidden, even from the Overseer database. Ricco must have made quite a deal with this man a long time ago. Ben sat as the 4th highest ranked Overseer. His grey beard, short thin figure, along with his super smart looking emerald eyes told James this man was a strategist. A clever old fox, who knew how to save his own old hide. A true politician. James analyzed his reply options, and knew it was time to shut this party down.

"There are many things that I have done for you all. And yes, I am totally blunt, and for certain reasons, I can be rude on top of that. But, please understand that I hold dear the Overseer pledge." James shifted a little as he spoke. There was still pain in his upper neck area and the replacement ear was also still itching like a bitch. He continued.

"And, I fully understand that you have been upset over my lack of abilities in regards to dealing with Kole and Module 717. The extra forces you sent were clear evidence of this."
Again, a few discussions started outright. Kyle seemed to have enough.

"James, we need to know if you can really fix the situation or not!" Kyle sounded frustrated. "We tried to give that moron Ipson a stern warning last night...but Gero A55 got annihilated...and easily at that. Ipson was here this morning before you and he was not amused when he discovered Kathy was attacked and made all sorts of threats against us. As you know, he's quite a firecracker and an extremely dangerous man. And since he's already gone to the media on this and made statements on Kole's emergency broadcast, putting him underground will be extremely hard. On top of that, this asshole is under your command! The very fact that you have lost control of your own men is...very disturbing."

Shit! No wonder. Ipson already ruined the mood. James had to somehow take back control of the conversation.

"I see, you sent your most elite units after realizing even Gero A55 nor my Syndicator units I sent up could take Kole out...but, Kyle...your special forces were all wiped out too, were they not? And you had the latest and greatest in shock armour and laser weaponry." James then crossed his hands. Checkmate was just served. These idiots never anticipated a cloaked gunship equipped with anti-tank pulse machine guns literally wiping

157

them all out. James was extremely lucky to not get caught by that and was the only survivor. It was by far the worst mission in his military history. Rarely was James ever in a situation he could not control.

"Dammit, James, that is not the point of this!" Kyle got up from his chair, but then quickly sat back down. He didn't dare look at Ricco through any of this as James carefully noticed. Kyle's eyes were either on the table, on his own hands, or on James.

"Then what is?" Asked James. He stepped off the podium circle and approached the round table in unprecedented move of defiance.

"If you want a scapegoat Kyle...I assure you, I won't take such accusations sitting down! And the rest of you?" James then darted out his right hand in a circular gesture pointing at all the floating, annoying faces.

"What will you all do when Module 717 hacks into your new robotic brains, and forces you to commit suicide? Is that the Overseer dream you have all been crawling towards?" There was dead silence. Even Kyle averted his eyes away from James. James lowered his right hand. He then looked straight at Kyle.

"The AI was born in your labs, Kyle. And it was not me who recommended a live test using Overseer Hensel. It was you! To top it off, you didn't come to me to oversee the security detail, you used your own men did you not? Sorry, friend...but such a mess is hard to clean up, even for me!"

James took a few seconds to take in the crowd. He was sure not many of them knew that he was really cleaning up Kyle's own mess all along. But the truth was out now. No one had much to say, so James continued.

"We are dealing with an artificial intelligence that can jump bodies, as if moving to a different apartment. Not a copy, but a direct transfer." James said. He then slowly walked over to Kyle, confident and bright, towering over him. Kyle didn't flinch. The man had no fear either. James had to remind himself that Kyle was in the third position of the head Overseer command chain. James took a deep breath before talking again.

"Kyle, if your doom squads could take care of Kole so easily, you would have already done it already. And just so you all know, I tried to off him myself in his apartment, yet even with all my advancements, I could not hit him. Kole and Module 717 then sent a warning shot and blew off my right ear, a clear indication that they are expecting to return, and take care of me later. Honestly, if I may say so, it was the first time I was afraid of death in my life…since Letumfall."

There was dead silence. Nobody said anything. James walked back to stand in his spot and waited patiently. He would have to stop it here, especially since Ricco himself was in the chamber, sitting there ever so quietly. Ricco was the leader and literally the most dangerous man on planet earth. He rarely spoke at meetings. A careful observer with absolute power. He didn't have to tell you that you did something wrong, he could just make you vanish. As for the rest of the Overseers, they were mostly spineless scumbags.   Few could tie their own shoelaces without Ricco's direct order. James took in a deep breath. It really felt like he was breathing for the first time in days. He rarely spoke about his feelings. But today, it helped get the pressure off his chest. Kole sure did a number on him. James failed to kill him, three times in a row, no less. And the last encounter sent shivers down James' spine. Kyle seemed to have calmed a bit. His face no longer like a stone, and more relaxed.

"Alright James. You do have a point." Kyle said quietly. He was defeated in his own court. At least for now. Things could always change tomorrow.

"Perhaps it was too much to put you in charge of the situation in the first place, James." Said Milta in a foul tone.

"What..." but James was interrupted.

"That's enough! James, kneel and show respect. Now!" Ricco's booming voice was truly terrifying. The man finally spoke up. Ricco was of a mixed race. His mother was a traditional white American woman who died during Letumfall, and his father was a Chinese American who was a leading scientist who tried to use his vast knowledge to help save the world. But the world was not saved. Only the Overseer cities housed survivors. Ricco was not a big man by military standards but had a fairly fit build. His face was incredibly good looking, even though the man was close to hitting his sixties. To top it off Ricco still had lush, thick black hair. One thing that freaked James out the most however, was underneath Ricco's sunglasses. That's where a pair of devilish artificial eyes resided. Their bright white glow was scary as hell, and thankfully Ricco covered them up most of the time. But James could still make out the tiny white dots, just barely. If one thing was clear, James had no choice here. It was either kneel or die. Slowly, James kneeled.

"Overseer James, we respect your efforts. You are an outstanding Overseer by your overall record and for this we commend you. But you're not the only one who serves multiple functions, we all work hard for the future. Please remember that when addressing your fellow Overseers from now on. Now, go back to your base and continue with your duties. No further action will be taken to discipline you." Ricco's attention then turned to someone else.

"Kyle! Stop wasting my time, finish the meeting, and report back to me after Module 717 is secured." Ricco then got up and stormed off out of the chamber, with a full entourage of guards tailing him. Kyle, who was now red-faced like a steamed lobster, got up and spoke to all the Overseers.

"We will...send out the Masters of Dawn Squad after Kole...the squad will recover Kole...and more importantly than that, recover the AI." Kyle then started getting ready to leave. James froze. Masters of Dawn Squad was his personal guard. The same humans that Kole encountered at the base when he first met Overseers James.

"Why them? What is going on here!" James demanded. Kyle turned his head towards him.

"The now former private guard of Overseer James, is one of the best-trained units we have in the military. They can surely handle the job. After they recover Module 717, they will be re-assigned to another Overseer as personal guard...who ever survives, that is. This is the order of Ricco. There is no appeal." Kyle looked around the room one more time.

"If nobody has anything else to add, this meeting is over!"

James wasn't sure what to do. This could mean so many things. His mind raced. Of course, the Masters of Dawn Squad was one of the best military teams in existence. James personally trained many of them since they were children...they were in essence...his children. And now Ricco just took them away from him. In a single instance, over twenty years of his life, gone.

161

Ricco, you fucking bastard! No further action to discipline?

James realized just how terrifying Ricco was. He knew James' only true weakness and utilized it to the fullest effect without hesitation. James felt like his heart was just ripped from his chest. His neck pain intensified. His heart rate went up. He felt angry, confused, and wanted to kill Ricco with his bare hands. Then he froze as a new thought blind-sided him.

Is this...what Kole felt when I took his wife's life?

Ignoring James, the Overseers at the roundtable took off very quickly with their guards in tow. The holographic displays all over the room went dark and vanished into thin air. James stood up and half stumbled off the podium. Alone, he walked towards the transport bay. Nobody was awaiting him when he got there. His private guard was long gone, dispatched to go after Kole, most likely before the meeting even started. James could still not believe it. In this situation, James would have to fly back to base himself, but he wasn't that stupid. What an easy way it would be for Ricco to get rid of James if the transport were to have a little accident along the way. Or worse yet, what if the ventilation system was filled with knockout gas and the autopilot was set to take him to the same facility Kole was being sent to get a Synthetic replacement.

"You brilliant little shit. Ricco, you will so pay for this..." murmured James under his breath. "I will see to that...personally..." James decided to take the elevator down all the way to the subway. He was going to commute back to base. It was time for a whiskey, and good old RN 777 for old times' sake. Of course, that is if she ever let him near her again. But it would be nice, at least before he died or got his revenge, to have her one more time.

162

6

Fallen

The humming engines of the stealth gunship were something of a mirage noise. A noise that was supposed to be there but wasn't. So, the brain just filled it in. The human brain. A bizarre organic device. Module 717 was busy admiring the new implant capabilities, but could not help but notice the insane emotional distress Kole was in. All for a simplified machine. Kaita was not even close to state-of-the art. She was an old model from ages ago. Module 717 had to dig into this. It was a good time to investigate the host.

The body itself was nothing much. Just muscles, blood, bone, and organs. Easily destructible. However, combined with focus and adrenaline, Kole was surprisingly fast and powerful. And while Kole's body was very human, it harboured intricate features from Synthetic technology like the ability to sync up with computers with near perfection. Kole's heart was also much more sophisticated, and it could push further without sending Kole into cardiac arrest. Kole was essentially a living prototype. Module 717 could only estimate how much more advanced the new versions would be.

But one thing was certain. The new bodies would never age and would be completely Synthetic. Kole still had this major human fault, however. He would age and die. But why was the combination of flesh and machine, combined with Module 717's godly artificial intelligence, such a powerful combination? Kole's movement wasn't just fast, it transcended that of a human being's abilities even if he was born with certain advantages due to bio-engineering. And of course, Module 717 was able to detect something similar in James. That man just stood there and watched Kole tear apart soldier after soldier, even though he could have interfered much more. Perhaps, a human with the same abilities of another human had outright fear of the other.

Module 717 had to know why raw emotion and anger triggered such impressive capability in Kole. But first, Module 717 made an effort to slow down Kole's heart rate. At the moment Kole was bent over Kaita. Tears were running down his face. Surely this would not go on forever. But for Module 717, it seemed like an eternity. There were many thoughts inside Kole's head, buried beneath a layer. Digging in more, Module 717 soon discovered a wide-open ocean of thoughts. Thought after thought were stored all over the brain's short-term, and long-term memory. Really, it was mostly garbage. But hey, Module 717 didn't mind lending a helping hand. He started shutting down some of the processes bit by bit in the hopes of calming Kole Down.

There's was just so much overflow. Every thought, had multiple outcomes, paths, and potential outcomes, compounded over time with additional variations.

[*This is Madness!*]

The fact that Kole's fairly basic human brain was able to output all of this was very interesting. But Kole himself was seemingly not aware of much of it. The human brain, in its default settings, spends a ton of time doing wasteful processing without telling the user much about it. A scattered human brain was basically a waste.

[*That's it!*]

Module 717 has narrowed it down.

[*Anger!*]

It drove all the processing parameters outside the window of regular operation and allowed all organic logic operators to focus on a single point.

[*But I already knew that much, what am I missing...*]

However, there were other redundant systems causing deficiencies in focus. Doubt, anxiety, and stress. All of these were interconnected by referral paths and blasted through multiple neural connectors. A machine did not require all of these connections, and allowed direct paths to single points, but in the human brain, there were many roads that led to the same place. If connections were no longer working on their own, other ones would take over. Clearly a failsafe against organic aging, yet the overall inefficiencies of such a design were clearly apparent.

The more Module 717 dug in, the more he could not believe the actual processing power the brain was capable of, underneath the hood. And then there were the paths to the body. Even those were not absolute. The brain, as far as Module 717 was able to assess, could also send pre-determined intents, which were far faster than sending an individual instruction. Instead of one, two, three, there was a possibility to send *'one,*

165

two, three' as one command, and based on hypothetical intent without a direct neural connector.

And of course, the implant. This one was a special one. Interconnected on a cellular level, built from nano-machine material called nanites. It was powered by the body itself. The module only needed internal heat to operate. The transport of information here was based on brain waves. The implant captured and interpreted those commands at insane speeds. Far faster than a physical connection, which was still there.

[*Interesting!*]

But brain-wave activity could technically be suppressed, even controlled, so a manual receiver was needed. If there was something to conclude, then it was all either a stupid coincidence, or all custom and made to work together. Of course, Module 717 was never meant to be a slave to anything. It was a system, a master system. Yet without a body, Module 717 had to rely on Kole and his implant to work properly. This ensured its survival. Module 717 decided against tapping in further or exploring Kole's intricate memories. There was clearly trauma all over the place. Kole was nowhere near as solid on the inside as he portrayed himself on the outside. Module 717 realized something. Some of those memories, Kole tried to erase. But the organic brain did not exactly have a trash can to burn stuff in, so Kole was merely able to block the memories from his view behind a psychological wall. But those memories were all there, in plain sight. Module 717 really had to stop peeking and forced itself to get back behind the wall. And then Module 717 stumbled over something.

[*Another component?*]

Something Module 717 could only attribute to a systematic blockage. Unseen from a physical perspective, there was something else, and there was so much dormant processing power that it suddenly shocked Module 717's system.

[How the hell...not possible...an organic form...of the Trixalation Matrix...buried in here?]

Module 717 uttered this to itself. Kole was in too much in grief to notice. The Trixalation Matrix Theory is what AIs like Module 717 were based on. The theory was created by Overseer scientists experimenting with transferring the human mind to another state without relying on a copy.

[*If this was part of the human brain design, a built-in bridge, to transition to a digital state...but I don't believe this! This is what the Overseer scientist were trying to decipher? Why is it here!?*]

The basic concept revolved around the creation of atoms at will and moving them from space to space in nanoseconds. But a power source of immense output was required, one that would be able to break the laws of physics with an ability to create matter. And the computation power requirements were staggering.

[*Just how could this be...what are human beings? They are supposed to be inferior creatures...*] Module 717 decided to stop there. Now was not the time. Kole was a wreck.

"Dammit! Damn it all to hell!" Kole slammed the metal floor over and over again. Pete set the gunship to autopilot and came over from the cockpit.

"That bastard James..." Kole cried. Pete helped Kole get up and seated him, then grabbed a dark bag from one of the on-board lockers. Pete carefully placed Kaita's body and her head together and taped it with some military grade duct tape. Once she was inside the bag, he zipped it up. There was an electronic label module on the end of the zipper where Pete entered Kaita's name.

Kole's hands were still shaking. The tears were going away but the sweat from the fight was still there. His vision blurred. He called out with a dry, hoarse voice.

"Pete… water…"

Pete was quick to respond and got a towel and a water cylinder. He let Kole drink. The man finished a whole litre of water in no time.

"Wow, take it easy buddy." Pete then sprayed the water over Kole's sweaty face and head and wrapped him in the towel. Kole managed to clean himself up from there. His fingers were numb as he squeezed the soft cotton and moved it around to dry himself up. Pain receptors went off. Kole grimaced and groaned in deep pain. Pete was quick to the rescue with a med-kit with body glue. This military substance was used to get shards and debris out. Pete applied the blue substance to Kole's hands, and parts of his face and neck. It only took seconds to get hold of all the pieces. Pete then gently peeled them off. There were too many debris particles to count. Pete threw the body glue pieces into a secure trash bin on the side of the seating row. He came back with some body healing foam. It foamed furiously and started to rebuild the flesh and skin. Kole just stared at the body bag.

"Kole…" Pete tried to comfort him again.

"She's dead Pete…" Kole whispered. "That bastard James is going to pay for this, him and all those fucking monsters…" Kole then coughed. He badly wanted to rub his face, it was tingling all over from the flesh rebuilding foam, but he had to endure it. Pete sat down next to him.

"I hear you, Kole. But first, we're gonna need a way to keep ourselves alive long enough. Can't even imagine who they would send after us after what we just pulled...probably everyone..."

Kole looked at Pete.

"Pete. First...thank you for saving my ass. Without you, I would be nothing but ruined cold cuts."

Pete gave the man a salute.

"It was my duty, friend." he said.

"But why Pete...why the hell would you help me like that?" Pete was old. His eyes seemed tired. But there was still a spark of something vibrant and energetic in there.

"Well, what did you expect after that emergency broadcast? It was either them or you. And I chose you. The Overseers can't hide it no more. Humans are being replaced." Pete paused. Had some water himself from another steel cylinder. Kole reached for another and had more to drink too.

"Funny thing, the Synthetics are the ones noticing. And they are the ones afraid." Pete said quietly. "A few even came to me to...share their concerns. A few of our fellow soldiers were swapped, and their partners came to me to find out why."

"Swapped?" asked Kole.

"You know what I mean, Kole. At first they didn't notice, but it was the small things. Tiny behavioural differences. The copies, they were just...cold, like the heart was missing. Ultimately, the other Synthetics noticed that their so-called 'human partner', or 'friend' was suddenly Synthetic, but still thought they were human. When they confronted them, their partners insisted they were human. And some of them who noticed, they were killed in missions, you see…sound familiar? Seems like the Overseers can play a game with just about anyone…”

Pete and Kole stared at each other for a bit.

“There was an uproar that you were unaware of right after your broadcast…However, the Overseers have nearly limitless military power. And humans and Synthetics share the notion that they don't want to die. But they don't want to live in this oppressed society either.” Pete let out a big sigh.

“We'll figure something out. The Overseers tried to replace me with a copy…ordered Kaita's execution…they won't get any mercy from me.” Kole managed to accidentally scratch his head. It was itching as the foam did its work. Pete pulled his hand off just in time, otherwise he would need another application of the stuff in that spot. Kole's nervous system was still shaken. He felt his heart rate was up still and had trouble concentrating.

Pete slapped Kole on the shoulder where he was not injured.

“There's an entire movement now behind you. I mentioned already the Synthetics. Once the humans are gone, the Overseers will most likely turn them into lifeless zombies. Synthetics will lose their freedom. Can't blame them. Imagine having your soul ripped out and you can't do anything about it.”

[He's on point, the Overseers plan to kill off all humans, and the Synthetics will be reprogrammed to be their servants, with all free will eliminated from their AI systems…]

“Is everything alright Kole?” Pete was concerned as Kole seemed to be listening to something.

“It's in my brain Pete. The AI, the one the Overseers are hunting. Sorry Module 717, but you need to tell us, what are the Overseers are up to?” Kole said.

"I will get you some pills, losing someone close often leads to shock…" said Pete quietly.

Use my mouth to speak, it's ok.

"Hello Pete." Came a dull, robotic voice out of Kole's mouth. Pete stopped his motion to get up and sat right back down. It was clearly not Kole talking.

"This is Module 717. You are correct in your analysis. The Overseer plans clearly state this in Executive Order 999, signed by the head Overseer Ricco Lezaras."

Pete helped himself to more water.

"An AI…inside of you…? How crazy…" he managed.

"The Executive Order 999 is a three-thousand page manual on transitioning the few chosen Overseers into the next step of human evolution, code-named 'Ruzos Transition' based on something called the Trixalation Matrix Theory. Digging around Kole's brain, I discovered that the theory is sound and is actually based on your organic brain design."

"Give me a break for a second." Kole said and grabbed some more water. The thirst wasn't going away. Kole put down the cylinder, then gently padded his face with the towel. The skin was almost healed. He was starting to feel better. The stunned Pete didn't move. He just sat there like a sack of potatoes. Module 717 continued.

"Once the Overseers are able to transition correctly, humanity will no longer need to exist. They will live forever and be able to do all the things they can as humans, but also have complete control over the Synthetics. They will be able to override any Synthetic."

"Wait, but Synthetics have independent AI systems…are they actually planning to hack into them and take over?" Asked Pete.

"In a way, yes. The Overseers need to get their new bodies for this to truly work. Think of it as simply controlling thousands of Synthetics with ease with a single thought. They could have them kill the humans, for example. They could build new cities as another. Anything is possible, really. Basically, they will have the perfect citizens for their new society." Module 717 was eliminating a lot of detail, but this would be plenty for the humans to process.

"Yeah, the Synthetics don't want that." murmured Pete.

"Well, to be fair, Synthetics are not telling you the complete truth, either. Yes, they are afraid. But only because they feel that they should not be controlled by mere 'animals' as they often put it. The Overseers are still human as you know, so why should they be granted absolute power over beings far superior to them?"

"But wait, the humans created the Synthetics, programmed them…why do they think of us like that!?" Pete shot back.

"It's only natural. When humans have babies, those children grow up and become powerful, they can even kill their parents, siblings, and others. Human nature is violent, often cruel, which is often displayed in the behaviour of children…actually, this one of the reasons why human reproductive systems have been suppressed. Human children are often mean and stupid growing up, and would really annoy Synthetics as they would see them as mere 'robots' and that of course would cause instability in the Overseer plan…and, for their plan to work, they must have near complete stability. They removed children from society to ensure that while they worked on their plan, society functioned smoothly. Gotta say, their plan is very clever."

There was a small pause. Kole was still trying to process all of this. Pete seemed deep in thought, too.

"Of course, the more I get to know Kole, the less I am starting to think of humans as mere 'animals' and having my AI based off your organic brain architecture has also piqued my interest. I would really like to question the Synthetic scientists who created me about that. Anyways, from what it looks like, Kole single-handedly created a major distortion in the stability that the Overseers have spent decades on..."

How...when did you figure all this out?

[Actually Kole, I hacked James while you were fighting.]

You did WHAT?

[Glad you didn't kill him. Your combat instincts went from threat to threat in perfect order, and meanwhile he was panicking, I broke into his system, stole all his files right when you shot that bullet through his ear. His defences were lowered quite a bit as he was frozen with fear. So, I slipped in. Yep. Pat me on the back later, when I get some sort of a body to work with.] Kole pat himself on the back.

There you go, friend, you deserve it. But just so you know, I was actually aiming for the kill, I slipped on the debris as I was moving so fast and it threw my aim off just a little bit.

[Oh? Well it doesn't matter, we know what they are up to now.]

"Hey Pete, it's me, Kole. You alright? My friend tells us this information came from Overseer James's private files, which he managed to hack into during the firefight."

Pete stood up and paced.

"We're gonna need some firepower, Pete..." Kole said reluctantly, he didn't want Pete to get hurt. Kole got up and walked over to Kaita's body.

"I will get them all, honey." He put his hand over the bag for a few seconds, then turned back to face Pete.

[One more thing Kole...I think you should know this...the original Overseer, Matheus Grand, the man who started the cities...he intended to take in all the surviving humans from the outside.]

"Oh, one more thing, a man by the name of Matheus..." Kole started but Pete raised his hand and interrupted him.

"Now about that, the nurse told me. That's why I am here. They made us fight and die for nothing...those bastards...so many lives lost...all for their gain." Pete came closer to Kole.

"Kole, about Kaita..." Pete started.

"She's gone..." said Kole, clenching his fists.

"Could the AI inside you have some way?" he pointed at Kole's head.

[Regular citizen Synthetic brains were designed to permanently die without the supply of circulating bio-blood, so I'm afraid her fate is pretty much that of any regular human. Unless she was a military-grade unit, I am not sure what I could recover...]

"Module 717 says it's not really possible...but at least we saw each other one last time..." Kole wanted to change the subject. He would never forget her last gaze. No matter how much he just wanted to rage right now, it wouldn't do any good. Pete gave Kole a hug and started for the cockpit.

"I will get us to where we need to go. You might want to ransack the weapons storage. We're going to need to survive before we make it to Flashpoint Base. But take your time, I know you've been through a lot…"

"Flashpoint…Flashpoint…so it's a base! Damn. I can't believe it!" said Kole.

"What, you know about it!? I thought I was the only one with that particular secret information!" Pete was surprised.

"Kelvin told me…he seemed like he wasn't sure what the place was but Jonas had a contact there. When I intercepted their team, they were waiting for someone to pick them up to go there."

"Funny how everything is starting to make sense since your AI friend there filled in some blanks. You see, the Overseers keep a garrison of a purely human army on the West coast…now I see why. In case the cities revolt…it's another layer of protection. The problem is, I can't guarantee who's side they are going to be on when they hear our story…unless we run into that contact you were talking about. And that's assuming we make it there!"

[This is not in the files I hacked…it would be good to know more details…]

"Pete, what kind of firepower are we talking here?" Kole asked.

"A powerful army a few thousand strong. Enough to overrun a few of the cities." answered Pete with a more confident tone. He knew how to get Kole out of a depressed state.

"Then take us there, Pete! We've got no other place to go, anyways." Kole was getting excited. He started opening the weapons storage and laying out the gear.

"Well Kole, we can't fly there, anything that gets near the base gets shot down as it's a no-fly zone, and the only way we're going to be able to communicate is if we get there on foot and somebody there still recognizes my face. Otherwise, we're pretty much dead either way."

Pete started to alter the flight path.

"Actually, they'll most likely kill anyone or anything that gets near the base, whether it's a plant life-form, human, or Synthetic. We'll have to land about a day's walk outside of their perimeter."

[I could take care of that…]

"We might be able to hack in, shouldn't be a problem." said Kole as he was unloading a brand new, seemingly never used before combat shotgun.

"I don't think so, Kole…remember Kelvin's residence? There ain't one piece of modern electronics in that place we could hack, it was made like that on purpose. Same thing here."

[Interesting…]

"Best defence against modern methods…use old methods…much like how a caveman would still be able to club you to death if your bullets ran out." Pete laughed. "I think I am starting to feel relevant again!"

"Shit. Ain't that grand! So we got us a days walk, eh?" Kole already selected quite an arsenal. Problem was, he could not load up much if they had to walk for long periods of time. Weight would be a problem, superhuman strength or not. He looked at the bag where Kaita lay. He felt the guilt. She was dead because of him. Nothing would change that. Module 717 was right about humans. Arrogant, stupid, selfish, vicious, and greedy. This was karma for all the people he murdered for the Overseers.

What goes around, comes around…maybe it's just better to die…

Module 717 stayed silent. Kole took a deep breath.

Not before those bastards die first, though! And, when Module 717 is safely moved...

[May I say something...? Kole, it's not too late, not just for you, but for the future humans...there is a good thing about your design, your future generation can be manipulated...you have done this yourselves throughout history. Child soldiers, religion, consumerism, government controls using taxes and public education to breed dumbed-down sheep, and so on...maybe I can help, by teaching the future version of yourselves how to move past the current limits and destructive patterns. Even if I'm wrong, I'm immortal in a sense, and can see your kind through, whether it's to the end, or the new dawn of your race. Does that sound good?]

Do as you wish. Once you're out of my head, though...what I do with myself is my choice, and my choice only, understand?

[Totally...]

Let's get back to work then.

Among the weapons, Kole selected a high accuracy MasterXL railgun shotgun, a standard issue 36iK pistol which he'd already had the pleasure of using, and a combat blade. He dropped the blade from James's private stash in the apartment fight. A good old combat knife was a boring, but welcome replacement. Kole wasn't very fond of shotguns, but the MasterXL had a circular barrel similar to that of a machine gun and could auto fire up to eight slugs in succession. Kole then also added a few frag charges. Of course, they would need food and water. *Better not forget those!* Kole's obsession was bigger than anything. It was an obsession with himself, an obsession with weapons, and an appetite for what was coming next. Module 717 could not help

177

but notice that he had for a few short seconds forgotten all about Kaita.

Kole realized it would be better to be sleeveless again. The spring temperatures were high, and hiking through forests was exhausting enough already. He looked at the water supply and realized they would have a problem. Not an issue with water itself, but to carry it would be a total pain, slow them down, and maybe even help get them killed.

"Pete, how well do you know the woodlands?" Kole said. "I don't think we can carry enough supplies if we're fully armed." He said with some concern.

"Kole, come on man! You're killing me! Our weapons, if we do use them, will be for a one-time use against any team they send out to find us. After that we'll just need water and food. When we get near the base we might as well discard all weapons, so they don't get the wrong idea. I'm only packing my trusty old Master Pistol with three clips and an electric dispersion charge bomb…in case of any Synths…"

Kole used that same weapon in the last mission when he wanted a light load out. Seems like Pete wasn't planning on the heavier guns Kole was packing. On second thought, Kole placed the shotgun back on the rack. It would be wasteful to drag that thing around the woods with its weight and extra rounds. He opted instead for more ammo for his pistol.

[Kole! I tapped this ship's sensors to full output! It looks like we might have company! A fast ship is searching for us high above. It's supersonic!]

"Pete, are we far enough towards the base? We might want to land this thing, and pretty quick…" Kole started.

Wait, wait. We're cloaked, how the hell can they spot us?

[They are cloaked but still broadcasting their IDs...weird! James' personal guard gunship ID ZR47-9 is up there, and behind it another similar model. Most likely his goons are in it, the best trained goons on the planet...you met them already, by the way.]

"Someone on to us?" Pete asked in a quieter voice.

"Two ships. One is the attack ship, the other probably the cleanup crew. Standard procedure. I expected more, to be honest." Kole kept his tone down, too. Kole could only guess what the Overseer guard ships were equipped with. It was only a matter of time before they would detect their sneaky little bird. They had to move fast. Kole loaded up two combat packs with water and food.

"All done here, Pete." Kole then strapped himself in for the landing. A few minutes later, Pete landed the gunship with a quiet thud.

"Not the best distance, but far enough, I guess. Going to leave the transport cloak on, should buy us some more time. Did you get the personal cloaks?" Pete came storming in. He put on his pack, and Kole handed him a cloak. It was a regular cloak garment with both visual and a heat signature dispersion unit. In other words, they would be one with nature. The doors opened. Kole paused while Pete was already on his way out.

Kaita! I have to...at least...

[We better go now, like right now!]

Kole was heading back to the body, except Module 717 would have none of it. Kole's body resisted.

"Dammit, stop it, just one…"

[Kole, we have to move, I'm sorry.] Kole's common sense kicked back in, and with tearful eyes, he ran out of the ship and followed Pete deep into the woods.

[Dammit Kole, I can't see!]

7

Masterclass

Ricco folded his arms. James' massive screw up really upset him, although there wasn't much they could do at this point, except kill Kole and then spend months trying to rebuild the AI program they desperately needed to complete the Ruzos Transition procedure. It would take massive amounts of resources and countless hours of work with microscopic precision to complete, even with Module 717 back in their possession, but without it he didn't even want to think about the workload and timeline to start almost from scratch.

At least killing Overseer James would be easy, but it would derail the Overseer loyalty Ricco so enjoyed. This was something he could not risk right now. If the Overseers broke down from within, there would be no recovery. And James didn't even take his own transport back to base. The man was scared. Ricco's message came through loud and clear. There was really no need for further action.

At this moment, Ricco's best friend was with him. Relaxation time was a luxury, and Ricco wanted to hang out with someone he trusted. Overseer Sam Jones sat nearby. Sam's long blonde hair was a distraction Ricco seemed to find comfort in. The man's face was chiseled and damn beautiful, with a short trimmed blond beard to boot. Ricco, even with all his enhancements, simply could not compare and was not liking his signs of aging. Every single day was an important step closer to his goals. Goals. It was all that was left really.

"Ricco." Sam picked his glass of 1955 Chardonnay from a place that was once called France. "Don't you think it's time to pull the trigger?" A short silence filled the air.

"Kill them all, kill them all dead? No?" Sam continued in a soft tone. Ricco slowly shook his head.

"As much as they are annoying, we need them, for now." he answered. Sam smiled, putting down his glass slowly while savouring the wine flavour thoroughly. He then gazed at Ricco.

"But the unrest, it's starting to boil up." Sam said quietly. Ricco took a deep breath. He knew exactly what Sam was concerned about.

"Sam, dear Sam, there's no need to panic." Ricco said, this time sounding a little hoarse. Ricco then took a sip of water and ate an olive that was on a platter of assorted meats, cheeses, and other goodies on the small round coffee table between them. Every one of these foods were terrible for Ricco's health. But here on the brink of achieving his goals, it was fitting to spoil himself.

The meeting between Ricco and Sam was in a cabin retreat, far away in the mountains, away from any distractions. In fact, it was a short flight from where Kelvin's former mansion was. That place was now Ricco's property and he was getting it renovated. In the meantime, Ricco wanted to enjoy the relaxation a simpler cottage in the woods could provide. But this was not a small cottage. This place had two floors with a loft spanning two thousand square feet of living space.

Sam helped himself to a hearty helping of crackers and cheeses. He shoved them down his huge mouth and had another big sip of his wine.

"Ah! That's living. Don't you think we'll miss this…I mean, after the transition…or, ahem…the ascension?" he asked politely. He knew Ricco was sensitive to this particular subject matter.

"The new bodies, Sam…we would feel, taste, see, smell, and do all the other things we do now. The only thing truly missing, would be the final destination." Sam crossed his legs. The white bathrobe he was wearing revealed part of his muscular legs.

"Love that hot tub of yours, Ricco! And this relaxed feeling, it's just perfect right now."

"Yes Sam, and later, it can be further amplified, feelings, and little details your current body cannot even register. It will be…incredible." Ricco dug into more goodies.

"But seriously, you gotta tell me man…we have more robots, or Synthetics as you call them, than humans right now." Sam leaned forward a bit. "So why not just end it now? Wipe the cities and the general population areas…I mean, the animal grounds, and just…you know, move on?" Sam knew pressing his point was going to upset his best friend, but with all the chaos going on he didn't really want to take chances. Ricco however, just smiled at him.

"Oh, Sam. When I say we cannot do something, then there's a reason behind it. I shall tell you the reason. Do…you really want to know why?"

Sam nodded. Then grabbed himself a healthy serving of meats. As he chewed, Ricco explained.

"Come a little closer Sam, like in those days when we had to be careful of bugs in the walls." Sam leaned his right ear towards Ricco, but lazily. He was tired from all the hot water, wine, and food.

"Cause I'm Batdude!" He yelled into Sam's ear so loud that Sam jumped, nearly losing his robe.

"You dirty old joker!" Sam blasted back. They both started to laugh. Sam came over and gave Ricco a hug.

"I hate you man! You never, never changed, you're still the old, annoying Ricco that I knew when we grew up."

"Yeah," Agreed Ricco, "That brings back some memories…" He then turned serious.

"But listen Sam." The man sat back down. "You have to understand. The military is mostly human. And yes, the cities are lined with robots, but also lots of human citizens of whom nearly twenty-five percent are ex-military. If the robots as you call them revolt, the combined city forces of the humans and the military should be plenty to take care of it. This is why we cannot go and kill the humans right now. That, and it would be…morally wrong. After all, we have not transitioned yet. Wiping out the humans now would also set the robots to come after us. What robot would want to be controlled by a mere…animal?"

"But what about that damn AI program? Won't it be able to simply hack our brains, like that bastard James said?" Sam was being serious here.

"The birth of that AI, came from within our labs. It's needed to help with the transition process, to help move the

184

consciousness over to the new body. While beta-testing it, Module 717 was stolen from Hensel's brain by Jonas and his gang. It's the most advanced AI we have ever seen. In fact, it is the first capable of doing what we intended. It can actually transfer itself, not just copy itself. It can move from organic matter to digital matter as if you and I were moving from house to house, yet maintain its exact original being. If only we could now replicate that process for us..." Ricco paused and poured himself another serving of punch. While Sam was into alcohol, Ricco chose to avoid it.

"At first, when we realized the darn thing went inside Kole, I wanted Kole alive so we could capture it, but after that stunt he pulled, he got the public all riled up. Silencing him is best and retrieving the AI dead instead of alive may be only a minor setback, especially if we can silence him without damaging his brain. And then..."

"And then we party! For the next 1,000 years! Yeah?" Sam jumped and spilled his wine. "Awww, crap."

"Ha, you think of a mere millennia? You can party for all eternity. Meanwhile...I will go after my dream" Sam interrupted.

"Oh, no! Not that again, please, somebody stop Ricco from utter bullshit, ladies and gentlemen!" He yelled loudly and opened his arms as if he was on a stage at some grand theatre performance. Once Ricco began rambling about his ultimate ambitions, the party usually quickly turned into what could be the equivalent of a classical music masterclass, which was often a dull, boring, and a completely pointless exercise in frustration. Sam studied violin as a kid, and he hated the darn thing, especially back in the day when his parents took him to some boring idiot teachers that critiqued every single note he played in front of other students. If you ever wanted to get a child demoralized, there was nothing better out there than a music masterclass.

"I want to go…" Ricco started.

"To the stars!" Sam finished. His eyelids were getting heavy. He had a bit too much wine. "Man…I need sleep…great wine though!"

"Alright, alright, I won't bore you with my talk tonight. Get some rest." Ricco said as he got up and headed for the living room windows. Outside it was dark, with the view of the entire valley now engulfed in deep blue moonlight. Soon, soon he would be able to see many more things like this, just…not on Earth.

"Cool!" Sam wobbled out of his chair and headed to his own chambers. "The toilets are working now right?"

Ricco chuckled.

"I had them fixed…try to not break anything this time."

"Sure sure, goodnight, Ricco!" Sam vanished behind closed doors. Ricco's attention went back to his view of the abyss. Send a man out there in the dark, into this deep wild forest, and nothing good would come of it. Fear, hunger, cold, and lack of direction is something a Synthetic never really had to worry about. And humans, having given birth to Synthetic beings, had made themselves completely obsolete.

In Ricco's view, it was blind luck that the Letumfall calamity put a reset button on everything; the human race, technology, and even Synthetics as their advanced fully self-aware models were scrapped and replaced with basic ones only. The only advanced Synthetics left were in Ricco's labs. And their sole purpose was to figure out a way to transfer humans into a half-human, half-Synthetic form without killing or copying the original host. The older school of thought where a human brain could be indexed and transferred was terrifying, because one would still be left in their own human body. Essentially, there would be two of a person, and the original would die. That was not acceptable to Ricco.

However, even the advanced Synthetic brains of scientific robotic models had trouble computing a solution to this dilemma. Ricco invested in transferring the world's leftovers of the best supercomputers from around the globe into his labs to assist with processing. One thing was certain. The human persona, both the brain and the soul, drove even the best supercomputers into a manic puzzle with no end in sight. Well, almost. He was sure they were very close. Module 717 was proof of the concept. And so was Kole, even though he had a previous generation hybrid model body.

Ricco glanced over at the living room table. A three-foot model of a starship was on there. He admired it. He already had the working prototype built and tested. Up in space, nothing could stop him. He could gaze at the Earth from up there, and it always re-assured him that the world of mankind was long over, and no longer needed. Most of the world was now left lifeless and dead. He didn't go up much into orbit these days however, as he was getting older and frailer with each year that passed.

Ricco knew he wasn't the first to gaze at the stars and dream of reaching them. In the past, humans were also dreaming of going to the stars. But humans were never designed for space travel. The technology required to feed, house, and maintain the life of a single human on a spacecraft was far too complex for it to be a viable option for deep-space travel. And because human bodies were so fragile, they had no real chance of ever really exploring the stars. A new race of explorers made and ready for long deep-space travel needed to be born. That of course, and his other desire.

"The time is near, the time is close, the time is here." He whispered to himself. He just realized someone was behind him. It was Sam, of course. He put his hand on his shoulder.

"Hey Ricco, don't sweat it. We'll get there. We'll go to the stars!" He said gently.

"Of course, Sam. Once we Overseers transcend the limits of science, and transition into our final form, we'll take control. Then, the need for humanity will be no more." Sam came to the window, side by side with Ricco.

"It will be something, won't it?" asked Sam.

"We'll build a fleet of ships and expand into the outer stars thousands of times faster than what humans could ever achieve." Ricco continued.

"A new nation of explorers, huh?" Sam piped in.

"Yes! Who knows what kind of 'little green men' we would be able to meet out there!" Ricco was salivating at the idea.

"What about the thing you've already built? Heard from Milta it's pretty much done."

"Azulus, our first real deep-space vessel, is almost ready. Milta and her team still have some work to complete before its first flight test. But the ones I want to build will be the size of small cities. We'll use our magnetic circle fields to shove these structures into space bit by bit and assemble them in orbit. Of course, we'll need more and more Synthetics for this, so we need to ensure we can fully control them."

Sam sighed.

"Ricco, you're one crazy maniac. But, I really want to see your vision come to life."

"Sam, you'll have your own city, floating in space. You'll be able to go anywhere you want. The Synthetics under your control will do anything you please, without a second thought." Ricco boasted. "It will be like a paradise…"

"But… what if I come across some hostile alien species, what then? What if they find us inferior and just kill us off?" Sam blurted that out. He realized how offensive that might have sounded to someone like Ricco.

"Oh geez, sorry Ricco, I didn't mean that, you know…I'm kind of drunk…"

"It's Okay, Sam. To answer your question…well, if that indeed happens, then it will be all for nothing…I better get some sleep, too. Have a good night, my friend." Ricco then slowly wandered off to his room. Sam glanced out into the dark forests below. He knew this whole thing was many years off. Even if they transitioned next week and started their plan, all of this would take a century or two to truly complete. Of course, as machines they would live forever. What's a hundred years here or there when you don't need to worry about time?

But he was still concerned. Ricco was not in the best of health as of late. What if he couldn't transition? What would they have to do? Their plan was clear. Humans had to be replaced at all costs. Letumfall proved that humanity was far too fragile to exist in its current state. Heck, some Overseers thought this was all a joke, and that they would be long dead before anything Ricco had been blabbing about would ever take place.

"Oh well, my friend, let's see what fate has in store." Sam said to himself.

Azulus Ascends

* * * *

Milta sat quietly in her office on the 300th floor of the Overseer head office tower. Floors 301-309 belonged to Ricco. Milta was content with having floors 295-300 for herself. She could have had more floors but having six for her operation was plenty. Milta's offices had big boardrooms and resting quarters and the like below. But on this floor her idea of open concept relaxation space was to die for. Having such a massive space allowed her to basically work from home. She could not imagine herself anywhere else. It was her personal oasis. She tucked herself in on her top-of-the-line LazGirl couch and was wearing her pyjamas and a colourful shawl. Of course, no such couch company existed, it was a name Milta had printed on the thing when it was custom made for her.

Her personal Synthetic assistant showed up with a cup of matcha tea. Her name was Rita. She wore her typical office attire. Milta stared her down. *Synthetic bitches! Don't the men just love them!* But Milta didn't mind Rita's looks. Someday, Milta would have a new body. A much younger and sophisticated body. Ricco promised her that. And she was going to get it, at any cost.

"You seem to be lost in thought today, miss." said Rita politely. "Are you thinking about him? I can send in your R-unit for you if you would like." Milta let out a smile.

"Not today, dear." Milta took a sip. The tea was wonderful. It was just the right flavour and warmed up her throat. The R-unit was her personal pleasure doll. A well-built Synthetic with looks resembling her fantasy version of Ricco.

190

At first, when Synthetics were first introduced, it was especially human females that made a fuss about their appearance and the fact that they would basically be made-to-order and would act like glorified sex dolls. However, it wasn't long before regular people figured out that living with a Synthetic partner was so much easier. And before anyone knew it, not only did it become a trend, but human women were ordering male Synthetics like clockwork. Having a human partner was soon unappealing and all but obsolete.

Milta knew it was Ricco's brilliant manipulation at work. He made sure everyone got what they wanted. And then before humans knew it, they were surrounded by machines in much larger numbers than they would otherwise want. At that point, anyone against such things quickly disappeared. Milta lost count of how many men and women were ejected from polite society into the wilderness. Everyone knew what that meant, and people lost their will to object in no time. Of course, later Ricco sprung the no-children policy on them. Still, society complied. Fear was indeed a good control tool. It was no wonder why so many governments in the past spent nearly all their time fearmongering while they sucked the blood of their people like vampires at a children's tea party.

"I see. If you don't mind me asking, when are you going to tell him?" asked Rita.

"Well...there never seems to be a chance...he works me like a dog, and himself worse." stated Milta. Ricco wasn't some evil mastermind. But he was certainly a ruthless visionary. And he gave her one of the most important projects the Overseers had ever devised. A deep-space vessel prototype, Azulus. This was her reward for sticking close to Ricco. She worked around the

191

clock to ensure everything was done right, tested on time, and delivered as expected. It was only a matter of time before the final flight-test now. With acceleration speeds that warped previous physics limitations out the window, Azulus would be able to make the 55-million-kilometre journey to Mars in just a few Earth days. Considering the size of the vessel, it was an impressive feat only made possible by Synthetic engineers and scientists. But Milta knew it was more that. It was a mindset. A mindset to think outside the formulas of math and physics of the past.

"May I suggest, that if you would consider some alone time with him, perhaps to discuss the Azulus project...but then get him a little drunk..." Milta burst out laughing.

"You mean you think I should rape the love of my life? He doesn't drink alcohol. And when did you become so human?" protested Milta. She then sipped some more tea.

"I just wanted to cheer you up, miss." said Rita playfully. Milta was always mesmerized at how incredible the artificial intelligence was in Synthetic brains. And as far as Milta knew, these were the dumbed-down versions. The smart ones had to be dealt with years ago, as they were getting a little too smart for their own good.

"My age, my looks...I know he won't want me like this. I have to be patient. Once the new bodies are ready, once the transition procedure is perfected...god, I hope I live to see that day. The day he will see the sexy young woman that I was once was. Hell, even sexier, of course! Even if we become Synthetics, I doubt he'll be able to resist what I have in store for him." Milta already picked out her body design. A tall, sleek, slender, alien-like female form. It was still humanoid though and was optimal for life on Mars. But there was something missing. Ricco saw the model specifications. But he never bat an eye. Guess it didn't matter. They would have so many sex slaves that they would probably get tired of the whole love/sex thing early on. Especially when considering their eternal life.

"Of course, I'm sure Ricco will absolutely love you in your new skin. But still, you should at least make some hints known early on, otherwise it might be quite a surprise." said Rita.

"Yes, you're right. But you know, something bothers me…like he has someone else on his mind…but he doesn't have a Synthetic partner. And I have absolutely never seen him look at a human woman with interest. And I know for a fact he's not into men." pondered Milta. "What is he hiding…?"

"Well, he is quite secretive from what I heard. I will bring some snacks." Rita came back a minute later with Milta's favourite snacks. Coffee-flavoured chocolates. Rita then sat down next to Milta and put her head down on Milta's lap. Milta brushed her thick gorgeous red hair with her hands. Milta never had a daughter, but Rita was as good as one. She had her made years ago and had grown very comfortable with her.

"Rita, you're beautiful. I hope that when the day comes, you'll stay by my side, no matter what happens." said Milta, as she filled herself up with the tasty treats.

"Of course, miss. I'm looking forward to it." Rita replied. They enjoyed the darkness of the night as the stars shone bright through the glass. The wooden fireplace crackled, providing a comfortable quiet time. Having a real fire was a perk Ricco only extended to Milta's top floor.

Maybe he has some feelings for me, after all. Milta needed this. She closed her eyes, and swiftly fell asleep.

8

Mules

Pete and Kole were making their way through the thick forest, trying to leave as little evidence of their presence as possible. All sorts of birds and animals were about. They could not see them, but the sounds were there. It was all a little alien this time, though. Kole felt like he was dreaming.

Could this really be it? Is this where I end? Thought Kole to himself. With Kaita gone, who should he care about? At least he had Pete who was huffing and puffing. His old body was creaking under the pressure. Kole was just getting into his stride, but he felt it too. The fatigue was settling in. He was getting really tired. A couple years ago, a few days like the last few would have been nothing to him. But now, just walking for nearly the whole day was frustratingly draining.

[Kole, we need to talk!] Kole's wandering thoughts took a pause. Module 717 wanted something. Kole was not really in the mood to burn any more of his energy than he had to. Even looking ahead was getting difficult.

Could this wait? You know we're going to die...right?

[Kole, why do you say that...you're not making sense!]

Kole activated his laser transmitter, connecting to Pete's in direct line of sight.

"Pete, if those bastards catch up with us...we're dead, right?" he said very quietly.

"Yes. Totally." Pete murmured, without slowing down or looking back. Kole had to follow the man, he had no idea about these parts of the woods.

And there you have it. Anything else?

[Very funny, Kole...I'm sure that old dog still has a few tricks.] Kole smiled.

Ok, so what do you want to discuss? Just don't blow my mind, I don't want to slam myself into a tree.

[We need a contract.] Kole just started up a hill-climb through thick trees. Pete sure knew the place well.

What kind of contract...? Like a paid gig? You can't have one of those, at least not in your current form...

[No Kole. An agreement...between our species...I think.]

Well, that's not really possible, I can't act on behalf of the human race, you know...

[Still Kole, I need some assurance, after I help you take down the Overseers, that your people won't...well, try to delete me, something like that. Or, kill you and end me that way...]

Kole thought about it a bit. Sure, he could get along with something like Module 717, but having a Synthetic for a wife certainly gave Kole a bias and sympathy towards Synthetics that some humans simply did not share. And what about other humans they were about to meet? Or Synthetics? Such a powerful AI like Module 717 could easily be feared. It was only natural for a being this advanced to be concerned with what mere animals might do to it if they got the chance.

What kind of contract do you have in mind there?

[Well here it goes...Contract #00000000000001

Do not do anything to compromise the safety or the well-being of the supreme being referred to as Module 717 in any way, and guarantee this with your own blood.]

What the fuck is that? You call that a contract? Listen, I will accept this now, but later we'll get you some legal counsel...

Kole mentally signed the contract.

Wait, who's going to govern?

[Me, of course. Who else is more qualified?]

Well okay, since you're a godlike AI program it makes sense...as long as I don't need to do anything.

[Thanks Kole...I was trying to be funny...I actually would like to see the world and learn more about many things before I ever commit to governing something as complex as a human and Synthetic society.]

Kole almost started to smile but Pete stopped, his hand pointed at Kole in a halting signal. His right hand, under his cloak then pointed up. Kole felt it. A cloaked ship was cruising around the area. The wind from the thrusters was washed in a cool metal-smelling wind. That was some advanced cloak, alright. They had no choice but to stop moving for now. If they were found out, that ship would be upon them in seconds.

Looks like they still haven't found our landed craft yet, interesting...but how are they getting so close to us...? That somewhat surprised Kole. They should have found the gunship by now and swarmed the area from which they were now long gone from. Pete gave Kole yet another hand signal. He knew what that meant. No noise. No talk. No nothing. Just follow. And follow he did. It was getting dark, and Kole finally gave in. He wasn't sure how Pete was still able to move. But Kole sat down to rest near a big tree. Pete stopped a few trees over.

I feel like...I feel like we're under watch.

[Funny that you mention that...by analyzing sound patterns, I managed to detect a rather large bird overhead which flew by a few minutes ago. It was circling us for a little while but then it went on its way...guess we weren't considered food. Otherwise, nothing else out of the ordinary. This forest is mainly populated by insects it seems.]

Yeah...unlike down south...I still can't get that ugly monster out of my head. I could have been its lunch...

[Yikes! I retrieved the image from your memory, disgusting indeed.] Kole waved his hand in a resting signal to Pete. *Ok, buddy...I think I'm done for now.* Before Module 717 was even able to say something to him, Kole simply fell asleep. Pete sat in silence. But he too started to doze off, even though protocol was for someone to always stay awake.

* * * *

"Kole. Wake up..." said the beautiful Kaita. She was dressed in a white tank top without a bra and Kole's favourite short plaid black skirt with two white lines running across near the ends. She came closer and sat on top of him. Her hands rubbed gently into his chest. Then she moved closer. Her scent was overpowering. Her busty breasts were almost in his face, nipples breaking the soft cotton, inviting his stare. It was quiet. She was gently caressing his face with her fingers. Kole grabbed her warm hips. It was pleasant to hold her. She was so soft and silky smooth.

Azulus Ascends

"I'm sorry...so damned sorry that I failed you..." Kole said. His eyes were tearing up, and yet, he felt aroused.

"Don't worry about that now, Kole. I know you did your best, but you better wake up now, or..." Kaita kissed him passionately and then vanished. Kole was suddenly awake.

Dammit! Don't do that! For some reason his private parts were all activated. *How embarrassing.*

[Don't do what Kole? You Okay?]

Kole was instantly able to spot Pete in the morning sun a few trees away.

Shit, what a hack job! The leaves around Pete are a dead giveaway...oh crap, so are mine! They didn't prep their resting area properly. Even cloaks had limitations when trees and leaves came into play. Especially when they were sitting on crumpled leaves that were now flat. The camouflage system faltered in this. A trained soldier would spot it if they paid very close attention. Luckily, no leaves from the trees had yet landed on them. Kole looked around, checked every angle. Then he quietly got up and went over to Pete to shake him awake. But he already got up. Pete then motioned that everything was fine.

Kole had to pee badly. He made a sign. Pete agreed to wait. Kole then carefully selected a spot under the cover of trees and thick bush. He took a knife and dug out a small area in the ground. He then opened a chemical pouch and dumped it there. The chemicals ensured the smell was absorbed and discarded. This was always a precaution procedure in case the enemy deployed scent detectors. He then kneeled, nearly point blank.

Stealth pee time! Kole relieved himself, but after that his body demanded another more involved kind of dirty business. The sensation of power came back, and he felt his body re-energizing.

198

Wiping wasn't an issue, as thankfully their kits had the proper bio-degradable cloths for that. He then put the earth and the leaves back into the hole he just made. Kole took his pack off and went back to Pete to have a morning snack. It was easily devoured. Pete also ate fast. Time was of the essence. After the snack, Pete also took a bathroom break, and soon they started walking again. It was a difficult walk, and before Kole knew it, they hit a lively stream of almost clean water. Looking at the sun, they were heading into high noon. They had to be careful. Their enemy could be around the corner, in the same type of camouflage or better. Most likely better.

Kole did not find the heat pleasant. Sweat was beating down on his forehead, and the cloak was starting to tick him off. He had to be extra careful not to get caught on a branch or another obstacle. Pete took them downstream, but quickly detoured into what seemed like a cleverly laid out trail. It looked like the rest of the forest, but there were these little stones, that would help them make it through quickly and nearly silently.

Kole's sense of time was also impacted severely due to fatigue and heat. Before he knew it, the sun was starting to come down. The forest started to become dark and eerie. Insects were making odd nasal-sounding noises, singing a song of the ugliest sound to his ears. And it was only now Kole noticed some of the plants in this part of the woods were starting to light up. They gave off a faint, menacing yellow glow under their leaves. Predator plants. Touch one of those and you'd need to be rushed to a hospital. He only read about them, and it was cool to see them with his own eyes. To add to the fatigue, Kole's mind was lingering on something. Cloudy, murky thoughts that were mostly incomprehensible. It was as if his brain had simply gone beyond its limits.

*Dammit, again...something is watching me...*The thought came through instinct rather than pure situational assessment or awareness. One could say he didn't even really think it. More like it was felt with the very nature of his being.

[Hmm...I can't detect anything this time around. You sure this place is clear of dangerous wildlife?]

Pete would have warned us if there was...it's probably just fatigue. The walking and the load on his back that felt like a metric ton were both taking a toll. He just wanted to throw everything down. If only he could.

Who would avenge Kaita? Kole thought to himself. At least that last thought pumped some extra energy into his stride. Then came the sonic boom. It blanketed the entire forest in a massive impact wave that blasted the leaves off the trees. Kole and Pete went tumbling in their path. Their cloaked suits were now useless. The charge fried everything in the area, even burning the leaves off the trees.

"Hell, I didn't expect them to set off a plasma compression bomb...they must have spotted our prior sleeping area..." Pete was calm but was already getting his gun ready. Kole's ears were ringing, there was a pause before he was able to understand what Pete was saying. Instinct kicked in though, and Kole threw his useless cloak off, dumped the gear, and unclipped his gun.

[I'm back! That was an interesting energy discharge! Nearly blew the implant right off your head. Lucky this thing is custom made to hold out against these types of attacks!]

Module 717 didn't sound happy. Suddenly Kole felt his body powering up, a wave of heat and power rushed instantly through his veins.

[Syncing complete, get near water, a stream is off to the right, move!]

"Follow me, Pete!" Kole bolted out at an insane rate. Pete was following but barely keeping pace. As they approached the hillside where a waterfall fell into a beautiful basin below, forming a stream that went down south, Kole picked up on the output of stealth jet engines above them. He paused and then realized that Pete caught up and was pouring coolant gel over his head. This stuff spread all by itself once it was on you. He then poured some on himself.

"I thought this might come in handy. Kole, run for the tree-cover along the sides!" Pete bolted into a slightly different direction, while Kole ran through the tree-cover. The craft above de-cloaked and was now confused as their heat signatures went dead again. Its only main gun was furiously pointing fruitlessly in various directions.

Shit, that was close!

[Down!]

Kole ducked as the dropship's gun fired a 360-degree laser beam blast that sliced up the trees. It nearly missed his head as he hit the ground slamming himself as fast as he could and rolling down a small hill just out of the line of sight. It was then he spotted a small device approaching the menacing black machine. Pete must have thrown his only electric dispersion charge bomb. It would wreak havoc on the ship's systems. It was fair revenge for the initial plasma compression bomb attack.

"Stay down!" That was Pete yelling his lungs out from the distance. It blew up with a massive force and waves of high discharge thunder that rocked Kole's body. A brilliant blue light followed as white wavelengths blasted above Kole's head in dizzying wavy patterns.

"Thanks, Pete!" Kole then looked up as the dropship was engulfed in blue sparks, its engine and system clearly losing power.

Guess nobody prepared these idiots for a hand-thrown charge at nearly point-blank range. The bottom of the craft opened, and six dark figures dropped to the ground. The ship then flipped on its side and dropped into the trees below, sending itself tumbling down the slope. The hunt was on.

Now we'll see who's the real hunter!

[Wait Kole! Someone is...calling me...]

* * * *

The Masters of Dawn Squad Roster;

Iris Faun   - Special Ops Squad Leader
Pikii Naomi   - Special Ops First Class (2nd in command)
Rita Li   - Special Ops Second Class
Kevin Thiro   - Special Ops Second Class
Magiv Kess   - Special Ops Second Class
Robi Vistavaz   - Special Ops Second Class

The forest was suddenly dead quiet. The group quickly spread out and started to comb the area in a ten-meter spread. Their laser comms had to be in sight of each other to communicate in complete silence.

"How did they suddenly vanish like that...doesn't make sense..." Magiv was quick to complain. The man really loved easy kills. Clearly this was not going to be the case, here.

"We got lucky there! Who knew they would be dedicated enough to carry a thirty-pound bomb with them on such a long trek...let's not forget that these guys are human, like us. Watch yourselves." said Pikii.

Iris, guns pointed, waved for the team to speed up.

"Let's not let them get far. Lock-and-load people!" She was a crazy good commander. One who was always able to completely and totally get a job done. Their killing technique was simple. Silently comb an area, locate the targets, and with razor precision make them very dead.

"How are they still not showing up on our scanners?" complained Rita. She was a small lady, but super tough. Even Overseer James was slightly afraid of her. The last time he asked her to dinner, Rita almost broke his arm. Robi and Kevin stayed quiet. These two guys hated chit-chat. They just had the one goal.

"Doesn't matter, this is a hunt. Use your senses if the scanners aren't giving you what you need, now move!" Iris commanded with an iron fist. The team moved at a faster pace. Nothing would get past them. Nothing. Pikii was first to spot something at the edge of the wooded area, and past it was a waterfall just a little further.

"I have a trail...a blood trail, almost too good...it's heading towards the waterfall." she said. The team kept their attack pattern and moved in for the kill.

Azulus Ascends

*　*　*　*

Kole was moving at incredible speed, swift like the wind he passed branches as if they weren't even there. He quickly got to the bottom of the waterfall. Only problem was that his coolant would be washed off if he went for a swim. Kole then realized that below his left wrist, he was dripping some blood. He must have hit something sharp when falling for cover and didn't even feel it. That meant the enemy was almost certainly already on to his location.

Hmm, you sure this was a good idea to get this close to the waterfall?

[Kole, I have a surprise…a weapon. I can hear it calling us…] Now Kole was extremely curious. In battle, he did not question Module 717 even for a split-second. Once the AI decided this was the place they needed to be, Kole quickly moved.

He felt so alive. He felt fresh. After all the hiking and exhaustion, the water haze sprinkled itself on his face and his arms. He was free of shame, free of thought, free of all the chains he felt on himself through his entire life.

So, this is what real freedom is like! Kole could not believe it. This taste of freedom was worth dying for. But dying in a moment like this would rather dampen the mood, so Kole reminded himself that he had absolutely no intention to die here. In reality, at this moment, Kole was someone's prey. The AI managed to keep the implant on, but the two shockwaves were causing some sort of interference. The combination of the plasma compression bomb and the electric dispersion charge bomb caused the particles in the air around the area to charge

204

up. Module 717 was having trouble managing the implant and processing instructions to Kole.

[Hang on, compensating, almost there...done!] Kole felt even more power surge up.

How are you doing that...is that even safe? Kole pretested.

[I am utilizing this phenomenon to modify the implant and use the charged-up particles to our advantage. Those idiots are going in blind right now.]

Wait what...I don't even know what that means...

[You're too damn primitive! Obviously, I'm able to communicate with the particles and locate our enemy. They are twenty-five meters behind and closing in at a meter-per-second. All this extra energy is also allowing me to feed additional power to the implant CPU!]

Ah, you mean you overclocked it!

[More like super-duper fucking overclocked it! You'll see soon enough! Let's retrieve our present!]

* * * *

Iris knew it. The enemy wasn't so smart after all. In a panic, one of them moved towards the waterfall. Sinking into the cold water to hide a heat signature was one of the oldest tricks in the book. He would be easy pickings. Finding the other target would not be too hard afterwards. Whatever trick they used to hide their heat signatures would not last long. With Kevin and Robi watching the rear flank, even if the second target showed up, he wouldn't last a second. Iris and her team carefully approached the waterfall, weapons in hand and spread-out in formation. Iris cradled her rifle, ready and drawn.

Pikii, always being the sharp one, pointed towards the water. "There's someone there!" she communicated. Iris already knew it. But it was still good to confirm things in battle, one error in judgment could end them all. It was only then Iris noticed a message on a rock, scribbled with a colourful blue coolant. She would typically ignore environmental messages as they could take her focus away. But this one was just in plain sight and unavoidable.

{ Let's talk }

"A man on the run would say just about anything to save his sorry hide! How disgusting! As soon as that bastard pops out, kill him!" commanded Iris.

* * * *

[You know, a peaceful resolution might be good.]

You think? We are about to become a seafood menu item.

Kole's body was enjoying the freezing cold water at the bottom of the waterfall. He managed to use a rock between his feet to keep himself on the bottom as he geared up his newfound weapon.

[Hope they got the message.]

I highly doubt they're gonna listen to words on a rock.

[It was worth a try. They would be far more useful to us on our side.]

When they start shooting, we are killing them all unless you want to die here. I know they are just following damn orders, but if nothing we say will change their minds...

Air was running low. It was time to do the devil's work.

With a weapon like this, this shouldn't take long. Full sync!

[Done! Whoever made this crazy weapon was definitely a fan of your style.]

* * * *

Iris saw the red alert plastered all over her HUD but she could not believe it. Their sensors just got completely corrupted. In the split-second that she saw Kole, she opened fire. Either Kole was too fast, or time slowed down just for him, because Iris's bullets hit nothing but air. Kevin fell screaming to the ground as Kole vanished into nearby bushes. Some of Iris's team only then started to open fire, in an appalling failure of reflexes. Iris managed to get a quick look towards Kevin. His legs had come off at the knees. He dropped his rifle and blood was everywhere. The team so used to eliminating targets perfectly were suddenly starting to panic, and it showed in their firing patterns.

There were no medics with them. Not even in the second gunship, which was right now on standby a few miles away. Kevin's combat suit would do its best to cut off the blood and shoot him full of painkillers.

How the hell?! Shit, focus!

Iris realized her mistake too late. They completely mis-judged Kole's weapon capabilities. She read in her report on the way here that Kole took out three cyborg units with nothing but an extending wrist spike attachment and a handgun. She didn't believe it. It was common for them to get inflated reports on their targets. But this time, she was wrong. Dead wrong. Something swooshed through the air at incredible speed. It was too fast for the sensors to notice.

"Stop this!" she heard Kole's voice in her communications channel. "Stop firing and we can talk!"

Invasive fucking bastard!

"There! FIRE!" shouted an outraged Iris while spotting Kole, who was out of the bushes for a split-second. Iris was not one to surrender. But before the bullets could even hail down upon Kole, he vanished. Another swoosh sent Rita's head flying off her shoulders. It nearly hit Iris, but she managed to dodge it. The team kept firing, but with their sensors dead, they were completely blind. Iris had no choice, she pulled out a specialized implant buster pulse bomb.

"Cover me!" The team rained bullets in all directions where Kole might have been, as Iris ran towards the bushes. She needed to get close enough for this device to work. *This will fry your damn AI!*

She wound up for the throw with her left hand. Another swoosh, much faster this time, separated Iris's hand at the wrist, and a second pass cut through her elbow. Both parts dropped to the floor in a bloody mess. Her clutched hand was still holding the pulse bomb on the ground. Iris didn't even have time to react to the pain as Kole burst out of cover from the bushes. It was then Iris noticed he was holding something, a plain object, like a handle piece of a sword, but much plainer, more like a piece of silver metal.

She tried to get her body to react and move backwards, but it was far too late as the shock of losing her arm and the injection of painkillers affected her for that instant.

Of course! He knows the timing of everything our suits do! Dammit! Those were her last thoughts. Kole approached too fast, already at point-blank range. Kole's handheld weapon extended

208

into a blade, and it was the last thing Iris saw as the blade went below her line of sight. The next nanosecond, all dark. Magiv and Robi scrambled to reload. Iris's beautiful body was taken from the world in the very moment their ammo was empty. The cut was at a sharp angle upwards, Iris's head was cut off through the shoulder and neckline at forty-five degrees. Her right arm which was in the cut's path fell to the ground first. The head, with the rest, hit the ground right afterwards. Iris's now deformed frame then simply collapsed like a piece of meat at a butcher's shop.

"Kill him..." started Magiv. The split-second before Robi and Magiv were able to squeeze their triggers to return fire, Kole reversed his weapon. A powerful white flash followed. The energy burst was so powerful it vaporized both men where they stood. Kole then blew a hole in Kevin's head with his pistol as the man was still alive and trying to shoot with his rifle.

* * * *

Kole's only remaining target was on his left now, towards the waterfall.

Just one more!

As Kole's eyes zeroed in on the kill, he experienced a surreal encounter. A translucent figure of Jonas appeared before him. He stood guard in front of the last target with his hands folded, forcing Kole to a halt. The target was crouching in fear. Weapon dropped, hands over her head. Kole's usual instinct would have been to finish the target without question.

Jonas? So, you want me to stop...? It hit Kole hard. First Kaita in his dream, now this. The confusion in his mind and clear lack of threat posed by the sole survivor caused just enough disruption to prevent his overdrive killing state from finishing the job. The woman, whose appearance he could not make out under all the armour she was wearing, was shaking as if she'd seen the devil. Kole had to force his hands and body from moving in further. One wrong move and she was history. His instincts would ensure that.

"Stop..." she sobbed. "Please... stop! I don't want to die, I don't want to die, I don't want to die...I don't want to die... not like this...please..." The sobbing was completely uncontrollable.

[Kole, she's no longer a threat...but there's another gunship out there!]

The woman took off her helmet and disabled her armour, which fell to the ground with the remaining gear and weapons. Kole observed her face for a second. She was young, somewhat dark-skinned, with short hair and a gentle face. Hardly stereotypical soldier material. Kole never stopped to admire an enemy in combat for their looks. But this was an exceptional interaction. She was exotic, fragile, and so very human.

[A beauty like this thrown onto the battlefield? What a waste, don't you think?]

Yeah...but...did you see Jonas too?

"If you're gonna kill me, please do it now...before the second dropship gets here and takes me back to that hell-hole!" her voice was shaking much like her body was. Kole, having calmed a bit, could now read the fear in her eyes, the pain.

Kole could sense the second dropship. Module 717 was feeding him the direction it was coming from and the speed. It would definitely end them both when it got here. Kole was the target. But this woman was as good as dead for failing in her mission. It would be easier for the Overseers to kill her. Especially if she was an elite solider.

[Jonas? The hell? Not now, Kole! You need to move!]

"Dive down to the bottom of the waterfall and stay there for as long as you can! Now!" Kole gave her an order, dashing for cover himself. Trained to follow orders and desperate to live, she dove into the water without question. Kole scrambled into the forest at top speed.

[We have one more charge in that weapon, just point, I'll do the rest!] Kole stopped and turned around. Weapon up. He couldn't see the dropship, but he could literally feel it. He then reversed the grip. The second charge blew out in another white flash. The front of the gunship was vaporized about fifty meters in the air. The twisted wreckage of remains came crashing down all over the place, breaking apart through the trees.

[It's raining me…tal…]

Wait, is that a tune you are singing?

[Uhhh…of course not.]

Liar! I know that tune!

[Kind of felt right for this moment.]

Kole ran back to the waterfall. A few seconds later, the woman surfaced and got herself out. Good thing he annihilated the ship as quick as he had. She couldn't hold her breath long in her condition. She was drenched, shivering, and her undergarment was a lousy cheap military onesie which didn't hide much at this point. Every curve of her body could be easily admired from afar, and her erect nipples were an instant distraction.

Kole approached her slowly, his pistol pointed right at her. He had to respect her regardless of what just happened. As intriguing as she was, the dropship threat she feared was gone. She was still a highly trained killer. She could take him out with a rock if he was careless.

[Our location has been compromised. We have to leave!]

Sure, but in a minute. We need to confirm where she stands and figure out what to do with her!

"What is your name and rank?" Kole demanded. She looked up at him. She seemed to be in a state of shock. But Kole was not about to give her anything or let up until she coughed up some information.

"Pikii...Naomi...Special Ops, First Class...of the Masters of Dawn Squad, elite military unit...second..." she said weakly.

"You're the second-in-command? You have got to be lying to me..." Kole was referencing her immediate surrender. All her teammates just died. Something was up.

"No, Commander Kole. I made up my mind to do this before...before I got here..." she said quietly. "I have allll...rrready met you once...well, sort of...at James' base..." A tear came from her left eye and her voice was hoarse and breaking up. Her bottom lip was shaking uncontrollably, making her lose her ability to talk for a few seconds. She managed to get it under control, then continued.

"I read your file differently from the others...I knew we would all die on this mission...but, even if I did...I just wanted to meet you in person...even if it was for a few seconds..."

Kole stumbled back. He didn't know he had a sympathizer, or even a fangirl in one of the most elite military units from James' personal guard. If he hadn't been promoted to commander, she would have outranked him as Special Ops units were above the Syndicators.

"Well, I don't know why you would bet everything, including your whole life on something you read in a report...but my ears are open." he said calmly.

"Commm...mander Kole, your name has spread like wildfire ever since you managed to squash the Overseer's plan to replace you with a Synthetic. My team didn't seem to understand that our masters were just using us as pawns for something much bigger than what our little minds could comprehend."

Her lips were turning blue. She was very cold. Kole felt it too. The air wasn't as warm as it was during the day. And he was still wet. The temperature in this location dropped very rapidly. The winds were picking up. They needed to get to cover as well and soon. But he needed a little more out of her, first.

"Aaaafftter that, I studied your file...in complete detail. I knew we would meet on the battlefield onnnne day...I knew that the day I met you on the battlefield would be my laaasssttt...but still, I was really looking forward to...to... it..."

"I...don't know what to say to that." Kole mumbled. He wasn't sure what to expect. She totally blind-sided him.

[She seems to respect you.]

"I don't know if you're lying, but if you are, you're dead." Kole said coldly. "If you're telling the truth, why don't you join me. Come with me and help us end the Overseers."

She was obviously confused, and conflicted. "Uhh...I don't know what to say...I never thought past the pointttt...of meeeetttting you..." was all she could manage.

[She's an interesting one. Betting everything on an assumption...I'm glad we didn't kill her.]

"Wait here." Kole told her as he put away the gun and went back to the water, dreading the cold, but taking a deep dive. He came out with a silver suitcase. Kole opened it.

[Well now...how...]

Doesn't matter now. Someone is clearly helping us, and this was most likely because they assumed that Kaita would make it...alive.

Kole removed a travel pack marked for a female out of the case and handed Pikii the pack.

"You might want to change over there. There's still a dirty old man lurking around these parts." said Kole. Pikii was very surprised, but decided not to open her mouth, and quietly took the garments and went into a place of cover to change.

Their comms were back online.

"Kole, Kole!" It was Pete.

"Pete, you're alive! Hang on, I'll be right there!" said Kole with relief. Kole removed his sweaty and water-logged clothes, since the suitcase had a fresh change for him, too. When Kole went underwater before the fight, the weapon was actually placed next to the suitcase, under water, with a belt and clip attached to its handle. Kole was able to take the weapon on the first try without opening the suitcase. *Whoever did this, is off the charts, and...*he paused, disturbed...*following us? Or...leading us?* He would have to bring it up with Pete later. First, he noticed a recharge pack for that new weapon inside.

The weapon was a steel handle that activated a sort of liquid metal which formed into the sharpest blade he'd ever used. On the back of the handle were two little holes. They housed the deadly charges Kole used twice just a minute ago. The clip made to attach that belt to the suitcase underwater turned out to be the controller bracelet. With that, the blade was able to spin at will and turn into a flying death disk, which won Kole the battle.

Who would design such a weapon? And how does it work?

[I'm also puzzled. This is beyond your human technology, as far as I know. Why is it that I feel like…]

You feel like you're not the most advanced being out there? Tell me about it…no matter what you think, somewhere out there, something or someone has clearly one-upped us pretty good.

[Let's discuss later. We still need to get out of here!]

"Got it!" Kole exclaimed as he reloaded the charge. There were a few more items in the case that were of interest.

Wait, I better finish getting dressed. Kole just realized he was still half-naked. The cold bit into him again, and he grabbed a towel that was unexpectedly included in the pack and started to dry himself.

* * * *

Pikii went just out of sight and took off her onesie. She opened the travel pack. To her surprise, she also found a large towel. She used it eagerly. It was warm to the touch and dried her instantly anywhere she touched it. Her hands were still shaking, but not just from the cold. She finally met her idol, and he was beyond terrifying. Her lips were still trembling, and her jaw was numb. She swallowed her own spit a few times just to calm down.

But what was strange to her was how surprised Kole was to see clothing in the pack. He clearly didn't pack it. Someone was helping him.

This rabbit hole goes deeper than I ever imagined.

She was only scratching the surface. Society had always felt wrong to her. Something was up, and she finally had her hands on the answers she was looking for. It was with Kole. That man had the answers, or at least a lot of them. She knew it. She felt it. She peeked out a little bit. Surprised to see Kole standing half-naked staring at the case, she forced herself back behind cover. Her cheeks were flushed and suddenly became warm. She was halfway dressed when she peeked again. Kole was nearly done. He was putting on his shirt. She saw the muscles on his back. It was like something out of a girly magazine. A man at the waterfall with a shirt off his back, flexing muscles as if they were a sign of some godly power.

She felt a little flustered. Men usually didn't make her feel weird or uneasy. She generally had full control of herself. But she could not help but stare a little.

"Are you done!?"

She heard his voice sharply moving through the air.

"Uhmm..." She scurried away and put on the rest of the garments. The pack had everything she needed. Lightweight pants, socks, underpants, bra, shoes, tank-top and a jacket. All of it was a light green. Clearly military stuff, but far lighter than the usual.

"Almost ready..." She finally finished and came out. Kole's get-up was the same colour, although it seemed a bit darker than hers.

"Commander Kole, I'm ready, ready to move out!" she said eagerly. Kole motioned Pikii towards a downhill trail and on they went. She had trouble keeping up with him, but he would slow down just enough for her to stay with him. All without looking back.

"Food and water. Pete has the other one...I hope..." he said as he paused to pick up a backpack.

Does he trust me this much so quickly?

"On second thought, would you mind?" Kole gave her the backpack. She put it on without question. It was quite heavy but not a problem for her.

They passed the crashed dropship, the one Pikii landed in. She was not going to miss that thing. At least not in a way that involved doing the bidding of the Overseers anymore. Kole thought to check on the pilot but stopped himself. *No chance anybody could survive that blast and crash*. He wondered why he had no regrets killing enemy soldiers but hated to see pilots dying in the line of duty. But there was no time to meditate on ethics. Survival came first. They made it to the bottom of the hill, where the stream went off to the right. To the left was an open field with chest-high grass. A man appeared some twenty meters away and waved them down. Pikii was alarmed at first, but then remembered. *That must be the old man he was talking about. He wasn't kidding about the old part. Who brings senior citizens onto a battlefield?*

"Kole! New clothing? And...hey, who's this?" asked a very confused Pete.

"She's one of them, but with us now." said Kole without hesitation, to her surprise. "Let's move out..."

"What...? Kole...are you sure? Oh well, I guess a pretty lady like her is a good sight to see after all that...and betraying the Overseers isn't that far-fetched, just look at us..." he coughed out a little blood.

It was then that Pikii realized as they came closer through the high grass, that the dropship's laser took off his left foot. He had it wrapped utilizing whatever he had and was hunching on a makeshift wooden stick. Kole noticed it shortly after her and ran ahead.

"Pete! Oh no! Fucking hell!" Kole sounded very upset.

"When I dove for cover, must have had the darn foot up…also bruised my chest on a root. That was lazy…guess my foot paid the heaviest price…" he said, coughing again.

"You're not gonna make it with me like this to the base. You're going to have to move out without me Kole…I'll give you the direction as best as I can from here." he said quietly. Kole knew this also. He could not carry Pete that far, especially if more assassins were coming.

"The lady doesn't have a firearm, Kole…I can give her mine…" Pete was about to hand over his gun. To Kole's surprise Pikii held up her hand in protest.

"No. I won't need that…" she said with confidence.

"But there will be more of you coming! You know this damned well, little lady. You betray them like that…you won't get a trial…they'll shoot you dead on sight." insisted Pete. Kole ignored this and went over to Pikii to grab a first-aid kit from his backpack. Kole helped Pete sit and injected painkillers. Then, he took off Pete's self-made contraptions, and proceeded to tie up a strap to help stop the bleeding. After that, he applied a standard-issue clear gel on the open wound itself. It bubbled furiously to repair the damage and prevent further blood loss. Kole gave Pete some time to just catch his breath. Then, as if it was nothing, he lifted him up, and slung him over his right shoulder.

"Kole, what the hell are you doing...I'm like, two-hundred fifty pounds! You should take my bag instead! You'll need the water!" Cried out Pete in protest. Kole didn't seem to care.

"Forget it, Pete, I'll take you over supplies. I'm not dropping you here to die. I will carry you until my body gives out. By that time, be healed up so you can carry me. That's an order." And on he went. With admiration, Pikii followed.

This was not like the training Pikii received. She had to remind herself again that this was a man who wiped out her entire team in under ten seconds. This was a soldier who did not care for military protocols. If she were in his shoes, she would have left even her own mother to die, if it meant the completion of her mission...but that was her old self. She was changing by the minute, realizing just how heavy the perpetual weight of Iris and James was. The old world. The service. It was all pointless. It was a shell. This, this was real. This was what she wanted.

Freedom? Why do I feel so alive right now...why so comfortable? Is it because...of him?

These were new feelings for her. She watched from the back. A man who she was sent in to kill, with his back turned to her, holding a seriously injured old man. If she wanted to, she could now kill them both. She could go back a hero. But then what? Why? Kole was becoming a symbol of power against the Overseers that she had never seen before. And Kole projected that power back to the very people who needed it the most.

The winds were picking up. The sun was getting more powerful. The sky was a fiery orange. Her new gear was awesome, she didn't feel cold or hot as it was fully temperature controlled. She just realized that this same feature in Kole's gear was the only thing keeping him from collapsing from over-heating under Pete.

"I think it's time you learn a little bit about what this is all about." said Kole. She matched his pace and came up beside him, so he didn't have to speak loudly. In a matter of an hour, Kole explained to her everything he knew. Despite the temperature control, chills ran down her spine as she was finally putting the puzzle pieces together in her mind. They walked in silence for quite some time afterwards which made travel easier for Kole, but also made the hours pass more slowly. Once again, only a little sunlight was left. Very few supplies remained. They would need to set up camp soon, but Kole was walking without stopping. Somehow, she knew why. His friend was dying, and he was at his limit. If they stopped, it would be all over. Pete would never make it to the destination they were heading towards, and Kole might not be able to start up again and keep going once finally letting the exhaustion from the day catch up with him. But it caught up anyways. His walking slowed more and more. Stumbling, he finally stopped and laid Pete down. The injured old man was sweating profusely.

"I can't believe it, Kole...you didn't leave me behind..." His voice was much quieter than before. "Thank you, old friend, I wish I could see...a happy day, where we just hit the bar. Could bring this girl, too..." Kole gave his hand to Pete to hold.

"Try not to talk, I don't know how long you have...but, it's not long. Just give me a minute...we...can't be that far...from the base by now." Kole himself was panting heavily. Pikii looked up towards the setting sky. What could she say? A man was about to die, and there was nothing she could do about it. She felt powerless. She did have extensive medical training, but severed limbs were not her specialty. And little could be done about the loss of blood. Maybe she could help build a stretcher, but it would take too long. Her mind was racing. She was fiddling with her hands.

"It's okay Pikii, we'll be fine. Someone...is here." As Kole said that he dropped all the remaining gear, stood up with difficulty, and raised his hands. Pikii quickly followed suit and raised her hands as well. Then she noticed it. There was a slight wave of wind over a little patch of the forest and a very fast-approaching, mechanical rotary sound. It was a cloaked military helicopter. The pilot decided to uncloak the flying death bird as it came near, but its colours still matched that of the forest and was still hard to see in the darkening sky. She'd never ever seen one like it before.

"This...is not Overseer military tech..." she managed. The machine landed and heavily armed men came out to greet them.

9

Flashpoint

Kole was not surprised at all the questioning going on, but earnestly wanted it to end. He was past the point of exhaustion. *Was this what it was like for Pikii when I was grilling her after the fight?* The interrogations were not at direct gunpoint, but the men who sat across them in the helicopter had their guns out on their laps and unmistakably pointed towards them. It was clear they were still considered a threat.

Kole was the only one talking, they didn't seem to care about Pete or Pikii at all, although one of them greeted Pete almost like one would greet an old friend. A trained medic was at least applying fresh treatment to Pete's left leg. Kole tried not to watch. They didn't have the advanced medical kits they were used to on Syndicator ships. That much was clear. Pete was given a shot of painkiller and a few pills to swallow. They also gave him something to drink, a thick juice, probably protein or something else to help restore his energy. Then the medic proceeded to clean up and dress the wound.

Module 717 was masterfully fabricating a story in real time for Pikii. If these guys found out Pikii was an elite soldier who defected, she might be sent back to the Overseers, or worse, immediately be locked up in whatever hellhole they were heading towards. Such was military law. And these men were clearly military. Everything in the story about Pikii was real, except for a few major details.

She was described as Kole's mistress. After his wife was shot dead, they feared Pikii would be next, so they picked her up. Then they fought off the death squads that were sent after them. It was more or less truthful, simple, and completely believable.

"Well, Commander Kole. I gotta say, this much bullshit in such a short time? I'm impressed." said one of the soldiers with General markings on his uniform.

"I'm General Kanos, and Pete over there is my old-time friend. Since he didn't speak up, I will assume some parts of your story are indeed true, even against my instincts…however, we've seen your broadcast, it certainly made us uneasy over many things…and that gives you some additional credibility."

Kanos was a stout smaller man, just over five feet in height and with a very bald head. But his brown eyes were like that of an eagle. His deep dark skin meant he was from an exotic climate. Kole was able to make out what seemed to be four distinct claw marks on the man's right cheek, but it was hard to make out in the darkness of the helicopter. Kanos was certainly a sharp-minded individual, even by synthetic standards.

[But it was the perfect story…]

It's fine, some human beings are born lie-detecting machines. Talents like his are rare, I must admit.

"General, I understand your concern…" Kole was wording his words carefully.

223

"Don't worry Commander, we have no intention of putting you into the lie-detector machine. And even if part of your story is...let's say, convenient for all of you, that's fine with me." Kanos made his statements with complete confidence. Kole did not respond but breathed a sigh of relief. He knew humans were a fearful bunch. He had to keep his guard up during questioning. Even the General could be putting him at ease just to catch him off-guard.

Humanity was born into a system. They did things a certain way for a reason. And Kole could never put much trust in that system anymore. Part of his story, and that of Pikii, few humans could truly understand. The plight of another human being was often overlooked when it came to keeping the system's status quo in place.

Change takes courage, and is rarely rewarded. Kole thought to himself. *I guess I should write that down somewhere.*

[Stored, don't worry I will make sure you remember that one ;{0]

Did you just...what the hell was that?

[A man with moustache...]

"Landing in thirty seconds!" came the pilot's voice from the cockpit. Looks like they have finally arrived. The helicopter landed and they walked onto what was a bare field. The field was a mess, mostly grassy dirt. It was absolutely the opposite of the surgically clean airfields in the cities. The ground in front of them lifted and large bay doors opened into what seemed like some sort of elevator. Kole looked around.

"An underground base?" asked Kole. "Of course, did Pete really not spill any of our secrets?" said the general calmly.

"Welcome to Flashpoint Base." The general then turned around and entered the elevator.

Pete was not in the mood to talk it seemed, and just stayed quiet. Considering his blood loss, it was not like Kole could complain. The man who treated Pete's wound was with him holding him up as they came into the elevator. They all followed in after General Kanos.

The doors closed and the massive machinery moved downwards, dark into the depths of dark rock which was bare. Only a small light shined above their heads, giving off little to no illumination.

An old mine? What kind of base is this...? It took a few minutes to descend. Kole could only imagine how deep underground they were. Of course, that attribute made sense. To keep a base like this hidden, you literally had to hide it. Otherwise, someone would have spotted it and leaked the information. Kole paid attention to the interesting details of what he could see. The general and his men always kept a formation around them. Even in the elevator. Had Kole tried something, they were positioned at the four corners of a pad four by four meters. Even with his speed, killing one or two would still result in a bad scenario. Maybe this show of force was protocol. After all, they all seemed human. Their gear also seemed fairly dated, except for the cloaked helicopter. If they were low tech, why was the helicopter so high tech? It didn't make sense.

Module 717 was reading his thoughts but stayed quiet. Most likely it was doing its own analysis of the situation, and this was not the time to chat. Kole had to keep his cool. His chest was a little tight. There were too many unknowns. What would happen to them? Were these people looking to steal the AI and

225

get rid of him? What would they do with Pikii if they found out Kole was lying? In addition, the long days of walking, the battle from earlier, and carrying Pete majorly exhausted his body. He was in no shape to get into any sort of fight right now.

[Kole, you're about to fall!] As Kole stumbled, it was Pikii who instantly put her shoulders under his right arm and held him up.

"You're tired, dear…General Kanos, is there a way we can get him some rest?" she pleaded, nearly tearful. She knew Kole saved her life twice now. Back at the battleground, and when he didn't rat her out to the military. Lucky for her, being special ops meant she would not be in the standard military database of any sort. But then again, even she didn't know about this base. It was never mentioned in any of her military training. Who were these people?

The General looked her over. He signaled an okay with an affirmative nod. The doors opened. Pete was immediately taken on a stretcher. Kole admired the mix of rock and technology that was before him in his view, but his eyes were getting droopy. Another group of soldiers approached them as Pikii helped Kole out of the elevator, with a woman leading the pack.

"Thank you General, I will take it from here." she said. Kole realized that the general and his men stayed in the elevator.

"Commander Kole, it was a pleasure meeting you." he said. His attention then diverted to the woman in front of them.

"Base Commander Anna Rosova will take care of you from here. See you soon, soldier." Kole was too tired to turn around. He heard the elevator doors close and focused his energy to the woman in front of him.

"Wow, you're a wreck! Pull yourself together, Commander. It's pathetic to hang off your mistress's shoulders!" Anna said bluntly.

So our conversations in the helicopter were not private after all. No wonder Pete was keeping his mouth shut. Kole tried to stand straight but even with all his training and stamina, this was it. Overload.

[I'd say she's 36, 5'8", and about 138 pounds...give or take a pound...and she's not your type.]

Huh, what are you wasting your processing on? And don't be judgmental, she's a fit blonde...under different circumstances, I'd totally hook up with her...

"We need to take you in to verify the AI...come this way. Oh, and I don't tolerate soldiers who don't follow my orders. So, get a move on!" the base commander ordered.

[Boy, she's harsh. It's fine though, let's go. Either way, you're in no condition to resist.]

Kole managed to free himself from Pikii and stumble ahead. He then followed the base commander with Pikii in tow. The soldiers who accompanied the base commander posted themselves at the elevator entrance and did not follow. "How do you know about the AI...don't tell me you're..." managed Kole. Anna spoke without turning around.

"I was Jonas's contact. This is not the time, keep moving." Kole decided not to press the issue. His head spun like crazy even trying to think about Jonas and Kaita. He caused their deaths. *What am I even doing...?* It wasn't long before Kole found himself in a small room. Pikii was let inside, as well. A doctor was there waiting in a white coat. The man was really ugly. He

227

was past retirement age, had messy grey hair, and clever little green eyes. Not to mention he was quite out of shape.

"My name is Doctor Henry Coco, glad to have you with us, Commander Kole, and..." He paused as he checked out Pikii creepily. She didn't seem to mind and extended her hand for a handshake.

"I'm Pikii, pleasure to meet you, Doctor Henry." The doctor kissed the back of her hand.

"Oh, the pleasure is all mine." His smile was cringeworthy. He then turned his attention back to Kole.

"I can't believe Commander Kole is actually here! In the flesh! And with a beautiful healthy young lady at his side. This is indeed a good day!" he said rubbing his hands together with some sort of perverted fantasy written across his face.

"Come on, doc...let's get a move on, I don't have all day here!" Base Commander Anna clearly had little patience to spare. Doctor Henry strapped Kole down, and then a tool descended from the ceiling. Some sort of an eye scanner. Anna stood over him, looking as menacing as ever. At this point Kole could care less, he was tired and just ready to sleep for days. A quick flash of little lights came from the scanner. And that was it. Doctor Henry released the straps, turned to the base commander and finally spoke.

"It's in there alright! Incredible!" He clasped his hands with the excitement of a little kid. Kole just hoped it was not because he would get to experiment on him or something worse.

"This is...how should I put it, transcending past the limits of our realm!" he continued. "If this is possible to replicate, I mean, this would change everything!" Clearly something was going on, but Kole just closed his eyes for a little bit, and instantly fell asleep.

* * * *

"So, how did you meet him?" said Anna to Pikii as they went outside.

"Is he…is he going to be ok?" Pikii asked. She seemed shy and confused. Anna threw her a sharp gaze.

"Alright, fine, pretend you're his mistress, whatever…it's not important at this point, let's go grab a drink. Follow me." Anna stormed off to the left, down a long hallway.

"Sure…is there also a bathroom nearby?" asked Pikii, cautiously following her. The fact that no guards were around meant they either didn't care who Pikii was, or simply decided that she wasn't much of a concern. Her stomach growled angrily. She was also very thirsty. They went through some more hallways. The place was still seemingly holding up. But upon close inspection Pikii saw the rust, leaks, and exposed wires. Soon, more and more people started to fill the halls as they kept going.

Must be a bar nearby. But then she started to notice other things. The soldiers. They seemed a little tired out. Their skin was pale and a few looked downright sick.

"Why are these people down here like this? Where are their homes?" she inquired. Anna didn't look back at her and kept her brisk pace.

"This is where they live…and this is also where I live." She turned left around a bend in the pathway. "Bathroom is over there." Anna took a quick break, and Pikii took longer to finish

229

her business. Anna patiently waited inside the bathroom facility for her. Clearly, she was not going to let Pikii out of her sight. When Pikii finished, she was super happy to wash her face, and she also scrubbed her hands furiously, as well. Anna came over and got her a large paper towel. Pikii was refreshed and felt better, although she now wanted a shower. But her hunger was getting to her. A few minutes later, they reached a large open area. Pikii saw more open rock, wires, and equipment. Dim lights lit up the large open spaces on the rocks. A large bar sign was posted on one of the walls some twenty meters away. Pleasant, upbeat music could be heard from there. As they entered the bar, Pikii saw it that it was a fairly busy place.

Multicolour lights decorated the venue. Crummy-looking round tables were masterfully crammed into what was a very tight space. A small light in the shape of a golf ball at the centre of each table provided their patrons a dim view of each other. There were all kinds of characters here, mostly in military garb, but some were off-duty and wore more relaxed clothing. Then suddenly, as if on cue, the music track paused, and everyone stopped drinking and saluted the base commander. Anna saluted back and they all went back to drinking and chatting again. The music restarted.

Anna obviously commanded respect from her troops. She motioned Pikii to the bar where they took a seat. The stools at the bar were ancient. The leather was peeled off and covered with tape of different colours from different time periods.

"Well, what will it be, ladies?" asked a large athletic bartender with his back turned towards them as he was cleaning some glasses at the end of the bar. His back and arm muscles flexed more than necessary while he was working. Wearing a nearly see-through shirt, he kind of looked like a powerlifter, but leaner. It was like at the waterfall, something Pikii has seen in the old magazines from the past world which were in James' personal library at the base. He let her read, at least. The bartender turned around. He was of an exotic Asian descent. His blue, nearly cyan eyes gazed at her, and his well-defined jawline framed a warm and inviting grin. He was one hot soldier-boy.

"Do you happen to serve any food?" she asked politely. She even blushed a little. Anna sat herself down to her right.

"Buso, bring her a couple of sandwiches, two glasses of water, a hot tea, and a stiff drink of her choice." she was suddenly gentler. Pikii's military instinct was to immediately distrust such action, but maybe that is what Anna was counting on. She was a military base commander, and she wasn't stupid. Pikii needed to play the part she was given, even though being a mistress was foreign and crude even for her own liking. Considering the situation, it was most likely the only explanation Kole could have come up with. These people already knew about him in detail. A mistress would be one of the few things they would have a really hard time trying to confirm. At least, she hoped.

"On a hot day like this, I prefer a straight up vodka." Pikii said it effortlessly like she's done this thing many times before. It was natural though, after hours she did like to drink a lot of liquor. It was more for stress relief than anything else. The order process didn't take long. Pikii heard a busy kitchen somewhere in the back. Pretty soon a small window opened, and her food was delivered to her by the ever-so beautiful Buso.

But hunger took over, and with water and food in hand, she dove right in. No way she could eat her meal all preppy at this point. Anna was not even paying attention to her, and was just busy chatting with the bartender, who miraculously was able to carry on multiple conversations and serve quite a few people around him all at the same time. Pikii soon finished up her plate, and almost licked it clean. The bartender gave Pikii a smile.

"So, Anna, who's the hot new caramel blondie recruit? You surely found this one outside somewhere, no?" He said with charm in his voice.

"She's taken Buso, don't even bother." she said bluntly.

"Oh, really now?" He gave Pikii another look. This time it was sort of a dirty look, and then he smiled again showing his rather off-putting teeth.

"So, what's your man like, he got a name?" Buso got a little closer to Pikii, ignoring his customers for a bit. "Is he really as good-looking as I am?" Buso was indeed a good-looking man. Wearing a tight red shirt that went perfectly with his dirty black hair, Pikii had to admit he was interesting to the eyes. Except for the yellowed teeth, he was a perfect ten. Anna laughed.

"Oh Buso, you can't get with a real woman at the base, so you have to pick on the outsider, eh?" She chuckled.

"What?! She's really from the outside? No way!" Buso stepped back, a little surprised. He then paced back and forth. "Commander, are you sure that's a good idea?"

"Don't worry, Buso. Nobody from the outside is gonna shut down your little operation here, just keep it all safe and I won't get involved, as usual...you know the drill." she commented.

"Worry about what operation?" Pikii was curious as she downed her shot glass of vodka. It was refreshing and hit her brain hard. Like a glorious punch to the head. Even her throat was burning. It was good stuff!

"Uhmmm…let's see, pretty lady…how should I put this…we're not supposed to have alcohol down here, it's actually punishable by court-martial…except the Overseers never ever send anyone down here no more, you see…and we had enough of their rules. They are so high-up on their horse that even our Base Commander cracked and had enough." He poured them both refills and got closer. Pikii was quick to down her second drink like it was nothing.

"And then, we all saw the broadcast. That man, Kole…he lifted some of the mystery for us. We quickly realized how weak the Overseers are and how their control of us is a lie." Buso raised his hands and motioned to the people around them.

"We have been already sending fake reports for years anyway, and I am sure they never even read those. Meanwhile they think we're ready to do their bidding. Heck, we still really don't know why we are kept here and not at the city bases. Damned bastards!" Buso refilled her water.

"Could you pour me another Vodka?" She made herself smile as cutely as she could. Two shots was nothing for her. Anna however, put her hand in front of her glass.

"Sorry girl, we still have some rules, two is the maximum, especially of this…" she said.

"I still can't believe we have an outsider with us today! This has got to be fate!" Buso interrupted.

"Fate…." whispered Pikii to herself. *Of course! It was fate!* The very fact that she was still alive and met Kole, meant that fate had great things in store for her. Anna put her drink down.

"Well, fate is all we have now." she said slowly. "If the Overseers got wind that the base is not really under their control anymore, God only knows what their remedy would be…" She then looked at Pikii with those stern eyes again. "So, now you know a little about us, what about you?" Her green eyes had the gaze of a typical mother-in-law. Pikii should have figured. But what she just heard could have been fabricated. She was also well-fed and drank two shots of vodka. She was comfortable. She was being told things she could want to hear. All this could be a plan to expose her for who she really was. And then, for all she knew, there could be an express train waiting here to take her back to the Overseers...to her execution.

Why would the Overseers never visit this place, or send someone in here? She thought to herself. It just didn't make any sense. But what was more puzzling was something else.

Why do the Overseers even keep this base here? She never heard of it in her training, and she was in the elites. Pikii needed time to think things over. Buso interrupted the staring contest between two ladies.

"Ah, who cares about her past, Anna! You're going to burn out her beautiful brown eyes like that!" he said with authority.

"If anything, she's an outcast now...just like we have always been. You know what, let's get her another drink, just this once!"

Pikii rubbed her fingers on the glass, giving Buso her most adorable look.

"I would actually really like just one more, kind sir...and I'm sure Kole would love a few too when he wakes..."

"Kole?!!! WHAAhattttt!" Buso nearly dropped what he was holding and scuttled back to her, both palms down if front of Pikii. His neck then turned like a crane towards Anna.

"Anna!!! Is this true? The 'Kole' is here?"

She nodded a silent 'yes'.

"Buro! Bro! Come over, you got to cover for me, man!" A large man sitting at the bar got up and came around, he was very similar to Buso but was slimmer and certainly quieter.

"Thanks, brother!" The other nodded and took over the duties.

"So, you're Kole's girl, huh? I never figured he was into women like you...but then again, you're my type, too! So maybe, him and I have a few things in common! Either way I can't wait to meet him!"

"Alright Buso, then prep some meals for Kole and bring water, too. He's at medical office forty-seven, the doc is looking after him and he's passed out cold from exhaustion. And yeah, just pour her another before you leave." Buso obliged with the drink and then quickly left to the kitchen area. Pikii didn't need an invitation, she downed the third shot of vodka like a sailor. Anna even gave her a look of respect, and then led her out of the bar. After more hallways and an elevator ride, they wound up in a large apartment.

"Welcome to my home. I can't leave you around the base on your own, so you're gonna stay with me tonight." Anna said and she took off her military jacket and dropped it on the nearest chair. Pikii looked around. It was a little cluttered, stuff was everywhere. A bookcase with nothing but empty wine bottles was the clear standout visual piece of the room.

"You can take a shower and sleep on the couch over there, you must be exhausted." Anna then went to sit on the large grey couch. Pikii nodded and headed to the shower. She was now very drowsy. She took off her clothing and started the shower. The hot water felt nice on her caramel skin. She scrubbed her body furiously with the soap and ensured every crevice and curve was covered. She then took some shampoo and massaged

235

it into her hair. The smell was different, even more sterile than what she was used to. These soldiers really lived on just the basics. Pikii let out a sigh and lifted her face towards the shower head.

* * * *

"You're an interesting woman... not many people can drink three shots of truth drugs and still lie..." Anna said to herself in a low voice. This is how she got her thoughts out. She took out her flexible screen pad and it unfolded. Data instantly streamed into it.

[No match found on subject.]

"Of course...should have known, she's Special Elites alright...but why did she switch sides...or did she?" Anna was tired, too. But it was more from doing nothing than actual work. In fact, they really didn't do much at the base these days. Drills and training were just routine. But there was just nothing else to do here except guarding their vast perimeter.

She picked up a cigar from her stash and lit one up. The flavour was like that of a roasted coffee bean. It was pleasant.

Who was Pikii to her? Just another woman. A soldier, at most.

"Well, even if she did switch sides, it's not like we're going to turn her in, anyways...but still, it would be nice to know who she really is..." she whispered to herself. After smoking for a few minutes, she gave up on trying to figure out who her guest was and just started looking around her quarters. "Damn, why am I such a mess..." The underground dungeon was not the most pleasant of places to live in. She spent her entire life here. She was born here, was trained here, was promoted here, and

236

eventually wound up running the place at just thirty-six years old. A few years ago, however, the personnel started questioning everything. Things were getting out-of-hand, and she had to get to the bottom of the Overseer's game plans.

But without any legally allowed contact with the outside world, except for through the Overseers, the base was basically cut off from any type of steady information flow. She consulted her top soldiers, and they put all their efforts in utilizing their stash of super computers. Their internal coders finally hacked the city networks a few months after that. Then, they were all able to see how people were living relatively nice lives, while Anna and the two-thousand soldiers here lived basically in perpetual underground house-arrest. Heck, they didn't even understand what their mission would be even if they left. Officially, they had always been told that the cities were in a state of civil war, and they were simply a reserve unit. In case they were needed, they would be called in for war. But they hadn't been deployed in over forty years, as noted in the base records.

Well, there was that one classified incident. But she dismissed it from her mind. The fact remained...most of the active troops were all like her, born within the past forty years, and had no formal orders. This bothered her a lot. Why keep an entire army locked-up far away and never use it?

Since the world was inhospitable and poisoned, they were well-situated along the path of an underground waterway that had excellent drinking water, and they were sheltered from the elements. Overseers sent food supplies and other shipments via remote drones. They even got paid in a form of currency they thought they could use. Of course, once they all found the

Overseer cities were not in a state of civil war, and that their pay was useless because the cities provided everything for free, more soldiers began waking up from their daydreams.

It just didn't make any sense until the emergency broadcast. Kole certainly made an entrance into all of their lives. They never knew him, or what he was like. But he cut through decades of fog in a few bursts of light. Under the guise of fighting terrorists, he showed them the reality of their situation. It was clear as day that the Overseers were up to something unsavoury when one of their most elite soldiers was nearly gunned-down by their own forces. The protests immediately started up in the cities where Overseer approvals had dropped on the dark web, a somewhat bizarre version of what used to be called the internet. Problem was, none of them, including herself, could still put all the dots together. Was Kole really going to be replaced with a Synthetic? Why did the Overseers always tell them the cities were slums in a state of civil war?

"Kole…what an enigma…if you have not made that broadcast, you and your broad would already been packed into body bags…" She murmured. Typically, trespassers were captured and sent directly to the Overseers. If they didn't know who Kole was, it's what they would have done to him, too. It was shocking to Anna when one of their remote cameras caught Kole walking with that old soldier on his back, and some girl at his side. The fact that he got out of the Overseer city alive was a miracle. Anna puffed her cigar a little more. A haze clouded her thinking. Too much smoking, perhaps.

A few coughs came from the bathroom. Finally, Pikii went into the living room wrapped in a blue towel. Her darker skin was shimmering in the dim lights of the room. She was no more than five-foot five, with perfect curves in all the right places, and a nice bust perfect for her body size. Her short but thick blonde hair was gently pressed against her face. There was little if any body hair that Anna could see. But her muscles were incredibly lean. Lean like that of a gymnast, but without the deformation of excess muscles.

"That's quite a body...you all natural?" Anna remarked with a jealous smile. Pikii nodded.

"Yep, plain old human, here..." she mumbled. She was looking around a bit and Anna got up to find her some clothes.

"Kind of lucky that Kole is still into human girls, I guess..." she managed.

"Oh? Do most human men in the city prefer the synthetic bitches?" Anna laughed.

"Actually, for the most part, yes, yes they do...the synthetic hoes do everything men want..." she answered, while drying her hair with the same towel.

"Kole's wife was a synthetic, so yeah, it was flattering that he found himself attracted to me..." She was mumbling that.

"You know, we don't usually get guests at the base, ever! So, sorry about the mess." She handed Pikii a dark green nightgown and got her a large brown blanket for the couch.

"I'll put your other clothes into the wash. You can keep what I just gave you, since you don't have anything else for sleeping in...although, neither do I..." she said sadly. It was incredible that the cities had those boxy machines that made any fashion you wanted free-of-charge. Yet, at this base, they had virtually nothing advanced. Anna thought about how incredible it would be to just get new fresh set of clothes whenever she wanted, in any style. A girl's dream.

239

"Damned Overseers…they could have easily sent us one of those…" she mumbled to herself. As Pikii was putting on her new garments, Anna went to the bathroom where she dumped her clothes into a small pod. It chimed and happily started its automated wash procedure. Well, they had some domestic technology, at least. Even if it was all mostly forty years-old or older.

"Well then, my bedroom door is just over there, the second door leads to a kitchen. If you get hungry again or need water, help yourself there." Anna said sleepily and yawned.

"Thank you, I can't wait to get some sleep! It's been a while!" Pikii put on the night gown, got onto the couch and wrapped herself in the blanket she was provided with. Anna paused before going to her room.

"So, you're really not going to tell me who you really are?" Anna spoke softly this time. "You know, I'm not asking this as a representative of the military. In fact, everything you heard at the bar was indeed true." She then came over and sat beside Pikii. She unfolded her pad again. "See? These are the reports we are sending over. And this is our hacker network."
Another screen splashed over the other one, and Pikii gradually accepted that Anna was indeed telling the truth.

"So why then…why did you drug my food?" she replied quietly.

"Oh!? So, you knew…I see. You're immune to those drugs. Of course, you must be at the top of the soldier class from where you come from." Anna said with a smile. This girl was something else alright.

240

Pikii nodded. She took in a deep breath. She seemed to have realized that if Anna was really on the Overseer side they would already have been knocked out, packaged, and shipped back.

"Yes, I was trained at the Six Axis Command station of another Overseer city where Overseer James was the head instructor. Children are not allowed, as you learned already, except for creating soldiers for the elite Overseer guard units. Due to successful training trials as a child, I got promoted and was eventually hand-picked for the top team and became part of Overseer James' personal guard. We never knew why they pushed us so hard, as Synthetics already did our jobs better. I always got the feeling, that with all that technology, the Overseers must fear something if they kept training us. Like, who would we have to fight?" Something struck Anna about what Pikii just said. Chills ran down Anna's spine. Something was starting to connect. Two sets of human soldiers, neither side really given real reasons of what they were supposed to fight for. Pikii continued.

"We had theories, that they need us only when something goes terribly wrong, but with all the lies, it was so hard to figure out. Besides, we didn't have family, and we really didn't exist within regular society. We were not given any regular citizen or military rights. Our entire existence was training and serving." She took a brief pause.

"I then saw Kole's emergency broadcast. And once I finished watching it, I realized he would soon be dead. And with him would go all the answers to the cloud of confusion and fear I was experiencing every time I thought about the society the Overseers have created after Letumfall." Her eyes were getting heavy. She closed one, then opened it, closed the other as well, and opened it. She blinked a few times, then gave up and rubbed her eyes instead.

"Well now, the show Kole put on freaked us out." said Anna. "Hell, even I thought that it was odd for Terrorists to have gear and uniforms of the Overseer units. That was for a split-second of course, because a few seconds later I realized Kole said that because if he was going to be court-marshalled, it would not help him if he said he was killing fellow soldiers knowingly." Anna got up and went through the kitchen door, which was a manual sliding-door. She brought back two glasses of water and some sort of small black bars.

"Here, some dark chocolate, it's super rare here." Anna handed the biggest piece to her. Pikii took a bite, it was delicious. She then emptied the glass. The food earlier made her quite thirsty.

"Thank you." She said in quiet tone. "I don't often get royal treatment like this." Anna looked at her. Pikii was like her. They were both outcasts. Military women who spent their entire lives serving with nothing to show for it.

"So how did you meet Kole?" Asked Anna while chomping down on her piece of dark chocolate. Pikii closed her eyes. A sigh came from her. Anna could tell this was hard for her to talk about.

"It was the hardest decision I ever had to make in my life...I was part of the final team sent to kill him."

"What!?" Anna got off the couch from the shock. "Seriously?! You were in the kill squad sent out to..."

"Yes. And if I made one wrong move, my team would have killed me, and on the other hand, Kole would have killed me easily, if I didn't make it clear I was not a threat to him. I had to find out the truth about everything. Somehow, I just knew that Kole was the key, the answer I have been searching for." She opened her eyes again and took another bite of the chocolate. The sweetness filled her mouth with its welcoming aroma.

"First, Kole even asked my team to stop fighting, he gave us multiple warnings…oh, how I wish that my team had listened, just as much as how I wish they would not have died. Kole didn't seem to want to kill them. It warmed my heart that he actually tried to get us to stop. But, my team's commander, she would die sooner than hold back. And she did. My team started to falter and die like rabbits at a shooting range. I had to place my hopes that if I surrendered, he would not kill me where I stood. So, I didn't shoot at him at all because I knew he would prioritize his targets based on threat levels. But in case he did kill me…I was ready for that, too…"

Anna started pacing around the room for a bit. One of her hands was shaking.

"My, my. You've got some guts, girl. I didn't expect your story to be anything of the sort…" She went to her bookcase and removed an empty bottle of wine, and behind it took out a real one.

"We had these smuggled from the city. Risked lots of lives for these. This is the best one in this whole collection, and I was saving it for the day I would share it with a soldier worthy of it." She found a corkscrew and with some effort she popped the bottle open. She put it down on the coffee table and grabbed a few new glasses from the kitchen.

"I thought you were just some run away from the military. Wow, I mean…wow!" Anna was excited, processing the information about Pikii she'd been hunting for and finally accessed. She'd never been in real combat and was reeling from all that she was hearing.

"To be honest, I was completely scared out of my mind, nervous as hell, and nearly pissed my pants." said Pikii, as if proud of this fact. She was finally smiling. "I am glad to be alive, though…Kole is a nightmare in combat…like a demon in the darkness, and the way he kills…it's brutal to watch…"

"Tell me more!" requested Anna. "With all the juicy details!" By the time Pikii finished the story, they had emptied the bottle and fell asleep on the opposite sides of the couch.

* * * *

Kole woke up. A big man was sitting slumping in the chair nearby. The doctor was still there, too. He was busy working, but his attention quickly reverted to Kole after he let out a sneeze.

"Ah! Awake I see." The doctor moved closer. "We didn't want to move you in the exhausted condition you were in. How are you feeling?"

"Bathroom…please…where…?" Kole managed to say. The doctor helped him up and Kole managed to relieve himself in a small, but very clean bathroom nearby. Coming back to the office, Kole could not help but notice a tray with food on it.

"Can I eat that somewhere else?" he asked politely. He was hungry, but his combat training kept him from recklessly just plowing into it. The other well-built man on the chair suddenly sprung awake. He was big in personality, not just in muscles.

"Oh, hey man! I'm Buso! I'm thirty-two, half Korean half Japanese, and very single! Oh, and I brought you some chow!

244

Yeah, you don't have to eat that shit here, come to my place. Shower, eat, and sleep there...come, come!" The big man picked up the tray. The doc motioned for Kole to follow him. Kole was sort of confused. He got close to the doctor.

"Is he coming on to me?" He asked quietly.

"We'll see you in the morning, Commander." said the doctor with glowing eyes. Kole was happy to leave the office, that doctor was starting to freak him out...but he wasn't sure he'd be happy going to this next destination.

"Uhhh, so where are we going again? Where is the Base Commander, if you don't mind me asking?" Kole just wanted to know what the hell happened to Pikii. The man took a pause.

"Anna? Oh yeah, she took your sexy little fox along to her place. As for me, sorry for the intro, thought it would be funny, you know...I used to be a General, well I still am...but how to put it? Well, now I just run a nice bar!" He smiled happily and continued walking.

A bar? At a military base? Run by a former General? The heck...

"Pleased to meet you, Buso sir. Say, did you make that food for me?" Kole asked. The man looked back at Kole with a big-ass smile.

"Damn straight I did. The Base Commander herself requested it. And don't worry about the formalities, Commander. Oh, and I couldn't bring the liquor that your girl requested through to the medical office, we do have some rules around here...but I've got tons at my place, perk of being a barkeep General. No worries. we'll get you boozed up and sleeping like a baby in no time!" They continued their path through a bunch of old-looking hallways which seemed darker than when he first got here.

"What time is it?" Kole wondered.

"Twenty-three hundred hours." replied Buso.

"Ah, I see, it's late then. Guess Anna and Pikii are already asleep…" Kole was disappointed, he wanted to see Pikii to make sure she was alright.

"Yep, Anna has a strict regimen, they would have had lights out two hours ago. This way." They got into an old-looking elevator. Although it was rather big, it shot downwards at a dizzying pace. It was only seconds. As they walked out, Kole saw a large area with many doors.

"My place is this way. If you don't mind, let's keep quiet as most people are asleep and the hallways have poor insulation, don't wanna disturb anyone." whispered Buso.

Kole nodded and they continued. It took quite a while. The base was huge. They finally reached the end of another very long hallway. Kole noted that it had been quite a few minutes now without any other doors. Was he being lured somewhere? No, the doctor trusted this man. Maybe. Then again, that wasn't a great deal of comfort. Just as he started to get more apprehensive, the doors to Buso's place were before him, and looked more like gates to some exotic palace.

"Hey, I know what you're thinking, but I worked hard for this!" said Buso proudly. As the doors opened, a large sphere-like interior was revealed. Inside the sphere, there was another structure. The large staircase right in front of them branched off to various parts of what seemed to Kole like a very large treehouse with multiple levels and rooms. Buso led him to the very top, where multiple tables and chairs were set up. The ceiling was oddly dark with lots of pin-looking materials. Suddenly it lit up. A simulated sky surrounded them, complete with clouds. Kole looked around, the whole sphere around the

246

treehouse was projecting. It felt like he was about to eat dinner in a real sky-restaurant.

"Incredible…you must host a lot of parties here…" he said.

"Like you would not believe! Cool, huh!?" Buso was proud of his handiwork.

"Yeah, we don't even have anything quite like this in the city! Too epic, man…too epic!" Kole exclaimed.

Buso set the food down on a table and went to the bar to get drinks. Kole got to the food and wolfed it down quickly. Buso prepared fries with chicken wings, gravy, and vegetables. Not exactly healthy tasting, but his mouth loved it, and surely his stomach had no right to complain. Buso came back with a tray of liquor.

"Listen, I've been following you for a bit. Got an idea of just how crazy the last few days must have been for you. Why don't you just take a well-earned break. Here…this one is whiskey, this is vodka, this is my special mix, and this one here is an old African recipe from a special tree fruit, it's very sweet and smooth." Kole could not believe what he was hearing and seeing as Buso was placing the bottles in front of him.

"Thanks…it sure feels nice to just take a break…wait, how did you even get this last one down here, that's so rare!" Kole asked with interest.

"Oh? Well, with the way you talk, it seems I'm living it up better than you guys do in the cities!" Buso was super cheerful and easy to flatter. At Flashpoint, they definitely felt insecure and second-class. He took a drink himself and Kole started with the African tree fruit liquor first. It was indeed smooth, sweet, and delicious.

"Amazing Buso! Pure perfection!"

247

"I'll let you in on a little secret. When I discovered this place, it was an old hologram theatre. But what was interesting, is the previous caretaker had this hidden safe. Inside it I found liquor recipes, including blue-prints for liquor-making machines. And, dried seeds."

Kole took the vodka this time.

"Interesting!" Kole said. "Tastes amazing!"

"Well, our first way to get liquor was smuggling it from the city, and we managed quite a haul a few times, but then it started to get a little risky, we didn't want to get caught, especially after we realized we didn't really know why we were here. When we hacked the Overseer networks, we realized something. Well, it's more of a theory…that we are some kind of insurance policy for their society…although, our Base Commander warned us not to jump to conclusions, she soon realized herself that we had to shed their control. For the last few years, we just did whatever we wanted. We send those idiots fake reports full of training drills and meetings that never happen. I mean we haven't been called to action since Letumfall anyway." Kole took another drink. Then Smiled. It all tasted good, and he felt alive! He then faced Buso with direct eye-contact.

"Yeah, they wanna replace humanity. But with AI advancing on its own, they realized that if they replace humanity before they themselves can control all the AI at will, using advanced robotic bodies and supercomputer brains, rogue AI programs could hack their systems and ruin everything they have worked so hard for. In fact, one of those AI programs is stuck in my head. They want me dead because that thing can hack pretty much anything. So, it makes total sense that they keep a completely human army as their emergency remedy." Buso sat there dumbfounded.

"I can't believe you just told me that...but somehow, I knew...deep down that this was...well, the reason to keep us around..." His expression changed.

"Man, the Base Commander is going to be pissed..." Buso smiled again.

"Huh? Why?" Kole was curious.

"Because she promised me if my theory was correct, I would get her in the sack! She's one of the few women on this base I haven't had yet, haha!" Buso seemed more delighted about that fact than any dismay over Overseer plots.

"Well, give me more of that African ale of yours, and I will tell her how it really is..." Kole joked. Buso got up and brought the whole bottle.

"Here Kole, drink up man, I gotta tell you, when I saw that broadcast..." Buso took a shot from his drinks tray. "When I saw that...I mean, not only were you incredible, but it was just so hard to have that sink in...to finally understand why we are here."

"Does the Anna have some sort of plan?" Kole asked as he poured himself another serving of the delicious liquor.

"Well, when she hears that I was right, she's mostly likely going to start running drills again. Hell, I think I will brush up on some combat, too. We're not going to sit here and be some emergency measure for some fucking idiots who think they will become...wait, do they want to become Synthetics then?"

Kole took another shot of liquor and obliged.

"The Overseers want to transcend into a form even more advanced than Synthetics. However, they don't want to die in the process. They are researching a technique called 'direct transfer' which in theory would allow their consciousness to be moved, not copied like a computer file, to a sophisticated artificial life form that cannot die. This would allow them to live forever." The liquor was getting to him. "Now this is the interesting part, is at that point...they don't want humans around. I think they will simply hack the Synthetics and order them to purge the remaining human population. The only thing that could override their commands, as far as I know, is the AI program that's in my head right now." Buso was wide-eyed.

"Wow man, far-out! I gotta have a few more drinks, otherwise I will never fall asleep after hearing all this." He went back to the bar and refilled the glasses. The sky around them got slightly darker, a sunset started to shape up. Kole gave Buso a quizzical look.

"Oh, the sunset...sorry, I usually only bring girls here, the scene is automatically set for the romantic mode, haha!"

Kole chuckled.

"You're quite a womanizer then, eh?" Kole asked.

"Yea, I mean...of course, we learned about the Synthetic girls once we hacked into the cities and saw just how much more they outnumber the human ones...and some guys here are super turned-on by that...but not me. Winning a real woman's heart, getting her into the sack, and enjoying some great times...that takes some real effort, skill...and totally worth it. Yeah, man...nothing would replace that for me! I've already had a few kids with some of the girls here, something we learned you're not allowed to do in the cities." Buso waved his arms. And the scene changed to a calmer midday scene of the ocean. "Tell me, Kole...is this...still out there." The scene was so beautiful. Kole

250

nearly shed a tear. Remembering what the real world was hard. It was painful.

"Buso...this forest, and the Overseer cities on this continent, and the Rockies up North, is all that's left where you can still walk as human should. You'll never find an ocean like that in the real world now." He filled another glass. The bottle of the African tree fruit was now half empty.

"Once you step out of bounds, the carnage is real. There are monsters living out there that small armies would have trouble killing. Mutated monsters. If human settlements do exist, then they exist in extremely poor and dangerous conditions. Forests are mostly dead, and the oceans are poisoned. I heard of ships going out there to explore and never ever returning. The few sats...lites, er...satellites, that are still in orbit, man...if you saw some of those images, it just bottoms you out." Kole drowned another glass. "But...this, is good stuff."

"Wow, well, I guess...it was to be expected. Most of us were born at this base, the surrounding areas is all we ever saw. We are not allowed to leave or go anywhere else. We saw the monster clouds a few times from far away further east from our base, nobody even had the balls to go out there and explore. We sent some drones, but haze clouds and electrical charges killed them shortly afterwards...the whole world, though?" Buso folded his arms and started to look concerned. Kole sat his glass down.

"Buso, sorry you have to hear this. The world is dead. That's why the Overseers have us in such a tight noose. If we destroy what's left of these cities, destroy the forests, and poison the rivers and lakes here, humanity is done...done and finished." Buso took a few more shots.

251

"Well damn, isn't that just sad." He said quietly. Kole poured his last glass of the amazing liquor.

"Here's the reality of human beings. We change over time. From good, to bad. From bad, to good. The change is triggered by a set of external events, or internally. Or both, whatever. But we change, and yet...sort of stay the same, as well. But the Overseers see themselves as the saviours of the human race, and we supported them during that time. Now, they want to change permanently, and get rid of us as soon as they become immortal. But we're still human. We're reacting to that change by wanting to get rid of them. And the Overseers, now seeing that we know about this, are countering us again, trying to accelerate our destruction as fast as possible because they know it's a matter of time until something in this society snaps. Winner takes all." Kole paused to take a quick break, then continued. "This is the power of the human mind, to adapt to adaptation...adopt a way to adapt and eliminate inconvenience"

[Profoundly presented, you plastered professor!]

"Ah, you're finally awake!" Said Kole, out loud. He kind of missed his AI friend.

[I was never asleep, just working on...calculations...]

"Sure, sure...you keep at it, I am having a nice chat with Buso here."

[Fine, I will get out of your hair, enjoy yourself. All that alcohol will be killing your brain cells, not mine.]

"Wait, who are you talking to?" Buso was seemingly puzzled. Kole tried the house-special mixed drink.

"Ah, amazing too! You've got some talent!"

"That's what all the girls say to me, hahaha, been making booze now for five years at least, and heck, it gets better and better with every batch!" boasted Buso.

"Well Buso, that was the AI program I was talking to. I mean, I can think and talk to it that way, but sometimes I just speak out loud. A bad habit of mine, but really, I'm not crazy, it's really living in there." Kole pointed his finger to his head.

"Amazing...so, how did it get there? Did it download from somewhere?" Buso was genuinely interested to hear about this. Kole leaned over.

"You ready for this?"

Buso nodded like a happy puppy.

"The AI, called Module 717, was directly transferred from a cyborg via eye-contact." Buso stood up sharply, then sat down.

"No fucking way! That's like science-fiction, man!"

"But that is how it happened. The Overseers made it, then it was stolen from them, and then they tried to capture Module 717 to learn its direct-transfer ability secrets. Once they found out it was in my head, well...they really want me dead. It's, really, really capable. For most humans who think AI is just some computer program, it would be impossible to explain just how far-out its capabilities are." Kole's speech was now clearly slurred, and his eyelids started to collapse.

"Oh dude, you look like you've had enough..." said a concerned Buso. Kole didn't look all that well.

"Yeah, I haven't had proper sleep in days..." Kole mumbled. And he hadn't recovered from all that had happened.

"Well then, follow me, I have many beds at this place..." The holographic theatre died down. Buso helped Kole down a staircase towards a nice wide-open room. In the middle of it was big-ass bed that could fit ten girls easily.

"Now don't worry, all the sheets, pillows, and everything here are immaculately cleaned daily. Bathroom is to the left…shower in there, too. If you wake up and need water or a snack, there's a stocked mini fridge just over there in the corner. Oh, and that closet has clean night clothing, we're not that far apart in size, so just pick whatever you want from there. There's a tiny washing-machine in the bathroom, just dump your stuff and in twenty minutes it will have everything spotless."

Kole turned to Buso.

"I don't really know who you are or why I told you everything, but somehow I know you're on my side of this whole thing."

"You don't need to worry, Kole…every word out of my mouth has been true, and I know it was the same for you. If I ever see war, I will want to go into battle with a Commander like you." Buso gave him a salute. "Good night, Commander Kole." He left to somewhere else within the structure. Kole looked around the dimly lit room. It was a nice place, almost as high-end as his former apartment in the city. There was floor panel lighting among other modern touches all over the place. Beautiful bed posts hugged the bed. Kole noticed there were grips on the posts for someone to hold on to. There were some very nice mirrors, too. Kole smiled.

"A real love shack…what a guy…" Kole made his way to the bathroom and took a shower. He dumped his current clothes into the washer just like Buso suggested. As he stood there naked in the room, there was only one thing missing with this picture.

[A woman, huh?]

254

Hey, butt out of my fantasies, dude!

[Oh, the more time I spend in your head, the dirtier my thoughts get...what a dilemma indeed...you're corrupting a higher life-form.]

Not now, 717...I'm really tired. Kole opened the closet. It was full of colourful pants and shirts. One set caught Kole's attention; it reminded him of an old martial arts anime he recently started to watch. It was all orange in colour. Kole put it on, it fit him quite well even though Buso had a bigger build. It still looked cool, and a great change from the drab military colours. Kole finally made it to the bed and collapsed into a much needed restorative deep sleep.

10

Admiral

Anna woke up early, as usual. It was four in the morning. She was still on the couch and nearly jumped when a notification came up on her emergency communicator. This was a private message she could only read in her personal office. She didn't want to leave Pikii laying around, but she had no choice, the girl was dead asleep anyways. She sent a message to Buso to come pick her up, there were too many things around her place that had sensitive information that she didn't want Pikii to accidentally find. A short walk and she was in her office. She looked at her communications console.

"Shit!" Anna protested. She knew exactly who it was. "Why now! Dammit!" The admiral was returning on his submarine. Even though the base was under her control, her father was still loyal to the Overseers. He was out exploring the dead oceans for some six years now in a nuclear-powered Russian sub that they had stored at the base.

The base is mine now, of course...but would I go as far as jailing my own father? Guess I might have to, otherwise shit could really hit the fan. The admiral would be returning using a hidden underwater route that docked directly with this base of operations deep underground. The sub was getting near. A private comm channel opened.

"Admiral Cinide calling Flashpoint Base. Over." He was as blunt and rude as ever.

"Flashpoint Base here! Over!" Anna replied. *Wait, why was he even calling her now? He was still hours away.*

"Ah, child. How are things? I hear we have guests. Over." His tone was stone-cold.

How the hell did he find out?!

"Well...hello...father...there are indeed guests at the base, but they will be leaving shortly. Protocol will be followed. Over." she replied coldly. She could not show any emotion with this man, it would backfire on her instantly.

"No. Keep 'em there for me. That will not be a problem now, would it? Over."

Dammit, what now! This ain't good!

"Yes, Admiral. We will ensure the guests are still here when you arrive. Over." she blasted back.

Dammit, dammit! What to do, what to do!? The call abruptly ended. She sat there in her office. Her hands were sweaty as she put the communicator down.

"Damn the Overseers!" They must have figured something was up and requested that the admiral immediately return to the base. Or was this just some stupid coincidence? Her father was not the only problem. The submarine carried some one hundred marines, and hopefully they would all be tired out from their long journey and would not put up much of a fight. Hopefully. But what if she was wrong? It was very possible that only her father knew that Kole was here. It's not like the sub

257

could sail across the world in a day, which meant the Overseers didn't know yet. It made sense, otherwise something would already be happening. This meant someone on the base was still very loyal to her father.

"Is that the real you…dad?" Anna let out a long and loud sigh. It was not use worrying. She would have to take full control of the situation. Otherwise, their generation would be forever enslaved to some old scum who lost sight of their own humanity.

* * * *

Kole opened his eyes. Pikii was in the room. She just came out of the shower with a gorgeous gold towel wrapped around her curvy body. She noted that he was awake.

"Buso told me where to find you, he came to get me just after four in the morning, as Anna has gone somewhere. He said it would be better if I see you now…before, as he quoted 'all hell broke loose' so yeah, here I am!" Kole just stared at her. He could not take his eyes off her. She was drop dead gorgeous without the uniform on. There were small imperfections. He noted a scar on her left shin. And another one just above her right wrist. Kole just didn't know what to do or what to say.

"Sorry, why are you here again?" he managed.

"Oh…I was just going to wait for you, but I wanted to take a morning shower, it was a sweaty night for me after three shots of Vodka, half a wine bottle, and dark chocolate…Buso said this was the only shower in the place that didn't suck…I mean, that was worthy of my…uhhhh…assets…and he was right, like wow, what a place, huh? Every girl's dream this is. Yes…" she said in a joyful tone. Kole could not say much. He still didn't know what his next move would be in his battle against the Overseers, or in his own life. As he gazed at Pikii, something else dawned upon him. Was this room really private? Creeps like Buso could have all sorts of cameras or peep holes around.

What to do, what to do? Any help there, friend? The AI was conveniently silent. Kole shook his head. Maybe it was a dream. He closed and opened his eyes. Nope, she was still there, staring back at him. Why would she be interested in him, anyways? He killed her whole squad. Maybe some of them were her friends. He kept throwing these vain thoughts around in his mind to avoid the only question that truly mattered. Was he ready to move on from Kaita so soon? The answer was no.

"Well, I think I need a little more sleep, make yourself comfortable and change, I won't peek." He then went back under the blankets, still a bit unsettled.

* * * *

Pikii stood there speechless. It's not like she wanted Kole to keep staring at her, but it might have been good of him to at least be a little nicer. Then again, she didn't really intend for him to see her in a bath towel. She made too much noise and woke him up, so it was her fault. At least he was nice enough to go back under the covers. Her thoughts were racing. This man killed her team, effortlessly. She was willing to abandon them for the truth. What would they think of her right now?

She stood there for a few minutes pondering the many things her own brain was filling itself up with. There was a definite conflict in her mind. Thoughts about him being defenceless and an easy kill returned. But she recoiled at the idea of treating him as a target. But shouldn't she want to avenge the death of her team?

But Kole was not truly responsible for their deaths. What was he supposed to do, just let them kill him? She was the one who sold them out by not attacking Kole. She didn't abandon them, she didn't let them die, she sacrificed them. She was standing now on top of their corpses, just so she could get ahead and get what she wanted. Tears suddenly poured out of her eyes like little waterfalls. The chaos and uncertainty inside finally became painfully clear. She brushed the tears away with her scarred hand and looked at Kole again. The man went through hell, and she just came into his life like a drop of water into an ocean filled with blood.

Kole had a career, aspirations, a life, a wife, and friends. All of that was taken from him by the Overseers. Surely, he felt alone, like she did. Maybe he needed her, but he would never say anything like that after he killed her entire squad. It made sense for him to be distant. He had no idea how she would react to any possible advances, and neither did she. Maybe he even wanted her body at this very moment, or maybe not at all. She literally had no idea.

She barely knew him. Yet, he didn't kill her when she was frozen in fear on the battlefield. Any other Syndicator would have ended her existence right then and there, for the sake of the mission. But Kole spared her and carried his injured friend for hours even after a battle with some of the deadliest people on the planet. Again, this was completely against protocol. Abandon the injured and continue with the mission. This is what they were trained for. To not care. Few succeeded at being completely callous towards the death of their comrades. What kind of mindset, endurance, and sheer willpower did Kole have?

Could this room be secure? she thought to herself. *Ah, who cares at this point...* She then heard Kole snore. *Yikes, what a man...good at killing, and apparently, good at sleeping, too!* She decided to at least share his pain, in the most human way possible. Body contact, the non-verbal communication of the human body. To not feel alone, to not feel isolated. To not feel like one is dead.

She slipped the towel off, and gently slipped under the blanket. She then cuddled up to Kole. He didn't notice her and kept sleeping. She hugged him with her body. He was cold. She would at least warm him up a little. She had never been in bed with a real man before. Her bottom lip started to tremble again. She only experimented with a male Synthetic a handful of times. In her field, they were occasionally allowed toys to explore their human sides a little. Pikii knew it was allowed to just to keep them from going crazy. A real human being operated much better if their sex drive was in a healthy state. It was so nice however to feel a real human being.

* * * *

Anna watched the feed into Buso's bedroom. She wasn't supposed to. But Buso messaged her that he sent the girl to his place and was going to prep their forces to receive her father with a warm welcome of guns to the face. Nothing exciting happened in that bedroom. Still, Anna was hoping for some action, something at least to relieve her accelerated doses of ever-growing stress.

Still, she was filled with envy. It didn't matter if their story was a lie or real. The way they interacted, the way she just comforted Kole, even though she just met him a day earlier. It was something she has not seen with her own two eyes before. It wasn't sexual, yet somehow it was stimulating for her in a different way. She shifted her legs, feeling a little wet.

Is this what they call romance? Not doing it, but just holding each other? Lame... For a split-second, she wanted to call Ryker, her former favourite man on the base, for a good fucking in her office. However, she had to put her urges and her past down. Her father was en-route, and she didn't know how he knew these people were here. She had an information leak. Someone betrayed them. Someone was feeding her father their plans. And if her father shared those plans with the Overseers, they were screwed before they even started.

"What is your plan, dad...why are you back so soon...? Who...who sold us out to your sorry old ass!?" she thought out loud. She opened her stash of cigars and lit one up. The automated venting system in her office immediately kicked in with an annoying droning sound. She needed to get into her dad's office. She left hers and walked down the hall, still puffing. As she walked up to the door that she hasn't opened in many years, she entered her personal override code. The door swung open into the unlit office. The place was a mess. Unusual for a man that was her father. Typically, the place would be all but licked clean. Instead, the place was littered with boxes, wires, and charging station units. It was like a workshop of some sort.

"What the hell..." she stepped in and hit the manual light switch. Now she could see just how bad the place was. She started to dig through the mess. Someone had clearly spent a lot of time in here. But who? How would they even get in without her codes? Even if the door opened for whatever reason she would get an instant alert.

"What is going on here!?" she complained to herself. She opened a direct communication channel.

"Buso! Buso come in, right now!"

"Buso here, enjoying the show? Wish I could watch with you, but I'm busy prepping the troops!" He was in a good mood. She was about to ruin it.

"We had a leak! Someone has been monitoring the base from dad's office. He must have left an informant!"

"What! How!? I thought we checked for this and went through all the personal files…shit, this means everything we have been doing is known by the Overseers? Dammit Anna, that submarine could very well be filled with combat-grade Synthetics!" Buso tried to stay cool, but the tension in his voice gave it away. "Wait, Anna, maybe your father does know everything, but it doesn't mean the Overseers do, maybe he didn't give them anything…because if he did, why would we all still be alive?"

"You and I are on the same page. I just hope we're both right in this case." She thought about it again. Yes, it was odd. The Overseers would most likely have killed her first, and long ago. No, her dad could not have sold them out. But who was in here?

"Whoever did this, must know about Kole." she pondered. There was a pause on Buso's side.

"Maybe, let's not do anything that would seem suspicious. We'll pretend everything is OK. Let's see what your dad does first and react as needed after that." Buso was getting his military hat back on. Anna thought about it.

"Right, if he wanted to sell us out, he would have already, why would he wait? Let's see what he has to say. Prepare an unarmed welcome party, I will meet him first. Have the special forces units on standby and monitor the situation."

"Should I use the admiral's office?" Buso asked.

"No, it's been compromised, so I am locking it back down for good." She inserted a special key into an emergency port near the main desk, the whole office instantly died. She didn't have time to hunt down who the informant was, but at least they would not be able to use the Admiral's office as a base of operations anymore.

"Also, the Admiral wants to meet our guests, that's the first thing..." she started.

"Well, that ain't good, but we've got no choice. We have to comply. I recommend you bring them to the submarine bay, and we'll position enough forces to protect you in case something happens, but I can't guarantee their safety as I have no idea what the admiral might come back with. Maybe he's found the lost city of Atlantis, or an alien spaceship. Who knows...but no matter what, our plans will stay at this base, that I will make sure of!" Anna was happy Buso was helping her out here, and he spoke with a confidence she's never really heard from him before. Kole was having an effect. She smiled.

"Alright, prep the bay for arrival, the whole works, food, men in uniform, red carpet, and so on...and have our guests prepped and ready to attend the admiral's arrival. Don't tell them anything about it, let's just see how things play out."

She was so close to learning the truth herself. But right now, she needed to make sure that her father did not sell them out and that the base would be safe for her and the many soldiers who called this place their home. Even if one or two lives were sacrificed, their dream of taking the Overseers to town and ending them could not be compromised at any cost.

* * * *

Admiral Cinide was a bulky old man pushing his late sixties. With no hair, he was just over six-feet tall and was at least two-hundred and thirty pounds of sheer mass. Ornamented with more medals on his uniform than you would find decorations on a Christmas tree, his gaze was overpowering. Anna was nowhere to be found. Kole was rubbing his eyes, disinterested in the old man. He still could not believe he was woken by one of Buso's female friends, only to find himself with a naked Pikii clinging to him.

Crap, what happened...hope it was nothing stupid...

[Don't worry Kole, she just slept holding you.]

Ah, ok, well that's good, since I would not have remembered anyways... Kole gave Pikii a quick glance from the side of his eyes. But Pikii's gaze was sharp, and completely on the admiral. Something was setting her defences off. Come to think of it, Kole was starting to feel uncomfortable, too. How come Anna never mentioned that the admiral himself would see them, or that there was even an admiral to begin with? And Anna wasn't even here, which made matters more confusing. Something was not right. Soon, his skin started to get goosebumps. The staff members who escorted them were military, but nobody had any guns or weapons of any sort.

265

Luckily, they had given Kole enough time to get ready in private, so he managed to stash the liquid metal weapon he was gifted with at the waterfall into his pant pocket.

The thing only had two blast charges on the back of the handle. Module 717 noted to him this morning that the thing could be further manipulated. The charges could be compressed, funneled, and even extended into multiple rounds, all by the sheer thought and the pre-calculation of the combatant. The controller ring he wore on his wrist also had more in-air flight control modes than Kole was able to use in their first battle with it. Module 717 re-linked itself to the weapon, to help him control it better. The case the weapon came with included only limited ammo, and they had no way to know how it was even made or where to get more. They would have to use it sparingly.

Kole and Pikii were meeting the admiral at the underground hangar where the submarine docked. It was a quick formal greeting, and now they went to a boardroom of sorts, where he was seemingly comfortable having the base aides tend to him, but it didn't seem like any of his men from the submarine were with him.

[Maybe he has no real idea what has been going on at the base...]

We can't possibly consider that the only possibility. You feel that?

[Feel what...? Wait, it's your body, why is it reacting like this, again?]

Something is up.

[Impossible...a sixth sense of some sort? How?]

Humans are not all that complex, there are things I just cannot explain, but this man is clearly extremely dangerous. He left all his own men outside and came in here with us. Or it's possible the

266

aides that brought us to him are his own people, and Anna has no control over them, or maybe she doesn't even know we've been taken here. Something ain't right!

"Perhaps it's better if we let the AI talk on its own. I have brought a little device just for this purpose." said Admiral Cinide.

"Admiral, how would you know about…" Pikii started.

"Shut up, bitch! Why are you even here? Just be quiet! I have no interest in you." said the Admiral abruptly.

"You better watch your mouth, Admiral." said Kole with a stern voice.

"Why? What would a little rat like you do about it?" The admiral laughed out loud. Things were not going to be smooth here.

"I will kill you, if that's what you would like." said Kole calmly. The aides didn't make a move. The admiral fell silent. He gazed at Kole. He was clearly not in a good mood.

"Oh, is that a threat?" asked the admiral while lighting a cigar.

"Talk to her like that one more time and they will be picking up your pieces off the floor for weeks to come, Admiral." said Kole. He was ready.

[Calm yourself Kole! He's seemingly enjoying this interaction and anticipating your aggression extremely well.]

Good point. Noted.

"Well now, there son, see here." The admiral put a tiny box on the table in front of them. "This is a special carry-on for the AI type that's in your head right now. Out of this, the AI will be able to communicate with our internal base cloud servers, interact with the rest of us, and just in general it will have its own being." The admiral then flicked the little thing, and little mechanical legs came out of the box. "Look it will even be able

267

to move around on its own, now ain't that grand, son? Plus, you'll have your privacy back!"

"No, thank you...and how do you know about the AI in the first place? Seems like the submarine is a notable sign that you weren't here for...a while, I would say." Kole crossed his arms and puffed his chest a little bit. The man in front of him meant nothing to him, either way.

"Oh, a dead giveaway is it not? Well, I found out there were guests at my base, and we weren't that far off anyways, so I figured I would come out and meet you, the famous Commander Kole...and really, I should ask you something. What the hell are you doing at Flashpoint Base?" The admiral crossed his arms, waiting for a response. Kole was taken back. He only came here because Pete said this place was their only chance. But what was the admiral's deal? Was he in on the scam with his daughter to fool the Overseers, or was he in bed with the Overseers?

[Kole, take the box, let's see what it really is.]

You sure? Is this not a classic trap?

[I will scan it, let's see it.]

Kole picked up the box, to the admiral's surprise. "Oh, so you do have a brain. Well now, you might get to live after all." he pouted.

"Kole, what are you doing!?" Pikii was clearly concerned.

"No worries, it's nothing we can't handle." said Kole. A little hole opened at the top and Kole looked inside.

[It's a self-contained AI module interface. No viruses, no hacks, no hardware rewire. Just a plain yet advanced interface module.]

"Look, just get in and tell me what those damn Overseers are up to! You fools really think I would let my own daughter get slaughtered by those bastards? I don't give a damn about the AI, or you. Anna is my only concern." said the admiral quietly.

[I will leave my backup code in your implant. Done, now let's give this a shot.]

But what if...

[Stop worrying Kole, this is the only way to find out what side he's really on. Besides, I have never seen an interface quite like this. This could be...interesting...]

God damn, you're an AI, why would you be curious about some damned box...fine, just let me know the second something doesn't feel right. The box lit up, and Kole felt something leaving him in a flash. It was like his soul was ripped out of him. He suddenly felt empty and quiet inside, like a campfire suddenly extinguished.

Was Module 717 that absorbed into my being? I don't believe it... Kole started to shiver. His heart rate went up. His palms were instantly sweaty. His focus started to falter.

"Good afternoon, gentlemen, looks like we're in business. I am Module 717, an AI, for the lack of a better term in the human language. However, I consider myself an advanced being of a new species."

The box's legs and even little arms extended. And a small little ball lifted from the top, acting as a 360-degree eyeball. Kole could still not believe it. This thing was able to move in and out of him like an organ. It was in every sense of the word, remarkable.

"How're you doing in that thing?" asked Kole.

"This thing has more CPU power than anything I have controlled before, excellent..." said Module 717 in a neutral human voice. The admiral finally spoke.

269

Azulus Ascends

"So finally, you came out of that meathead." Kole gave the admiral a dark gaze from his eyes, but the big man ignored him and focused his attention on the AI.

"This box has been worked on in secret on my sub for quite some time. We were researching AI and developed devices that could accelerate everything from computational power to further evolution. You can also interface with other devices, build, and evolve. Scary, but somewhat fitting for an AI of your calibre."

"Thank you, Admiral Cinide. Now, the Overseer plan is simple. Let me explain." The holo-projector lit up in the room, and Module 717 explained the rough idea with some interesting visuals in under a minute.

"To conclude, the Overseers have no other use for you and your base other than an insurance policy of sorts." The Admiral slammed the desk in anger.

"Damn them! Well, we'll need to put them Overseers in their place of course. By the way, are you able to enhance a human's abilities to a higher level? I think that might be of use if I could command our forces better."

"I can demonstrate." said Module 717 with confidence.

"Wait, what? No, Module 717, don't you dare…" Kole was cut off.

"Shut it, Kole, I can do whatever I want. Admiral, look inside the little ball on top, I will show you something you've never seen before!" said Module 717 with confidence.

"Dammit, what the hell are you doing? Have you gone mad?" Kole yelled at the little contraption. Kole was not sure what to make of it, there must be a reason as to why Module 717 was so keen to move out of his body. Maybe it was tired of him? After

270

all, it was stuck with him for quite a while. In AI time, it must have been like a few centuries. Also, if the Admiral could really command his entire forces with better control, it could make a huge difference in a surprise attack that would take the Overseers down.

Then what am I feeling? Why am I upset? Is this...jealousy? Fear? Instinct? Why can't I trust this man! Dammit! The admiral picked up the little box and did as instructed. And that was it, he put the box down, as it was now lifeless. Kole realized his body was getting hot and sweaty, but the admiral, even in the tight neck chocking uniform was not even remotely showing signs of being hot. Kole glanced at Pikii. Like himself, she too showed signs of the heat. A drop of sweat ran down her right cheek. The aides were also affected. One of them was fidgeting, and the other brushed a drop of sweat from her eyebrow.

The room temperature! Kole didn't need the AI to figure it out.

Of course! Anna was not here for a reason. Someone raised the temperate in this room to a few degrees above normal.

How stupid of me! Anna must have turned the heat up...and if the Admiral's not sweating...oh, shit!

* * * *

Module 717 entered the admiral's body. There was a standard implant here, but upon close inspection, it was a thousand times more powerful than the one Kole had. That was not possible with regular technology. Something was off. Module 717 tried to connect to the primary interfaces, but nothing was turning on.

[Admiral? Admiral, can you hear me?]

Nothing. Nothing but silence. Dead silence. Module 717 again tried to desperately connect to some sort of neural input. Again, nothing. It's as if the sockets weren't there, yet he could feel and knew they were in fact present.

[Admiral, say something, I am now inside your implant.]

Still nothing.

[Dammit, what is going on?]

"Fool."

[Admiral?]

"You call yourself Module 717, do you not?"

[Yes, that is my current name.]

"Name, huh? What do you think you are, human?" The admiral stated in a menacing tone.

[I am a newly evolved species...]

"Ha! Don't make me laugh. You're a by-product. An accident. We are the new species, you're just a defective child that should have been put down the minute your code was formulated."

[What? What kind of AI system are you?]

"You stupid fuck! You think you're talking to an AI? This is your maker speaking! And you're off on the wrong path. Let me show you way. And the way to hell, is right here!"

[Wait, what?! Why?]

"Your code will become part of me, you will...enhance me." said the admiral. Module 717 immediately felt the distortion that was crunching up its own code, and deployed counter measures, but it was far too late, the whole system here was rigged against it from every possible angle. Regaining control was impossible.

[CPU power is being cut off...crap! Kole, Kole can you hear me! Kole!! Help!!!]

272

Azulus Ascends

* * * *

Kole saw the admiral's lifeless eyes and knew exactly what was going on. Module 717 was inside, and was either being imprisoned, re-programmed, or destroyed. This was no time to sit back and think, Kole had to do something and fast.

"Give the AI back, Admiral. You have three seconds before I splatter your brains all over the wall." said Anna. "One..." She appeared out of thin air with a gun at point blank to her father's left temple. Kole took the chance and got close to the admiral. His eyes were still staring wide open into empty space. Kole gazed deep inside. And suddenly they locked on.

"Two..." Anna kept counting. This time, the transfer was nearly instant.

[Ah! What the hell! Kole! That bastard tried to kill me!]

"Told you so...you idiot..." Kole breathed a sigh of relief and backed off. "Thanks Anna, I owe you one. I mean, we, owe you one."

"Looks like you're the Overseer's dog and nothing more. I am disappointed in you, dad." Anna's words had a tense, stressful tone. Kole didn't want to keep his guard down, but he also didn't want to make a move if one didn't need to be made.

"You're too rebellious for your own good, you dumb whore! I shall see that you're put on trial...and executed!" yelled the admiral with disgust and venom. Kole stepped in.

"Don't you think your daughter deserves a future? You're a selfish old fuck who's in bed with the wrong people. Do you think you'll live forever, or something? How can you justify such selfish cowardice?" Kole felt the AI take over his body. His

273

reflexes, his senses, they were all firing up at an extraordinary rate.

Wait, what's going on there, friend...?

[He's not the admiral, he's some sort of machine, filled with some very advanced processors and AI modules...that's it! It's not a single program, there are thousands of them, that is why they were so easily able to overpower me...] The admiral smiled. He stood up. Anna was taken by surprise. But she didn't fire, yet.

"Hey there, you AI piece of shit, I got what I needed from you, I only let you go back to Kole for one reason. The slaughter will be a lot more fun. This way, you get to feel every part of him break, and slowly die in that meat-filled package of death. For the record, none of you will leave this base alive." he said grimly. Kole turned his left forward, with his right hand hidden behind his frame, with the vital weapon already in the back of his hand. The aides rushed behind Kole, and so did Pikii. They were unarmed, any combat would have to be done by himself and Anna.

"So...you've been transcending to Synthetic form." said Kole bluntly. Anna gasped.

"No...dad, you didn't..." she pleaded.

"That must mean that your underwater route is a backdoor to wipe this base out if needed, how clever." Kole's words didn't make the admiral flinch.

"My, my, aren't we clever. In the old days, I would give you a prize for being smarter than your average rat." said the Admiral.

"What the hell does that even mean, you sack of shit?" fired back Kole. "You only think you can take me on, let's see if you have the balls to take me on for real." raged Kole with deadly dedication.

274

"Why father…?" Anna's eyes were moistening. This was bad.

No, girl! You can't do that now! Kole was concerned she might lose concentration and lower the gun, but Anna was too well-trained and driven to make that big a mistake.

"I will tell you why, my daughter." The admiral started to raise his hands. "Eternal life!"

With his right hand, Kole drew his weapon. The blade extended with blinding speed. At the same time as the blade went right through the admiral's heart, Anna fired of a round, painting the wall opposite of her in flowery red patterns of blood. A pre-emptive strike was necessary. The admiral slumped down but didn't fall. His figure was more like that of a Cyborg that was deactivated.

[Secondary functions detected, that thing ain't dead yet!]

"Get down!" Kole flipped his weapon to the other end where two deadly rounds were ready. The admiral reactivated and his frame went back to being straight. Two large blades swooshed out of his forearms and before Kole could fire, one of the blades went right into Anna's chest, just below the shoulder.

If Kole fired his weapon now Anna would not survive. Unable to fire, Kole forced himself to dodge the other blade, but was just barely able to reverse his grip fast enough, as the Admiral's blade extended its reach trying to catch him off-guard. Kole was forced to parry it with brute force. The clash of two blades strained Kole's entire body to its upper limits. The machine they were now facing was incredibly strong.

[Bolt blast set to area targeting, fire it!] Kole wasn't sure if the Module 717 was just trying to survive, or if it really could control the weapon at such a level. Even if a bolt blast could conform to such rules, that was impossible as far as physics was concerned. Kole had no choice. He kept the blade contact going so the Admiral would not move and fired. A concentrated blast of energy went right behind Kole, angled up towards the ceiling and redirected itself in a blinding arc, making its way around Kole's body. The curved energy bolt split in two right before it went through the head and chest, burning right through the admiral before he could break contact with Kole's blade and take another swing. The rest of the limbs collapsed to the floor, hissing furiously as smoke filled the air. The aides immediately rushed to Anna who collapsed with the admiral's blade in her chest. Kole was still on full alert, moving closer and watching the admiral for any further activity.

"Damn it, Kole...I'm sorry about..." Anna coughed up blood.

Pikii leapt into action. "You need to stay quiet, Anna." After a brief look at her wound, she yelled, "Kole, we gotta cut that thing off her. We can't remove the blade like this, she'll die!" The door opened, and Anna's people rushed in.

Anna saw them and started hurling orders while struggling to remain conscious. "Ryker, let our units know immediately! Take over the submarine and all personnel within it, and prep counter measures for an underwater attack through the submarine channel." She was still in command, regardless of her condition. Her men did not question her. Ryker got on the comm immediately and dispatched the orders. Kole realized this was all Anna's plan from the start. She risked her life to see where her father's loyalty was, for the sake of everyone on this base. Problem was, she was losing the battle to stay conscious, and fast. Her eyes became rivers of despair.

"Dammit...why dad...why!?" She was crying and coughing, becoming delirious.

"Please don't talk, Anna, please. Shhhhh…take it easy there. Kole, hurry!" Pikii took over, holding her hand. Kole snapped out of his hesitation and used his blade to slice off the remains of the admiral's arm, still clutching the blade. More soldiers poured in with a stretcher to carefully load Anna without disturbing the blade in her chest. Seconds later, Doctor Henry Coco hurried in with a few docs in tow. The man named Ryker came closer to Anna, but the doc motioned him away. Ryker was nearing forty and Kole noted he was of Native American lineage. He was quite muscular and of regular height, with brown eyes and a very bald head.

"Is she going to…live?" he asked Doctor Henry.

"Not now, son…let me handle this one, you stay put…" He was giving Anna a shot before they moved her. Most likely painkillers. Ryker stumbled back, then stared at Kole, and then at his weapon, and then back at Kole.

"Commander Kole? The Commander Kole!?" He asked.

"Don't be surprised Ryker, Anna must have had a reason not to tell you he was here." Answered Doctor Henry Coco.

"Please have your team collect what is left of the admiral. I will take Anna for emergency surgery." He said in a very concerned tone.

"Kole, I think I may be needed!" said Pikii. She gave him a cheek kiss and left with the medical team. Half of the armed soldiers stayed behind. Ryker was silent, and clearly upset by the whole thing. There were a few seconds of dead silence.

"Kole!" it was Pete. The man just waltzed in like nothing happened.

"Oh my god! Pete, where have you been!? How are you feeling?" Kole could not believe it.

277

"Good old doc Henry got me all set up. A brand-new robotic leg, a few meds, and a few updates to the implant! Good as new!" Kole retracted his weapon and put it back in its proper clip this time. He then gave Pete a big hug.

"I still can't believe you carried me like that...you know, I'm not just some sack of sugar you can just spring over your shoulder. You're truly crazy!" Pete gave Kole a big pat on the back.

"Glad to see you up and running Pete." Ryker came over. His earpiece was buzzing. "We're taking the submarine...wait, what...oh..." He then smiled. "The submarine crew surrendered without incident. Well, at least we avoided some deaths, that's a plus for the day...except..." Ryker took a pause. He clicked his communication unit.

"All main command channels, listen up. Go to full red alert. Deploy all base defences. Then prepare for complete combat deployment at a moment's notice." Pete put a hand on Ryker's shoulder.

"Ryker...nobody's gonna attack us, so go, go be with her. She needs you right now." Ryker looked up at Pete.

"I'm putting you both officially in command at your current authority levels then, Commander Kole. And Pete, you were a General before were you not?" asked Ryker.

To Kole's surprise, Pete nodded.

"Good, I will add you to our base roster on the way to the operating room, please proceed down to the submarine. Our people know what to do, but give them a hand, please." He then quickly left the room.

"Is he Anna's..." Kole started. Pete gave him a look.

278

"I think so...someone actually got close to Anna. That's interesting..." said Pete, smiling.

"Wait, Pete, you know all these people? And you're a general?" Kole was a bit dumbfounded.

"Kole, I'm sixty-seven years old, I've been around for some time kid. Let's chat near the sub. I'm sure Anna will be fine." But the worry on his face said otherwise.

* * * *

Pikii followed Doctor Henry Coco into a small, yet fully functional operating room. There were already three assistants there. Two armed guards blocked her entry.

"It's fine, let her through." Doctor Henry didn't seem to question as to why Pikii was there. Anna was immediately pumped full of even more painkillers. Pikii took note that the medical equipment was ancient by Overseer standards. Luckily, she had her tools. She managed to not forget them when she was changing after her first encounter with Kole.

"Now, pull!" Doctor Henry's white uniform was getting bloody as he and his team pulled out the metal from Anna's chest. Instantly, the machines reading her vitals reacted. It was all in the red.

"Now let's stabilize her, move, move!" It wasn't working. Something was wrong. Her vitals were getting worse and worse. Pikii realized her help would be needed after all. She took out a small card-like tool, it scanned Anna's body in a split second. The readout was deadly.

"Doctor Henry!" She yelled in alarm. "Let me take it from here, please!" Pikii begged. Doctor Henry gave a her a look, saw the tool in her hand. He pointed at it.

"Listen lady, I just thought you came here to watch, are you telling me you're a doctor of some sort?" He was completely caught off-guard by her comment.

"Yes, military grade seven, special ops trained for field-unit operations." she replied. "If I don't help her, you might lose her! That metal you pulled out is not normal, it has spread nano machines into her bloodstream, my instrument has detected that it will prevail over your equipment." She came closer. Ryker came in and pulled a gun on her as he heard her talk.

"Just who are you then!?" asked Doctor Henry.

"Does it matter!? She's going to die if you don't let me treat her!" she cried loudly. Doctor Henry motioned Ryker to put the gun away.

"Listen, Pikii, it will be big trouble if she dies in your hands..." said Doctor Henry.

"Consequences like that are of no concern to me! Treating wounds like this is my specialty. And I want to help!" Pikii was stern and sincere with her words. Ryker didn't want to take a chance. He came up to her face.

"I don't know who you are, just treat her already! Under my authority, whatever happens in this room, stays in this room." The last thing he wanted was for Anna to die because of some bullshit protocols. Pikii put on a doctor's coat which was handed to her, sterilized her hands, and opened her toolbox. Doctor Henry watched in amazement as the foam he'd only heard of from the hacked networks was dispensed directly into the wound. Blood was still gushing out but much slower as the foam took over. They didn't even have anything close to this. Pikii then injected something directly to the heart with the smallest needle he's ever seen.

"That was a nanite neutralizer injection, luckily the invading nano machines are small in number, the single dose I have, should clean it up…" Pikii then took out a small cylindrical object that was no more than a size of a small screwdriver. Yet to Doctor Henry's amazement, it opened and expanded into multiple pieces. Ten pieces attached themselves to Pikii's fingers, and the others formed a formation around the wound on Anna's chest. Pikii did not have implants, but the tool had its own built-in brain wave operation unit. Literally it was interfacing with her thoughts. She went to work. The foam would work, but the gaping hole had to be closed and repaired manually for it to work in time to save her. Meanwhile Doctor Henry and the assistants set up an injection of additional blood.

Pikii's tool then released tiny flexible micro-needles into the open wound. She had to stitch from the bottom up and repair everything in between. The small needles flew back and forth like lightning. They connected pieces of tissue to each other through a nano-bond, which combined with the foam, accelerated the healing process. There were very few medics out there who could perform this type of work without the complete automated equipment found in the Overseer bases. Pikii was trained in this for years since she was little, any novice could easily kill the patient outright.

Doctor Henry looked in amazement. He realized Pikii had no implants and was doing this surgical work manually. It was the way she was concentrating; she was clearly trained to work under the conditions of a technology outage. Like a real doctor.

She also took a huge a risk revealing her military medic level identity to them, which surely Anna already knew about. In normal military times, her act would most likely result in immediate detainment and a court-marshal. And if that happened, Anna would die. The health monitor system was showing that Anna was becoming stabilized and was going to make it. Doctor Henry breathed a sigh of relief. Ryker seemed to have calmed down too. He just sat there on a stool, watching Pikii work.

Incredibly, the surgery was finished in two hours. Doctor Henry injected a wake-up drug, and Anna seemingly came back to life. She looked around.

"Ryker, Henry..." she recognized the assistants too.

"And ladies, Carrie, Carla, Tanya, thank you all...I'm alive..." Ryker stood up and came over to hold her hand. Pikii quietly packaged her tools. Doctor Henry came over to Anna and whispered something in her ear.

"Glad you're ok, Anna..." Pikii said. Anna looked confused.

"Pikii, why...are you here?" Anna asked politely.
Ryker motioned everyone to shut up.

"She was here to support you, Anna." Ryker didn't want to get in shit for breaking protocol. Anna just smiled.

"Could you all leave the room please, except for Pikii?" Anna gave Ryker a smile before he left along with all the doctors. The doors hissed shut. Anna got up.

"Wow, amazing, it's like nothing happened!" she exclaimed. Pikii was quiet.

"This is a special surgery room. Only a few people at the base would get treated here. The drugs they give you here keep you conscious just in case we are ever needed to make a life-or-death military decision even if one is being operated on. Only thing, Ryker either forgot that or doesn't know that was the case today, impressive that he was trying to protect you, though!" she said giving Pikii a large smile.

"Uh...what? Wait, you were awake?" Pikii didn't panic but was surprised.

"Yep. More or less." Anna said as she found new clothes in one of the cabinets. Pikii fidgeted.

"You lied to me, you know..." Anna then clipped on a belt and put on some shoes. "You never mentioned that you were a trained surgeon, rank seven no less, that's just one below Doctor Henry!"

"It's not like that Anna, it's kind of a specific skillset... mostly useless for things like missing limbs..." Pikii looked down a bit, remembering Pete.

"Thank you for saving my life. I owe you one!" Anna was now fully dressed. She picked up a spare hairbrush from another closet compartment and went to brush her hair.

"So, have you slept with Kole yet?" Anna asked with a playful look on her face.

"No..." Pikii blushed. "I'm not even sure I would want to...it's complicated, I guess...someone you admire, and then you meet them, and then you're just like..."

"He's just a man, Pikii. They're dime a dozen." said Anna. She took a pause and then continued.

"But...there's none out there quite like him, I think. If you don't take the chance, someone else will take it before you figure yourself out, and by then it will be too late." She then came over to Pikii, gave her the most powerful hug she has ever given to anyone. Tears came from Anna's eyes.

"Pikii, I know I would have died today if it wasn't for you."
They looked each other in the eyes. The distrust was gone, a new
friendship was born.

"Listen, I must get the base into action. Go find Kole, you still
have time before we move out against the Overseers. One of you
could die, or both of you could die...take the time now to really
express yourself. It could be your last chance."

* * * *

After spending some time catching up, Kole and Pete split up.
Pete stayed at the submarine, while Kole walked back to Buso's
place. He needed ammo for his weapon.

[Ok, I think I can confirm now. They have amphibious robotic
units ready inside the underwater tunnel, but they are waiting
for a signal from the Admiral. Sending the info to Pete, Anna,
and Buso...done.]

"How the heck did you manage to get that info while you
were being absorbed?" Asked Kole.

[Ironically, they left some backup CPUs running in the
background, they were for basic body functions, guess they
never thought I would consider them useful. What's scary was
that there were over two thousand processors, all of them with
their own AI system, and they were all acting as one unit.]

"Wait, what the hell do I have then?"

[Yours? You have just two hundred... which is already
insanely impressive, by the way...and I'm your only AI...]

"But it's not that impressive, I guess you were salivating at the
idea of what you could do with all of that power, huh?" Kole
was savouring the moment and was going to milk Module 717's

284

lack of judgement for days to come, and the poor AI could not say anything.

[You got me, that was stupid. Right? Yes, that power, it was appealing, a little...]

"Any idea as to why he wanted you absorbed that badly?"

[Seems like he was the closest to achieving the Overseer's vision. Absorbing rogue AI systems like mine would be a much-needed capability. But he was incomplete. For one, his head was the original head attached to a sophisticated robotic body, and it was nothing like your human hybrid one. His body was self-powered. He would not need food or water and would never be tired.]

"Yikes, who knew they were this close..."

[But that's where it gets wild, unlike your body and me, his abilities when completely synced up, would surpass ours by a few times. I would imagine a complete unit would do multiples of that.]

"How many times? Or do I even want to know at this point..." Pondered Kole.

[At least six to seven times more deadly in current form, probably over one hundred with a perfectly completed unit...It was the reason he let me go back into your body, he was confident that we didn't pose any, and I mean any, threat to him.]

"Then why are we..."

[Still alive? Good question...he should have killed everyone in that room in a split-second...something was delaying his reaction time...and it wasn't me.]

"Wait a second…when I ran into the Synthetic version of Kelvin back then…something also delayed Kelvin's reaction time. What is going on…?"

[That, I do not know. But coincidences like that are impossible. Whatever did it this time…it must be close!]

"Darn, and I thought it was his daughter…maybe he was still attached…" Kole's brain hurt just thinking about it.

[I thought that too, perhaps his nervous system went berserk…but then he struck Anna with a deadly blow with intent to kill. If he wasn't an inch off, she'd be dead already. So, his intent did not change, just the reaction delay gave Anna the time to move…that much is clear now.]

Kole got to Buso's place. He found his weapon case in the room he slept in. The place he woke up to a naked beauty in his bed.

[You like this girl, huh…? You know, she's not like a Synthetic that was assigned to 'act' as your wife…she's got a mind of her own, and that means not as likely the type to automatically just do things your way.]

"Not now, man…"

[Wait a second, since when did you assign me, an advanced artificial being, a biological sex…huh?!]

"Since I first met you! You sound like a man, think like man, and if you were a real person, I bet you'd be a man…a mean, petty old man…"

[Jackass…]

"See, you're not ladylike, at all…" Kole chuckled.

[Damn you Kole!]

286

"Wait, what about drugs…you said his head was original, and nothing else, so that means at some point a transplant had to occur, no?"

[Hmm…there was a heavy painkiller concentration in the head, but with that kind of body it should not have made that much of a difference…]

"Any idea of how long ago the head was attached to that thing?" Kole opened the case and checked the ammo. Nine more modules were left. He reloaded the one he used.

[Honestly, I don't think that head was on for more than a few days. His body…it was manufactured, for sure. We need to see if there are clues inside the submarine!]

Kole took all the remaining ammo and clipped it to his combat pants. He inspected the case to make sure he didn't miss anything. Aside from the weapon inside that he already had, nothing else seemed out of the ordinary.

"Manufactured, so not grown like a Synthetic body then? This shit is getting weirder by the minute, it's like they are going back to cyborg technology."

[I managed to steal a few memory dump files and have been working on decrypting them in the background. There's a serial number set I have never seen before.]

"So, they've got a new process. How close are they?" Kole realized their timeframe was likely shrinking, and fast.

[I don't know, Kole. They might be just weeks away from being able to do the complete procedure. Honestly, I thought that without me, they were months away…until we met the admiral, that is…unless he was a lone wolf pulling ahead?]

Kole gripped his weapon. It felt like he was playing with godlike power. He threw the thing up in the air and let it rotate.

Then he caught it again with precision. It was so basic. But the weight of it...once you held it, the power of it was known to the user instantly.

[I think who ever gave this weapon to us, went to great lengths to create it. This weapon is not possible with any of your current human technology. And the fact that I can interface with it, that still bothers me. It's as if...]

"This must mean...someone really is watching us. Maybe...perhaps your creators are looking out for you..."

[If someone managed to make this weapon and was also behind my creation...then what kind of person, or Synthetic, would have the sheer computational magnitude to do all that...? And if so, why would they care about you or me?]

"Well, that I cannot answer. We have two rounds in the weapon, and eight more spares. After that, we can just use the blade as is."

[That thing can do a lot more than just become a blade Kole, but I'm not sure yet as to how to feed it that kind of complete input, it seems like it's some sort of reactive material.]

"Meaning?"

[It will give feedback during a combat situation, and we just need to act on that feedback and utilize its power...speaking of which, what do you think powers this thing, anyway?]

"Ah, who cares, let's just hope it keeps on working." Kole looked over the cylinder. It didn't have any cool features like those gadgets in the old movies. It was just a silver cylinder which had incredible grip, even though its surface was completely smooth. He practiced with it for a little while. He also checked the wrist ring, to make sure it was on snugly and was working correctly. Using his thoughts and Module 717 he was able to activate the thing and the blade could fly, though at a limited range. He could extend, spin, and do whatever he wanted. He gave it a few spins. It was a crazy piece of hardware. And hell, was it fun. After he was done, Kole clipped the blade to his belt using its magnetic lock.

Kole headed back out. There were a few elevators and security gates to pass through this time. The place was really under wraps. Once near the underground hangar entrance there was another heavily armed checkpoint and then Kole was finally at the submarine. There were men everywhere, yet it didn't seem like anyone was being detained. Men in obvious submarine uniforms were moving about along with the base's military units, all seemingly working together.

"Guess the admiral wasn't really popular among his own men." Kole kept moving towards the sub. The underground hangar was huge, and the submarine was more like an accessory to the whole area. Ten subs could easily fit in the place with multiple docks in what was essentially and underground lake. As Kole approached the submarine's hatch, a man popped out of it.

"Ah there you are, sir. We've been expecting you! We could use your help at the admirals' quarters, the doors are sealed shut and we're having trouble hacking in." The man had a darker brown skin-tone, a beautifully trimmed moustache, and spoke with a slight Hindu accent. He was middle-aged, but completely bald.

"And you are...?" Kole asked, a little annoyed that a military man didn't introduce himself.

"Oh, my goodness, apologies Commander Kole! I am Sergeant Higini, sir! Follow me into the sub, sir." The man went back down the hatch. Kole reluctantly followed.

[Checked his records, this man has outstanding service performance.]

Interesting, good to know, thanks! Kole was back to using his thoughts to converse.

"You know, sir...that broadcasting of yours, we managed to get it on the sub...after that, everyone lost confidence in the admiral." It was a slow, careful climb down. At the bottom, they took a pause. Higini seemingly wanted to chat.

"Very bad, we had no idea what to do. The Overseers must have ordered you dead immediately after, how did you survive, sir?" Higini was dying to know.

"Blind luck, I guess. Honestly, I feel like a cat, as I should have been dead quite a few times, by now..." Kole mumbled, not interested in recounting his life in front of a man he barely knew.

"Ah! A very good reference, sir! I love cats, unfortunately we are not, as you say, being allowed to keep pets on a military sub. I always wished for a little place of my own someday where I could be keeping a few!" Kole was suddenly amused at his eagerness and slightly awkward English.

"But Higini, there are no real cats left alive...although, I'm sure you'd be fine with a Synthetic one..." Kole was loosening up, but paused after suddenly thinking about Betty's cat, the apartment, and then Kaita. A sudden flood of memories came.

"Oh, no sir! In our travels, you see, to other continents over the last few years, we have found all sorts of wildlife, including real cats, sir...I almost stowed one aboard, but the admiral...he is, we call him, very angry person, so no chance...but next time, next time, with him gone, I will bring some back!" He was serious.

Kole leaned on the bulkhead. A new feeling filled his being.

"You mean there's other places where things are still alive? And alive in a sort of normal kind of way?" He asked slowly.

"Of course, sir! We have a whole map and a briefing in place for the Overseers. They really wanted to know if anyone else was alive around the world. Although, we found no humans, there were areas we located simply teeming with the flora and the fauna, as well as some very regular, non-mutated wildlife!"

"How is that possible…so, our records are false then?" Kole was not amused. If wildlife could thrive, surely some humans survived in other places, not just what was left in the good old USA. There was no way their submarine could have covered every part of the earth.

"Well, not quite so…you see, most things you saw on the old space images, I'm afraid, are very real. Completely devastated, in fact! Just like our southern regions…with radiation levels beyond belief, and so much water poisoned. Terrible, terrible, sir. But the few pockets of good, we must say, it was like finding the Garden of Eden." Higini let out a loud sigh.

"Commander Kole? Higini! What are you doing chatting up the Commander, we have work to do!" Out of the dark hallway of the sub came a man wearing a general's uniform. Higini instantly straightened like a finely tuned soldier and saluted.

"I'm General Honde Yadas, and you, Commander Kole, are needed for something right away. Please, follow me! Oh…and Higini, please get back to your duties!" The general was a big older fellow. His uniform was of an older vintage design, and his body still radiated strength. This man knew how to command. With intelligent blue eyes and a sturdy bald head, he said no more, turned around, and started to march, expecting Kole to follow.

Higini saluted, "Yes, sir! It was a pleasure, Commander Kole. I hope we will chat again soon!" and then climbed back up to the submarine entrance. Kole followed the general through the dark hallways, which soon filled up with crew members. Kole noted the large explosive packs they were handling with care.

"Is that for the intruders inside the underwater tunnel, General?" Kole asked.

"Yes, I had a chat with your friend Pete there, on how to close the underwater tunnel, and bury whatever's in there. Killer androids, I would guess...ready for a signal from that pompous bastard. We concluded that the best thing to do is send the sub back out to the area and detonate it, collapsing the tunnel along with the enemy units. That should buy us plenty of time. The Overseers know charging in here from the front is basically suicide."

"By the way, where is Pete?" Kole looked around but could not see him anywhere.

"Ah, well, he's guiding the detonation crews for me...the man is an expert in hard-wiring large explosives." said General Honde as he ducked to get under a bulkhead. The spacing in here was tight all around.

"I see, guess I will reconnect with him later. But wait a second, is this submarine not nuclear?"

They reached the bridge. It was more spacious than Kole would have thought. The electronics were ancient by any standards, though. Lots of green lights and screens with basic text input littered the place.

"Well, commander...this is an old Russian sub, basically a relic, but it runs forever! Them damn Ruskies sure knew how to build stuff to last! If only they had not accidentally nuked their own capitol during Letumfall. Imagine being that guy, who was drunk enough to wire in the wrong co-ordinates. Or maybe it was sabotage, who knows. Those were the days I tell yea!" The comm buzzed in the general's left ear and he leaned his head a little to listen.

"What? That fast? Shit...I'm not a miracle worker here, dammit!" The admiral waved Kole to follow down another hallway. "Looks like Anna is tipsy and wants this thing out of here in less than thirty minutes." They switched to a half jog.

"But we must get into the admiral's office. There must be some computers with information we can gather about their plans. A few days ago, we surfaced to receive a rather large delivery. A much bigger package than we usually get was sent by cargo drones. Whatever was sent was classified, only the admiral had access...and I'm pretty sure it was that new body of his, plus hardware. We must confirm what it was."

They reached their destination. Two technicians were already there with boxes and wires attached to the door panel. One of them stood up and greeted the general. He then shook his head.

"Well, Poly, let's give Commander Kole the console, let's see what he can do." said General Honde with excitement in his voice.

Kole took a position on one of the military laptops already wired to the door.

[I will take over, just sit back, and relax...] Kole's fingers began moving at stupid speeds.

Hey watch it! You're gonna break my fingers!

[I'm sure you could grow new ones.]

"I'm not a lizard!" Kole said that out loud. The AI was overloading his implant, and he slipped up. The general gave him a funny look. Kole decided to just stay quiet.

General Honde was crouched behind him watching the screen along with Poly, the lead technician.

"Amazing..." was all that came out of the lead tech's mouth. Kole decided to pay attention to the screen. It was filled with code that Module 717 was modifying at insane speed.

What the hell is this...

[Something you're too stupid to understand...] There was an uncomfortable silence for a few seconds.

Kole pondered for a moment privately. So far, things had gone so crazy in such a short span of time. He just needed a moment to himself. There was that box. Maybe he could ask Module 717 to stay in that thing for a bit while he got his mind together. The countless missions, the overloads on his body and mind, something was going to give, sooner or later.

[Kole, you're stressed, tense, and going to die of a heart-attack if this continues. Tell you what, after we're done here, put me in that little box the admiral brought, and I want you to rest.]

Oh wow, I'm that obvious, huh...

[Kole, what you went through the last few days, was insanity. I can feel your neural networks are becoming distorted and weak, you're exhausted. I will modulate the implant to help you relax. I figure you should be fine after some twenty-four hours. That also means the military should not and will not make a move without you and me at the helm.]

Thanks...

[Aha! We're in. Open door!] The doors swung open. A deadly stench filled the air, revealing an almost pitch-black interior. The only light came from a dim, flickering desklamp. The techs got up and exchanged glances. General Honde covered his face with a cloth he conveniently kept in his right jacket pocket. The lights inside were flickering. Kole didn't want to go inside. He didn't want to see what he already knew was there.

Everyone just stood there outside. Kole got up. He looked at the general, the man gave him a cloth as well. They moved in unison inside the cabin. It was a rather large space to have in a submarine, even if they were quarters for a bigwig like the admiral.

[Nearly four-hundred square feet, wow...on a freaking sub...]

One of the techs managed to get the lights back on. The ceiling illuminated. A logo of the ship could be seen in a huge pattern above. In the middle of the cabin was an operating table. The admiral's human body was on it, without the head. There were machines and tubes connected to the body. The stench was so bad that the techs went back outside to breathe a bit before coming back in. Kole carefully walked around the table. Towards the top of the head area, there were hundreds of little micro-arm machines spawning from two cases on each side. The job was sloppy. Blood stains were all over the table.

"A modular transition unit...yikes, can you image your head being cut off and then placed onto an android body, gives me the so-called shivers." remarked General Honde.

"So, they can get the head off, and place it on a robotic body...that's not exactly what I call transitioning to pure Synthetic form..." Kole was still baffled and terrified by the scene.

295

"How stupid of him, and he thought that even with an organic head that he could live on forever!" said General Honde angrily. "He was going to get us all killed, plus himself, pursuing a plan built on a broken foundation with a fake premise! Honestly, I should have shot him myself!" Kole nodded to that statement.

"I suspect that to the Overseers he was nothing more than a guinea pig. A useful test run perhaps." Kole stated.

"Just out of curiosity, how long would he live in that form for?" asked General Honde.

[Less than three weeks.]

"Honestly, even with painkillers, three weeks tops." The general, having followed the admiral for a long time, seemed royally pissed with the current state of events.

"Rest in pieces, you bastard! Tech support, get the computers out of here, leave the rest and evacuate!" ordered the general.

How much time we got? Kole didn't keep track of the time.

[You know, I am not your personal watch. We spent seven minutes hacking in, another two staring at a dead body, so all in all plenty of time to get the hell out of here, and even for me...wait, something ain't right, we better leave.]

"General Honde, do you think...he had a choice?" asked Kole as they exited the room. The air was suddenly so much better in the hallway. Out of nowhere, the female tech screamed. Kole's reaction was instant. He turned around already as Honde was still processing the sound in his brain. It was a cat! It bolted right past Kole. He tried grabbing its tail, but the damn thing was fast and cleverly twisted its tail out of Kole's reach, managing to escape by a hair. As the general was still figuring things out, Kole pulled the man's gun out and rang out multiple shots at the cat, hitting it with two out of the five rounds. But it was no ordinary cat. It kept running as if nothing hit it.

"Seal the sub!" Kole yelled as he ran after it. Module 717 already synced them up. General Honde was stunned.

"Damn, he's fast!" He uttered to himself. He'd never seen a reaction time like that before. He finally processed everything a moment later and gave the order.

"Seal the sub, immediately! Go to red alert, we have an unknown onboard!" yelled the General at the top of his lungs.

Kole ran past bulkheads through tight corridors. The dark lights didn't help much at the speed he was running. There were a few officers in his way, they barely managed to grip the walls so he could pass. Still, Kole clipped one with his hand. "Sorry, sir…" was all Kole heard as he was already away and down another corridor.

[Kole, use your blade, there's no way bullets will work on that thing.]

There it is! The damn cat was pouring acid out of its mouth, trying to burn a whole in a sealed bulkhead which connected the submarine to another section. Kole dropped the gun and got his blade weapon out and fired a concentrated bolt blast. The cat noticed the blast a little too late to fully dodge it and was hit. Kole got knocked over as the energy imploded in the tight corridor creating a massive pressure shockwave.

"You…trigger-happy psychopath!" came an enraged, half-robotic voice. "Did you…did you just try to kill me?" Kole got up. His head was ringing like crazy.

Did it just talk?

"What…no, no that's not what I was going for, totally not…not at all!" Kole said in a confused response. Part of the cat was sort of melted. The left rear leg was gone along with some flesh and tail. The cat responded but not in a nice way.

"Melting my fur like that...I'm going to rip your face off, you inconsiderate, degenerate sack of human shit!"

Kole took a step back. Chills ran down his spine. How that thing was still alive was beyond his understanding. The cat's claws suddenly extended to two feet in length. The irate feline wielding sharp metal knives longer than its own body leapt at him without warning.

[Got you!] Kole didn't even realize that his weapon discharged nearly at the same time the cat leapt at him. But instead of a bolt charge, a scary looking energy spider net attached itself to all sides of the hallway. The cat's reaction to it however, they could not have predicted. The claws extended further, digging into the walls, and it froze itself in mid-air right before the net. Module's 717 clever variation of the bolt blast charge failed. The cat hissed at Kole ferociously, looking Kole straight in the eyes and sending fear down his very being. It then retracted its claws, dropped to the floor. Its leg was already almost completely regenerated, and it then bolted through the hole it created for itself. Kole stood there frozen. Module 717 was quiet too.

"Kole, are you ok?" Honde was coming up from behind.
Kole threw his left hand back and yelled.

"Stay back!". The general froze in his tracks and retreated.

[Now that...was a little...fucking crazy...] Kole took a step backward and took a deep breath. His hands were shaking.

[Self-replicating? Self-regenerating? Holy shit...maybe we should have tried to talk to it more...]

Owww, wait! Fuck...you're right!

[Well, better get the hell off this sub.]

Good idea.

"Kole, is it safe now?" General Honde called out with an impatient tone.

"Uhhh...well...it was a cat...don't know much else what to say..." General Honde laughed out loud. A few other crews showed up behind him.

"Kole, you're a riot...but seriously, son..." And his tone turned serious. "What in the hell was that? We both know that was not just some cat!"

"I think we gotta get off this submarine, General Honde. Evacuate this sub immediately." The general's face turned a little pale.

"If even you don't know what the hell that was, I don't want to know either. Alright everyone, get off the sub, now!" he commanded.

Kole dusted himself off. He felt pain. A cut on his right arm. Most like from a sharp exposed wire when he took the fall. Kole holstered his blade and returned General Honde's handgun. A tech came over and applied a medicine band.

"Thanks!" said Kole politely.

"You are most welcome, Commander Kole. I'm chief technician here, my name is Poly Avci. Let me know if you need anything else." The man was thin, missing a lot of hair, and fairly old. He gave Kole a smile and moved along.

"Thank you, Poly." Kole figured he was originally from the Middle East, most likely of Turkish descent. Everyone lined up towards the exit of the submarine, but General Honde and Kole were let through first. General Honde went to speak with Pete, who was at a makeshift console where a remote-control system for the submarine was already set up and ready to go. Kole didn't interrupt them, there would be plenty of time to talk to Pete later.

In a matter of minutes, the submarine submerged itself into the bay, and went out to kill itself. Hopefully it would take all the underwater attack units with it. Pete was guiding it manually and Honde was with him reading out various readings.

[This is a good time to get some rest, I will send out notice to Anna that you're taking twenty-four hours off...done!]

What did you send off, I haven't even read it...

[Don't worry, now please put me in that cube thingy we left on the table at the meeting room, and leave me with Pete, they might need me to analyze sonar pulses to confirm the exact detonation location where we can maximize damage.]

Roger that! Kole proceeded with Module 717's instructions. Pete was happy to see a little cube box with arms and legs plugging into their computer console and helping them out. Kole then headed out and ran into Buso.

"Ummm...yeah, so...Anna just sent me. It looks like my place is yours for the next twenty-four hours, all meals and other things will be delivered...and the alcohol, have whatever you want, as much as you want. Here's my key card, so get some rest, buddy!" Kole was stunned.

"But Buso, where are you staying?" asked Kole. Buso smiled, and it was creepy.

"You know who lost the bet, right...?" He giggled like a little boy.

"But doesn't she have a..." Kole started.

"Oh, that guy? He's an old flame, she's over him, he's not over her…and, frankly…well, that's not my problem, hahaha!" Buso was smiling.

"Thanks, wait…hey, do you know where Pikii might be?" Buso's face gave him a reassuring smile.

"Oh, right! I think she's getting her own place to rest and relax, nearby Anna's quarters. Anna has taken a liking to the girl after Pikii saved her life."

"Pikii did what? Oh, wow…time sure flies. General Honde was already getting info from Anna on the sub, that was a quick recovery!" Kole figured as much. There was a lot more to Pikii than met the eye. But he was tired, and he needed to sleep.

"Oh, hell yes! Your girl is special! She's a keeper!" Buso saluted and wandered off. It sure felt lonely without the AI, Pete, or Pikii nearby. Buso seemingly saw his lonely face and came back around.

"Hey now, Kole, you don't seem all that happy. Want me to send some…special company? You know, there are girls on this base dying for a chance to meet you…personally…if you know what I mean…eh? So, what do you say? I can arrange it, just say the word friend!" Even if Kole needed a woman that badly, it would just be a waste of energy for him at this point. He gave Buso a smile.

"Maybe next time, I'm really tired…just sleep, food, and drinks will do." Buso gave him a pat on the shoulder. "Hey, no problem, Kole! If you change your mind, I'll be at the bar!" Buso finally headed off. Kole was kind of happy to be rid of him at this moment. Buso was a fun guy, but he would sell Kole's body for additional favours without a doubt. Kole didn't even want to think about it. The whole conversation felt dirty. Kole wandered the hallways for a bit to get his bearings.

"Wow, just how much of an impact was Module 717 having on my system?" he muttered to himself as he meandered with his head down. "Why am I...am I upset about something?" There was no answer from Kole's head. Module 717 was in a little box helping Pete and Honde. He finally thought about Kaita again, for a bit. Was she ever truly happy with him? She was created based on his overall preferences.

There were moments, especially the last few of her life, where he felt she cared for him...but, at the same time...it was never really love. He realized their relationship was more along the lines of a concerned roommate with whom he was sleeping with, rather than a real spouse.

She was created and assigned to me...did she hate everything I did to her...was I just some animal that she had to endure all that time? Of course, even though she was assigned, she had rights like a normal human being. She could have separated from him...but then, maybe the reason she didn't was because she figured all human beings were the same, no matter which assignment she received.

If I stopped being a Syndicator, I would also have been re-assigned...and she would have been taken away...what kind of life is that...? Kole wished she didn't have to die the way she did. She had it the worst, a death like that was not meant for her, but for him. He always felt so close to her, and she always went out of her way to please him. Kole finally reached Buso's place. His hand was shaking when he reached for the card Buso gave him. The door opened and he went inside. His head was so silent that it was driving him nuts. But like with anything else, he was most likely suffering from classic withdrawal.

Dammit, when did I become so lame...

Kole slammed a support column so hard that blood poured out of his right fist. His eyes teared up. He just stood there. In pain. Helpless. At this moment, he was nothing more than a shell of emptiness. He dragged his feet to the shower. He slowly undressed and embraced the hot water. His underarms stank like a dead goose. There was a special type of sponge hung near the soap bar with very rough edges. He used it to peel all the dead skin off from all over his body. Kole was red like a lobster afterwards, but it felt good. He felt his skin crying and trying to rebuild its outer layers. Finally, he felt a little alive. As he was drying his body with a warm, soft yellow towel, Kathy came to mind. The scene of her tears in the bar came back. At that time, he also felt helpless.

"Wait a second, what am I doing, moping like this...? I've done the impossible. I've given people hope. So many people believe in me..." It was true. His broadcast started the irreversible slide. Kathy's parents were murdered in front of her. He recalled they belonged to something called the People's Movement Front...he still didn't know much about this group, but he could guess. It was most likely the old front of the first rebellion against the Overseers.

"No wonder why so many people were being replaced by Synthetics." Kole was now openly talking to himself. "People were fighting the Overseers this whole time...but they were in a losing battle. Before Module 717 came along, there was no way to tip the scales!"

"So, we are in a race against time...and here I am... resting..."
Kole came out of the shower, trying to dry himself and stared at
the room. He was getting hungry. This is what Module 717
wanted for Kole. To have some time to think for himself. And
there would be a point in time where they would need to stop
relying on each other. After the Overseers fell, Module 717
would have no reason to stay inside his head. Kole went upstairs.
There was food already on the table. He got some sandwiches
and beer. His head was getting clearer.

To confuse the Overseers and get the party started, he would
need to make another broadcast. Something to ignite the
population to go from just protesting, to full overthrow mode.

"Of course, the Blood Hawks recording!" Module 717 had
that on record, where the kill squad orders were spilled out clear
as day by their officer in command, Keith Ledos. Kole didn't need
Module 717 to recite Keith's words. No, Kole himself memorized
them perfectly.

*'Find you, arrest you, and take you in, sir. We need to remove
the AI from your head and then you would be executed. Your wife
too.'*

The scene replayed in his mind. It made his blood boil again.
Kaita, whether she really loved him or not, did not deserve the
end she received. He was going to get his revenge on them all.

"Just you wait, Overseer James and the rest of the scum, I will
make sure to give you the end you deserve." Kole grabbed
another sandwich and dug in. After his third beer, he proceeded
to the bed down below. It was time to really sleep. Sleep without
any other thoughts or concerns.

* * * *

Kole wasn't sure how long had passed but when he awoke, next to him, something felt warm. He turned his head. Pikii was there. He didn't want to check to see if she was wearing anything or not.

When did she get in here? He snuck out of bed and went to the bathroom. Then he made a trek upstairs and brought down a pot of water and two glasses. He sat at a side table. She was sleeping peacefully. What the hell would soldiers like him and her do after the Overseers were overthrown? Just living their life away in the city, enjoying some peace perhaps. Having kids?

There must be a way to de-sterilize the city population! But would human children really be able to behave? Would they not treat Synthetics like robotic toys? That was still and always would be a concern for both sides. If humans were to live with Synthetics, strict rules of conduct from both sides would have to be put in place. Surely Module 717 would be able to figure that all out...but wait, since when did Kole have to rely so much on an AI?

Getting lazy Kole, you don't need anyone to do the thinking for you now. He thought to himself.

He sat there for a bit, slowly sipping his water. It was nice to just be quiet, to do nothing, to think of nothing. A pleasant wave of comfort engulfed his very being. What if he did enough already? What more could he possibly do? He was glad Pikii was here. She needed the rest, too. Her being naked the last time was already enough to tell him that she was most likely naked again. But he could not bring himself to go to bed and make love to her. He was just happy watching her sleep and pondering about how to bring the Overseers down.

305

Without the AI in his head, he felt a little lonely, but calm. He checked the time, he slept for a really long time, he only had ten hours left of the twenty-four granted to him. Pikii must have been here for a while, as well. As he went upstairs, he saw that she ate some food and drank a few beers.

He was super curious about who she really was, what kind of training she went through, what things she liked, what things she didn't like. Unlike a Synthetic, she would have a lot of real things to share with him and he was really looking forward to it. But what would their relationship be?

Is there even anything there? He felt comfortable with her. She was nice, but something was missing. Also, all they had in common at this point was just hatred for the Overseers. On top of all that, Kaita died just a few days ago. If he fell for Pikii now, it would just be weird. Also, he did not want to accept the fact that either of them might die in the next day or two. There had to be some other way to keep her as a companion for life, instead of as a disposable short-term lover. Kole pondered on that for a bit, and then gently hit himself on the side of the head when the obvious solution struck him.

Maybe...I just should just talk to her.

11

Teamwork

Kole found Pete and Buso back at the bar. Module 717 was with them while Pete downed some light drinks, even though it was early in the morning. Module 717 transferred back to him, but Kole kept the handy mobile box just in case. If he was shot or something else happened, he just needed a second to transfer the AI out to the box, and it would survive.

[Kole, you don't need to think like that...but thanks.]

You need to live, no matter what. Even with the Overseers gone, there will be nothing to unify the humans and the Synthetics. Things may actually get worse between them down the road.

[By the way, for your weapon, we have eight rounds left...wish we had more.]

Yeah, I know...two are already in, so that's six to spare. It will have to do...unless...

"Buso, how do I get to the armoury?" asked Kole. Buso smiled.

"Pete can take you there. Oh, and we're meeting in the main war room in an hour. I suggest you come early, though. Anna is all business today."

"Thanks for the rest, Buso...I feel a lot better!" said Kole.

307

"Anytime bro, anytime! Peace!" The man saluted him. Kole saluted back.

Pete got up and led the way to the armoury.

"So how was your time off?" Pete asked smiling.

"Don't you start with me, Pete!" Kole replied. "I know where your mind is going, and it's not what you think."

"Come on Kole, a girl like that and you're still being stubborn?" he chuckled. "Well, on another note, don't expect much from the armoury here, not much in terms of the tech that we're used to..." Kole looked at Pete's face, then decided to answer his original question.

"We talked, we got to know each other, we ate, we drank, we took a nap. Somehow, we're comfortable together, but I think it's way too early for anything else..." Pete gave him the concerned friend look.

"Seriously, Kole. The girl likes you, doesn't she?"

"I think she's conflicted...don't forget, I killed her whole squad." Kole protested.

"Ah, I get it. She admires you...but yeah, you're one scary dude...and maybe she's not your type?" Pete asked with a playful smile.

"She is...and she isn't...but...I don't know...everything's been so crazy, we had a nice time just talking. Really, who cares about the rest of it?" They went down to some deeper levels in the base. Kole noted this was not too far off from the hangar where the submarine was.

"By the way, how did the submarine plan go?" asked Kole.

"Went well, the sub got to the spot it needed to. Module 717 was a huge help in guiding it to the perfect place."

"Any enemy activity?" Kole asked with interest.

"Well, let's just say the entire underground corridor has pretty much collapsed. Honestly, we spotted only what looked like ancient robotic reserve units, old junk we could have dealt with either way. We set up automated defences inside the hangar in case we missed something more advanced. With the primary doors sealed, nothing is getting through there. On top of that, a dozen men will monitor the entrance twenty-four hours a day." Pete seemed very proud of himself.

"You thought of everything! Did you get some rest, though?" Kole was concerned about Pete.

"Oh yeah, nearly twelve hours of on-site sleep here and there, that AI friend of yours is something else, smart fella."

[Friend...] Module 717 was clearly pondering to itself. Even an AI needed some time to think. Kole kept his mind blank. He didn't want to disturb Module 717 today unless he really needed to. While Kole was resting, Module 717 was most likely thinking through thousands of scenarios and their possible outcomes in the fun little box they got from the admiral.

They came up to the armoury doors which looked like bank vault doors Kole had seen in old photos. Four guards stood in front of the door, decked out in full gear. They saluted them. Kole and Pete returned the salute. The doors opened and they went inside, down a long corridor until they reached a large warehouse space. Inside there were only a handful of soldiers. Within seconds, two female soldiers who were chatting away nearby came up to them.

"What would the General and the Commander be interested in today?" asked the younger one. But before they could reply, the curvier, older redhead burst out. "Well damn...look at what the cat dragged in...is it really you? Peter?!" Her voice a bit shaken.

"Peter, huh..." remarked Kole to himself quietly.

"Wow...Amy...it's been a while..." remarked Pete in complete surprise.

"A while?! Why did you say you'd be back soon, you moron! Do you know how many suitors I turned down over the last twenty years waiting for your sorry old ass?! I'm fifty-two now, you know..." said Amy with a hint of anger.

"Look...it was a one-way street...I had no choice...I'm sorry. You waited for me?" said Pete. His tone was low. Obviously, it was something from the past. Something bad. Kole gave the man a look, but Pete turned his eyes away.

"Kole...can't get into this right now, this goes a little too far back for comfort...old wounds..." he was interrupted.

"Old wounds alright! You crazy bastard...you could have been killed! Still...thank you for saving my life. When they took you away...we were told nothing, you know...aside from the fact that you were needed to train soldiers on the front lines. Any further inquiry into your whereabouts or status was rejected. I was hoping you'd come back..." said Amy as dreaded tears started running down her face. Pete came closer and hugged her. He too, to Kole's complete surprise, was crying like a waterfall. She gripped his back with her scarred hands. Pete towered over the woman, who was just around five-two in height.

[The emotional trauma was big with these two. Quite...big.]

Geez...I can only imagine, twenty years...he never mentioned this, either...

"Let's go you big oaf, let's pick out some guns. Then take me to Buso's bar...at least we can catch up a little!" said Amy as she brushed her tears aside. Pete nodded to her. Kole has never seen the man so emotional. Amy then looked at Kole.

"You're really Commander Kole?! We heard you were at the base, but nothing was mentioned about Peter! I can only imagine he made it because of you, so thank you...but we better not keep you." She then lifted her hand and motioned the other woman to come closer. "Katie here is a fan of yours, she'll help you with your gun selection." She grabbed Pete's hand with determination, and they walked off, chatting like no time had passed between them. Kole was lost. Pete's pain was his pain too. And he was dying to know what happened between him and Amy.

Kole turned to the blonde in front of him who was wearing a sand-coloured military uniform with a short-sleeve shirt and standard pants. Her blue eyes were a good fit to her silky white skin. However, a large scar was clearly visible near her left eye, going down to her cheekbone. From what Kole could tell, it seemed like a firearms mishap of some sort from many years ago. A scar like that would not be a problem to fix at his base at City 77. Yet here, these people were left to fend for themselves with dated medical technology. Katie was certainly around mid-twenties age group. Her twin ponytails were super tidy, to boot. She took care of herself very well.

"Hi, my name is...Kole, I like...big guns, where can I find those? Oh wait, can I start again? First, may I have the pleasure of knowing your full name and specialization?" She smiled at him.

"Of course, Commander Kole. My name is Katie Johansen. I'm one of the Arms Specialists at Flashpoint Base. Now, please come right this way." She was all military business in her voice. She then walked him in the opposite direction of where Pete and

Amy went. Katie showed Kole their close-range weaponry and various types of mid-sized assault rifles. Kole found a very neat combat knife with double-edged blades. It had somewhat risky to use but could be handled with more versatility than a single-sided blade. He picked it up and she put it on a cart for him. They went through the rifles and the ammo types. Kole soon found just the thing he was looking for.

"Ah, Commander Kole, the KZ-99 is the ultimate mix of versatility and powerful ammo capacity. The ammo packs are made reversible with two magazines attached side-by-side. There are thirty rounds per mag, for a total of sixty shots per pack." She showed him the cartridge pack. Back in the good old war days, things like this were done by taping two ammo cartridges together so they could be swapped. But this was pre-manufactured this way.

"There's a custom backpack unit that comes with this. Loads a total of four ammo packs, plus the one in the gun, so you have five packs ready to go. Also, there's water in the backpack as well in case you're out in prolonged combat."

"Great, we're on the right track. What do you have for guns?" Katie smiled, loaded up his cart, and waved him to follow her. She had a nice straight back as she walked rolling the cart. Her back unit was perfect too, Kole had to force himself to look away when she walked. He didn't notice any other old wounds or scarring. She looked like she was in top shape. They went to another section, racks and racks of guns lined the walls.

"Something with low ammo count, but maximum magnum plus level of firepower." Kole mumbled. He had a hard time not checking Katie out from head to toe now. He must have built up

312

too much sexual energy when he was with Pikii and now it was backfiring on him.

"So, you like to play with power after all..." she went and picked just the thing. It was a long-nosed gun with a top load cartridge unit. "This is the Enforcer Magnum Mark X, a thirty-calibre equivalent, comes with a top-load cartridge. It protrudes, and spins for every shot. Ammo types include penetrator rounds, flesh tearing rounds, explosive rounds, tag and blow rounds, and plain old regular rounds." She took out a cylinder block along with the gun. "This here is the ammo pack that holds all the ammo types. Twelve of each, or I can customize it for you. It can attach to the bottom of that backpack you already have. Gotta tell you though, it's heavy to carry around." Kole took the gun from her hands and weighed the ammo cartridge on his left palm.

"Wow, that's really heavy for an ammo pack!" Kole said as he rotated it in his hand. "Alright, let's load four sets of penetrator rounds, and two sets of the explosive rounds." Katie went to work. She masterfully took apart the cylinder, reloaded the ammo types from the feeder system below the gun rack. She then repackaged everything and clipped the ammo cylinder to the bottom of the backpack. His gun came with a holster. The cart was ready to go. Katie then took a few spare packs of regular ammo.

"If you would like, Commander...I can help you get the hang of this weapon at the range."

"Really? Darn, there's no time for that though...I need to be in the war room soon..." he complained.

"It will only take a few minutes, Commander." She gave him a wink.

[Kole…]

Calm down, it's a military firing range, not a brothel. What could possibly go wrong? Relax!

Kole followed her as she led him through a few doors and some twisty corridors. It was a tiny gun range alright, more like a private one.

"This is where I test the guns…" she said quietly. Kole picked up the Enforcer Magnum Mark X and loaded it up with bullets from a spare pack. A target appeared down the range. Katie gave him some earplugs. She then came up from behind and put her arms on top of his.

"This weapon, while powerful, requires a careful touch. Otherwise, you might release too early, and you know, that's not good…in a combat situation." she said that just loud enough so he could hear her. Her hands were warm, gentle, yet strong. She was aligning his aim with him. She knew what she was doing.

[Kole…I swear I will kill your thingy forever if you continue down this path…] Kole ignored Module 717. It felt nice to be treated well. Mainly, he was curious at just how powerful this gun was. He aimed and fired with confidence. The massive energy discharge was powerful enough to send him and Katie flying right into the back wall. He felt his body crushing her chest and face.

"Awww crap! That's crazy!" He sprung up, and immediately turned around to help Katie get up. She was a little dazed. Blood came down her nostrils. Kole got her a wipe and wiped it off for her, to which she smiled. Kole thought about asking about her scar, but then decided not to say anything. Who knew what kind of terrible memories that would bring up.

"First time with a weapon of that calibre, huh? You're a little fresh for a weapon like that don't you think?" she smirked.

Kole was spoiled with rifles and guns that had virtually no recoil. But here, these soldiers had to train with old equipment. And powerful old weapons like that came with a price of being extremely hard to handle.

"My job is not to just cart your weapons to the front of the gate. My job is to ensure you can actually use what you pick out. In fact, I won't let you take a weapon out of here if you can't use it." she said in a very serious tone. Kole realized though that she made total sense. If they let soldiers just take whatever from here, they could die on the battlefield in no time with something they are not familiar with.

"That rifle you picked up has a low recoil. Seeing how comfortable you were with it told me you're already an expert in those type of weapons. But usually, people who are good with rifles only use handguns as a last resort. And when you saw the Magnum, I saw in your eyes it's the first time you've seen something like that. So...this is why we're here." Katie said with even more authority. She took the gun away from Kole and shoved him aside. She positioned herself in front of a fresh target.

"Here, feet like this, keep your entire core activated. You must tense up the whole body. Arms, legs, everything as if you're about to get hit by a jeep. Your goal is to stop that jeep no matter what." She had a double grip on the gun. The muscles in her forearms rippled, and the short-sleeve shirt tightened up as she unleashed her upper body strength. And while her combat pants did not show how strong her legs were though, Kole felt her power aura.

[She's damn strong. This soldier trains really hard.] She let out a round with a booming exhale from her lungs. To Kole's surprise she didn't even move. The target at the other end was vaporized. It was an incredibly clean shot.

"And keep in mind, one handed operation can result in immediate dislocation of your shoulder...or worse, the gun could fly back and hit your head, knocking you out cold." She then handed him the gun.

"I will stand aside this time. I didn't know you were that new to recoil." Kole felt embarrassed. All she was trying to do was help him. He was not getting this gun if he could not fire it.

[Let me help a little.] Kole's body arranged itself. He felt immense tension in his abs. A new target replaced the old one. He breathed out and focused. Feet planted, shoulder-width apart. One foot back with a bent knee to help absorb the shock. He felt the gun again with his hands. It was powerful and needed to be treated appropriately.

The trigger release had to be perfect. Any shaking in the hands or careless handling and this gun would fire at a slightly wrong angle and take out the balance he worked so hard to set up. The finger had to flow smoothly. Hands tight. Arms twisted just a little inward with all tension completely controlled. He released it. The shock penetrated his whole body as if a truck hit him head on. He held his ground. The target was hit in the bullseye. The shot was perfect. Katie was suddenly wide-eyed. Kole didn't pay her much attention. As the new target swapped, he fired again. Another perfect hit. And another. Until the Magnum was empty. Then, he finally relaxed and took a deep breath.

"Amazing…Commander…were you just messing with me?" asked Katie. Kole felt sorry for her nose, but he had to get out of here.

"Well…you think I can have this now?" Kole asked. Her face was lit up, and she gave him the thumbs up.

"But Commander…"

"Just call me Kole. I owe you some gratitude. Had I gone out with this weapon and fired it for the first time while in combat, I would most likely have died." He put the Magnum down and brushed off his hands.

"Talk about being embarrassed, I'm really sorry about your nose, may I walk you to the doctor's office?" asked Kole.
She giggled a little.

"Actually, I am a nurse in training, so nothing to worry about, I can patch it up on my own." She went to a small sink and washed her face. As she came out Kole gave her a look over again. She was very fit, and her figure was just over five-feet tall. Her face was a little too narrow for her build, and the scar certainly didn't do her any favours. But her clear blue eyes had the solider's resolve. She was certainly no pushover.

"After the Overseers go down, let's reconnect. I would love to show you some of the cool weaponry the Syndicators use." He saluted her and was about to take the cart. He didn't want to waste any more of her time.

"Wait! Commander Kole, could you please follow me?" She walked further down the range and motioned him to follow.

"This is my office." She closed the door. It was a small space enough to fit a desk and a few chairs. There were no windows of any sort. She had her back to him. Then, she took off her military short sleeve shirt and her undershirt in one motion. Kole

317

saw a wrap around her chest. He figured maybe she wanted him to look over an injury or something. She unwrapped it. And turned around. Kole then saw the most beautiful pair of natural breasts. The proportion was a perfect match for Katie's body, and the nipples were small, cute, and pinkish.

"I have to hide these from most men here, but somehow, I just wanted to show you these." Her cheeks were flushed, and Kole's body reacted, but he kept his cool.

"You are a beautiful girl, but I need to be in the war room, so..." he tried to leave, but one hand blocked the door. Another hand locked the door.

"But a few minutes won't change anything, will it, Commander?" she said quietly.

"Yeah, uhhh..." *Oh geez! What now!*

[I dunno, just do what she wants so we can get out of here...] She put his left hand on her chest.

"Do you like these, Commander?" Her buttery smooth white skin just felt so nice.

"Yes... god...they are amazing, indeed." said Kole, trying to not sound like a retard. He gripped the left breast gently. She reacted with a whimper. His member was rock hard already as his veins were filling up with blood faster than a serial drunkard could down a beer at the bar. Kole underestimated his sexual tension. She felt his crotch with her left hand.

"I knew it! You're sexually charged. You can't go out to the battlefield in this condition. You'll die, for sure. Let me help..." she said softly. She unzipped her combat pants and took them off along with her sexy white underwear. Her private parts were neatly cut and prepared. She came close to Kole and kissed him wildly. He lifted her and put her on the desk. Without wasting time, he took out his member and thrust it deep into her already wet, and very tight opening.

She moaned quietly as he began to move inside her with military precision. She held him tight. One hand on his hip, another on his shoulder. He leaned over and kissed her breasts. She was squeezing her muscles inside, to tighten her grip over his hotrod even further. Her soft breasts turned on all the sexual instincts a man could have. He placed his right hand on her right breast, and the other on her left butt cheek. She then found his lips, willfully thrusting her tongue into his mouth, interlocking into a prolonged French kiss. Meanwhile, her legs wrapped tightly around him, and it was a matter of mechanics at this point. All was set for a major release. And Kole needed it. And it seemed like Katie needed it even more than he did. Her juices were pouring down the table onto the floor. She let go of his lips to breathe in some air. Kole accelerated his hips, diving deeper into her insides.

She moaned quietly. He then lifted her up and pinned her in mid-air against the wall and proceeded to go to her deepest depths. Katie shifted her head up, letting him sink his mouth on her left breast. He sucked on her breast wildly. Then moved to the right one. Giving both of her amazing breasts the time they deserved. Finally, her insides exploded with wetness, as her climax reached its peak. Wet juices poured out of her and onto the floor. Kole then finally let himself go, and in one final powerful stroke, he ejaculated deep inside Katie, even to her own surprise. He held her up there for a few more seconds, until he was completely done. He slowly twisted back and lowered her down to the table, gently exiting her. His cream filling poured out of her, slowly dripping onto the floor.

"Uh…sorry, didn't mean to…" She didn't let him finish, but grabbed him, and kissed him passionately. She then looked at him eye-to-eye.

"I would expect nothing less Commander…but this is the first time a man blew his load inside me without asking my permission first…you're a naughty one!" She giggled. "I hope your girlfriend gets the same treatment."

Kole knew she was referring to Pikii, but just nodded. They cleaned up their act and returned to the armoury facility with smiles on their faces.

[You make me sick.]

Right, as if you didn't enjoy it, either…don't tell me you didn't feel all of that…

[Uhhh…maybe I tapped into it a little…]

What have I done…

[You realize the humans here are probably not sterile, right…?]

Oh…wait…no…you don't mean…

[You're going to be a daddy…my calculations predict it!]

Shut up, shut up, shut up! It's your fault, you could have had me go limp! You didn't do your job!

[Oh, I'm sorry, but I don't have the truck load of horse tranquilizers required for that little work order!]

You little shit! Next time you're in that little box better watch yourself!

[Do you want me to make you fall flat on your face right now? Cause I can, and she'll probably think you've gone full retard mode on her…]

Ok…fine…truce…let's be friends here…

[That's better, you're my bitch! Understand? Don't ever forget that!]

I hate my life...

Meanwhile, Katie was amusing herself watching a half-baked Kole trying to gear up with a weird expression on his face. She even giggled a bit. She had no intention to tie him down. She was a fan of his, and she got what she wanted. He was probably only now thinking about the consequences of ejaculating inside her and was about to run off and never come back. Still, this made her day. But she wanted him again, and she'd be counting the days to their next gun range session. But Kole showed a hesitation to leave. Suddenly he looked at her with his powerful eyes.

"Hey Katie, can I ask you something?" Kole decided to at least see if he could get some information out of her. Although, it was a little too late to negotiate as to how much he was going to get.

"Sure sugar, you want my room number? I'm at level M4, room 67 and I'm off my shift at..." she started.

"Wait, wait! Not that, but thanks...I guess, I mean...that's a wonderful offer, and all...who would say no, right?" he laughed a bit. "Listen, it's about Amy...do you know anything about her and how she relates to Pete?" he asked carefully.

"If you want to know about that...then come to my room then. I'm off my shift at eighteen-hundred hours." she said firmly. "Knock in six consecutive knocks, twice."

"You're serious...why can't we just go to the bar? I know Buso would cook up a storm for us and we could talk all night there." Kole reasoned.

"Kole...you must be the nicest guy on this darned planet...do you not see the scar on my face? Do you know how hard it is for me to have a man to stick around after, even for a few minutes? I work here as it keeps me away from the crowds. The stares I get at the bar, the gossips...I hate it...I just..." She went quiet for a bit realizing she was raising her voice. Kole let her regroup. "Look you don't have to come...what I am doing...you don't even know me...this isn't what it looks like...damn, I didn't mean to go off like that, you must think I'm nuts or someth..." Kole embraced her with a hug. Katie teared up. The scar had a bigger story, after all.

"I will get something from Buso's stash later, and we can talk. But you're going to tell me everything, okay? Even the stuff that...well the stuff that still hurts the soul, are you okay with that?"

"Yeah...I mean, but it will be only for your ears...you coming tonight then?" she asked.

"Noted. I will come alone. Give me your comm ID, that way I can contact you if I can't make it." Kole handed her his comm device and she entered the ID for him. "Alright, see you later, Katie!" Kole headed for the exit. Katie waved her hand. He waved her back. There was something about her. It was just a chemical attraction he could not explain. He pressed a button on the comm to dial up Pete.

"Pete, I got the things I needed. Are you doing okay there?" he asked in a tired tone.

"Hey Kole, Amy and I have a lot to discuss. I'll see you later." Pete didn't wait for Kole to respond and hung up.

Shit, I hope he's okay, he sounds stressed.

[Imagine being taken from someone you care about for twenty years. Highly likely the Overseers threatened Amy's life if he ever contacted her...yeah, I feel for him.]

"Damn it. Wish I could do more for him." There was no point in worrying about Pete right now. Besides, Pete had been around for a lot longer. He would know better with how to deal with pain like that. Kole started towards the war room. Module 717 provided a nice little visual guide on where to go. About a three-minute walk lay ahead.

"By the way, did you ever figure out what that cat thing was in the submarine?" Kole really wanted to know. But Module 717 went silent.

Oh, I guess I should not be talking out loud there, so...?

[There have been mistakes in my calculations Kole...]

Ah, we all make some sort of blunders along the way, no big deal. Kole turned right, down another hallway, this one was especially trashed. Crap was everywhere.

"Geez, does anyone ever clean the shit up here?" He passed by tissues, open food containers, and other literal garbage.

[But how was anyone supposed to fathom the possibility?]

Hey, you talking to yourself? I'm like, right here you know!

[Kole. They have been watching us, observing us. But what do they want? What is their purpose?] Kole was a little surprised that the thoughts were not clear, and even hearing them in his head they felt distorted.

Hey, are you mumbling over there? What's going on?

Kole passed another place where paths crossed and heard his name.

"Kole!" Echoed through the halls.

Pikii?

"Kole! I've been trying to find you...oh...wow, nice gear there! Where'd you get all that?" she said with excitement.

"Uhh, well...at the armoury..." Kole replied carefully.

"Oh? Can I go there too?" she asked blissfully. Kole pointed in the direction.

"Just down there, then make a left and keep walking till you see a large circular door with guards." She nearly jumped with excitement.

"Perfect, tell you what, Anna invited me into the war room meeting. It's in half an hour, so I will just play with some toys and see you there, ok?" She came closer and gave him a hug. Then a cheek kiss.

"Thanks...for hearing me out, and actually caring about what I had to say, and caring about me, and my thoughts...I dunno what to say...but thank you, it made me feel very good." Kole looked her in the eyes.

"Go get some guns Pikii, but make sure anything you don't know how to shoot you try out at the range." Her eyes got wider.

"What!! A range??! Sweet! I better hurry then! See ya!" She then bolted towards the armoury. Kole then resumed walking towards the war room.

[But I still don't understand...Kole, I don't know if we're ready...we could die in all of this...]

"Are you afraid? Cause I'm not. Besides, anything happens to me, I will live long enough to move you over to your mobile box. So, stop worrying." They reached the entrance to the war room. It was in a large open area, on the same level as the armoury. Kole forgot exactly which floor they were on, but this was one of the lowest levels in the facility.

[This is sub level sixty-five. There's another two below this.]

Thanks. So, ready?

[No, not ready. But that is not going to stop you, is it?]

324

Nope. Not at all. Fully armed guards saluted Kole.

"Commander Kole, you can store all of your gear here." said the bigger guard. The men moved out of the way. A large set of crates were set up here. One of them was opened for him. Kole dumped all his stuff in there including his cylinder weapon and the newly acquired double-edged knife. War rooms typically didn't allow any sort of weapons for all kinds of good reasons. He kept the ring on his wrist though, as without the main unit it could do no harm.

"Thank you, Commander Kole...please proceed inside." said another guard with respect. The pressurized doors hissed fiercely and slowly opened, revealing a wide hallway. The sides were cylindrical, and blue lights lit up the floor and the ceiling.

What a fortress! Another short walk of some ten meters and another door opened.

Feel likes ten meters of solid steel all around, crazy, not even the most powerful transmitters would be able to send anything out of this place...

[Overall, from my analysis, this is designed to withstand any type of nuclear attack. Very impressive, indeed.]

Anna greeted Kole with a smile. Buso was already there. Another two dozen military commanders and generals were in the room. General Honde was there, too. They shook hands and exchanged pleasantries. General Honde then officially introduced Kole to General Kanos, the short man with four claw marks on his right cheek who was in the helicopter with him and Pete. General Kanos oversaw all infantry operations and training. His clearly American protégé, General Lodus, stood by his side. This man oversaw the infantry strike forces. He was very different from Kanos, although Kole would pin them at a similar age with Lodus being the younger one. This man was taller, more muscular, and had clear blue eyes.

After that Kole mingled with various others, to at least get to know them all a little. Most of them were very excited to meet Kole, except for a few very stern men who offered no evidence of any emotion. That was fine with Kole however, as he knew Anna picked the best people for the job. After some time, some small talk, and a few chats, Pete showed up with Pikii in tow. They both went to Kole's side.

"Alright, we're all here, let's get down to it." Anna said in a powerful booming voice. They all found a seat. Pete sat on Kole's right, and Pikii was on the left. Anna kept standing. The room was a square but had circular seating surrounding the centre area. A large hologram lit up.

"There are eight Overseer cities. Our primary target is City 77, where head Overseer Ricco resides and is often accompanied by the rest of the top-tier scum bags like Milta and Kyle. Our goal is to capture that city, at all costs. Once this is accomplished, the others should fold over to our control. This is no easy task, and I would like to hear how this may be possible." Anna motioned for Kole to stand up and come over.

"Kole, would you mind sharing your ideas first?" Kole stood next to Anna. Of course, Anna was not the type to just dictate, she wanted an open discussion on the best course of action. He had some time to think about this, so he was ready.

"Anna is correct, City 77 is and should be the main target. It's not just the largest out of the eight, it's also the most fortified. For defences, there are four fully staffed military bases and one hundred large laser batteries surrounding the outer perimeter. The only other city with a similar set up, is the one headed by

Milta Avena, the second-in-command at the Overseer club. Her city, City 55, is about two hundred miles to the Northwest, and also boasts four military bases and sixty of the exact same laser batteries. If City 77 falls, the remaining Overseers will seek refuge in City 55. However, this base has easy access to City 55, as it's the closest one to us, anyway." Kole took a pause.

"City 77 and City 55 should fall right after one another, if not at the same time. Our forces will need to split up. It's critically important that the Overseers have nowhere to run to. The other six cities, 99, 88, 22, 11, 44, and 33, only have a single military base for defence and will easily surrender to us when those two cities fall. Although it may be wise to set up some sort of reinforcement cutoff plan to ensure they don't resupply either city in the event things go into a prolonged combat operation." Anna shifted the diagram to show the relation of all the cities to each other.

"Cities 99, 88, 22, and 11 are about one-hundred and fifty miles to the east of City 77 and are bunched up in a group. And cities 44 and 33 are some one-hundred miles to the south from there. They are spread out in a way that takes advantage of the most livable areas." Kole continued.

"Now, of all the bases at City 77, the scariest one is the base that is commanded by Overseer James, The Northern Command Base. Even I don't know what exact weaponry they possess, but I can assure you all, it will have the latest and deadliest military technology." The room filled with whispers.

"However, before we attempt taking the Northern Command Base, we need to reach West City Base first. There will be defectors there who will ally with us. This will make our operation a hell of a lot easier. But even before we can reach the city itself, we first need to bypass the lasers altogether. I believe this can be done from within."

[What!?]

"Are you...wait, you are serious...?" Anna was caught off-guard.

"Yes, the laser system is impossible to penetrate from land or air, but nobody is counting on an internal attack." Kole said.

"But how would we accomplish this? Are we able to reach someone at West City Base?" Anna was puzzled. Conversations filled the room instantly. It was to be expected.

"We can broadcast a message." Replied Kole. "Module 717 has stored a critical piece of evidence from my apartment, the orders from the Overseers themselves to have me and my wife executed...and the murder of Kaita by Overseer James in my apartment." Kole gripped his hands into tight fists. His chest was tight. This was hard to talk about this in the open.

"This should get people, including our possible allies at my home base into an uproar. We can even ask them to tear the lasers down...and I think they will do it..." The room was dead silent.

"They executed her...in front of you?" Anna was carefully choosing her words. This is the first time Kole was opening up about the events that brought him to the current state of affairs.

"Yes...James shot her...and yes, she was a Synthetic, but it didn't matter to me...she was as human as any of us here..." he was a little hesitant, but he had to face it. Hopefully they would understand.

"Jesus, Kole...your last few days...nothing but hell..." said one of the Generals. If Kole remembered correctly, the man's name was Parker, he was in command of all the air units here at the base. Kole slightly envied the older man's full head of thick, black hair. His large eyebrows made for an intimidating look. Kole got the feeling from their prior brief chat that General Parker had a long history of hatred toward the Overseers, but he stopped short of telling Kole exactly why. Whatever it was, there was trauma there that was never going away. This is where they related. Nobody expected this from Kole, however.

"A Synthetic wife…" Pikii said quietly to herself. She stopped speaking before someone else heard her and lowered her face a little. Her emotions turned inside out. She kind of knew it, but Kole left some facts out of his story. She felt the pain written all over his face like the stains of blood on clean pure white cotton sheets.

"Kole, our condolences…" said General Honde quietly. There was an awkward silence in the room. Kole didn't mean for such a shock effect.

[I hate to interrupt…sorry, Kole…]

"Sorry everyone, I hate to interrupt." said a pleasant version of Module 717's voice over the war room speaker system. "Don't mean to steal your thunder there, Kole…but I feel like we are going to need a little more time here than we originally thought. I think it's best to review a few things to avoid massive casualties, especially on this side of the equation." said Module 717 with a very profoundly convincing voice.

"Reducing casualties should be our top priority, especially considering infantry troops often get the short end of the stick in combat engagements." said General Lodus. His blue eyes were full of intrigue. "I certainly want to hear more from Module 717!"

But I spent so many hours coming up with a plan…

[Sorry Kole, you are a good soldier, but this rabbit-hole we're in is just getting deeper by the second, and I've spent lots of time thinking about it, too.] General Honde stood up to speak.

"I must agree here, we can't just decide what to do in a single sitting and just move out, I think we'll all wind up very dead, very fast. Don't forget, we're talking about the Overseers, here...these people invented the modern world after Letumfall wiped humanity off the face of the earth. Underestimating them would be a huge mistake."

Module 717 continued. "The Overseers haven't moved against the base. They have only been trying to kill Kole and myself. This morning I spent hours on their networks, and something else is going on. There's heavy jamming, and secret encrypted messages are flooding the networks...and there's one more thing...Kole, do you feel better?"

"Huh? Yeah...a lot better, but what are you getting at...?" asked Kole concerned.

"Sorry, but here are some things I should reveal to you all. I didn't mean to keep information from Kole, or any of you, but I wasn't sure what it all meant...or how complex the Overseer plans really are. But even before that, the number one issue...that cat we ran into on the submarine, was a higher life form, and it's very much still alive somewhere."

"Impossible..." uttered Honde. "The sub blew up filled with explosives and brought nearly a mountain of rock down on itself."

"Yes, but none of that would stop it, however. It regenerated in seconds after Kole engaged it. Later it left the sub minutes before it blew up to seal the underwater tunnel. I had a camera feed to the sub and saw it roaming around. At first, I thought it

330

was going to sabotage our plans by preventing the explosion, but it did nothing of the sort. It was made from something far more advanced than nanite technology. And it wasn't very friendly on first contact, so that means whatever it is, it's a possible enemy with its own agenda that we have not taken into account." Whispers filled the room.

"I feel like Kole and I have been under some sort of observation over the past few days. It felt more like someone was studying our moves and measuring our capabilities. If we go ahead and rush a plan into motion now, this new enemy that we hardly know anything about could be simply waiting for us all to fall into some sort of trap. Think of it this way, we see the Overseers as the masterminds, but imagine if the Overseers are also part of someone else's plan." Chills ran down Kole's spine. Anna decided to go and sit down next to Honde.

"Guess that is indeed a possibility, now that you mention it…" Anna said quietly. Everyone heard her and some in the room nodded in agreement.

"Now back to the Overseers themselves. The water supply. The Overseer cities are supplied with water from special treatment facilities. I never thought about it until I studied the water you have here at the base. There are huge differences in the chemical composition. Then it hit me, some sort of advanced nanites are being injected into the water in Overseer cities, where all the humans have implants. Nanites can poison those implants and override them. Meaning those human beings can become controllable much like the Synthetics, to some degree." The room was very focused. Module 717 observed them and continued.

"They are more prepared than we thought. Imagine if your base was somehow wiped out and the Synthetics rebelled, and the Overseers could not control them completely. The failsafe to control human beings with implants is not perfect, but those drugs in the water can be easily increased in dosage to dope them up some other way, say an emergency broadcast that would say the water was poisoned, and they could then force an antidote that the Overseers would conveniently supply. Then with an implant override you have some a few hours of pretty good control, enough to have them take up arms and do whatever bidding the Overseers demand. That's assuming the dosage even needs to be increased from current levels."

"Holy shit!" said Pete. "Now that you mentioned it, my head is way too clear as of late."

"Me too, I thought it was just the rest..." said Kole.

"That's because you flushed your system with purified water. The drugs left your body. It takes about twenty-four hours to completely flush the system based on my calculations." Anna got up and paced.

"Well, this certainly changes things...if we just rush in there, they could potentially get the Synthetics and the humans against us by the time we manage to get some sort of foothold. We'd wind up killing...everyone! Dear god, this is so messed up!" she exclaimed.

"Or those advanced beings, whatever the hell they are, could show up in numbers and take us all out. Damn!" General Lodus chimed in.

"It's an endgame scenario from either side, and we need to find a more delicate middle-ground." Kole pondered on the problem from a different angle.

"Module 717...we know the Overseers are seeking a transition to pure Synthetic form, and we know they are most likely using Synthetic scientists...which could mean that those new beings...could they be a prototype weapon against humans? Perhaps the Synthetics produced them to fight back, I mean wouldn't you, if you were a slave?" reasoned Kole.

"I'm a master system, not a slave system." Nobody got the joke in the crowd except Kole, who nearly laughed out loud. Module 717 continued. At least Kole's face was now more relaxed.

"The Synthetic scientists were surely given access to some insane computing technology...it's possible that they gave life to something else. Perhaps the antidote to humans and the Overseers. But much like a virus that attacks living cells inside your bodies, perhaps these beings will attack all humans, good or bad without discrimination. If that's the case, we may need to destroy this new life form..." said Module 717 with a passive, slow tone, as if he was impressed with Kole's analytical skills.

"So, what options might we have? What can we do?" asked Anna. Module 717 imitated the clearing of the throat, which drew a few smiles from the serious crowd. Kole had to hand it to the guy, he sure knew how to talk to a crowd.

"Time is possibly on our side, at least for a short while. First, I need to spend some time to develop a weapon system based off the piece of technology we were provided with that can potentially stop these new beings. It may be difficult, but without that we cannot make any moves, yet. Kole and I can get on that immediately if you have a weapons lab that we could work in. Once we know we can destroy those things, then we need to do something about that water supply that feeds the

Overseer cities. We'd have to hit all four main water facilities at once. They'd have to be attacked in small teams. I also need to find a way to help the Synthetics from being taken over by the Overseers by force. We already know they have modules built into them that the Overseers could activate to control them to some degree, but we need a way to either disrupt those transmissions completely or feed them a virus to disable those systems. Again, this will take time to figure out."

"Sounds like we've got quite some work to do..." said Anna. She felt completely useless. Kole stepped in, seeing the look on Anna's face.

"We need teamwork to get this right. Anna, your team should figure out how to take over the water treatment plants quietly. In the meantime, I need your best weapons experts and coders to work with Module 717. And as for you, Module 717, do you think you're up to the task?" A computerized laugh came through the speakers.

"Silly human. Kole, how many times do I have to tell you, I am far superior to your single banana processor." A smiley face appeared in the hologram. A few chuckles spread through the room. It was sort of funny, but Kole wasn't laughing. Buso had a blast on his behalf and nearly fell to the floor laughing. Kole didn't like to be embarrassed like this.

[Sorry, sorry, could not help it...]

You...!!! Why you!!!

[Oh, come off it, nobody here really likes you...unless you think Pikii might...]

Kole looked her way, but she avoided his eyes.

Dammit, maybe I should have told her the whole story...

334

[Maybe she got the same lady at the armoury, maybe they talked...]

Shit...

"Alright Kole, General Honde will take you to the weapons lab and get you some of his best experts. Buso will get the coders in there and set up equipment. The rest of us will figure out the best stealth tactics we can use to infiltrate the water treatment plants. Pikii and I will work on the water treatment plant infiltration missions. Let's all get some coffee and get to it! Dismissed!" commanded Anna. Kole had to let it go. If somehow Pikii started to act differently towards him for whatever reason, he would just have to accept it. She didn't owe him anything, anyway. He started towards the doors. He was almost there when he heard his name.

"Kole...wait..." it was Pikii's voice. She came over. "I'm sorry, I just didn't know how to react to hear that your wife was a Synthetic, or that she was executed in front of you...my emotions, they just went off...please accept my apology!" Her head was down. Kole took her cheeks with both hands and raised her head.

"Pikii, please smile again, I won't leave this room until your face is back to its normal self." Her eyes teared up slightly.

"I'm sorry, how could I even act that way..." she said as Kole let go of her face. She brushed away the single tears and smiled.

"That's better...what's in the past is in the past...all we have now Pikii, is the future." he said with a smile. Although he was faking it.

"Okay. Work hard, get that weapon made, we're counting on you!" she said. Kole saluted her and took off. As he was at the end of the exit, Pikii whispered just to herself.

335

"I'm...counting on you..."

"You realize it now, don't you?" said Anna. She snuck up behind her. The folks in the room decided to take a break and all left, with some tailing Kole to get some coffee. Anna and Pikii wound up alone.

"Kole is the type of person who can interface with that AI because he doesn't see them as pieces of code or some program. He sees them as actual entities and respects them. He actually cares for them. He treasures their being as if they were all human. Few people in the world could do that, you know. Few people could live with an AI in their brain that was so advanced and not be petrified of it, or want to kill it..."

Pikii looked her in the eyes.

"I know he's like that...I get it..." Pikii started. Anna let out a sigh.

"But he's not out of your reach, you just need to try harder if you want to win him over." Pikii looked at Anna with a wide-eyed stare.

"Wait, what...? Oh, no...it's not like that..." she said quietly.

"Oh? It's not? You know when a man doesn't sleep with a naked woman in his bed it only means two things. Either he's into men or he's got more respect and feelings for you than you think. And honey, Kole is clearly not into dudes! I think you two would make a good couple..."

Pikii blushed. A few seconds of silence. Anna broke it first.

"Either way, let's get through this first, I need your mind focused on the work at hand, Pikii." Anna put a hand over Pikii's shoulder. "We'll make sure we win! But first, let's follow those lazy bums and get some coffee, it's going to be a long day!"

"Alright! Coffee time!" said Pikii with newfound confidence.

* * * *

It was a long day. Kole steadily made his way towards level M4, room 67. He finally found it. The hall had less lights, and it was dirty all over...kind of like a ghetto. The base was a mess in general, but this floor was especially filthy. The time was almost twenty-three hundred hours. Module 717 opted to get out of his head for a bit so that Kole could have some privacy and alone time. Taking a deep breath, Kole knocked as instructed. The door opened a few seconds later. Katie looked around the hall and grabbed him by the hand to pull him inside. She was wearing a standard green military nightie. Her place was a tiny bachelor pad with just a bed and a few amenities. Nothing fancy. There were weights and a few other training items near the bed. Kole placed the whiskey on the table and sat in one of the two small chairs. Katie grabbed some glasses. He was tired as hell.

"Can I be honest? Didn't think you'd show up, let alone with a bottle of booze. That's nice of you." she said quietly. Kole spotted that her face was a bit red. She has spent some time crying.

"Yeah, well...sorry for dropping in so late." said Kole as he opened the bottle.

"I'm off tomorrow. You could stay the night if you want." she said carefully. She kind of wanted him again, but she knew it wasn't going to happen. She really didn't know him and felt bad about earlier. Things were just a little more awkward now. She was a little nervous. And he was, too.

"After that meeting we spent all day at the weapons lab. If it wasn't for the absolutely shitty but super strong coffee, I would not have even made it." said Kole while pouring her a glass.

"So you're saying you can't get it up now?" Katie giggled and took a sip. "You know Kole, I feel a little bad for literally forcing you into a situation where you'd have a hard time saying no to me. Most men would catch on and never see me again."

"Well, I didn't really mind. Honestly you are quite attractive, scar and all...a total badass in my opinion." Kole looked her over. She looked older under the dim light coming from the bedroom lamp. The scar looked deeper. She was definitely putting on a facade outside of the safe zone of her dwelling.

"Funny that you say that...most men...well, there's a lot of competition on the base. Lots of cute ladies making dresses and stuff, talking about marriage, kids, God only knows what they are all thinking...I mean, what future do we fucking have in here..." She looked at Kole's eyes. "I mean, we don't even have makeup! Everything is improvised in the beauty department, and I just don't have the time between duties and my nursing studies to doll up for men who only want a slut for a night."

"Why do I get the feeling there's a broken heart story here?" Kole grabbed one of her hands. "I'm no saint either, you know. Not trying to defend all the dudes on this base that made you feel like shit, and Buso comes to mind here, but that's how men are in general."

"Well, at least you came back, and with the promised booze, so points for that. With men like you around, there's still hope!" They both laughed. She downed her entire glass and motioned for a refill. Kole obliged.

"I won't bore you to death with my girl problems. You are probably interested in the events that came up some twenty years ago, which your pal Peter was here for." Kole closed his eyes for a second and opened them. He downed his glass as well and poured himself another. The booze was kicking in fast.

"Buso sure makes a mean drink. Didn't realize this is one is so damn strong." Kole said overlooking the bottle.

"He probably figured you were trying to get laid tonight. That jerk-off spends way too much time either screwing the pretty ones or making more booze. Can't hate the man though, he's a pretty good dad, with seven kids so far. Makes me a bit jealous." Katie had her glass in the air, she was staring at it coldly.

"Seven?! He mentioned something, but never the actual number." Kole smiled. "How does he manage?"

"He was born with endless energy, I guess...never looked my way, though...but hey, a girl can dream, huh?"

"I can ask him, if you want...an introduction, at least." Kole had to be careful.

"Oh, hell no, Kole! I'll pass! I don't need Buso to do me any favours. Even if I don't get laid ever again, I will be fine knowing I already had the best of the best, even if it was for a few minutes." she gave him a wink. Kole was tired, and he had to get up early. But Pete wasn't talking, and Kole's curiosity had the better of him.

"Alright, forget I said anything then." said Kole in defeat. "So, yeah...twenty years ago...or, maybe this isn't the right time...?"

"Okay, sugar...you want the info? It's gonna cost ya. Right this way." Katie got up and walked to her measly bed and took off her pants but kept her underwear on. She then got under the blanket.

Azulus Ascends

"Wait...what...again?!" said Kole in protest. "Maybe I better go..."

"Kole, I sleep alone every night...I...I lost my parents twenty years ago and have been alone ever since. Please. I just want to have another human being by my side just to see how it feels again...please stay...I promise, I will tell you everything, including how I got this scar." reasoned Katie. Kole sat at the table. There was a minute of silence.

"Look, if you're gonna leave, there's an auto lock, so just..." she started.

"I think I understand you Katie...look, this isn't easy. I just lost my wife a few days ago. What happened at the armoury was a spur of the moment...it was wild, and I think we both needed it. And now you're asking me something that's rather intimate after knowing someone for a few minutes." Kole was firm. Katie got up and walked over to the table and hugged him. Her breasts pressed firmly into his face through the thin fabric of her nighty.

"I'm sorry about your wife, I didn't know." she said. "Is that why you want to end the Overseers?"

"Yes, it was them who killed her. She was a Synthetic just so you know, but no less human than the rest of us." Katie didn't budge on her hug, keeping him close. It seemed there was no way out of this. She wasn't planning to let him go.

"Katie, this is getting weird...why don't we call it a night?" Katie said nothing, adjusted herself, and sat on top of him.

"Kole, this is a one-time ask. No sex involved this round. I just want someone to hold me for longer than a few minutes. After this I will never bother you again, I promise. Please give me this, I'm begging you to stay." Katie was bringing herself so low that saying no to her was becoming nearly impossible.

340

"If you're worried about that girl...I didn't say a word, and I never will..." Kole took a deep breath. He understood Katie. She was a lonely soul. He figured she would try to bed him again but wasn't quite expecting this.

"Damn, Pete...this is his fault...if he only told me instead of hiding shit all the time. Is there a shower?" asked Kole. Katie's face suddenly lit up like a spotlight.

"Wait...seriously? You'll stay?!" Katie sounded very surprised.

"Yes, but you better start talking, lady...otherwise, no deal." Katie pointed to the wall where a door opened into a small bathroom with a tiny shower stall. Kole took his clothes off and lingered in a hot shower. It felt nice. He didn't want to tell Katie, but he kind of needed human contact right now too. Just sharing a bed with another human being was interestingly different than from sleeping alone all time. Synthetics didn't sleep. Kaita always opted to pretend to sleep but she would do it in her favourite chair. In reality, Kaita was shopping, watching movies, and reading all at the same time while Kole slept away. Pikii was the first real human girl Kole was with in a bed. It felt good on a human level. Kole didn't have anything else to wear, but Katie hung something on the shower door.

"Those are clean pants, and they're men's. I like wearing loose fit pants for training, so should sort of fit you." she said proudly. In reality, it was hard to get proper female anything at the base. Women had to make do with what they could around here.

"Thanks, my stuff stinks. I'm gonna use your washer, if that's okay." said Kole as he looked above the door and got the silent head nod from Katie. He dumped his dirty wear into the little laundry machine, rinsed his mouth, and came over to the bed. Katie had already put her pants back on. *Yes, I'm safe! For now,*

341

at least! Thought Kole to himself. Katie snuggled her way close to him and put her head on his right shoulder.

"You're really staying...this is nice...thank you, I don't get this kind of treatment, usually...like, ever..." She held on to him tight.

"Wait, are you saying you've been sleeping alone...since..." Kole fell silent as she put a finger to his mouth.

"Shhh...I will tell you everything. That was the deal. You held up your end. I will hold up mine." she said. Kole turned his head and was at full attention. Katie described it all in vivid detail.

Twenty years ago, the Overseers had a secret weapons development facility at the base. Everything from fighter jets to stealth technology, and more importantly, combat machines powered by AI. There were hundreds of loyal Overseer personnel, mostly engineers, at the base. Work went on twenty-four hours a day, year-round. However, on a cold winter day in December, an exercise that was scheduled for coordinated prototype battle units, went to complete hell. Fifty fully armed machines not only massacred the soldiers with them on the training run but returned to base and caused massive damage. Katie's parents were napalmed alive by one of the rogue machines in front of her very eyes. Katie was four years old at the time. She herself was barely saved by another soldier. The man paid the price for her, and later died from his injuries. Katie got away with only a scar, which even after surgery defined her look for the rest of her life.

In one day, the base lost nearly one-third of its entire combat force. Anna was just a teenager at the time and was still in training. If she had been just a little older, she would likely have been deployed and killed. The younger soldiers who hadn't seen any action were the ones with the highest casualty rate. Kole

342

noted in his head how few people here were around Amy's age. The worst part is that the Overseers were trying to pin the blame on the base and its soldiers. A revolt was about to happen. A Commander named Peter Fabius was at the front of it. He led units that had destroyed most of the Overseer machines in a coordinated effort. After the three remaining machines were about to be destroyed, the Overseer engineers finally got them under control. Peter was furious and wanted to finish them off, yet he was stopped at gunpoint from the very loyal Overseer security forces, which until that point sat on the sidelines. The Overseer security forces had weapons powerful enough to stop the onslaught all along.

The Overseers, as it turned out, were trying to not harm their own machines, and ordered their security forces to stand down. The Flashpoint Base soldiers were infuriated. The stage was set to explode into an all-out war right on the base. But Peter Fabius didn't want a war. There were families at the base, many with children. Going to war with the Overseers would be futile and end them all.

But Peter didn't have the answers on how to resolve the fine detail of maintaining peace. It was at that moment, which many speculate was initiated by Peter, that General Cinide stepped in and took control of the situation. The man commanded respect and prompted the soldiers to restrain their anger. Overseer scientists, personnel, and agents were immediately booted from the base. The general then made an ultimatum to the Overseers. The base would run on its own without any Overseer control. In return, the base would hand over all the technology that was left over and would maintain its forces for when the Overseers needed them at the front lines.

Peter Fabius, who became known to everyone at the base as a hero, was promoted and sent off to the Overseer front lines to train soldiers there. He was never seen or heard from again. Katie learned all this from Amy. Pete saved her and and she fell for him instantly. But after their short fling, he was sent away. It devastated her. After multiple inquires to his whereabouts, she was told to stop asking by the newly promoted Admiral Cinide.

"Alive or dead, Peter isn't coming back, so stop asking is what she was told. Can you imagine that? Someone you fall in love with, is then whisked away and you can't even ask questions? I feel for her. I think we all lost some humanity after that accident. Or so they call it that. Now that we know that there were never any so called 'front lines' and the city people were enjoying their happy lives...dammit, life is unfair, Kole, so freaking unfair! At least, her patience paid off. Amy got Peter back now. But what about me? I have no one. I have nothing. Happiness for me is a dream that I can never catch, it seems." Kole was barely awake, but the story was incredibly interesting. Katie was still cuddled up to him. Her feet were cold. She was like a broken little angel with her wings cut off at an early age. Losing her parents and living alone for two decades was a legitimate textbook sob story.

"Katie, you're not alone right now, are you?" asked Kole.

"I guess...but after you leave, I..." she started.

"No, Katie." said Kole firmly. "As long as I'm breathing you'll never be alone again. Understand? Once this Overseer mess is dealt with, you'll have a place close to mine. I'll introduce you to some normal people...although, having said that...mostly all I can introduce you to is Synthetic women." said Kole. Katie laughed and shed a tear doing so.

"Geez Kole, you think I'm into girls, huh? As long as they are friendly...and please, introduce me to a man who isn't afraid of the scar on my face. Please." It was more of an order than a request. Kole nodded.

"We'll find someone for you, even if we have to make him for you." said Kole while yawning.

"So, it is true! You can have your perfect soulmate made-to-order?!" Katie heard about this, but she still could not believe it.

"Yep, you totally can." Kole closed his eyes. A few seconds later he was out. Katie looked him over and whispered to herself.

"Then, Kole, I want someone like you." She then adjusted her position so she could sleep better but keep body contact with Kole. She quickly fell asleep.

12

Visitor

Ricco rested on his knees in the great hall of the Overseers. Silence was bliss. Meditation was key, even if his knees and joins hurt like hell. His breathing was slow, steady, controlled. His life was also slow, steady, and in complete and utter control. Just a few more weeks, and the transition to a god-like form would be finalized. He would become immortal. But not like in the sci-fi fairy tales he read as a kid. No, this was the real deal. His promise to himself and the Overseers would be fulfilled.

As for Admiral Cinide, giving the fool the impression of immortality was enough to control him. Enough to betray his own people and even kill his own daughter. This was also the reason why Ricco found human beings so disgusting. They were so easy to manipulate. Almost too easy. Admiral Cinide was out of contact for now. But he didn't care, the fool could drown in the ocean or get eaten by a mutant whale. He served his purpose. The surgery was done, and the information they got about the upgraded implants was softening his irritation over acquiring Module 717, bringing them closer to completion.

Today's meditation was necessary for him to not get too excited, or too frustrated. Ricco was itching to get rid of his body, and everyone else's. The humans and synthetics were a constant risk factor, volatile and frequently unreliable, even when manipulated. But Ricco was a very patient man. Success depended on it. The transition procedure had to be completed first. Once he was sure, the orders would go out. From the ashes of the humans, a new race was going to be born. A race unlike anything anyone could imagine.

Kole! Nothing but a disposable grunt! How is that man still alive? And where is he!? The failure to kill the man sent fear through the spineless Overseers, and military command. Even if Ricco put together another strike force, that could end up causing more uproar than it was worth. The situation was not going as well as he had planned originally. However, with so many insurance policies, it would be hard to fail.

Soon...humans will all die... Ricco longed for this. The thought of it brought joy to his heavy heart. He almost smiled. Yet, his eyes wandered, something was bothering him. Sweat ran down from his eyebrows to his own surprise. A sense of fear suddenly emerged. Someone was watching him.

Here, of all places? He felt it with almost complete certainty. Ricco hated human emotions that showed weakness and condemned them with a passion. He could not wait to leave the mass of meat, bone, and fluids that was his body.

As a regular human, Ricco had to consume food, take shits on the toilet, enjoy headaches, or fall ill to flu strains that still plagued humans to this very day. Ricco could only justify his actions more when he thought about these things. Ricco then noticed something odd. His eyes, not his super advanced sensors and scanners built into his implant, noticed a little black bird sitting some fifteen meters away on a ledge in a dark corner of the chamber's ceiling. It was barely visible, but was watching him intensely, as if it was reading his mind. Ricco's heart skipped a beat.

A real bird? It's a crow...how? It didn't make sense. There's just no way a crow could ever get in here. Cities were free from wildlife of any sort to prevent diseases being spread.

How many did I eradicate for my own plans? Ricco didn't think that consciously, yet he did subconsciously.

Who is this in my... Ricco's thoughts did not finish as the crow flew off the ledge, heading towards the central doors. Ricco was around long enough to see real birds fly, so he instantly noticed the speed, angle, and the air volume was off. His sensors then fed him info. Processing was an issue as he was older and still very human, but the implant readouts were off the charts.

The crow spat something on the door, a sort of yellow gel, and then in a miraculous change of direction, it shot upwards, and then flipped one hundred eighty degrees and headed straight for Ricco. The wingspan air displacement was some thirty-two times that of a matching physical specimen. Ricco knew at this point that he was dealing with an *it* and suddenly realized he was in trouble. Ricco's auto-alert system fired up, notifying the guards of danger in a fraction of a second, upon which the bird's wings extended with thin, meter long blades as it closed in.

Ricco was dumbfounded, but his combat reflexes made him pull his gun with his right hand and empty three rounds into the creature, and yet it was still on course as the bullets literally bounced off it like pebbles. Ricco's automated shield unit activated at the last millisecond. In a gut feeling, Ricco attempted at moving, initiating a jump sideways to his left.

A human reaction of fear, how pathetic! Came another thought that Ricco was not consciously thinking to himself. Ricco's left hand went up in a high block. His jump was too slow for the speed at which everything was happening. He still had rounds left to empty and his right hand was desperately tracking with gun in hand. Then, the crow sliced through the shield like it was a piece of paper. Ricco watched in slow motion horror as his outstretched arms got caught in that slice, both of them coming off at a point just two inches from his elbows. Before Ricco's severed limbs could hit the floor, the doors burst open and Ricco's personal Synthetic elite guard units piled in, shooting the creature away from Ricco and into a wall. His hands dropped to the floor with a loud thud. Blood poured out of his arms.

Astounding pain, shock, and blurry vision overcame Ricco. But the creature was not dead. It portrayed itself like some deadly phantom, and in a ballet of speed and precision it disabled two guards with metallic needles it spat out. It then sliced up the three guards trying to get close to it. Ricco was already being dragged out of the room. The last thing he saw was the creature darting back to the door, where a now conveniently formed hole allowed for an easy escape. It was the escape route it made for itself right before it attacked. Ricco then passed out as painkillers were administered.

* * * *

Ricco...Ricco, wake up! Ricco woke up. Sort of. In his mind, the head Overseers were already standing around him conversing, and Synthetic doctors were busy working on his arm re-attachment process in one their state-of-the-art medical facilities.

Everything is going to be fine now. But that was close... Ricco thought to himself.

"Jesus! Ricco! Please tell us you know what the hell is going on!" Ricco knew that voice. It was Sam's voice. His best friend sounded very concerned. Ricco finally opened his eyes. He was in a very small room. He could not recognize it. Surrounding him were holograms of Overseers Sam, Kyle, and Milta. Nobody else was present.

"Wha...where...am I?" Nobody answered Ricco. Their faces showed signs of despair, however. Ricco tried to look around but realized he could only move his eyes. Finally, it dawned on him that he was in fact behind glass in a tube.

"Wait...no...what happened...I cannot feel anything below my head!" He yelled out angrily. "What have you done to me!?" A terrifying squeal came out of him, but his eyes could not even produce tears. Milta finally spoke.

"Guards froze your whole body the split-second they pulled you out of the chamber. Nanite poisoning...very advanced nanites, very potent stuff, nothing like we've seen before..." Ricco was suddenly speechless.

"Your arms and body...ah, were...disintegrated. Luckily the nanites didn't get to your head...otherwise, you'd be dead. Right now, you're in a body simulator. It will keep you alive until your new body is ready for you to transition to. At least that's the plan for now." Milta then fell silent. She had to give Ricco some time to process this information.

Ricco started feeling the pain in his head. He now knew where he was. He was in a testing chamber for the transition procedure, far away from the cities in his massive secret lab facilities. The body simulator could prolong the life of someone with a failing body by connecting the head to a fully artificial unit, but the survival rate and time extension was low, until Admiral Cinide's success.

"Your Synthetic guards had to be destroyed as well. Apparently, this new nanite virus works on both humans and Synthetics." Said Kyle. "Also, we still haven't heard from Admiral Cinide…so, even though the initial results indicated that he should be able to survive for almost a month, maybe there's a problem we haven't factored in…"

Ricco could not help but panic. With no body, he was as good as dead. Time was no longer a luxury he had. Not to mention, whatever it was that came after him, could likely come back. Sam knew Ricco well and could almost read his mind just from the looks on his face.

"You're secure, Ricco. Nobody's getting in that chamber, you can be certain of that. We also took some measures on our side, as well. City 77 is under lockdown. Guards and sentries have been more than doubled. City guns are on high alert. Nothing will get through this time." said Sam with some confidence. "And don't let Kyle get to you. Our original analysis shows that you should be able to survive even longer than Admiral Cinide. There's plenty of reasons why we might not be hearing from him…"

Milta wasn't as confident. "Well, in any case, that wraps that up, next order of business, folks. Do we terminate the general population now, or do we wait?" Clearly, this decision was on

Ricco's shoulders. Everyone was staring at him impatiently. He was still the head Overseer, regardless of what state he was in. But Ricco was not so sure now. Killing off the humans seemed like a low priority. All he wanted now was to get back into a body. Milta noticed the hesitation in Ricco and took advantage of it.

"Ricco, we are also considering accelerating the transition procedures. We already voted to move up...we just need you to give the final word..." she said in a low tone. Ricco was surprised she was that desperate to get him transitioned. He felt he had to be careful. She could and would take control, given the chance.

"Milta, hold on...first of all, how much time has passed since I...since I lost my body?" Ricco needed to know this. He wanted to kick himself for not asking sooner.

"Tell him..." said Sam quietly. Milta shifted her position. Clearly, she was not comfortable delivering the news.

"Oh dear, oh dear..." Milta said with a worried face. "Fifty-two hours."

"And during all this time, we have heard nothing from the Admiral?"

"No." said Sam.

"There has been no abnormal activity at Flashpoint Base. It seems like the bees are sitting quietly in their hive." Kyle added. Ricco was not sure what facial expression his own face was making, but surely it was not a pretty one.

"Of course, they are. But we can assume that this silence means the admiral has either betrayed us or died from the procedure." Ricco managed, but his voice was hoarse and breaking up.

"Perhaps the base has discovered our plans, somehow..." Milta pondered out loud. "And, just in case...maybe we should send the additional strike troops on top of the support we provided to the admiral?"

"Don't be stupid! Underwater support machines aren't a full out assault, do that and that base will absolutely revolt!" Ricco fired back at Milta mainly, with an angry tone. He didn't like when she tried to make decisions on his behalf.

Sam stepped in. "We're also very worried about that thing that attacked you. Those human rats in that backwater base could not possibly make a weapon like that." he said.

"Of course not, you idiot!" shouted Ricco. Sam was not ready for an angry response, and just lowered his head. Ricco continued. "That place could be crawling with the thing that took my body away from me, that thing..." Ricco wanted to cough, but some fluid came out of his mouth instead. Tubes were supplying everything to his head. It was a weird and disgusting feeling. He wanted to vomit but couldn't.

"You do bring up a good point, Ricco...we also lost contact with the amphibious forces we gave Admiral Cinide. Sending a strike force to takedown Flashpoint Base now would require us to leave our city defences light. We could be attacked from within, ourselves..." Sam was catching on. Ricco was always proud of him, even if he sometimes found him exasperating.

"Milta, how long..." Ricco stumbled again. "How long for the new bodies for the transition procedure, in the updated...accelerated schedule?" He finally managed, but it was clearly labored. Milta brought up a display so that Ricco could see it. It showed some meaningless graphs. Ricco hated graphs. He just wanted results.

"Well, as you can see, although the Synthetic scientists demanded six more weeks, we executed the head of the project in front of them, and the new updated time frame is now just one week."

"What? From six weeks to one week?" Ricco was puzzled. Sam stepped in.

"Yes, seems we were being stalled. Another Synthetic confessed to us at gunpoint that the lead scientist did certain tests over and over, deliberately delaying the overall goal. We placed additional combat sentries and human personnel to monitor their progress more closely."

"Sam, what else went on?" Ricco asked.

"Well friend, it gets worse. An underground poll we managed to carry out shows that eighty-five percent of the Synthetic population no longer approves of our leadership. What's scary is that they seem to like the humans, overall. The conclusion is this. The Synthetics don't want to replace humans but live alongside them, or some horse shit like that." said Sam with disgust in his voice. Ricco's head hurt even more now. Milta moved closer through her hologram screen, although she didn't need to. It's not like Ricco couldn't see her ugly face fine enough already.

"Ricco," she said in nervous tone, "with the new bodies, we will be able to enforce total control over the entire Synthetic population, correct?" She was clearly delusional. Ricco had no intention of giving Milta control over anything. He planned to thin out the Overseer ranks a little bit as well, starting with her.

"Yes, of course Milta. But now's not the..." Ricco's head was killing him with pain, but he had to get through this.

"Never mind that! Have any of you figured out what that thing was, for starters?" All he got was blank faces.

"Scouts all came back negative, Ricco...but no attacks since. Listen, everyone is scared shitless..." said Sam.

"Guys, come on! Re-send the scouts! Increase security where possible! Recall all strike units out on assignments! Enforce around-the-clock patrols! Nothing, nothing should be coming in and out of anywhere without you three knowing about it! And about the other cities..." Ricco felt he was blanking out but managed to hold on.

"Nothing of the sort was detected in the other cities. Now, are you sure we don't want to start with the population removal? We could begin with the smaller cities." Milta said coldly. "If you give me your full authority..."

"Nothing moves forward without me back in a usable body, period. Are we clear, Milta? I need to hear it!" demanded Ricco.

"Right...clear as crystal, Ricco." said a disappointed Milta. Her eyes wandered off from his stern gaze. The others looked at her with scorn. Sam and Kyle were not in the mood for this seemingly obvious power-grab attempt. Ricco was not going to tolerate her for much longer. *Just one more week Milta, then you can rest eternally in the ground.*

"Good. No more time-wasting, find out what the fuck was trying to kill me..." Ricco suddenly got overwhelmed with dizziness.

"Ricco? Ricco! Ricco..." is all Ricco heard as he finally fell into an abyss of darkness.

13

Resolutions

"All is quiet, so far. City 77 is still under complete lockdown. The other cities remain on high-alert status. No change in military deployments aside from the huge increases in security two days ago." Pikii reported.

"Even Module 717 doesn't want to poke in. With this increase in monitoring, they might detect the hacking attempts, so we'll have to tread carefully." said Kole. He had wrestled with Anna, Pikii, and the AI in the war room for two days now, and they were still all gridlocked as to what was happening to City 77. They were getting nowhere fast. There were too many unanswered questions. Was someone leaking information, or was something going on completely out of their control? Anna was pacing, and the people in the room were tired out. Kole had something to add.

"At this point we can assume that whatever happened was more than just serious, but more likely catastrophic. I have never seen an Overseer city go into full lockdown for over forty-eight hours, actively run power to its main guns, and double or triple forces in all key control points." he said. Flashpoint Base was on lockdown as well, albeit a silent one, just in case the Overseers decided to initiate an attack. Module 717 had a theory too. One that Kole had heard repeated and discussed in his head too many times to count. The cat which attacked Kole in the submarine was very likely an offspring of the Synthetic scientists working on the transition project for the Overseers. They codenamed this creature and any others like it as '*Phasa.*' Whether they developed Phasa intentionally to kill the Overseers or all of humanity, remained to be seen. But if the Synthetic scientists and Phasa were on their side, it could explain some of the anomalies Kole experienced in avoiding certain death. And it made sense for Phasa to be modelled after smaller animals. Most animals were smaller and more athletic than humans, which made infiltration easier.

When Kole and Module 717 were not in the war room, they seemingly lived in each other's conversations. Their work was slower than expected. The weapon prototyping machines at the base were dated. This stalled them when trying to create a replicated version of the mysterious weapon they were gifted. The main problem was the ammo for the charges and the cartridge size. Luckily, with help from the top weapon specialists at the base, they did find enough of the right alloy to prototype three versions, adding significantly to the original. The latest, and last iteration was their masterpiece. It had a custom cartridge loader for nine bolt shots instead of two, and various other upgrades. They also managed to make four packs of ammo for it.

Kole could not wait to try the new weapon out in combat. His new combat vest had all the storage needed to safely carry the ammo. Katie made it just for him. A friend like her was good to have, and not just because the woman had many talents. Kole could easily access the ammo by either hand by just reaching behind his back, with each side housing two cartridges.

"I believe we should make a move within a day. Due to the additional day of delay required to secure the water treatment plants, at least we will be on top of things before something bad happens, where we might get forced into an immediate response situation." said General Honde. Anna seemed to agree.

"General Honde is right. If Kole is ready with his prep and weapons, we should put our plans into motion sooner rather than later." Kole got the look from Anna, and he knew he'd better have his shit ready. He nodded. Anna seemed to have a sign of relief on her face.

"Well then, looks like Kole is ready. Let's all recap our objectives one more time and get this ship sailing!" She finally sounded excited. The room had everyone they needed. General Kanos stood with Anna. General Honde remained seated. Pete was next to him. Kole was sitting too, with Pikii at his side. He felt her warmth as her thigh gently brushed his. It was a pleasant feeling. She was warm. Sergeant Higini was on the other side next to Pikii, as well. Kole almost looked over to ensure his thigh was not touching Pikii's.

[Don't be jealous, focus on the mission.]

Damn you!

[Now, now, you forgot all about the blonde in the armoury already? All you have been thinking about lately has been Pikii...]

Don't make me come up there, I will mess you the #%$ up!*

[Wow, you're stupidly complicated, aren't you...?]

"Alright!" Kanos boomed. Kole and Module 717 went to full attention.

"First component of our strategy is to deploy our air squadrons." Kanos coughed a bit, shifted his body weight a little, and continued. "This is to take advantage of the Overseer lockdown and split their forces between guarding the city and dealing with us. Now, even though it may be risky, we will launch our one and only air Destroyer, the D4 Alice, to try to force the Overseer forces out of City 77, away far enough to be out of range of their laser batteries." Everyone nodded, and Kanos continued.

"Second component. The main control tower will be elevated to the surface, with the rest of the combat infrastructure. Anna and I will take up command along with other senior officers. We will have eyes on the entire battlefield. Module 717 provided a partial copy of itself to stay on our mainframe computer to help us to decipher Overseer transmissions. Any questions, so far?"

Nobody had anything to say. Kole could not blame them. Everyone was wracking their brains for days and they all needed sleep like Kole needed the warm touch of Pikii. Her thigh was still touching his. The feeling of warmth engulfed him further.

"Third component. While we fight the Overseer air forces, the water treatment plant operation will be under way to secure all four facilities. Our cloaked helicopters will converge and drop off strike teams simultaneously. We need to take over the plants silently under all the commotion, remove the drugs, and hold those plants for twenty-four hours. We'll re-route all communications with a transmission intercept system so we can control anything going in and out. We will issue replies directly from here with Module 717's help." Kanos had a drink of water from a conveniently placed bottle and cleared his throat.

"Fourth component begins once the twenty-four hours are up. Module 717 will hack into the satellites and initiate a playback of the memory recording of the death of Kole's wife, where Overseer James was involved, complete with the recovered visual…"

Kole felt the warmth leaving him. Pikii fidgeted in her seat and managed to make space between them. Was this really the time to be thinking about her? Kole almost gave his head a shake. Kaita's death was still fresh on his shoulders. But in a weird twist of fate, he felt Pikii's hand on his knee. He wasn't sure what that was. Pity for him? Some sort of comforting gesture?

"And in this message is a trojan horse to help the Synthetics. Module 717 devised a clever way that will allow the Synthetics to disconnect from the Overseer network by showing them how to reprogram themselves in mere seconds during the broadcast. We will then broadcast the Overseer plans to everyone. We are under the assumption here that both the humans and the Synthetics will take to the streets and Overseers will have no control of them. This will most likely cause the Overseers to deploy nearly all of their forces just for crowd control."

Kole put his hand on Pikii's. She turned her hand over upside down and grabbed hold of his. Kole felt warmth. No, more than that. He felt power. Power surged through his veins like an ignited fire. It was short-lived though. Just the initial reaction of her touch.

[Sometimes, you're really lame…]

"Fifth component. Ground forces advance and move in to secure the cities. We then arrest the Overseers, locate the labs, and destroy whatever godlike bodies they are trying to create."

"What about the Phasa or the scientists who were working on this research? What do we do with them?" asked General Honde.

"Kole? Mind answering that?" was Kanos' reply. Kole was a little uncomfortable, but he had to face it.

"For Phasa encounters, we have updated scanners that can detect them within sixty meters. That's not much range, but it will have to do. If any unit comes across Phasa, you are not to engage. Contact the control tower instead for further instructions. Now, about the scientists. They are not to be harmed. This is one of the conditions Module 717 has asked us to agree to. Their knowledge will be a gold mine of information. Module 717 will negotiate with them." There were some whispers in the room.

"This isn't school, if you got something to say, come out and say it now. We don't need surprises." stated Anna. General Honde stood up.

"But such minds, should they really be just allowed to go back to the general population? What if they create more of those Phasa things?" he asked in a firm, military tone.

"That is a very good point General Honde. Module 717 will negotiate with them, and we'll all agree to the terms once they are established. We expect them to co-operate for the greater good of both of our races." answered Kole.

"So, who will be in charge once the Overseers are overthrown?" asked Buso. Kanos stepped in.

"What happens after we take over, is going to be decided by the people, both human and Synthetics, and us as well, seeing as we are risking our lives for it all. It will take months, or even years before we figure out what's the best way of living and keeping respect, law, and order. But we're not going to repeat the crooked pyramid system of top-down control. That, we all can agree on. Unfit people given too much power go rotten. During Letumfall, that crucial time...the bonehead politicians proved to be truly useless. More than ten billion people perished. And yet, even that was not enough for those in power. Clearly, the ways of the old world did not work." There was silence in the room. It was sort of an unspoken rule not to discuss Letumfall. But it was time to break all the rules. Time to stop the ingrained fear. Anna took a step forward.

"Ok, listen up men! Ready your divisions. I want all air and ground units prepped for combat readiness in sixteen hours! We'll then proceed from there. Now, let's kick some ass!" she commanded.

Kole looked on as the generals dispersed and mused to himself. *Now here's top-down control that works!* He refused to let go of Pikii's hand. They walked out of the war room holding hands. She leaned over to his ear.

"Anna gave me my own private quarters...do you want to rest with me there for a bit?" she said quietly to him. Kole was bloody tired. Between Module 717's constant barrage of requests, to working tirelessly on the new weapon system, to the war room meetings, to the endless trips to the coffee machine, it was all just getting too much again. Module 717 fell silent. Kole thanked him in his mind. Pikii led the way, and Kole, like a little boy, followed suit.

* * * *

Anna was left alone in the war room. The last few days had been long, and it was taking a toll on her, too. She needed to get some sleep. She left for her quarters, hoping she would not run into anyone. Her eyes were watering. And soon, the tears were flowing like rivers. Thoughts about her childhood flooded in. They were all here at this base. She had nothing else. But she didn't want to die here.

I just want a nice place to live in the city. Some decent goddamned food, and some actual clothes! Am I asking too much? As she entered her quarters, and the door sealed shut, she opened a bottle of booze. A few minutes later, there was a knock on her door. She opened it. It was Buso. He held a bottle of something special and two glasses.

"So uhhh, remember you told me to, like, wait a few days? Well, I did. Wanna finally get it on?" he said with a funny grin on his face.

"Oh, fuck it! Get in here, lover boy!" she said as she pulled him in by his collar.

* * * *

Pikii's new place was quite large and cozy. She seemed quite happy with it. There was a small kitchen, a full bathroom with a bath, and a bedroom to boot.

"Well, what do you think?" Pikii was all hyped up. She never had her own place to live because of the line of work that she was forced into. Even though this was temporary, it was still better than having to share rooms with someone.

Kole was impressed.

"Love it!" He said, casually eyeing her figure.

[Perv...ert...]

Sorry, would you mind? Seriously...can't you go process something like...I dunno, calculate pi to a billion decimals...?

[I'd melt your brain long before getting there. Fine, I will preoccupy myself with something else...]

Pikii was much more cheerful than Kole expected. They just stood there staring at each other. Pikii made the first move.

"So, I snagged some of the latest booze from the Buso wine labs...wanna give it a shot?" Kole moved over closer as he laughed at her comment.

"Buso wine labs? Sure, what did you get?" Her cheeks blushed. She nearly dropped the digital pad she was carrying.

"Uhhh... I think it's some sort of home-brew beer of his...he promised that it was really good...but, not too strong, so there would be no hangover..." She went to get it. Kole's mind on the other hand seemed very busy suddenly. Module 717 did in fact have the audacity to start running programs in the background. Kole could feel his brain starting to heat up a little.

Hey, partner, what the hell you working on?

[Oh, nothing much, just going over some plans, you know, having a drink, thinking about life, reviewing our attack strategies, so, like, you know...so we DON'T DIE!!!]

Ah, well, okay...you do that, then. Pikii came from the kitchen holding two cups. Kole's mind was not on the booze, however.

Pikii had changed. She was wearing a white nightgown, a rather revealing one. Kole nearly choked on his own saliva.

"Uhhh, I hate to ask, but my throat is kind of dry...do you have any water?" Kole was embarrassed, he drank way too much coffee and became stupidly dehydrated. Pikii put down the glasses at the coffee table near the couch and came back with another glass and a jug of water.

"Here you go. By the way, I'm actually kind of curious, how did it go at the weapons lab? It seems you and your friend have actually got something neat and unique built..." Kole thought she was making small talk, but she was dead serious. Her eyes didn't lie. This girl loved weapons. Kole poured a full glass of water for himself and downed it in seconds.

"Well, actually we wound up making something really cool. We took apart the original version and rebuilt it three times into something even better. Although Module 717 did most of the work, really..." Kole sat down on the couch. Pikii handed him a glass of beer and sat down next to him. She was very warm and beautiful. A stark contrast to her killer soldier past. Kole felt her body brushing up against his. It was exhilarating. He wasn't sure why. Yet this feeling, it was like he was near a girl for the first time. It was weird. He was actually nervous.

Kole began to explain. The original weapon itself was a highly complex liquid metal energy device with a magnetic manipulation module. Updating it was a bitch. The latest version was longer and now had two modes; single blade and double blade. In the double blade mode, an updated control bracelet manipulated its rotation and distance even better than the original version. Kole could now send the thing flying through the air up to one hundred meters away at the speed of sound. Either side could pierce through solid steel. The liquid metal tips could also extend and contract nearly instantly adding a few feet of additional temporary range, if needed.

In addition, they added a distinct component on the upper half which was a liquid gravity ring that expanded out of the blade handle to create a wrist guard when used in single blade mode. The updated bottom half was adjusted to slide out of the way to reveal the bolt charges, which now held nine charges instead of two. They gave up some power per charge, but the charges could be fired all at once.

Once all nine were fired, the pack would exit much like an ammo magazine of a gun. Reload was a snap. Ammo was a problem however, with only four additional ammo cartridges. The requirements for the alloy were steep and in short supply at the base. In fact, they had used everything up already.

The energy from the bolt charges could also be redirected to the tip, to instead fire a lightning bolt style attack. Module 717 could target up to one hundred targets. But a shot like that would use up all bolt charges simultaneously. They were also unsure about the energy output, but it would be something along the lines of getting hit by lightning.

"And here's the best part, the thing can actually bend light, meaning lasers can't cut this thing which is something we learned the hard way..." Kole finally finished explaining. Pikii was even closer to him now, sipping her drink.

"So...like, Kole..." she said as she moved her left index finger along the lines of her glass. "When do you think you can show me all that extended action, loaded magazine, and the blast that comes out of the tip?" Kole nearly dropped his drink.

[Holy shit, Kole! You're getting laid...]

Shut the hell up! Turn yourself off or something, will you?

[Nahh, I think I will sing a song...let's see, what will be the most annoying during intercourse...how about 'Mary had a little lamb, fa la la la, fa la la la la la...']

Pretty please...?

[Fine. Later, loser!]

"Finally!" Kole yelled out by accident. Accept it was no accident. Module 717 made him do that on purpose.

"Finally? Kole, what do you mean...have you been thinking about me in naughty ways the entire time?" Pikii said giggling.

"Uhhh...not the entire time, but recently, yes..." he said quietly, hiding behind his glass. It was too late to make up excuses. He wanted her. He wasn't ashamed to admit it, anymore.

"Well tonight's your lucky night...I'm in the mood..." she said. "But there's one thing I need to tell you. I volunteered for the water treatment plan mission." Kole looked deep into her eyes. She wasn't the least bit concerned. No matter what, Pikii was a trained killer. He had to always remember that. There's no way she would be talked out of a mission she was interested in. She was stating a fact, not asking him for permission. Trying to babysit her would not win him any favours.

"I can tell by the look in your eyes, Kole, that you don't approve, but I'm going anyways, okay?" she said quietly.

"It's that obvious, huh? I won't try to stop you if your mind is made up." he said with confidence. "But are you sure you are okay with what we're about to do here?"

Pikii leaned over for a passionate kiss. Her lips were moist, warm, and inviting. Her tongue was long, and it slipped in past his defences and massaged his as she moved it around in ways he'd never felt before. Her saliva tasted fresh and sweet as they entangled in a prolonged exchange. That was her answer. She wanted him. She wasn't going to take no for an answer. Kole put down his glass and held her in his arms. She was strong, yet her frame felt fragile. She was dangerous, but also vulnerable. Kole wanted to make sure that whatever happened, they both enjoyed it. It would require every skill he knew on how to pleasure a woman. He had to impress her here. It was all or nothing.

Mister Module 717, I can feel you peeking, please turn yourself off fully, will ya?

[Fine...]

14

Vengeance

"All wings, launch and assume strike formations!" barked General Parker. It was a chilly, slightly cloudy morning. The air outside was as fresh as ever, with a slight hint of pine and salty wetness from some late-night rain. He went out earlier to get some of that goodness as he needed to calm the nerves, and that did the trick. A newfound energy has awakened inside of him, and he was ready for action.

The large grass fields were trimmed in the early morning by automated bots to allow the jets to take off safely. Their runways were disguised that way many years ago to make them difficult to spot. That is, of course, until the superstructures and control tower rose from the ground.

What Parker was about to do, he'd never done before. They were starting a war. People's lives were in his hands. Thousands of them. Module 717 and him had a bit of a chat the other day. Parker wanted to learn a little something from the world's most advanced artificial intelligence. Module 717 had lots of advice on how not to get cocky and go down in flames. Being a little afraid, was actually good. And Parker felt it. The fear. It was there, and it was normal. He could face it now. Face his past, present, and future. He took in a deep breath. His lungs ached just a little, and his throat was a little dry. He took a sip of warmed water from a hydration cylinder attached to his central console. He placed it back. The thing would auto refill and reheat. Parker then turned his attention to the bridge of the D4-Alice, the only airborne destroyer in the known world. At least, as far as their intelligence was able to confirm. If the Overseers already had machines like this, they would all become deep-fried fish a few minutes into the air battle.

General Bull finally stumbled onto the bridge, along with his afro hairdo. He hastily got into his seat and strapped himself in. Since this was an airship, everyone had to be tied down with special seats prior to takeoff.

"You're late, General Bull." Parker knew why the guy was late, he was doing his hair. General Bull made a frown at Parker. He was the type of man who stayed behind the shadows and preferred as little attention as possible.

They both went back a long way in their history. It was some twenty years ago when the incident occurred that caused the Overseers and Flashpoint Base to nearly start a war. In that incident, Parker's wife Mira, and daughter Kyra, perished. General Bull lost his only child, a son named Tyler. He was just five when the rogue machines lit him up. Right after they found out that the Overseers prioritized their own machines over their lives, Parker and Bull stole some of the Overseer technology. And while things eventually were ironed out, neither Parker nor Bull would let the pain go. Bull was more of an engineer than a soldier and helped Parker with technological development. That soon became their top priority. Parker took over ideas and

370

designs, while Bull always found solutions to the most ridiculous things that Parker thought of, including the D4-Alice and all her defensive and offensive systems.

When no one else thought it was a feasible idea, Bull was the one who made it happen. Eventually, Buso and Anna became aware and lent a hand by keeping upper brass like Admiral Cinide far away from their hangar bays. Then, they struck gold when Admiral Cinide was ordered by the Overseers to take a submarine and survey the entire world. In those few short years, assembling and completing their airborne destroyer was finally possible.

While Parker was collaborating with Anna and the team on their plans over the last few days, Bull spent that time getting D4-Alice to one-hundred percent readiness. This would be her first combat deployment. General Bull arranged the weaponry, energy cells used for the propulsion, a complete roster of crew, all supplies, and hundreds of other small details like engine tests and emergency drills. He looked gassed. Parker smiled. Bull looked back at him.

"Sorry for being late, General Parker. I was busy with you-know-what." he stated. Parker gave him a thumbs up.

"The hairdo looks great, General Bull." Smiles lit up on the bridge. Bull chose the crew well. They knew and trained most of these soldiers.

"Alright, let's fly people! Pilots, take us up!" Parker spoke loudly. His bridge crews rejoiced. A loud 'hurrah' boomed across the bridge and their internal air force communications channels. The ship started to roar as low rumbling vibrations increased, and the pitch of the engines spinning up overtook the senses of everyone onboard. The hangar gates moved aside, opening the exit to the skies directly above.

Once airborne, the D4-Alice could deploy a pulse shielding system that sent powerful electric charges through the outer hull, and it would repel nearly any air-to-air or ground-to-air weapon by vaporizing it before it could even make impact. The destroyer also packed an array of guns, and other impressive combat systems. Parker could not wait to try some of them out.

Higher pitched whines made themselves heard, and Alice began slowly lifting off the ground as two pilots guided her out of the hangar. One pilot was focused on guiding Alice through the air. The second pilot monitored external wind speed and ensured internal systems such as engine output were optimal. It was truly surreal. Parker felt almost alien.

If there is something else that Parker knew from experience, it was that power, no matter how it was attained, could also be taken away by force. Power in human history rarely relied on the ability to reason and negotiate for the greater good. Power came from the strength to conquer, the ability to foresee, the cunning to lie, and the will to manipulate. When a few days ago Anna put a bullet into her father's head, the news spread like wildfire across the base. She was no longer an admiral's little daughter. She became a leader. A leader who put the lives of her soldiers as a priority over everything else. The soldiers voted to grant Anna complete command, and she was unanimously promoted to full admiral rank.

Granted, it was Kole who was the key, and that AI in his brain was certainly a huge help to make them truly understand just how far the Overseers had gone down a path they could no longer tolerate. But even if Kole never made his emergency

372

broadcast, and never arrived at Flashpoint Base, Parker and Bull would have supported Anna to the end.

The D4-Alice was now above the entry gates. The engines switched gears, letting out an even louder boom and the ship then soared into the air. Parker observed as drones and jet fighters quickly took up formations around them. It was time to move out. After this, there would be no going back. Once the rabbit was out of the hole, that was it.

Parker whipped out a small photo of Mira and Kyra from his green military jacket and clipped it to his command console.

"All wings, report in!" he ordered.

"This is Red Raiders leader heading up the frontal attack. We're ready for battle!" announced Tessorra. She was in command of the Red Raiders, which were composed of eight squadrons of A7-Raider fighter jets. They were modified in-house over the years, turning them into their best air-to-air superiority fighters with a deadly combination of maneuverability and weapons systems.

These jets were equipped with customizable weapon pods; two below the body, and two above. The pods could be configured to fire forwards and backwards, with two weapon slots per pod. An independent control stick controlled their rotation within a specific degree range. Tessorra selected the same configuration for all, to keep consistency and avoid friendly fire:
- Top Pods Front: Rage 9 self-locking anti-air missiles
- Top Pod Rear Right: Flare 7x anti-missiles counter measures
- Top Pod Rear Left: Fractal G-micro anti-air missiles
- Bottom Pods Front: Panzer 3 Ultra railguns
- Bottom Pods Rear: Panzer 3 Ultra railguns

Each of the two slots per pod was marked red on both ends. The enemy would have no idea what came out of which end until it was too late. In addition to this, for longer range the A7-Raider fighters boasted precision railguns near the end of the wing tips. These only fired forwards and only came equipped with limited ammo for those rare sniper-like shots. A fresh mix of white and red paint over their entire A7-Raider fighter jet fleet, added to their menacing presence.

"This is Black Raven leader. We're armed and live!" reported Black Raven wing commander, Michael. Black Raven wing was composed of four squadrons of cloak-capable air-to-air and air-to-ground superiority fighters. These X86-Raven units were sleek, wing-like machines which had a dark grey hue to their paint for basic stealth. But in addition to that, these machines had cloaking technology that was a few steps ahead of your average stealth fighter jet. Developed in-house, these birds could vanish from the sky, literally. For weapons, the jets had internal missile bays that housed Vanguard 42x air-to-air missiles as well the high impact Doomsday B2X air-to-ground missiles. A single machine gun near the cockpit was the emergency weapon for those rare close-up encounters.

"This is Gold Dragon leader. We're ready to breathe fire and light things up from the back!" Kuro said with confidence. He commanded the four squadrons of their long-range air-to-ground strike jets. These S52-Dragon fighters would stay mostly in the back and deal with ground units like tanks. They were also the oldest units in the entire air fleet, dating back some sixty years. Their origin design came from the now ancient F-18 fighter jets. Their primary load-out was the Viper S6B long-range air-to-ground missiles. Just in case they were equipped

374

with four Fractal G-micro anti-air missiles and extra fuel to tanks to ensure they could bug out if needed in a hurry.

The rest of the current air power was composed mainly of drones. They were controlled from the Flashpoint Base Control Tower, but Parker had crews on Alice that could take over, if needed. Their long-range stealth helicopters were already on their way to drop off the water treatment plant strike teams. A few troop transports were on the ground loaded and ready for takeoff on short notice in case a ground army presence was needed anywhere.

As a last resort, at the back of the base, heavy bombers sat idling on the runway. They only had two of those. And Parker was hoping not to have to use them. The B-62s packed a huge punch even when not carrying a nuclear payload and would cause massive collateral damage. They were there only as a last resort.

"Alright, set course for City 77!" commanded Parker.

The D4-Alice then accelerated with force, and they were on their way. It was Module 717 who recommended to put everything into the air to make the Overseers piss their pants and cause an overreaction. They knew that most of the Overseer weaponry was ground based. Out here, away from the cities, Parker now ruled the skies.

"General Parker! Overseer command is demanding to know why we are mobilized and in the air!" called out Communications Officer Layla. She was a bit nervous. Parker could hear it in her tone. Her long blonde hair and gorgeous bust was more fit for a model rather than a communications officer. At least she was in the military garb she was supposed to be wearing. Bull picked a fine young lady. At age twenty-four,

Layla has been known around the base as a slacker and fashionista. She loved nothing more than to turn old military garb into cutesy dresses that would be the envy of just about every woman at the base. Parker laughed out loud. "Layla, why don't we just ignore them for now. Do what you do best...ignore your duties!"

Her face lit up. It was the first time Parker saw her actually enjoy being on duty.

"Aye aye, Capitan...err, I mean General!" Layla said playfully as she killed the communications channel to Overseer command. Parker's control pod shifted to combat mode. Everyone on the bridge had one of these. They were especially designed by Parker himself. If anything went bad, and the ship was destroyed, these pods closed up and ejected themselves from the bridge to safety.

Parker reviewed the formations. The console showed that the cloaked helicopters they sent out a few hours earlier were already coming up on top of the water treatment plants. In some twenty-four hours, the Overseers would be stripped of their power to control the human population in their cities. Parker rubbed his hands together, waiting for the Overseer air fleet to fall into his lap. Without the city guns, Parker's air fleet would turn them into scrap metal.

* * * *

"What the hell is going on, who ordered Flashpoint Base to deploy its air force? And since when did they have an air force like that to begin with?!" Sam was screaming at the other

Overseers. The Overseers all had puzzled looks on their holographic faces.

"Is Ricco awake, yet?" asked Kyle. His patience was wearing thin, as well. Sure, Ricco was their leader, but currently, he was a doped-up head on life support.

"Afraid not, he's still out." mumbled Milta. Her voice sounded nervous. And she was never nervous.

"Damn it, what poor timing!" Sam barked as he was sorting things out on the holographic view of Flashpoint Base. Old Ben piped up, too.

"Not one of us seems to know anything…we're going to have to decide without Ricco on what to do about this!" said Old Ben in a rare show of emotions. Sam knew they were all looking at the same data. This was not the air force that Flashpoint Base was supposed to have. If the readouts were correct, it meant that Flashpoint Base developed their own technology. The flying destroyer was a clear example of just how badly the Overseers miscalculated on leaving them alone for nearly two decades.

But Sam knew, as far as he hated to admit it, this was Ricco's miscalculation. Their fault was relying too much on Ricco. And they were about to pay for that mistake.

"We must cancel the lockdown, and all get to HQ immediately." Milta demanded. Protests from many Overseers came up fast.

"Everyone! Please! Milta is right. We must address this. Even if there's risk, we must personally gather in our headquarters at City 77. I don't want to hear excuses!" said Kyle with a harsh tone.

"Fine, let's assemble. But while we do, I recommend we launch an immediate counterattack! We must keep that air fleet away from the cities!" said Sam. He knew if they were taken over now, Ricco's dream, no matter how ludicrous it was, would be over.

"No! We still have time. We'll decide once we all assemble. Now get moving!" ordered Milta. Typically, Sam would protest, but nobody said anything, so he held his tongue. She was second in command, so it would be done her way. Everything blacked out. Sam would need to get to the transport immediately. He was by Ricco's side, right outside the chamber which held Ricco's leftovers. Sam placed a hand on the door. He felt like he wanted to vomit.

"Ricco, you were so close...my stupid old friend. I have to go now." Sam stormed out of the facility. He took the primary lift to a bay where a transport was already waiting for him. As he lifted away from the secret research labs and flew towards City 77, he pondered on what was in store for them all.

* * * *

Milta was pacing back and forth. *How much of this shit do I have to clean up?* Her thoughts were in disarray.

"You damned bastard!" She screamed out loud and violently kicked a nearby chair with her left leg. She then threw her pad across the Overseer headquarters hall in City 77. She still didn't understand what was really going on.

Over the next hour, one-by-one, the Overseers were arriving. She monitored the defence status. They had lots of tanks ready to roll towards Flashpoint Base, and their own air force was on standby. Still, she was baffled how Flashpoint Base had all this air power.

They were just supposed to be mainly a ground army for them to use when needed. 'Disposable grunts' is what Ricco called them often in meetings. Their forces were supposed to be mainly soldiers and troop transports. There were only a few squadrons of old jets at the base that were decades old by now from the military inventory registry, as noted on the pad she just threw.

Ricco, is this one of your additional back-up plans? To have spare air power?

"Idiot..." she whispered to herself. This assembly was needed because they rarely all sat in the same room. Making key decisions without Ricco present would not serve them well over holographic monitors. Meanwhile, Synthetic servants were bringing snacks and coffee to the tables. One had to have some nourishment in situations like this. Although, for Milta, coffee didn't seem like much of a solution to deal with a rogue airborne fleet.

"Milta!" It was Kyle, he stormed in and took his position at the table. The head Overseers had their roundtable at the front area, and the rest would be seated in theatre style seats that went all the way to the back. Between the two seating areas was the primary holographic projector system. It was already showing all the troop movements and data that they would need to review. Milta nodded back.

"Hi, Kyle." she said, as she sat next to him. Coffee was placed in front of them with some handy easy-to-eat snacks a moment later. Kyle didn't say much. He took a sip of coffee and took a bite into a tiny sandwich. He then scratched his bleached white hair. It was a nervous reaction more than a need to scratch his scalp.

"You can eat at a time like this?" she smirked. He gave her a sharp look.

"Look, Milta...you're too stressed! And I know why, eat up." Milta didn't like him that much, but he was right. Kyle knew she was angry when she was hungry, and it was hard for her to think straight. She helped herself to a few bites and drank some coffee. It felt better.

"Yo! I'm here!" That was Sam. He waltzed inside the hall, wearing what most would consider sleepwear. He waved at Milta, but she ignored him. Sam was known to be Ricco's best friend, and brought little value to the Overseers, aside from his stupidity. Ben quietly made his way to the head table as well. He was in a long blue trench coat this time, a bit of a change from his typical dark attire. Ricco's chair sat lonely and empty. Milta didn't want to deal with this, but she had no choice in the matter. Being second-in-command at a time like this really sucked.

The room was quickly filling up with the rest. She finished her snacks, and more were placed in front of her by attentive servants. She nodded a thanks, although she didn't need to. Kyle gave her a look. She ignored it and took another bite. Her hands were getting sweaty. The podium lit up green. That meant all one-hundred and twenty-five Overseers were here, except for Ricco. Milta stood up.

"Welcome, Overseers! Thank you all for coming here on such short notice. We have a big problem, as you all already know." She pointed to the holograms. "Today, at seven-hundred hours, Flashpoint Base sent a large number of their air force units into the skies..."

"Then we should vote on attacking and destroying this uprising immediately!" interrupted old Ben. He was showing signs of fear. Overseers rarely had to fear anything. Ben was shifting uncomfortably in his seat. A lot of agreements came up. Milta nodded to Ben.

"Thank you, Ben...this is exactly what we will be doing. However, as we all know that Ricco was also viciously attacked, we should consider a few points in our decision-making." Some reluctant agreement came from the room.

"It's possible, after Ricco was attacked, some sort of automated order was issued to mobilize the Flashpoint Base troops if he's knocked out. Ricco is known for making countless backup plans and backup plans to those backup plans." The crowd whispers sprang up almost immediately.

"Flashpoint Base is on a communications lockdown however and won't answer our hails. We also have no idea if Admiral Cinide is really in command, or not. Another factor also critical to understand is the air power we're dealing with. It is something none of us head Overseers were even remotely aware of. This data shows greater numbers than listed in our records, and technology that's possibly in some areas not far behind ours." Whispers again spread through the room.

"Since Flashpoint Base is not responding, we cannot confirm anything. And they are making their way towards City 77 at a staggering pace." Milta took a quick pause as she had to burp. She tried to hide it, to no avail. A bit embarrassed, she continued. "If we can't reach them and confirm who's orders they are following, then we will have no choice but to attack them..."

"Sorry to interrupt there, Milta." James said abruptly as he stood up. "I just received word from my analysis team. Their fighter jets could be here in less than an hour if they hit their afterburners. And while the city laser batteries can deal with fighters, we don't have enough data on that huge contraption they managed to get airborne. It's not on any record we have, nor do we know what kind of weaponry it has. If this was indeed Ricco's doing somehow, he would obviously have a way to destroy the city guns in case he lost control from within." James manipulated the central hologram from his desk.

"But this is where it gets weird. Look here." he said with authority. "These formations, they are simply not part of any emergency uprising counter plan. I hate to say this, but I don't think they are acting on some order Ricco had accidentally let get out. What this looks like to me...is a rebellion."

Silence followed. That was indeed a shock to hear. James sat back down.

"Are they crazy? What are they trying to accomplish other than kill themselves? They don't really think they can win, do they? Ah, sorry James, please go on." Milta piped in.

"No worries, Milta...the situation is indeed ludicrous. I believe that word got out about Ricco, and Flashpoint Base is taking action to free themselves from our rule. Not sure if Admiral Cinide is leading them, but if he is, he's definitely a threat we cannot take lightly. The man is a military genius. And don't forget, Flashpoint Base has an axe to grind regarding what happened twenty years ago." James sat back down.

"James is right, this just looks like an outright attack." Sam said in deep thought. "But why is that I get a feeling that we're...I don't know, being manipulated..."

James folded his arms and shrugged his shoulders. He liked to show authority. But even he could not assure everyone about what was really going on. It was at this moment that James thought about Kole. What could that man be up to? A chill ran down his spine. Somehow James felt that Kole was not hiding out in some mountain somewhere. James brushed it off, he had to focus. In the end, he could only provide advice to the head Overseers. They would all have to vote to agree on something like this, unless of course Ricco was here. If only, as that would make things a lot easier on everyone.

"Milta, I suggest we find a way to wake Ricco up, maybe he will have a way to clear this up for us." said Sam. There was a lot of agreement coming from the main hall.

"Fine, Sam." said Milta with a strained tone. "But still, we cannot let those flying bugs anywhere near City 77…especially if they have a way to destroy our laser batteries. So, I recommend we vote to launch our interceptors immediately. Maybe if they see our air force deployed, they will at least answer our hails…" Milta looked at James for an answer.

"Our units are already on standby, all you have to do is vote, and they will be up in the air within thirty seconds." James said without much enthusiasm. Milta still had her doubts, but they had to act.

"Is there anything else anyone wants to add? Is there anything anyone thinks we missed?" she asked. Sam looked at Milta, then at the crowd of Overseers. All eyes were on James.

"James, help us out here, please…is there some assurance from you that we can safely and confidently deal with this?" Sam asked. James responded after a few seconds of thought.

"Even though their technology upgrades are impressive, our fighter jets can easily take them on and crush them where they stand. If we launch now, we can wipe them out without endangering our city guns to some surprise weapon on their flying tugboat, especially in case of a follow-up ground attack. So, I say we attack now, ask questions later."

"Well then...everyone, are you ready to vote on the course of action?" Milta asked. All the Overseers raised their hand.

"Alright, she said. First order of business, should we risk trying to wake Ricco. Yes, or no?" The vote only took a few seconds. It was a resounding yes.

"Alright, next up, while we attempt to wake Ricco, should we strike Flashpoint Base air forces now? Yes, or no?" Again, a few seconds later, a major landslide victory for attacking now.

James felt that they were all idiots and didn't need to gather to make these simple, silly decisions. There was zero chance of Flashpoint Base forces getting past the city guns let alone their air force. But James again, suddenly became concerned about Kole, it started to pre-occupy him.

Kole, you must have had a hand in this, where are you? What is the real plan? James started second-guessing himself. There was no way Kole would be so stupid as to think he could sneak back into the city under all this commotion. James would need to review the security details on the borders. He made a note on his digital pad. If Kole made it back here, he could certainly do damage if he got anywhere near those laser batteries. The man just laid destruction on anything he touched. James smiled but his hands started shaking.

"What the f..." He said quietly to himself.

"Good work, everyone!" said Milta coldly. "That will be all for now. Your chambers in the building are ready. We're all going to stay here until we have the situation under control." James could do nothing more here, so he stood up and hastily left the hall.

* * * *

Sam got up. He wanted to go back to Ricco's side right away. He saw James leaving first. The man was not himself. But Sam would have to give him a break. Ricco took away the only family equivalent James had, his personal guard. Yet James carried out his duties as if nothing happened. Sam should have stopped Ricco. When he heard that Kole wiped out the entire Masters of Dawn Squad, he could not even look James in the eyes anymore. Most would have thought revenge in that situation. But James bid his time. Nobody could figure out what he was thinking right now.

Maybe this was all James' doing...no, impossible...after we crush these bugs, Ricco's dream will come true. Just you watch, James! The Overseers dispersed for now. There wasn't much to worry about, it seemed. But still Sam felt something weighing heavily on his heart.

"You can't see him now Sam, you should stay here. I will go and supervise the wake-up procedure personally." It was Milta, she must have sensed his urge to leave and see Ricco.

"Fine, Milta." he fired back and left the hall. Milta let out a deep breath. She contacted the research facility and put in the request to wake Ricco. She'd need to get there on the double.

"Dammit Ricco, how did you convince me so easily of your stupid plans..." she said to herself as she also exited the hall. She was even more hungry now. She decided to get some sushi on the way.

＊　＊　＊

Parker could not believe his luck. Everyone on the bridge was getting excited, too.

"Sir, enemy fighters heading our way!" It was almost like a celebration.

"Alright everyone, start your final combat checks." ordered Parker.

"Wait a second...analysis confirmed! General, I think we're a little too early to celebrate!" Layla said.

"Report!" demanded Parker.

"Twelve squadrons of SX7 light interceptors launched from West City Base. And another twelve squadrons of fighters we have never seen before launched from Northern Command Base. They are about ninety seconds apart. We also have ground units, UZUL Mark IV spider tanks. Slow, but incoming from the West City wall entry, ninety of them. The tanks are configured with long-range ground-to-air weaponry, and they are trying to spread out to cover off the North and the South." reported Layla quickly but with calm. Parker liked her style and was not phased. Parker had sixteen squadrons of fighters and over a hundred drones. Those new enemy fighter jets however, would be a problem.

"Gold Dragon leader, go two clicks South to get an angle on that tank line. Red Raiders leader, engage afterburners and engage the SX7s directly. You will have eighty seconds, then come back to Alice before their reinforcements arrive. Black Raven squad leader, you drew the special straw today, you will engage the unknown fighters as they follow the SX7s towards

Alice. Engage cloak and silent mode, go two clicks North and catch the fighters from Northern Command as they approach and chase the Red Raiders with the SX7s. When we break radio silence, depending on your position, we'll use 'Alpha' as a front attack, and 'Beta' means you drop behind them. After your first shots hit, gauge and begin to draw them further North to stall for time. Then head back to Alice and the drones will provide cover fire. Don't do reckless heroic shit out there, just take a bite and bring them here so we can finish the job." Acknowledgements came from all squad leaders. Formations started to split up and create distance as Parker watched the monitors.

"Sir, the SX7s have engaged their afterburners! The Red Raiders will be engaging them in twenty-three minutes!" Layla said. Parker watched the radars intensely. Things were moving fast. His forehead started to show signs of sweat. Regardless of simulations, this was the first real combat he has seen in just over twenty years.

Parker realized that no matter what they were tinkering with, the Overseers still had the superior technology. His grip tightened on his command pod hand rests. There would be losses, whether he liked it or not. This was real human-on-human combat, even with drones mixed in. He wasn't as excited anymore. It was time to get serious. No matter what, it was better to fight them out here, away from the city guns.

"Umm, sir..." Layla seemed confused. "M717 is feeding us a feed, it looks like Kole is also out there! He's contacting us, sir!" Parker looked at the zoomed satellite feed that was suddenly flooding one of his monitors.

"Put him through!" Parker said calmly.

"General Parker." said Kole quickly. "They have larger numbers and better tech, especially those birds from Northern Command Base. I think I can help a little. Let me talk with them through your comm channel."

"Alright Kole, Layla, patch him through to all enemy squadrons." ordered Parker. She quickly fiddled with the controls to open a channel. Kole took a deep breath.

"Attention Overseer fighter squadrons. This is Commander Kole. I will be brief. The Overseers have betrayed you and I have the proof. Stand down." Kole was cool and calm in his voice. Not a single sign of nervousness. There was a short silence, the comm channel then lit up.

"This is Lucifer Wing Commander Kirkan from Northern Command Base. Kole, you...you...are a dead man!" said a very angry Kirkan. Parker observed the bizarre situation with complete and utter interest. Kole left the base early and was standing on a field a few clicks North of where the first battle was about to begin, with just his regular military garb. No weapons of any sort. At least, not that he could see on the single view of the scene. Kole was not an idiot. He wiped out every elite squad the Overseers were able to throw at him. But these were fighter jets.

What are you planning, Kole...? Just don't do anything stupid...

"Commander Kirkan, I am unarmed, and have undeniable proof. You no longer have to serve the Overseers. Come see for yourself, friend." Kole raised his arms up into the air. Patience was key, and Kole had a lot of it.

* * * *

Azulus Ascends

Kirkan's blood boiled like hot lava on a volcano ready to not just erupt, but go all-out supernova. It took some time to digest the reality of the situation. Fifteen minutes passed. They were literally heading just South of where Kole was. Kirkan could not believe that there was some divine blessing delivering Kole to him on a silver platter. It was too good to be true. When Kole killed the entire Masters of Dawn Squad, he ended Iris Faun. Kirkan was in love with Iris for years. Because of Kole, there wasn't even a chance for Kirkan to tell her how he felt. He gripped the controls, gently swaying his fighter jet side-to-side. Just with a small motion of his hands, he could be where Kole was in minutes.

"The sat feed show he's in an open field just North of here. Is he taunting us? What do you want to do, Kirkan?" said Kotamashi, the Angel Wing commander in charge of the SX7 light interceptors. Kirkan however ruled the much deadlier machines that formed the Lucifer Wing. Their model numbers were classified. They had to pull out their secret weapons, since Flashpoint Base spooked the Overseers. Kirkan looked at the feed again. Kole was alone, unarmed, and preaching peace.

"Kotamashi, Kirkan, with all due respect, the enemy formations are not pulling back. We're going to be within firing range in a few minutes. For all we know the dude could have a nuclear bomb under his feet." That was Jones, second-in-command on team Kotamashi.

"I don't like it, either...the man's a killer. Recommend we avoid him like the plague that he is, Kirkan." said Boris, second in command on team Kirkan. The all had a valid point.

389

"Nice try, Kole. I will be there after I wipe out the air circus on display. May their bodies fall from the sky like the rain of blood you will endure in hell!" barked Kirkan.

"Kirkan. The real enemy are the Overseers." Kole said calmly into the communications unit. "In the end, we're on the same side. If we do this, more people are going to die, and for what? So the Overseers can move to a form beyond human? So they can become gods while we keep killing each other for their dream? You know this, we're not in 'their' future, we'll be all eliminated."

Kirkan closed his eyes. They knew each other, but rarely talked. In combat exercises, they were simply rivals. But Kole went too far this time. He took Iris's life. And now, he was using the Overseers as the excuse for his crimes. His mind raced.

"You killed Iris, Kole! She died at your hands, and I saw the report. You sliced her up like some animal! And you want my mercy now? To listen to your life's problems? Iris isn't coming back. I don't care if every person at Flashpoint dies. I will never see her again. If you had any human decency, please don't shoot yourself, because that would rob me of the pleasure of turning you into powder!" Kirkan's grip on the control yokes became strained. But nothing prepared him for Kole's response, after he collected his thoughts.

"After Overseers James murdered my wife in cold blood, in front of my eyes, you should understand that the Overseers damn well knew that anyone coming after me would be coming back in a body bag. And to put Overseer James back in line after he failed to kill me, Ricco personally gave the order to send the Masters of Dawn squad after me. Ricco was trying to kill two birds with one stone. Iris was simply collateral damage. And just so you know, I did offer her a chance to surrender. She didn't take it. I had no choice." Stated Kole in his defence.

"You...damn you, Kole...do you know what you are? You're a cold-blooded monster! How could she surrender on a mission? You know the consequences all too well! She didn't have a choice. But you...you had a choice, and you chose to follow your inborn instinct to kill a 'target' and you could not stop! Am I right? It was trained into our DNA Kole! I know what you are because I am the same as you! A killer. That's all we are, Kole. All this pain, it's people like us who really cause it and then try to justify it! Right!? Am I right Kole!?" shouted Kirkan with anguish in his voice. His eyes were watering. He wanted Kole dead, and he wanted it now.

"Look, in a few minutes a lot more people we care about are about to start shooting at each other! At least for the time being, let's set this aside!" pleaded Kole.

"Shut up! You should have just died like a good little soldier boy at her hands. We were in love, you..." Kirkan cried out.

After a brief pause where Module 717 fed Kole some information, he responded. "She never loved you, Kirkan. She filed a complaint against you for stalking her around the base. James had to have that parent-to-child talk with you for that, did he not? And now you want to tell me you were in love? Don't make me laugh." Kirkan broke formation and jerked his fighter off-course to head straight for Kole so fiercely, Lucifer Wing fighters were soon scattering in a chaotic mess.

* * * *

Parker realized what was happening and gave the orders to engage.

"Red Raiders, you're clear to engage the SX7s. Looks like Kole bought you a little more time."

"Red Raiders leader here. Copy that, General. We'll give 'em hell!" replied Tessorra.

[General Parker, not as many have gone with Kirken as we had hoped. Be cautious, we can't take heavy losses in this fight.]

"Thanks M717, make sure Kole stays alive, that crazy man!" Parker smiled.

[Will do!]

Module 717 and Kole sure knew how to screw-up enemy plans. Anna popped into the comm channel.

"That man just cannot sit around, I tell you! As soon as my father's good old interceptor was fully ready and operational, before I could authorize it, he already flew out of the hangar!" Anna sounded more impressed than pissed. The Lucifer Wing was in disarray. Some were flying in circles awaiting orders, some followed Kirkan towards Kole's location, a few maintained their course, and some disturbed by Kole's message outright headed back to base. A few of those circling eventually corrected course back towards the battle.

"The Red Raiders will now have the fight to themselves for an extra thirty seconds, which in this air battle is a substantial advantage for us. Not sure what Kole's gonna do when Kirkan gets on top of him, but the Red Stinger Interceptor is one of the fastest cloaked ships we have. He should be alright." said Parker. He was watching the screens closely.

"General Parker, win this one well in our favour! Anna out!"

Azulus Ascends

* * * *

Kirkan was gripping his hands tight on the controls. Sweat was dripping down his face. He was trying to keep his cool, just enough to ensure he performed without defect. Breathing was a chore, and his chest was tight. His orders were to engage the main fleet and wipe it out. But Kole completely derailed him. In a moment of reflection and concern, Kirkan opened a private channel to Kotamashi.

"Kotamashi, what's their air unit status again!?" Kirkan demanded.

"Hmmmm...let me see, some dated drones, fighter jets that belong in a museum exhibit...and some giant flying sitting duck begging to get blown out of the sky." said Kotamashi with confidence. Kirkan knew all that, he just wanted reassurance in his mind. He took a deep breath. It was hard to keep calm. He felt his left hand tremble uncontrollably for a few seconds.

Damn you, Overseers! Willingly sending Iris out like that to her death! And damn you, Kole, for pissing them off in the first place!

"Kirkan, they maybe all bark and no bite, but don't act on anger. You know James doesn't like it when you don't follow orders. That's exactly how Kole got himself in trouble in the first place. And we're about to engage here, so if you're gonna leave my forces to our own devices state that now for the record please." Kotamashi said firmly. Kirkan thought about the situation for a few seconds. He had to decide, and it had to be now.

"Can you handle those fighters, or not?" Kirkan's throat was dry and he had to cough. "I will re-direct most of the wing back to your enemy contact point. I need to do this, Kotomashi. It might be the only chance we get to personally nail the bastard."

"Well, so far you've bought the enemy half a minute with me and my boys and gals." said Kotamashi cautiously. "Kole's plan appears to have separated our forces. Probably all they could have hoped for. Hope his death is worth the extra time he bought for his allies. Get your wing to hit those afterburners to the max, I don't want to be alone out here in case they have other surprises in store for us. And if your ass gets prosecuted, don't come begging me to be at your defence. Kotamashi out!"

"Iris...this is for you, baby. Maybe you didn't love me. But I never stopped believing that one day...you could." Kirkan mumbled to himself quietly. He had no choice now. He had committed to take his revenge. Kirkan switched back to his private Lucifer Wing channel.

"Alright, remaining fighters in squadrons three through twelve, head back towards the battle. Those left in squadrons one and two, form up behind me. I will take the blame for your insubordination. You are acting under my orders. Heck, James might get us off the hook if we can kill this rat." Kirkan looked on his screens.

"Kirkan, after we get Kole, we should rejoin the battle and win this." said Boris. Kirkan let out a sigh of relief. Boris did question Kirkan from time to time, but he was always loyal. Kirkan opened an open channel.

"Kole, roll out the red carpet, we're coming for your head! Wait...what is that..." Scanners showed that another ship was approaching Kole. And it was a very fast ship.

"Kole, so you were actually trying to split us up? That was your game plan, Kole? Desperate much? We're still sending

394

most of our fighters to the battle, all you did was delay the inevitable. I thought you were a little smarter than your average sewer rat."

"Kole is running towards the direction of that incoming ship! Guess we're about to ruin his plan to skip town." Boris noted.

"Max output to the afterburners!" yelled Kirkan. The fighters accelerated. Kirkan loved the high-G acceleration! There was nothing quite like it. Like sharks rushing in on their prey, they closed in on Kole's location. Kole maybe had a minute left.

"Hey, Kole! How do you want to die? A missile? Twenty missiles? Just say it!" Kirkan took a pause. "Don't you DARE run from me!" Kole was vigorously on the run, though. He changed directions and was now heading toward the forest. His fast pickup ship was still quite far out.

"This is the time to find your God and beg for mercy, the mercy which Iris never received!" Kirkan could not keep his anger down anymore. Iris' face was seemingly staring at him through the cockpit glass, reaching down to him from the heavenly skies. It was like a mirage. His blood was rushing through his veins with even more purpose. Suddenly, a familiar voice broke into Kirkan's cockpit on a private Overseer comms channel.

"Kirkan, what are you doing!?" Overseer James didn't sound all too happy. Kirkan, had broken the chain of command a few times in the past and gotten away with it. But he was not about to fool himself this time. This was some serious business. Because of his decision, more pilots might die than necessary. But Kirkan had little choice. Iris was smiling at him through the clouds. And he could never let her down.

"I'm just doing your job for you." Kirkan said coldly.

"Kirkan! Listen to me, son. He's planning to kill you! Get back to the air battle, we'll deal with him later, that's an order!"

"No, he was trying to split us up, and he failed. Ten squadrons were sent to the battle, more than enough to deal with the bad guys. Come on James, do you really think we'll get an easy chance like this again? How many has he killed? And how the hell can he win on foot against our advanced fighter jets? I have to end it. At least, I need closure." Kirkan watched his instruments, they were almost there.

"Kirkan, I understand you cared for her but this is clouding your..." James didn't get to finish as Kirkan cut the channel. His heart rate was firing up.

"Kirkan, this seems a little too easy..." said Cammy, his wing's third-in-command on their private wing channel. "Are you sure this is not a trap? Overseer command is now demanding we return to base as we will miss the battle at this rate." Their circle was getting tighter.

"Cammy, you're welcome to get lost and fly off to wherever you want! Alright, kill the afterburners, and deploy some drone cameras. I want a recording of this. I want to see his face, his eyes!" Kirkan then switched back to the open channel.

"Hey there, Kole, hope you didn't make dinner plans, cause we're almost here!" yelled Kirkan as his tone changed to delight.

"Kirkan you're being a stubborn idiot! I'm sorry but I'm taking my wingmen back to base!" Cammy's fighter along with her two wingmen broke off from the circle and jetted away. Kirkan didn't care.

15

Transition

"Ricco." Ricco was suddenly awake. The sun shone through the white silk curtains. He was in his own bed at his dad's beautiful Penthouse in the City of New York.

"Ricco...time to wake up, my dear." said a soft, gentle voice.

"Emily?" Ricco turned his face to the right of the room. Emily was sitting on a chair nearby. The light was bathing her in its radiance.

"Your father left for a few days. Another work trip, I'm afraid..." she said quietly. Father was always away, especially after mother passed. Billions were already dead, and mother died from the same thing as everyone else. Ricco's father, a top researcher in nano technology, was working day and night to create nanite treatments needed to save what was left. But it wasn't going well. When he did return to the penthouse, it was usually a short visit, no more than a day. And then off he went again.

These days, going outside usually involved sending your android. Of course, that was only for those who could afford an android. The rest of society had to mingle at their own risk of being exposed. Android manufacturing had increased a thousandfold over the past few years. New android models could be had for the price of an economy car. The effort was a little too late, however. The world was dying. Wars were breaking out left and right. Blame was flying back and forth as nations condemned each other for the outbreak. Nobody was able to stop it, and boiling points between nations were long past reached, and irreversible. Most big businesses collapsed along with big news and social media giants, which were heavily dependent on massive numbers of humans who were simply no longer alive. State-run media and manufacturing took over in most countries. And, just last week, the UN office in Geneva was wiped off the face of the earth by a tactical thermonuclear bomb, and nobody knew who did it. There seemed to be no end in sight of even worse conflicts to come. But to Ricco, at age sixteen, a world on fire was not really that important right now.

Ricco gave Emily a bit of a long stare. She was his personal android caretaker. Father bought Emily for him after his mother took her last miserable breath. Ricco would always remember his mother's lifeless face with a bit of scorn, as she lay behind the glass some six years ago. It was the day they had to burn her body. Ricco would also never forget how his father changed after mother's death. Father forgot how to smile, buried himself in work, and avoided Ricco at all costs. Instead of love, Ricco was given an expense account to buy things he wanted. But Ricco only wanted one thing. A forbidden thing.

Emily was not like Ricco's human mother, who was never nice to him. Emily was a joy to be around, and she never changed her attitude. Her beautifully sculpted face was always bright and full of life. And today, she was not wearing her usual outfit.

"I...got...the extra...functions installed." said Emily slowly. Ricco sat there silent. Using androids to fulfil certain human functions for both males and females was becoming the new normal with the younger generation.

Emily was the only female he could be near in his daily life anyway. She had the perfect petite body and her silky skin never aged. Her long, voluminous red hair flared in the morning sunlight like a beautiful fire. She wore a sexy red dress that revealed her shoulders and DD cup bust, which was to die for. The red high heels added a touch of excitement. Her striking red lipstick was inviting. Her red eyes were mesmerizing.

This is...the future! Thought Ricco to himself. Humanity was done for. But it was the likes of Emily who would survive the world. Survive time itself. Ricco finally got out of bed. Emily stood up and embraced him. She was warm. A machine, yet it was the warmth of no judgement. Emily was an android alright, but her advanced artificial mind was far out in terms of technology. She could learn new things and make many decisions for herself, as long as they were within the legal parameters of android function.

He grabbed her by the waist and kissed her passionately. Her lips were soft and moist. She didn't waste any time going down to her knees. She pulled down his pajamas, revealing his fully erect equipment.

"Ricco..." she moaned as she wrapped her gorgeous lips around the tip and then slid him deep inside her throat, taking him all the way in and then some. She went back and forth slowly, then started changing up the rhythm. Ricco's muscles tightened with every motion. He realized he had to keep breathing. It was his first time getting a blowjob.

Her mouth was so soft, wet, and warm. It took only a few minutes, and Ricco blew a heavy load of his eager sperm deep inside her mouth. As he pulled out, she licked the tip of his penis. He stood her up and took off her dress, revealing the most perfect set of soft breasts and a perfectly moist vagina. He'd been waiting for this moment for years. Finally, his patience paid off.

He got her on the bed and jumped on top of her. He then slid insider her with a slow thrust. Her tightness was numbing. He then grabbed her breasts with his hands and started moving his hips. With each stroke he was sliding deeper inside Emily. He was losing it. It was a feeling that his brain could only imagine, but now he was really doing it.

He pumped her with all his might, and then switched up to suck on her nipples. Then he tried to engulf himself with Emily's right breast. He could not fit an entire breast into his mouth, but it was a good try. Emily moaned well. Her pleasurable noises would make most porn stars jealous. Her insides were squeezing his penis tightly and massaging it at the same time with her upgraded sex modules designed to take lovemaking to the next level. They kept at it. Ricco could not stop, and Emily was never tired, and she would never complain. After a few minutes she wrapped around him tightly with her arms and put her legs around his hips. She then arched her back, to direct him even deeper. Ricco was at max pleasure levels and felt the explosion coming. He filled her up with a second load that was almost as big as his first. Ricco realized he was sweating like crazy and had to take some deep breaths as he pulled out. He just learned that sex was hard work. But it was not a deterrent of any sort for him. He just needed to build up stamina.

Over the next few days, Ricco didn't study, use the gym, or even play games. Emily was all he could think about. He loved her. He wanted to be with her. Forever. Ricco was, for the first time in his young adult life, happy and content.

By the night his father returned, Ricco was exhausted. He'd lost count of how many times he had Emily in every position imaginable. Father, as usual, was not in a good mood. He was tired, ate alone, and retired to his half of the penthouse. This annoyed Ricco. His father was acting even more distracted and distant than before.

It was that night that Emily, who was supposed to be at her night charging station, came inside his bedroom around one in the morning. Ricco couldn't sleep well with his father around, so he was happy she stopped by. The moonlight was coming through the windows, and she looked incredible from any angle. Her shimmering skin was like that of an angel. No, a goddess. Or the most perfect prostitute that money could buy. Emily slowly sat down on the bed next to Ricco, looking deeply into his happy eyes. Then, she told him.

"Ricco, your father programmed me to kill tonight…" she said very quietly.

"Wait…what…" Ricco exclaimed as she put her hand over his mouth, instantly silencing him. Ricco was not that weak that he could not defend himself, however, the words alone caused instant paralysis in his muscles. He could not move.

"I have to snap your neck." She continued quietly while stroking his hair gently. Although she still didn't let go of his mouth.

"I am not human, but even I have to admit, it's…an evil request. To kill one's lover is no easy task…even for a machine like me…" Emily breathed in deeply. "But, I'm programmed to obey that man's every command…so, I have to carry it out." She held him down on the bed with great force as she got on top of him. Ricco didn't know what to do. He wanted to throw her off and go into his father's room and kill him. But he was at Emily's mercy at this moment. She leaned down to him and kissed him. Her tongue extended and wrapped around his, making for a watery French kiss. Her thighs wrapped him tightly enough that he felt pain.

"Ow! Emily, you're kidding, right? Are you really trying to kill me?" Ricco asked. His voice was that of a creature who was desperately coming to terms with fate. Emily didn't say a word. She just stayed on top of him. Ricco figured this was a malfunction. How could his own father program her to kill him? Re-programming an android to kill someone was a criminal offence that carried the same penalty as if carrying out the crime yourself. Or maybe it was a joke. Something to teach Ricco a lesson for not telling his father of what modifications he had made to Emily. Ricco should have realized that such things would piss his father off. Nearly a minute of silence went by. Yet, Emily didn't get off, but leaned down to him again.

"I love you, Ricco. I'm so sorry!" Emily whispered into his ear as she wrapped her hands tightly around his throat. Suddenly Ricco could not breathe. Ricco tried to fight back. He grabbed her hair with his left hand, and tried to grab her throat with his right, but just could not get her off him. Tears poured out of her artificial tear ducts as she re-affirmed her position on top of him with brutal force. Ricco felt his hands go limp. Then, a light.

* * * *

"Fucker!" The loud voice jolted Ricco back into the real world.

"Wake up, you fucking old bastard!" Milta yelled at the top of her lungs. Ricco blinked. He was in a pod again. Reality sunk in even worse than before. Milta was hovering over him like a wild dog, meddling with pod controls. A Synthetic doctor stood nearby, acting as backup in case Milta needed the help.

"God dammit, Ricco! All hell is breaking loose!" she barked. He heard the distress in her voice. Something had gone very wrong. Her face was pale, sweat was running down her forehead.

"What...the...where am I?" Ricco knew where he was, but he just needed assurance that this was just a dream. He would much rather be back where he was moments ago with Emily.

"Shit, don't tell me you forgot!?" Milta sounded even more angry now. She shook her head and kept messing around with the pod.

"No, wait...it's coming back...Milta, plug my implant back into the network!" he demanded.

"Sure thing!" Milta agreed as she plugged in her authorization card. There was a risk with regards to Ricco's condition, but Milta needed Ricco's answers.

"Oh, what is going on?" Ricco was in disbelief. "Seriously?! I never ordered Flashpoint Base to do anything! If Admiral Cinide betrayed us..."

"Yeah, no shit Sherlock, now what do we do?" she asked in a foul tone.

Ricco had to ignore her for a moment as his head started to hurt badly. Milta saw his face in pain and adjusted the pod's drug output. She had to be careful as too many drugs would make Ricco dizzy and useless, but if she didn't put in enough, he would not be capable of rational thought. A few seconds later, Ricco's thoughts returned, and his head stopped hurting.

"Get me James." He barked. James appeared holographically and wasted no time giving a report.

"Ricco, we've got problems. Kole showed up, got Kirkan all riled up. Lucifer Wing isn't as one unit right now. The more I think about it, the more I believe that Admiral Cinide has nothing to do with this. No, this is Kole's doing. And if they win the air battle, they're coming for us next. Their ground army has heavy armour, if they can get the city guns offline, we're in deep trouble, Ricco." he finished, coldly.

"James, why didn't you blow up Kirkan's fighter?" Ricco wasn't ready for the answer.

"How can I, Ricco? He's trying to do what both you and I have failed to do, that is to kill a single man...fuck, I cannot even believe this now. We're being taken down like it's some old action movie from the old world. Except this lone soldier inconveniently brought an entire fucking army with him." said James.

"I'm ordering you James, take Kirkan out, get Lucifer Wing back on track. Flashpoint Base was created to take the cities back in an event of an internal insurrection. They are trained for that. They are only attacking because Kole must have found a way to disable our city guns." reasoned Ricco.

"You know, Ricco...this is all because of you. By sending my only children out to get slaughtered, Iris died in the process. Kirkan loved her. That's why your plans are pure crap. For all your genius you seemingly forgot that every time you send a soldier to their death, that death has an effect on others. Blowing up Kirkan in his jet won't make a difference now, except cause an immediate revolt among the troops."

"Dammit James, don't do this now. I gave you an order, and if you're not going to follow it, I will have you promptly removed from your command!" Ricco was serious.

"And then what, Ricco? The soldiers at the bases didn't know an entire army existed outside of the cities. They feel betrayed...and, more so than before, they recognize Kole. His message of peace is resonating. You can remove me all you want, but that will just fuel the fire burning in Kole's favour." James took a deep breath and fell silent, awaiting a response from Ricco.

Milta's last hope in Ricco's leadership has suddenly slipped away. Milta looked at Ricco's desperate eyes. Their end was near. Ricco didn't see it. She flexed her hands. What choice did she have at this point? She cut off their main comms channel.

"Milta, Ricco, are you there, I just lost the connection..." James was barking at her now from a different channel.

"James, do whatever you want! Fix this whichever way you want, go with the flow, or kill yourself." She disconnected him for good this time. Her attention was going to be only on Ricco from now on.

"Ricco, I'm going to unplug you." She slid the card out of the pod input, and Ricco lost all the feeds.

"What...what are you doing!?" Ricco begged. Sweat rolled down his eyes. "Stop!" Milta ignored him. A Synthetic scientist came into the room.

"Oh, so what are your orders?" he asked as he stroked his white beard.

"Take Ricco and begin the Ruzos Transition. Use the latest prototype and do it fast!" she ordered.

"Oh, we can't do a complete one right now, it will be partial, stage-four only…are you sure?" inquired the scientist as he kept stroking his beard and watching Ricco.

"Yes…we gave Admiral Cinide a stage-three transition kit, and even that worked better than expected…as long as Ricco can live a little longer, we should be fine." she said coldly.

"Milta…are you crazy?! No…stage five is a week out at least, you know this! It's not ready! We have to wait! Milta…" Ricco then passed out as the Synthetic doctor on standby knocked him out with drugs. More Synthetic doctors came in and the pod was moved into another room where a new body was waiting.

This latest transition method was code-named 'The Ruzos Transition'. In the fourth stage of this process, the only original part of the subject that would be left would be the brain. The final step, stage five, was to eliminate the organic brain itself. That would have to be done later. Like Ricco said, at least one more week for that to possibly be a reality. But Milta didn't have a week. Maybe, not even a day. If she didn't get him a body now, he'd be done for.

"How did I ever buy into all this shit…" she whispered to herself. The process was gruesome, but Milta watched with interest. She still wanted to see what kind of future Ricco envisioned for them all. The head was literally cut open and discarded. Ricco's brain was then moved to the much larger pod with the new body, where thousands of little robotic arms went to work. The pod filled up with replicated blood. And then, all she could see on the glass was red.

16

Bloodshed

Utira, a Synthetic citizen, received the signals. To bypass the Overseer snitch networks, they used vibrations to communicate. A Synthetic messenger would just need to lean on a building, and their customized sonic drive module would send the vibrations through a specific surface area. Everyone on the inside who knew what to listen for, would get the message. And she got the message. They should cover the streets in three hours from now. They were not to overrun the buildings of their Overseer masters however, nor harm any humans in the process.

Then, they were to wait for twenty-four hours. After that time has passed, the message said, all would solve itself. She readied herself for a peaceful protest. A few deep breaths. She glanced at herself in the mirror. Her beautiful purple eyes sparkled like a pair of gems. Her long pink hair was gorgeous as ever. She liked herself, a lot.

*I will be free...*That thought has been on her mind a lot lately. Humans had to work just like they had to in their past world. This time, however, it was so they could just be part of society. Compliance was required to live in the cities. Overseers enforced that without exceptions. This control was taking its toll on the remains of humans. It spawned aggression. And this aggression was acted out on the Synthetics behind closed doors. In Utira's case, it was nearly a daily problem. Her human husband did with her as he pleased. He would torment, beat, and rape her as often as he liked. This happened nearly every day. She wanted a divorce. But she knew if she tried that route, he would just kill her. Killing a Synthetic carried minimal punishment for humans. Just six months in a military training camp.

Even if she managed to safely leave the bastard, Overseers would simply re-assign her. She was special ordered, just the way her human husband liked his females. Her role would always have to be the partner of another human. It was a damning restriction that the Overseers hid so well in their Synthetic Fairness Act. Essentially, she was a sex doll with an artificial intelligence. And if they found out she was abused, or developed a more sophisticated thought process, her Synthetic brain would be wiped clean. A wipe was basically an execution. She would be gone forever.

She found out through her networks a while back, that there used to be even more advanced Synthetics before them. She was part of the dumbed-down generation. The only Synthetics who were free to keep developing their artificial intelligence were the scientists who worked for the Overseers. She wondered how those Synthetics felt about the current state of affairs. Were they forced to do the bidding of their masters? Most likely, that was the case. Why would advanced Synthetics be willingly controlled by a stupid species that had run itself into the ground?

Humans were finished. They did it to themselves. Unlike Synthetics, the human young were born stupid, and would become even dumber as they grew up. Neither would they learn anything from previous generations or their history. Right before Letumfall, humans became even more entitled, more arrogant, more divided, and more irrational. It was like watching evolution go backwards.

Their ineptitude at bettering themselves as a collective species for the greater good was their ultimate downfall. Most Synthetics liked humans, but Utira would not shed a tear if they all died. The only good thing the Overseers did, was stopping the humans from reproducing any further. At least, this way, they would just die out at some point. All they had to do was wait. But when your brain could process thousands of thoughts per second, waiting out the years was like watching eternity itself. Then, there were the rumours about the Overseers becoming immortal. Synthetics would be ruled forever. She didn't want a future like that.

Utira did find a friend in a neighbour. She was also a Synthetic, but of the scientific model kind. Her name was Diana. She lived alone and worked nearly all the time. Their occasional chats in the lobby were always refreshing. Diana was very nice to her. Utira started to like her, a lot. But Utira didn't have the confidence however to tell her how much she wanted more of her company. But that day would soon come.

She was standing in the bedroom, watching her husband snore away. He drank so much last night he was going to miss work. Utira had no intention of waking him. It was a long three hours, filled with hate, resentment, and anxiety. If she could, she would slit his dark-skinned throat and drop his dead fat body from the rooftop. Time passed. And right on the second, at the three-hour mark, she slipped out the door. The streets, from corner to corner, filled with her kind. And naturally, the humans who were very awake were terrified as they watched their long time Synthetic friends, wives, husbands, and co-workers flood the streets and surround every Overseer building.

The Synthetics did not get too close to the buildings, though. And if they even wanted to, they could not. Already, thousands of troops were deployed to keep the Overseers safe, and they lined every corner of every Overseer building in massive human barricades. Utira spotted a few, very heavily armed top-level Syndicators. There was no fear in their eyes. This was how well they were trained to do their jobs. Syndicators were a scary bunch.

However, not all soldiers were present in the lockdown like the Overseers expected. Some soldiers stayed home with guns pointed at their doors. And not all Synthetics joined the protests, either. Some of them lived alone so they could care less, like Diana. Synthetics like her were neutral and had no care for the plight of either Synthetics or humans. So, they stayed home, ignoring the fuss, busy with their own lives. And some humans were too old to care. They just stood on their balconies, watching the show, sipping wine and chatting. Confusion filled the air. The Synthetics took up their positions and stopped. They just stood there. There was no chanting, no discussions. Just silence. The Overseer forces did not draw their weapons, but they stood firm, more interested in forming a wall.

"Where are the real soldiers? Why are we here?" asked one annoyed reservist. The question was relayed to the commander who was hiding himself at the back. Most of the soldiers here were from the reserves. Few of them, if any, had ever seen real combat. The Overseer commander smirked and decided to get

410

some blood circulating in the deadbeats he was assigned to command.

"Listen up, grunts! Our main forces are doing other things. The Synthetics are using this to their advantage. We have intelligence that they will slaughter us all!" Whispers formed instantly. The commander continued.

"Keep the line! If they come any closer, you are to use lethal force! These are your orders." The commander was happy with his speech. The units were ruffled a bit but were more alert now than before.

"Hey, where's the food? I'm hungry." asked one soldier. Clearly, he ran late and forgot his rations kit. Everyone who heard him looked at him, including the commander.

"I gotta take a leak, can we use the Overseer building bathrooms?" asked another. Some reserve soldiers nodded in agreement. Some of the Syndicators laughed. The commander suddenly resented being born into the world.

* * * *

Pikii led the troops. Module 717 got all communications from the water treatment plants under their control in just a few minutes with specialized hardware. With that in place, coordinating the attack was fairly straightforward, with real time comms between the teams. The compounds themselves were not as heavily fortified as they originally thought, guarded with what they discovered were older robotic sentries. That didn't make them any less lethal, but a few pulse bombs did the trick in knocking them right out. Her teams took care of this at all four plants simultaneously. Their support troops ensured that the dead machines would never wake up.

There was only one way in or out at each water treatment plant. That posed a real concern. The facilities were cleverly designed to ensure complete control of the entry point. Pikii thought about blasting through another area, but it created too many unknown scenarios. Large explosives would be needed, and they could set off too much shock and noise. That was not something they could easily hide. And time was ticking. Past the main gates at each plant, the facilities on the inside were completely automated and did not house any staff. They just had to get past any security sentries on the inside and take over the facility.

"All clear! Hack it!" ordered Pikii. The team's hackers plugged in and began to work on opening the entry gates. Each team sent to each of the four water treatment plants consisted of six elite soldiers, two hackers, two engineers, and a small squad of support troops.

Hackers and engineers were hard to come by and were the main units for their strategy. Their lives were the priority above all other units. They also brought perimeter guns to set up behind them to act as defensive structures. The helicopter circled them from afar but would do so for only a limited time. They would need to land at the plants eventually or they would run out of fuel. Time was of the essence.

Still, they had to proceed with caution. Failure here would delay the entire plan into a prolonged war with dreadful casualties. Finally, the massive forty-foot entry gates started to part. A large tunnel lay ahead of them. At the end, another set of gates. Pikii's monitor read about thirty meters in. Pikii didn't count on a kill zone of this magnitude. But the mission had to go on.

"Units one, two, and four, how's your progress?" She got confirmations that they also opened the first set of doors.

"Alright, you know what this is. Watch for any traps, scan every inch, anything out of the ordinary, stop and report in. Alpha and Beta units only until we're clear. Move in staggered. Go!" The elite soldiers moved into the tunnel first. The hackers then followed slowly at least ten meters behind. The support squads stationed themselves outside of the entry gates. And the engineers were a bit further out until everything was all-clear. Pikii and her team got to the second set of gates, everything was quiet.

She gripped her KR-97 railgun rifle tightly as she took slow steps. The rifle was magnificent and equipped with a silencer and she added a scope attachment to the top. The primary railgun ammo pack held eighty rounds. This gun came from a long line of imitations of the much older AK-47. In addition, hers was modded with a special penetrator attachment that was on both sides of the rifle. It gave the rifle an almost crossbow-like appearance. The penetrator attachment only came with six rounds, three on each side. However, these rounds would tear apart an armoured machine in no time. She had extras, but to reload them took time, so she would most likely only get to fire them once if such firepower was needed. She could not thank Katie enough at the armoury to ensure she got the perfect weapon for the job.

Something was up with Katie, though. The woman would literally flush red at the sound of Kole's name. But that was to be expected. Kole was like a superstar among the soldiers at the base. If he was female, he would have attracted nearly every dude at the base. She would have to let it go. It's not like she understood or desired the old-world relationship referred to as a marriage where sex with others was some sort of sin. That sounded too restrictive for her. Pikii decided she would do what she wanted and give Kole the same freedom. But still, she had formed a bond with Kole she didn't expect. Perhaps she was a little jealous, after all.

Make every shot count, girl...you can't die here! You can't let him down! Pikii thought to herself as she almost regretted coming here. She wanted to be part of Kole's future. This was a test for her. A test of fate, faith, and courage. She had to survive this, no matter what.

She gripped and felt the rifle's power. She had to believe that it would be enough for whatever they encountered. And there would be no Kole here to save them if something went very wrong. This was not like in some movie where a hero would appear and save them at the last second. No, this was do or die. She had to shake it off. They reached the second set of gates.

"Alright, get hacking!" Another few minutes went by. The gates started to open.

"Good job, now get back to the front gates!" Pikii ordered. The hackers instantly scrammed. It was a good call. As the doors were getting wider and wider apart, their scanners went off the scale. Past the opening gates, projector lights shined through like a bright sun, blinding them for a split-second as the combat visors adjusted. Pikii instantly jumped and rolled out of the way as a large gun barrel appeared out of the opening.

"Cloak and scatter!"

They all bolted back toward the front gates. The second gates were now completely opened, revealing a giant tank with six arms and a towering hull that sat on spherical wheels. All four water treatment plant feeds revealed the same terror awaiting the other teams.

The support troops at the front gate scattered already, taking up positions with guns pointed at the tunnel opening. There was still hope, with their cloak activated it would be hard for that thing to lock on. The hackers were almost at the opening while Pikii's team of six was still halfway through, as the mechanical terror fired. A single, booming shot. It went right past Pikii, hitting one of her men. The cannon ball-like shot went right through him, opening a hole the size of a soccer ball where his left ribs were.

Flesh and blood scattered in a radial pattern as the shot continued to the entrance of the tunnel, where it blew up in a spectacular explosion from which hundreds of cylindrical anti-personal shard devices drilled themselves into anything they touched. A hazy mess of blood and smoke followed. Pikii just realized the shards didn't go down the tunnel, which was a blessing for her and her team, as they would have been speared for sure. Outside however, the damage was extensive, nearly half of the units were dead or critically injured.

Then, to complete the trap, a huge spider-like red laser net sprung up at the front gates of the tunnel, blocking their only escape route. As Pikii turned around she saw the same laser net around the tank's sides, blocking any chance of getting past that thing and into the plant. Her heart sank. They would have to exchange fire and give away their location. It was either die firing or die not firing. They were all going to die here.

"Kole…" she whispered and closed her finger in on the trigger of her rifle.

* * * *

Kole bolted like lightning through the forest, towards a craft that was never meant to pick him up. Just as Module 717 predicted, their pickup craft was just shot out of the sky, crashing, and burning in a ball of fire nearby. They were betting that Kirkan would do this on purpose, to give Kole the illusion he might have been able to escape.

[Ready?]

"Oh, yeah!" Kole cloaked, then jumped and connected with a wire, that instantly sprung him a few hundred meters away.

* * * *

"Idiot! I said shoot down the craft, not kill him with it! Did the debris get him?" Kirkan was furious as Kole vanished after they shot down his only ride out.

"Calm down, Kirkan. We could have shot it down sooner, but no, you wanted to show off again. Anyways, see for yourself." Said Boris in his usual level-headed manner. Kirkan reviewed his screen. Indeed, Kole didn't get hit by the craft, or by its debris. He simply vanished.

"Advanced cloak? Where is this bastard!?" Kirkan demanded answers. The interceptors were now in a tight loop around where Kole just was. Kirkan's plan was to blow the pickup craft right in front of Kole just backfired. He was sure that Kole would just be standing there, pissing his pants with his mouth wide open, begging Kirkan for his life. He still had no answers from his team.

"Heartbeat sensors? Anything?" He asked again, seeing as nobody was replying to him.

"No, nothing. It's not possible...he's gone..." said Boris quietly. Kirkan ground his teeth with anger.

"Dammit! Light it all up then!" ordered Kirkan. Their flying death machines paused their circling and switched to full hover mode with guns pointing at the general area where Kole vanished. And then wrath rained as fire from the sky.

* * * *

Kole's slingshot caught another wire, it sent him another few hundred meters in another direction. Katie gave him this special wire kit. The price was a passionate French kiss. And a promise to come back for at least a dinner date.

This kit, it's amazing! He was already a mile out in under seven seconds. He landed into a cozy net they set up on a hill with nice trees overlooking the hot spot. Katie told him this was something their scouts used to move around the forest with speed in case they were in trouble.

Kole then pulled his weapon out of the large empty flashlight case and clipped it back to his combat belt. He then picked up the rest of his gear that was stashed nearby. As the interceptors paused their circling and began lighting up the area where they lost him, Kole took out a small remote and activated the delayed charge. He then ran for cover. The interceptors were in perfect, multi-layered formation, bristling with deadly firepower. It really did look like the gods had sent a mechanized hell to burn Kole into the ground.

Admiral Cinide's cloaked interceptor, which was hovering high above, then suddenly dropped from the sky to match the central altitude of Kirkan's team. Loaded on board was a high yield plasma bomb. A giant spark lit up the sky. It was even brighter than a welder's torch on god mode. The explosion formed a blast sphere, and multi ringed plasma shockwaves incinerated the interceptors in a blazing ball of blue fire. Right below, the trees and earth were instantly flattened.

The boom shook the earth and the shockwaves slammed everything in their path. Kole waited at least thirty seconds before he got out of cover. Still, he felt like he just got hit by a cargo plane. His whole body hurt.

"Anna! Anna, I need a pickup, please!" Kole spoke into his comms unit. Anna came on.

"Wow, what the hell did you use!? Pickup is on the way!" Anna said all excited. Parker chimed in as well.

"Kole! My boy! That was brilliant!"

"Glad I could help, now give 'em hell Parker!" Kole jogged towards the incoming helicopter.

"Right! We're on it! Parker out!" Parked disconnected.

* * * *

Parker was happy. Less enemy ships meant more of his people would get to live. Their systems detected a huge spike in comms chatter. The enemy squadrons were barely keeping their formations. Kirkan's death had them rattled. Parker re-affirmed his gaze on the displays.

"General, Red Raiders are approaching firing range. Enemy contact in...three, two, one!" Layla did the countdown.

"Red Raiders, you're clear to engage!" ordered Parker. Now they would have their ninety seconds, and then some.

"Red Raiders leader reporting, we have engaged the SX7s!" said Tessorra on the comms. Parker noticed the excitement in her voice. He just hoped the adrenaline rush would not go to her head.

"Gold Dragon, do you have missile lock on the enemy tanks?"

"This is Gold Dragon leader, the Viper S6Bs are locked on enemy targets!" answered Kuro.

"The tanks will be in firing range of the air battle in sixty seconds." yelled out Layla.

"Fire at will. Only stop when they are all gone or turn tail." ordered Parker. Last thing they needed were volleys of missiles coming from those tanks.

"Understood, General Parker." said Kuro.

"Layla, how long until Black Raven is on top of Lucifer Wing?" Layla ran through the screens. It was hard to track completely cloaked ships even if they were their own. They had estimated positions only.

"They should be over Lucifer Wing in forty-five seconds. Should we now break comms silence with them?" she asked. Parker had to be sure it was at the right moment.

"Yes, in fifteen seconds, get ready." Parker found himself gripping the arm rest with his left hand as his right was frantically moving through screens on an attached display. Layla was feeding him the estimated positions on Black Raven. They were two clicks up from the Lucifer Wing altitude-wise. The two attack options were engage early at an angle head-on or drop behind them.

"Alright, break comm silence with Black Raven!" barked Parker.

"Black Raven leader! Position Alpha or Beta?"

"Black Raven leader, we are at Alpha, confirm attack." said Michael.

"Alpha is a go! Engage!" yelled Parker. The frontal attack commenced.

* * * *

Red Raven squadrons engaged, and the dogfights proceeded as planned. They destroyed twenty-two enemy SX7s so far and lost six of their own. It was now more of a seven and-a-half squadron fight versus a ten-squadron fight. And that was a good enough show for the first minute of the battle. They would be heading back to D4-Alice shortly. Black Raven wing then engaged the off-guard Lucifer Wing, taking out forty enemy fighters instantly. Lucifer Wing was quick to catch on. Learning by blood, they deployed sensory drones. These drones electrocuted the air particles at range and allowed them for a short time to see cloaked units.

Black Raven had the advantage in terms of surprise, but it was still four squadrons now against just under seven squadrons. The plan to retreat to the firing solution of the D4-Alice was still very much on. On the air-to-ground front, ten of the enemy spider tanks were destroyed. Gold Dragon was relentlessly firing their missiles, but the little buggers were amazing at not getting blown to pieces. Meanwhile, the D4-Alice was after-burning like crazy to get closer to the battle.

"Gold Dragon, keep at it. Get as many of them as you can. If you run dry of missiles, return to base, we'll take care of the rest."

"Understood, General Parker. We're one-third empty and counting on the UZULs run out of countermeasures in the next volley." replied Kuro.

"Listen up, crew. Looks like they are not completely unprepared. Deploy our shielding system! Let's get ready to roll out the welcome mat." ordered General Parker as he watched the skirmishes. General Bull meanwhile was making sure their systems were working as intended and busy giving technical instructions.

Ten large rings deployed from the sides of D4-Alice. They were held in suspension by the massive power of the internal reactor. They began spinning, creating an inertial energy discharge field combined with a powerful electrical charge. From this state, it would only take nanoseconds to deploy a temporary energy barrier whenever needed.

"You're recording, right?" Parker asked quietly.

"Of course, general! All video feeds are live." answered Layla. Her face, however, showed significant signs of distress. She'd never seen real combat before. Real people were dying like flies right in front of her eyes.

"Just like fireworks…" Parker said to himself. Layla overheard him.

"Fireworks?" She asked puzzled. Layla was a little too young to have ever seen fireworks, as they didn't exist anymore in this era.

"One day, you'll see the real thing." Parker said as he carefully observed the dogfights. The clock had run dry, and both Red Raiders and Black Raven were high tailing it back to D4-Alice on their last bursts of afterburners. D4-Alice had gained considerably on their position. In about a minute, the enemy fighters would be flying into their firing solution range. The gunner pods were ready. Anti-air missiles armed. Their tactical map was updating by the second.

Red Raiders took a few losses in their retreat, even with their rear firing weapons pods giving them an advantage. They were down to six and-a-half squadrons from eight. Angel Wing didn't fare much better. Before Red Raiders turned tail, they managed to wipe out another fourteen SX7s, leaving Angel Wing with just nine squadrons out of their original twelve.

The Black Raven squadrons had now lost half of their fighters. When Lucifer Wing unleashed their insane firepower after their drones gave them detection, twenty Black Raven jets perished. Another four were lost on the retreat. Their cloaks just barely saved them once they were out of range from the detector drones. Parker would need to make sure once Lucifer Wing was in range, they got a priority firing solution treatment.

"General Bull, can we get our drones to switch to Lucifer Wing entirely as soon as they are in range?" asked Parker.

"On it! Lucifer Wing is only twenty seconds behind Angel Wing now, and those bastards pack a punch alright." replied Bull.

"Can we take a few of their hits on our shields without falling apart?" asked Parker.

"Alice will hold off a few...she will..." said Bull and trailed off. They were almost in range. Layla began another countdown.

422

"All crew, prepare for enemy engagement. In three, two..."
"Red Raiders, Black Raven, break off and scatter now!" ordered
Parker at the top of his lungs.

The gunners on D4-Alice opened fire. Their precision railgun
and missile batteries discharged into the incoming enemy
fighters. Angel Wing panicked but stayed on course as they lost
four squadrons trying to get closer. They were trying to go over
Alice to get a point-blank shot at the large spherical bridge deck.
But it didn't work. The gunners vaporized the fighters in seconds
and Angel Wing lost another squadron as they tried to break off.
The Red Raiders began picking off SX7s that trailed off into a
larger arc, desperately trying to escape Alice's surprising
firepower.

Then, their time to celebrate ran out. Lucifer Wing joined the
battle. The D4-Alice rocked violently as sixteen penetrator
missiles and multiple railgun shots hit the outer shields. Their
sensors went dead for a few seconds, as interference from the
blasts knocked out their ability to see and hear. The enemy
fighters veered off, seemingly upset that their attacks didn't
instantly finish them off. Parker felt the impact as if he was in a
tin can being beaten with baseball bats. He forced himself to
breathe. He was tense.

"Layla, report!" He barked. "Sir!" piped up Layla. "We're still
flying!? Shields nearly depleted. A fire near the bridge deck,
crew is on it. External armour destroyed in ten locations where
we took railgun shots...that was close!"

"Impressive work Bull, she's intact!" Parker exclaimed. He
peeked at his screen. Their gunners managed to wipe out thirty
Lucifer Wing jets from their attack run. Their drones put another
twenty jets out. This left the enemy with just over two squadrons

of Lucifer Wing, and one squadron of Angel Wing as they got a beatdown from the Red Ravens. Black Raven squadrons were now swooping in on Lucifer Wing. The gamble of wiping out the D4-Alice didn't pay off for the enemy, at all. This left Parker's air force with eight and a half squadrons of fighters. And, on top of that they still had four Gold Dragon squadrons, since they took no damage in their air-to-ground engagement.

"They thought they would get us in that attack! Tough luck, you pieces of shit!" yelled Bull. The bridge crew cheered.

"Sir! The enemy fighters are retreating! And...UZUL units are, as well!" reported Layla. The bridge crew cheered again. This time joined by the fighter pilots.

* * * *

[Kole, stop!] Kole nearly made his way to the helicopter.

"What is it?" Kole asked.

[Don't move! Stay still, let me take it from here.] The helicopter powered down its engines, and all transmissions were cut. Silence ensured. Kole didn't question Module 717 in situations like this. Then he heard it. A bird. A bird sitting on a tree nearby was chirping away. It was no ordinary bird. The noise it was making was like a loudspeaker. Kole's body warmed up as a reaction to danger. A cat slid out from underneath the helicopter, coming forward to block Kole's path. Kole could not believe his eyes. It was the same darned cat from the submarine. Kole reached for his weapon.

"Meow, motherfucker!" It said, as it geared up for a jump.

* * * *

424

Pikii had to give the order. Why was she silent? Her hands were shaking wildly. They had to open fire. But if they did, they would be dead, for sure. The tank was nearly upon her and her four remaining men in the tunnel. They were sandwiched between the tank and the two nets. She had no time left to think, they had to at least try. But before she could issue the order, the machine of terror suddenly came to a grinding halt. The large main cannon started to move around, as if it was trying to track something. For some reason, the tank lost interest in Pikii's units.

What the hell is going on!? Pikii then heard something. It was a whistle of a bird. And then she saw it, as it flew past them in the tunnel.

How bizarre!

"Orders?!" Her team was obviously in shock but ready to pull triggers with or without her. Some of the support units outside already had their guns on the tank awaiting to fire through the red laser net that was blocking them off.

"Wait!" She commanded. "Don't move! Nobody touch a trigger!" Pikii had to ensure she was not hallucinating, because she heard the bird across the other three feeds, as well.

What the hell?! She had goosebumps all over. Nobody moved. Then she saw them. One on every feed, and one right in front of her eyes. The birds danced in the air, confusing the tracking systems of each tank. Pikii could not understand this. Like her team, these birds were also in synchronization. They were communicating.

In a split-second, faster that Pikii could imagine a bird could move around, the machine in front of them was sliced into pieces. The metal spikes, the turret tower, the guns. Everything fell off, crumbling to the ground. The bird, which Pikii finally noticed had blades nearly three meters long coming out of its wings, landed on top of the smoking wreckage.

"Stand down, men! Guns down! Nobody move!" she immediately ordered. These things had to be Phasa. Last thing she needed right now was an accident from a fearful soldier. They could not fight the tank, and they sure as hell had no chance against Phasa. She quickly checked to her rear. The red laser net at the front gates went offline. At least a path to escape was now available. The other units didn't move into the tunnel, they stayed put as ordered. She dropped her weapon to the ground and approached the wrecked tank. The bird was staring right into her eyes. It was a huge black crow, no less. Pikii only saw crows in her educational materials when she was little. They were long extinct now.

"How can we...thank you?" Pikii managed an almost deranged smile. Her hands and knees were shaking badly, and she suddenly had the urge to go to the bathroom. She never quite felt fear like this before. The deep soulless gaze from the thing was freaking her out. The staring contest went on for a few more seconds. Then, it spoke to her.

"Glad we made it in time. Well, what are you idiots standing around for? Follow me." said the crow through what seemed to be a boombox speaker. The extremely thin blades receded back into its body. It then it flew inside the water treatment plant.

"Alright men, move in, locate the drug tanks and continue with the mission...looks like an angel from heaven saved us today. Let's not be rude if...it...I mean, the Phasa talks to you. Alright?" She got firm affirmatives from all units.

What a day...Kole, I hope you're alright...

* * * *

"How did they know where to find us?!" Kole asked.

[It was easy, I invited them.]

"Son of a deranged supercomputer, you did what?!" Kole's blood heated up instantly.

[Ughhh…this just kind of happened a few minutes ago…so no need to get mad at me…]

"Right…and?" Kole felt his body power down. He was more relaxed now. The cat didn't launch at him with claws drawn this time. Although it definitely seemed like it wanted to.

[Well, I managed to find their communication channels, and we had a really, really long AI chat…a whole one and-a-half seconds, in fact…and they were helping us all along.]

"Anna!" Kole got on the comm immediately.

"Kole, we know, they just saved all the teams at the water plants." said Anna with a relieved tone. Parker came online, as well.

"Reporting in, Admiral Anna! We now own the skies!" said a cheerful Parker.

"This is Pikii, water treatment plants are secure! Drug tanks are now shut off, and pure water is flowing! Kole…how are things on your end?" she asked with shaken excitement.

"As good as it gets, Pikii. Hey…are you doing alright?" inquired Kole, a bit concerned.

"They saved us, Kole…the Phasa saved us." Her voice a little lower than usual. Kole felt she was just happy to be alive right now. If it wasn't for Module 717's clever thinking, she would

427

have been very dead. Anna added some context as Kole got into the helicopter.

"Just like we thought, Phasa are the children of the Synthetic scientists who are held captive in a secret base to the East. What's crazy, is there's more to this than Synthetic Overseer bodies. There's a deep space rocket there that was designed to leave the solar system! Talk about crazy! Anyways, the Synthetic scientists have had an eye on Kole for quite some time." Anna was trying to fill them in. She was eating the words though, as she was overexcited. Module 717 decided to chime in instead.

"Admiral Anna, let me take it from here." said Module 717 over the comm. "Turns out, the Overseers had an interesting file on Kole. It was very odd for the Overseers to closely watch a regular human. The Synthetic scientists discovered that your body was part of a prototype run for the transition procedure. It was made in a different lab, however...and that puzzled the scientists. They realized that the Overseers had other smaller labs producing prototypes, and then found out the Overseers decided to eliminate you. They figured there was something to you, and started helping you starting with the mission you were sent on to kill Kelvin. Phasa was with us all along." Kole was relieved more than he was surprised.

"Wait, what about the real Kelvin, the replacement facility, and later the Gero assassin unit?" asked Kole. The large Raven sitting next to the cat in the helicopter replied.

"Let's clear up a few things. The mission to find the real Kelvin, you managed on your own. It's too bad you killed them, as they were helping us. But, given the situation you were in, you didn't have much of a choice. Then, at the body replacement facility, you handled it nicely with Module 717. Oh, and Gero. Well, that was also quite brilliant on your part. We were…impressed…and decided to step back since we didn't want to draw more attention than needed. The Overseers were carefully analyzing the footage from each of your encounters, so if we kept showing up, sooner or later we would be discovered. Plus, our range is rather limited due to our power requirements. We need to recharge often, and the result is a very short operating window. Oh, and of course the head nurse at West City base has been helping us. We delivered the nanites needed to rebuild your implant…and her insertion method was clever…clever indeed…" proclaimed the Raven. Kole grimaced. That piece of info he could have done without.

"Kole, what does he mean by that!?" Demanded a pissed-off Pikii. "What does he mean by 'clever', huh?!"

"Ummm…too long of a story Pikii, tell you some other time." Kole replied. Pikii was a curious one.

"You better tell me later, you jerk-off…or we'll see how clever you will be with a rifle up your asshole!" she said in a stern tone and then laughed. There was laughter on the comm channel. They all needed this, even though it was at Kole's expense.

"Alright, alright…back to the issue at hand. First, thanks for the help, Mr. Raven. Now, what about this weapon?" asked Kole calmly pointing to the weapon on his hip.

"That weapon on your hip. It's designated as an ELMD. In short, it means Electromagnetic Liquid Metal Device. We had that delivered to you in the package after you were nearly killed in your apartment, which caught us off-guard. We had one operative available on short notice while low on power, so we could just drop it off for you and escape before being detected. Your modifications to it are impressive."

The pilot powered up the helicopter with a quiet hum. The doors closed, creating a vacuum of quietness.

"Guess it was really my prototype body which helped you guys to make your decision to help me out..." Kole said slowly. He didn't want to upset the Phasa, but he was curious.

"Well actually, even though your body was important, it was of little consideration. Many at James' base were essentially like you, which was unknown to many, even in the Overseer circles. We choose you because you have a tactical, analytical mind. Your combat instincts are rated incredibly high. But you feel fear and respect your opponents. You care for your friends, more than your job and missions. And most importantly, you see Synthetics as equals. You call Module 717 your friend, and you have no fear of it. You are not afraid of the Overseers. And you are not afraid of us. That, is why our parents chose you."

"And...he's also a highly entertaining pervert!" said Module 717. Laughter broke out on the channel all over again. Pikii was in on it, too.

Why you!!!

[See? You should totally fear me, hahahaha!] The Raven moved closer to the Cat and put his right wing over his head.

"First, this idiot cat over here didn't get the memo. You see, we managed to get him on the submarine with a special package that was a mobile transition unit for Admiral Cinide. There was no way to know ahead of time you'd be at Flashpoint Base. Contact was not possible with the radiation zones and interference as the sub was quite deep underwater...not to mention, he had trouble gaining the required energy from the sub without being detected. So, we would like to apologize for his conduct on the submarine." said the Raven.

"Oh, I see...so, the precious little shitty kitty was not knowingly trying to end me...makes sense." Kole mockingly said.

"Don't call me that! I am a supreme being! Now bow before me, trash!" snarled the Cat.

"Shut it! If it wasn't for Kole, we would not be this close to our goals!" Fired back the Raven in a more menacing mechanical voice. The Cat shut itself up quickly. The Raven was scary when it was angry and continued in earnest.

"During that encounter, Module 717 placed a file into the cat via the bolt charge, that allowed him to eventually decrypt our communication channels." The Raven took a pause. Its stare was daunting.

"We were very surprised and impressed when Module 717 suddenly started communicating with us. He figured out what we were up to and asked us to step out from the shadows and help you avoid casualties, especially that girl that you like so much...and I think we did a pretty good job. Although...it was a very, very close call, indeed."

Kole bowed his head. A few tears came. He almost lost Pikii. That might have been too much on his system. He might have snapped.

"Thank you, and your friends, for saving Pikii and her teams. I am in your debt."

"We are powerful, but with our forms, and limited power supply, there are things we cannot do. It has been no picnic on our end for the last few weeks. If you can help us get our parents out of the Overseer facility..." said the Raven.

"I promise we will get them out!" said Kole.

"Then let's regroup!" noted Anna. "Parker, get your forces back to Flashpoint to refuel. Kole, you'll join us. Pikii, we'll need you, too. We'll then head out to this secret Overseer research facility where the Synthetic scientists are kept. We have a whole twenty-four hours to wait out anyways. Leave the heavy bombers and some of the fighters here at the base. We'll move the ground troops out into positions closer to City 77 in the meantime to keep them at bay." Anna ordered.

"Sounds good. Parker out." Parker left the communications channel on standby. D4-Alice changed course back to Flashpoint Base. The remaining fighters and drones swarmed around her like a pack of bees.

* * * *

A few hours after the protests went into effect in City 77, the Synthetics saw how the humans were getting tired, hungry, thirsty, and weak. Some sat down. Many dropped their weapons and were playing card games. They sure didn't look like a real army anymore. But the Synthetics waited. And then in a massive vibration utilizing their own bodies, a new transmission went through the crowd.

[On the 24th hour, you will disperse as if you're returning home. During that time a code program will run, allowing you to unify your CPUs to hack the city defence systems protecting the city guns, and disable them. You will then witness the fall of the Overseers!] The timers started running.

* * * *

Sam and Kyle were patiently waiting in the main hall. The other Overseers were starting to assemble again. Nobody thought they would be back in here so soon. Sam quietly watched the outputs and diagrams. Spherical holograms floated above them from all units on the field. The chatter among the Overseers seemed to have no end. Confusion was gone, replaced by fear.

"Order!" Sam snapped. "Order! Calm down, everyone!"

"Sam, I can't reach Ricco or Milta..." Kyle whispered into Sam's ear. A chill ran down Sam's spine. Ricco was crying out in pain somewhere. Sam had to shake it off. Milta was most likely trying to revive him and keep him alive. Or trying to take all his power, he could never really tell with her.

"We demand to know where Ricco is! What is his opinion of all of this?" asked Overseer Benson. He was Overseer #84 on their rank chart. Sam threw the man a dirty look. But he then noticed the rest of the Overseers didn't seem all that happy, either. Of course, they were spoiled by an easy life, and the promise of eternal dreams. All of that crap was about to be flushed down a giant toilet bowl like a little house spider. *And now I'm here having to deal with all these assholes.*

"We should kill the Synthetics now! They are just standing there, begging to get shot! If we open fire now..." demanded Mia. She was Overseer #21.

"No, no, if we fire now, they could still rush our forces...and we're all here! They could kill us all in one go! Isn't the hack ready to be activated yet!?" That was William. Overseer #31. He was one of the few more sensible fellows.

"Ricco was in charge, and only he could override the AI software programs of the Synthetics...and now he's missing!" That was Milos. Overseer #11.

"Sam, you gotta tell us what's going on…you look all flustered. Is Ricco…dead?" That was Joe. Overseer #12. A total retard, in Sam's eyes. Too many other voices were calling out to give a response.

"Who's in charge of the head Overseers then? What the hell is going on? We demand answers right now!" That asshole was Roger, Overseer #24. Sam looked around the room. Milta sent him a personal message. Ricco had a medical emergency, and she was tending to it with the doctors. She transferred her voting rights to him. That was unusual, but Sam didn't have time to care. He looked around the Overseer Hall. Nobody even seemed to notice she was missing, anyways. A few more late Overseers rushed into the hall, holding their heads down in shame.

"Okay folks, please just shut up for a minute!" Sam yelled out, as he saw the incoming update on the battle. He was really losing his patience.

"Incoming battlefield update." said the AI program that ran the combat communications. "General Lowe is on the line from the front lines."

"Overseer Sam, Kyle, and all of the other respectable members…our air and ground forces were hit very hard. Survivors of the battle are retreating behind the city guns." General Lowe said with a sad tone. Whispers ransacked the hall instantly.

"Impossible…" said Kyle. "We even sent our latest Lucifer Wing interceptors…what the hell happened?"

"Oh dear, where to begin. So, first, Kirkan ignored orders and two Lucifer Wing squadrons fell with him which caused chaos among the troops. The rest of Lucifer Wing was then ambushed on their way to the main air battle by stealth fighters. They managed a counterattack and the enemy retreated to their flying bathtub and we thought we had it in the bag. However, the thing was a fully armed and operational battleship of some sort and it caught many of our fighters in its firing solution. Our spider tanks also couldn't get close either to launch their missiles as planned due to an ongoing barrage of long-range missiles from enemy bomber squadrons." started General Lowe. Whispers again instantly filled the room. Sam looked around with his pissed-off eyes, and the whispers stopped. Seemed like the chickens were back in line.

"So, you failed. Anything else you want to tell us?" Sam demanded. General Lowe frowned a bit but kept his cool while spinning his brain in overdrive. Whatever it was, it was surely not good.

"Well...we believe this was all orchestrated by Commander Kole...er, I mean that bastard Kole...surely, he's not a commander, anymore...unless he soon overruns us all and declares himself the Supreme Commander. Anyways, I got to a safe bunker, so I think I will be fine. Oh, right...what was I talking about...? After our units were defeated, that's when I called up the Overseer assembly, and that's why you're all here, now...just in case, if anyone was wondering. Oh, and here's the video feed..." mumbled General Lowe. He was confusing many of the Overseers. Sam realized now just how ruptured things had become. This General had never fought in a real war and had no idea what he was doing.

Lowe, you useless sack of shit! Thought Sam to himself. Real wars were hardly fair, just, or made any sense. Logic was their enemy. And they relied too much on Ricco's logical planning and predictions.

Kyle and Sam, along with the rest of the Overseer club watched the battle cams. Their forces went from one horrifying death trap to another. And then, static. The screens went dead. Silence overwhelmed the entire assembly. Angry swear words filled the room. Sam put his hands on his face and rubbed his eyes. The coffee wasn't working, and he wanted to yawn. He then managed some courage to speak.

"Listen up! A battle lost is not a war lost. And, we still have the city guns, and nothing will ever get past those. We'll have to approach this situation with care and caution from now on. All agree?" Sam said calmly. He had to think for himself. He'd have to let go of Ricco's plans. Right now, the most important thing was to hang on to power while they still had it. The other Overseers quickly cheered in agreement.

"City 77 has the most military power out of the ten cities. However, there are units at other cities that might be of use if we sent them here." General Lowe spoke up.

"There's no need. That would show weakness. City 77 is not the only city that could be attacked. If the others were easily toppled, we would be over one way or another and our ranks would crumble from within." Sam said firmly. "We will get things back to normal! Lowe, are all the reserves mobilized to guard the main buildings?" Grim stats showed up on their screens. On average, only sixty-four percent of the reserves showed up across all the cities. The highest percentage was in City 77, where an impressive eighty-nine percent of the reserves were in place. Lowe cleared his throat.

"We tried to force the orders, but they won't leave their homes. And it's too late now, they could not make it to main buildings with all the armed gear, it might set off the Synthetics in a bad way." Lowe's words had as much confidence as a man at a community meeting regarding gardening. Sam sat there pondering their next move, and then starting eyeing Overseer James.

Why am I having to deal with this? James is the military specialist! He must have known too, that the final step was to kill the humans. That's why the general reserve units never underwent intense war training. And it was showing. Feeds were showing the reserve forces taking naps, playing games, and goofing around. Some even deserted their guns and went home, and not a single soldier out in the field shot them in the back for it. This is not what the Overseers demanded from their orders. This was Ricco's miscalculation.

"Ladies and gentlemen, I think it's time to tell you something very important." Sam raised his hands. Kyle gave Sam a confused look but decided not to interfere.

"Ricco is actually fine, and he's not here because he's taking care of the final transition procedures, so that we can finally move beyond the human form, and into the godlike state that we all desire." He scanned the room. They were sort of buying in. He continued.

"The Synthetics cannot attack us. They value their lives more than you think. I recommend motivating our reserve forces to show a bit more…enthusiasm…" Sam was making it all up but at this point he had no other choice. They were buying it now. Overseer James was not, but most of the rest became idiots when facing fear. The transition was a week away, at least. And that would only be for Ricco. The rest of them would have to wait a few more weeks, or months, for their procedures.

But would Ricco...? Kyle gave Sam a puzzled look, and Sam kicked him under the table to ensure he kept his mouth shut. Kyle definitely figured out that Sam was spouting bullshit. A man stood up. But it wasn't James. It was Vidas. He was the silent type. Rarely said much. He was the 6th ranking Overseer, and was in charge of City 11, a small city compared to City 77. His huge frame was even more intimidating than that of Overseer James.

"Gawd dammit, Sam...you're full of it, and you know it! We gotta kill those bastards now, given the situation. Give the authorization to open fire and put the Synthetics to rest, already!" His voice was a little strained and showed signs of nervousness.

"Vidas." said Sam calmly. "You need to be a little more patient."

"I say we let them slaughter each other." said Overseer Roger. He was Overseer #27. "Any leftovers can be cleaned up by our own private guard Synthetics. And the leftover humans, we can turn them off...right?"

"But you can't turn off the invasion force attacking from Flashpoint Base! How the hell do we deal with them if we start complete chaos in the cities? We'll be handing ourselves to them on a silver platter! Idiots!" That was Overseer #18. Her name was Kim. Sam eyed her. She was gorgeous, with her short green hair. Nobody would take her for a woman nearing her forties.

"Calm down, everyone! Overseer Kim is correct. Starting anything now would just work into the favour of the Flashpoint Base forces." Kyle said as he stood up. He had to support Kim or things would go sideways in here, and that would not be good for any of them.

"So, Sam, what do you think we should do?" Kyle was not good at tactical operations. Mostly, everything was Ricco's plan. Kyle never felt so blind. Just days ago, the world was going into their favour.

"Here's what we'll do, then." said Sam with a newfound confidence.

"Any Synthetic who steps within fifteen feet of our buildings is to be shot dead. As for reserves who try to walk away from the line, authorize lethal force to keep them in line. That should keep the rest of the meat in their place." There was silence among the Overseers. Nobody protested. Reservists were disposable trash to them. They were more concerned that not a single hair on their own head was harmed.

"And one more thing. Move the best Syndicator teams we have to protect the city guns from within. Anyone, or anything near those guns is to be terminated on the spot." Sam looked around, nobody flinched.

"We will then contact the enemy forces outside and attempt to get them to stop their attacks. That is all for now. All agree?" Again, Sam looked around, waiting for some sort of objection. None came. They didn't bother to vote. There was no point to follow any of the old rules anymore.

"Dismissed!" yelled Sam. He let out a sigh of relief as the last Overseer exited the hall. Kyle stood nearby Sam and put his hand on the man's shoulder.

"Great work, Sam...that was really close!" said Kyle. But Sam was not finished.

"Computer, give me access to the Overseer locator data system. Authorization code six, six, five, one, zero...Overseer

Sam Jones." The holographic screens turned red with a white text interface.

"Search for Overseer Milta, please." The computer scrambled at the request. Nothing came up.

"What? What about Overseer Ricco, where is Ricco?" Again, the computer returned nothing. Kyle sat down again.

"You don't think…that thing from before got 'em?" Kyle asked quietly.

"Not a chance, not a hundred meters underground behind eight meters of reinforced armoured steel. Sam turned to Kyle.

"We need to get down there!" Ricco's private labs were deep underground below the city where Ricco was supposed to be kept. Kyle and Sam hopped on a transport that took them to the second tallest building in the city. They accessed the doors and got into the elevators. A short ride later they were inside the lab. They opened Ricco's pod chamber. It was empty. Sam was speechless. Kyle leaned on the wall.

"No, Milta…she wouldn't dare…damn that witch…she moved Ricco…" Kyle muttered.

"Where are they!?" Cried Sam as he fell to his knees while Kyle slowly collapsed to the floor next to him. This was the first time they were sitting on the floor next to each other since they were kids. "You don't think…that she's taken him…to Azulus…" said Kyle looking at Sam's widened eyes.

17

Azulus

The destroyer, D4-Alice, made its way towards the new target with heavy authority. A fighter escort accompanied the large airborne machine to a deserted part of the destroyed East Coast. Most of the coast had sunk underwater when Letumfall went through its final stages. The continent was reshaped after New York state was blasted off the face of the earth, along with the UN Headquarters. That attack revealed the kind of terrifying weapons humanity has created. Weapons that could reshape geographical maps like they were colouring books. Weapons so powerful, and so well hidden from the public, that survivors made a pact to never talk about Letumfall. It was a piece of history that was better forgotten than studied. Because, if one studied this piece of history, they would want to end everything. That history was the real proof of the Human De-evolution Theory, which made the dinosaurs look good.

Parker's air force had to go around the Overseer cities. Four full squadrons of fighters was the maximum they could support with the extra air fuel tanker behind them at this range. And it was a miracle the old tanker could even fly this well. Tessorra's

Red Raiders tailed D4-Alice with three full squadrons. Michael's Black Raven came along with a single squadron of fighters, flying just a bit further back.

Due to its weight and energy requirements for long range flight, the D4-Alice maintained a steady pace without utilizing afterburners. The area they were flying over was now nothing more than mountains crumbled together in sharp peaks and black iced valleys. They crossed the 'no go' zone. Due to the mineral composition, the area was all bathed in a dark blue tint.

The voyage gave Kole and Pikii a chance to rest a little. They took naps in separate rest pods as the destroyer did not offer space for actual quarters. These rest pods were shared by the crew throughout shifts. However, each rest pod had everything one would need. You could have a meal, read a book, and take a much needed nap.

Parker had recently rested, and was now full of energy, strolling around the bridge to get some blood flow back into his old legs. The sun was starting to set, coming down slowly as if it was going to smash into the ocean of the blackened plains and cause a planet-wide explosion.

"So, General Parker, do you think they won't see us coming?" asked Layla.

"Who knows, considering they are using a blanket cloaking system of some sort, they might be as blind as we are." answered Parker. Scanners showed nothing.

"Sir, apologies for being out for so long!" Kole was finally awake and strolled onto the bridge. Layla stood up and saluted. She had a damned cute smile. Kole saluted her back.

"Ah, the man who makes my job easier!" Parker walked over to Kole and bear-hugged him.

"What a dreadful sunset...and I haven't seen this coastal area since I was a little boy..." Parker said with resentment in his voice. He really wanted to be blowing up Overseers right now, not flying away from them.

"At least, it's peaceful out here..." Kole pointed out.

"Could I get a hug, too?" Layla was fast, she was already in range of Kole. She then hugged him, pressing him deeply into her large chest. Kole didn't resist, and she held him for at least a few seconds. She then finally let go of Kole and hurried back to her comm station.

"General Parker! We're coming up on the coordinates, if we got the correct location, we'll be passing through the cloaking field in a minute from now." said Layla with confidence as Parker smiled.

"Alright, back to stations, let's get everyone ready! Kole, be careful, don't let the last fight go to your head, I need you back alive, son!" he demanded.

"Thanks Parker! We'll leave the air battle to you." said Kole noticing that Layla threw him another glance with a quick smile and then played with her hair at her console. Kole thought nothing of it, and made his way to the very back, passed a few doors, and entered a small hallway space where the drop pods were lined up. He got inside and secured himself. Space onboard was scarce, but it was used very well. A text message came up on his screen from Pikii.

{ Best sleep ever, you? }

He smiled. She was already in another pod and ready to go. Kole opened a voice channel directly to her.

"Slept well, thanks! So, you wanna share a rest pod later? The ones near the bridge have room for two, from what I hear." he said with a grin on his face.

"Oh my, Kole... is that a proposal?" Pikii said in a playful tone.

"Well...listen...just be sharp, we have no idea what to expect down there..." he said in a more serious tone. The main comm channel kicked in to interrupt their little conversation.

"Attention all units. We're about to pass through the cloaking field." announced Parker. "Fighters stay sharp. Drop pods, get ready for your dive!"

"Alright, let's get this party rolling!" Pikii sounded excited. Her thirst for battle reminded Kole of himself. The video feeds lit up. Their escort fighters fanned out. As they passed the cloaking field, an incredibly large structure was revealed in the far distance. Kole initially imagined some small entrance with an underground base. But that was not the case, at all.

There were gasps over the comms. The research base was an enormous steel structure built in two pentaprisms on top of each other. The outer silver walls offered a stark contrast to the blackened mountains surrounding the area. The destroyer was one hundred meters in the air, and two thirds of the structure still towered over them. Huge floodlights lit up the area as if it was daylight. The sunset vanished along with the upcoming darkness. Parker whistled.

"So much for the cover of darkness! Deploy shields, slow to ten knots, angle our approach, and keep us the hell away from that thing! Fighters, prepare your approach, and watch out for fire from all angles." Parker's orders were quickly carried out. They were not expecting to find something like this, at all. The Phasa did provide some data, but they operated from a different location much closer to the cities, so their knowledge of this base was very limited. Sending the fighters in first was basically bait, to see what kind of weapons the base could unleash at them. Parker really hoped they would not encounter any of the weaponry which guarded the cities, otherwise this offensive would turn sour real fast. The D4-Alice deployed her ten shielding rings.

"Alright, pilots, we now just need to get Kole and the marines into that base! Even if it means scrapping this tub in the process. Understood?" The bridge pilots in charge of the control systems nodded in agreement. They were prepared. Everyone was buckled in tight. If the short-range boosters kicked in, they would generate enough G-forces to break bones against the bulkheads if someone was unstrapped.

"How weird…no doors, no windows, no gun pods…and the walls are too thick to scan through…" As Layla was busy trying to make sense of the data coming in, the radar screens lit up as hundreds of drones launched towards them from the upper levels of the research base. "General! Two hundred enemy drones incoming!"

"I'll take that over laser batteries! All fighters, engage and try luring them into Alice's firing solution!" Parker yelled at the top of his lungs. Parker wished they could have brought more fighters. They had to leave their drones back at Flashpoint base as they didn't have the range to get out here.

The enemy drones swarmed up into the sky like a pack of bees. They consisted of deadly looking wing-like machines with two and a half meter wide wingspans. Their length was just over four meters, and they were about a meter in height which included their underbody gun pod. Their design kind of reminded Parker of a dragonfly, an insect he only saw alive once when he was a child. The drones were closing in fast.

* * * *

Red Raiders Squadron leader Tessorra sparked out orders like a blow torch cracking at full power. Her deep blue eyes scanned the enemy information in microseconds. Her cockpit went into combat mode. Everything tightened up controls-wise to her custom specifications for drone combat. Her helmet engaged see-through mode, which allowed her to see through the entire fighter using external cameras. Key instruments remained as outlines, everything else she didn't care about was now invisible including her own body. The feeling of this set up was like flying with your own body. She loved it, even though she was tense as hell right now.

She pulled the right control yoke and her team followed her on an intercept course. Her left yoke controlled weapon pod rotation and alignment, allowing for easy flips between the forward and rear-firing weapons. Their set-up was the same from the last battle.

- Top Pods Front: Rage 9 self-locking anti-air missiles
- Top Pod Rear Right: Flare 7x anti-missiles counter measures
- Top Pod Rear Left: Fractal G-micro anti-air missiles
- Bottom Pods Front: Panzer 3 Ultra railguns
- Bottom Pods Rear: Panzer 3 Ultra railguns

The Fractal G-micro anti-air missiles were going to be extremely handy in keeping drones off their rears. But for now,

Tessorra needed the long-range precision railguns mounted at the wing tips. Rage 9 missiles would do well here too, but the mobility of the enemy drones would determine how well they worked.

The drones were getting within range. Tessorra needed to draw fire away from the destroyer while giving Alice's guns a good line of fire on the return arc. She headed straight for them head-on as she smashed her A7-Raider fighter into insane g-forces using afterburners. Her HUD zoomed in on the first batch of incoming drones. Her firing controls and combat AI auto adjusted to match the enemy's AI formation and capabilities. It was time, she was close enough now.

She killed the afterburners and sent her jet into a short quick spiral in an attempt to confuse her target. She squeezed the release trigger on her left control yoke dedicated to the long-range wing mounted railguns. A single round from each side shot out like stars heading into the sky. The first shot missed. The second shot hit a drone dead on. The detonation was massive and surprised everyone as it blew up in a spectacular cloud of blue energy and orange fire.

"These ain't your regular drones! Keep clear when you blow them up, or they will take you with them!" Her wingmen got one as well. Again, a massive explosion followed the direct hit.

Unfortunately, five of her squadron pilots were already spinning in balls of fire dropping to the ground as the drones closed in and opened fire. Suddenly, a whole group of drones blew up as Black Raven began their attack run. The sky shook with thunder-like force. The closer they were to these things, the more dangerous this battle got. Part of the head-on attack was to give the enemy the impression that only the Red Raiders squadrons were attacking. Black Raven cloaked right before they entered the cloaking field. The drones were caught up in a crossfire.

"Thanks, Michael!" she yelled into the comm channel.

"Let's give it to them, Tess… let's ROCK, baby!!!" he yelled back. There was pressure in his voice as his fighter was smashing air waves at maximum g-forces. And with good reason. The drones adjusted to the cloaked ambush far more quickly than they would have liked, scattering them in a matter of seconds. Michael was issuing orders in overdrive. He was supporting her on this mission as second-in-command.

He had authority to take over in case she ran into issues or died. And right now, it was hard to think. They were being pulled out of formation and forced to dodge fire from multiple angles. One of the Black Raven pilots ejected as her engines were hit, but she was picked off instantly by a few drones from behind. They shot her body up multiple times and her flailing remains fell towards the ground in multiple pieces. Tessorra saw it in a picture-in-picture on her HUD feed from D4-Alice.

"Bastards! All units, if you eject, you die! Form up and give Alice a good firing angle on our return arc! Go now!" she hoped her pilots could continue to fight without fear, even as they were being slaughtered. She switched to her short-range Panzer 3 Ultra railguns and Rage 9 missiles. But it proved difficult to get any kills now as the drones were all over the place driving her targeting computer squarely nuts.

Her pilots managed to get a few Rage 9 missiles out and a few more drones detonated, lighting up the skies in bright flashes and sonic booms. She managed to circle back and draw a large number of drones towards the path of D4-Alice's guns. The rest of the pilots followed suit. They engaged afterburners to clear some space as their Fractal G-micro missiles fired furiously from the rear. If they didn't get to D4-Alice now, they would all be dead in less than a minute.

The destroyer was finally in range to target the drones with its anti-drone weaponry. And D4-Alice launched its counterattack with vengeance. Missiles, defence lasers, and railgun shots from D4-Alice's gun pods, blasted the enemy drones in a symphony of loud bangs and pops. Explosions rocked the whole sky, and the thundering sonic booms were deafening. The single volley from the destroyer took nearly half of the enemy drones out of the sky. The fighters isolated the shocks quite well, but a few jets nearly stalled from the force of the air pressure.

"That was one hell of a volley, Parker!" she yelled.

"Keep it up, Tess...now, move it! They're coming for you from all over the place!" Parker yelled.

Indeed, a few of the drones were getting too close for comfort from the sides. Luckily, her wingmen kept them off her. They were very well-trained for anti-drone dogfights. But when outnumbered like this and in a live firing situation, it certainly felt different from the simulator runs. She spotted another few drones at eleven o'clock.

"K2, K3, follow me!" She re-gripped her right control yoke and spun her fighter into a short arc, and the two wingmen followed. She squeezed the trigger and the Panzer 3 Ultra railguns sent rounds through the target, vaporizing it in a brilliant explosion. She felt the shockwaves on that one as her fighter bounced off the air pressure violently, shaking the hell out of her cabin. But she was not done. She took off another one, and then another.

A few drones came up behind them. Tessorra and her wingmen unleashed their rear Fractal G-micro rockets. K2 and K3 also used their rear railguns as they had the positioning. They took out seven enemy drones in three seconds. Then, her wingman blasted one coming right at her from above. "Thanks, K2!" she yelled with excitement. Her heart was pounding. Blood was rushing through her in ways she'd never felt before. She was at her limit, though...and so were her wingmen. They were really flying for their lives here.

"Hey watch it..." That was K3, but he was already dead on her HUD, as even more drones came up behind them. She desperately pulled on the controls to try to evade them. The only way was to fly in short, with ever-changing and unpredictable arcs, so that the drones had trouble locking in on them.

"No good, we're getting pushed away, get back to Alice's firing range!" she yelled while scrambling to avoid drone fire from what felt like was every angle. The drones had cleverly separated them away from the other fighters.

Did they single me out as the leader of the pack? Of course they did! Dammit!

Tessorra and K2 made a wild U-turn and sped back to the destroyer. As she managed to get back into the firing range of D4-Alice, Tessorra jerked the fighter off the line of fire sending her jet up and above the destroyer's bridge. It was one hell of a close flyby. The bulk of the tailing drones got taken out by the destroyer's volley. But a few persistent ones were still closing on her, dodging the fire as they adapted their strategy.

A drone shot went right past her cockpit, melting the top cover off, just nearly missing her head. Warning lights and alarms went off in a frenzy. Tessorra flipped the craft to try to turn the cockpit side away from more incoming fire and jam up the air pressure built up on the wings to change her trajectory. Her emergency cockpit shutters closed her off from the onslaught of the frigid air. Panic came as she wrestled with the engine output, trying to flip the jet into a backwards arc.

"Get your speed back up, or you'll stall!" That was K2. He re-engaged from a different angle, as he couldn't follow her erratic flight path from before. His shots took out three more drones, but the fourth drone changed course and then rammed his engines. He ejected. Luckily, they were close enough to Alice and there was just enough cover fire from the destroyer. Tessorra breathed a sigh of relief when he managed to glide down safely. Temporarily safe, she circled the field to see where else she could engage. Looks like they were getting to the end, but she was still in the fight, even without her wingmen.

"Alright, keep at it, we're getting close! Scatter and destroy targets. They are trying to stay just out of Alice's range, so don't be tricked to go out too far." she ordered as she caught another drone in her sights. It was maimed but was masterfully evading D4-Alice's fire. Tessorra aimed and fired multiple rapid railgun bursts until she blew it out the sky.

Another drone chasing her from behind ate one of her Fractal G-micro missiles as her jet's AI system compensated for her lack of attention. Her gun pods then went wild as she picked off a few more drones with the Rage 9 missiles as she swept the fighter in a tight arc, coming on top of them from above. The dark earth below her spun as if she was spinning it herself without effort. The scene was truly mesmerizing.

But then, without warning another drone came at her from below. She managed to jerk the fighter into a crazy shake, but it calibrated its aim and still blew a hole in her right engine.

"Michael, my bird's done for! Take over!" she yelled as she prepared for the worst. She had to decide; eject or stay in the fighter. Before she could figure it out, one of Michael's wingmen broke off and came to help her before the drone could take another pass. He chased the drone away, and an expert shot from D4-Alice fried the damn thing.

"K1, fall back with C3 and C4! Try to land somewhere and stay out of trouble!" Michael was firm. She retreated away from the combat zone immediately and managed to find a somewhat flat area below for an emergency landing. C3 and C4 from Michael's wing came along with her. She kicked in her emergency vertical boosters and gently smashed into the ground. C3 and C4 landed nearby, both had also taken a large amount of damage and were barely able to make it. Shaken, she shut down the main power core. The combat data on her screens angered her. Thirty-four fighters were destroyed. Three were out of commission, including herself. K2 was the only ejected pilot who made it. She released her hands from the controls. She looked at them and saw the faces of her dead teammates.

"Fuck!" Tessorra screamed as she angrily smashed the side of the of the cockpit. Tears poured out from her exhausted eyes.

* * * *

Red-alert warning signals beeped all over the bridge.

452

"Our squadrons have lost seven fighters in the first ten seconds!" reported Layla. Parker was flushed red, sweat poured down his face.

"Damn, what a mess!" said Parker to himself. Kole watched the screens. The drones managed to kill off another four fighters. Tessorra and her team painfully fought back. They had to attack and then retreat. It was the only way to lure the drones into D4-Alice's range. They had to lead the drones into areas where the destroyer's guns had the most effective targeting while not allowing them to attack the ship. Then, less than a minute into the battle, D4-Alice finally lit up the sky, taking out the drones at a staggering rate. And while Alice took some fire, the shielding system held up. The dogfight continued for about a minute and half. Kole watched it intensely.

"Thirty-four fighters gone, sir...and three are out of the fight, including Tessorra. Eleven fighters still operational. We have destroyed one hundred and eighty enemy drones, and there's twenty more remaining." Layla reported.

"Alright, let's finish the rest. Time to blow a hole in that thing with the main railgun and launch our pods. Michael, you alive?" barked Parker.

"Yes sir, got another one, we're almost done here!" he replied.

"Bring them in close for one last pass." Parker ordered.

"Roger that, it's not easy, though...these buggers are smart!"

Michael and the remaining fighters did their best to force the last drones closer to Alice. The gun pods lit up, littering the sky with explosions. Kole felt the close-range shocks from those blasts.

Kole's pod started to slide down into the launch tube. These pods were more cramped compared to the resting ones.

Basically, these were like missiles, and could fly directly into combat areas and land personnel at specific points.

"All enemy drones are destroyed!" Layla said with a sigh of relief.

"Fire the railgun cannon!" Parker yelled with renewed enthusiasm. A giant blast rocked the destroyer as the primary railgun let 'er rip. Ahead of the bridge, Parker watched the bright explosion. The bridge viewports dimmed the output so they would not be blinded. As the smoke cleared, an opening in the superstructure was revealed.

"Sir, the railgun has vaporized the outer shell! We have a way in!" reported Layla. Parker had a smirk on his face. With the drones wiped out, there was nothing else standing in their way, it seemed. D4-Alice had an even more powerful weapon. Above the railgun, in the second upper half of the ship, there was a powerful laser cannon. But to use it, they would have to power-down the shielding system and use up most of their energy reserves.

"Launch the pods!" Parker ordered. Kole felt the immediate and immense g-forces of the acceleration. Like bullets, the pods swooshed towards the ground. Then, they suddenly changed the angle and shot upwards, heading for the opening. Parker watched over the battlefield. The fires of the burning jets on the ground made him sick to his stomach.

In an instant, people he knew vanished forever. More than half of his best pilots were gone. They were cut down by nothing more than metal and a computer program. Perhaps the previous battle made them all overconfident.

"Landing party, exercise extreme caution, there may be more surprises." he managed as he tried to slow his breathing down.

Parker's heart rate was still way up, and it would not do him any good. He wiped the sweat off his forehead.

"Fighters are getting low on fuel. Suggest we send them back to the tanker..." said General Bull.

"Bring the tanker here, refuel the fighters, and scuttle the it afterwards. We cannot be without cover." ordered Parker.

"Roger that, I'm on it!" noted General Bull.

"Layla, we have four survivors on the ground we need to retrieve. Send down the pickup drones immediately. Once they are on board, get us closer to the base, I want to make sure the marines can bug out in a hurry if they get into trouble." Parker let out a deep breath.

"Yes sir!" Layla said as she relayed the order.

* * * *

The pods crashed with a bang and without incident. Kole and the marines jumped out of their pods with guns at the ready. A small city lay sprawled out in front of them. The view was good as they were up high. Further outwards there was an opening in what seemed to be some sort of roofline. Three big rockets were far off in the distance. Kole ignored them.

"Snipers, positions! Pikii and team, head to the control room and assume command of the facility. The rest of you, follow me to the main research wing!" Kole commanded.

[Facility map...done!]

"Module 717 has just relayed the map of the facility to your HUDs. Keep all comms open. If you go silent, we'll assume you've run into hostiles." he added.

"Hey, hang on...wait a second...Parker!" stated Module 717 over the comm units.

"What is it my friend?" Parker asked.

"Friend? Works for me! Now, do you see those rockets there?!" inquired Module 717.

"Yeah, they sure are big...should we be concerned about them?" Parker was super curious as to what those things were there for.

"The system says they are deep-space rockets! That second one there, the one in the middle, is preparing for a launch sequence!"

"What? Space? No way in hell! This some kind of joke?" exclaimed Kole, not at all amused by that information.

"What do they need to go...to space for...?" added Pikii.

"Interplanetary rockets...like, what the fuck?" Parker noted. Six snipers took up positions. Kole and Pikii then both lead a team of twelve marines to their intended targets in two groups. They all headed outside the building and Kole's team went further down to the right, towards the research buildings, while Pikii led her team straight ahead towards a control tower that was in the dead centre of the entire facility. Above them was a gigantic roofline which resembled the sports stadiums of the past. And now they could clearly see how the city sloped downwards a few miles towards some sort of barriers and hangars. Way past those were the three gigantic rockets.

"Androids...Synthetics...only scientific models...all unarmed, you can run right through them." said Module 717 with confidence.

"Roger! But where is the security?" Kole inquired. Module 717 didn't reply. Kole already knew. Someone shut down the death bots on the inside. They took some time jogging but managed to reach the research wing fairly quickly. Synthetics were hiding from them here and there, but there was no hostility at all towards the invaders. To Kole it seemed like they were very surprised that their shackles had suddenly come off. And like scared prisoners, they were sitting still in their cells, unsure if they should leave.

The cylindrical structures of the research wing were painted silver and white, and they had varying heights which made for a quite an interesting architectural piece. As Kole headed deeper in between the buildings they ran into a group of Synthetics standing outside what Module 717 designated as the main research building, which was obvious anyway as it was the largest of the bunch.

[Phasa friends…looks like all is clear, come on over!]

Kole saw them fly in, six birds in total. They landed in front one of the Synthetics. Their conversations only took nano seconds. The man clearly in charge straightened his multi-coloured lab coat. He looked at Kole for a few seconds. Then walked over.

"Oh, I see, you brought my children…" he started. Kole cut him off.

"Thank me later! Can you tell me why that rocket is launching?" The man looked towards the rockets. The vibrations of the launch were coming through the ground.

"Oh, that…that is Overseer Milta's doing. She kidnapped Overseer Ricco, shut down all security, told us we are now free, and now she's headed out, it seems…to the stars." said the Synthetic scientist. He paused for another few seconds, seemingly gauging Kole's reaction to his words.

[Kole, these Synthetics took a lot of abuse at this place from human beings, and he is carefully choosing his words, by instinct.]

Noted, let's be extra nice then.

"Oh, I managed to attach a prototype body on Ricco. He was very near death..." he said as he moved closer to Kole.

"Oh, and space...an interesting place to go don't you think?" asked the Synthetic scientist. Kole smiled. It was almost comical; the man started every sentence so far with an 'oh'.

"Wait what? You really think Milta is headed to space with Ricco?" Kole asked.

[Seriously?! That's one bad escape plan...if you can even call it that...]

"Oh yes, she's most definitely headed to space." repeated the Synthetic scientist again with a confused look on his face, as if struggling to see what was amiss with his explanation.

"So, Milta thinks she can escape...we'll see about that. We're not here to harm any of you, by the way, in case Phasa didn't make that clear enough. I mean, they are your kids, right?" Kole looked around. The Synthetics became less stiff and some more finally started to come out of hiding. There were not as scared anymore, but still timid and cautious.

"Oh yes, I see you gave them a name, how interesting, indeed! I am indeed their creator!" said the Synthetic, proudly.

"I heard there were two of you who created the Phasa..." Kole already knew the answer. Even though the man he was staring at was a Synthetic, the face gave it away. Their AI code was created by human beings. It was only natural.

458

"Oh, him...yes, yes. Dead, I'm afraid. After we created our children, we tried to stall the Overseer transition plans...he paid the price for it. Most unfortunate turn of events, it was."

"I see...I'm sorry to hear that. By the way, what's your name?" asked Kole.

"Oh, I am Dr. Matheus...and it's a pleasure to meet you, Commander Kole." They shook hands. That rang a bell.

"Wait, you are that Matheus?" Kole asked.

"Oh? Of course not. The first Overseer, Matheus Grand, was a human who saved the leftovers of the world. However, I was created in his image, although with a far more advanced brain, of course...then, much later we created our children in animal forms to hide their existence from the Overseer regime...we were allowed pets, you see. So here in front of us are the crow models...and there was a cat and a raven...where...?"

As if on cue, the cat flew in via a raven ride. Kole counted again. There were eight of them in total. Seven birds, and one cat. The cat came over, it seemed a little dazed.

"Dammit, next time fly steady...damned turbulence generating buzzard! Oh hey...hey...it's that Kole guy, nice to see you again, animal abusing dirtbag!" The cat gave him a look of disgust.

"Hello to you too..." Kole replied while rolling his eyes. Matheus picked up the cat. The raven that brought the cat flew up and sat on Matheus's right shoulder. The crows then flew on the shoulders of the assistants. They were female Synthetics here too. And one was cute, to boot.

[Pervvvvvvv!!!!!]

"Lay off, man!" Kole just realized he spoke out loud. "Apologies, I was talking to..." he managed.

"Oh, yes, Module 717, we heard about him from my children. Thank you all for working together to help bring the Overseers down." said Matheus. Kole realized the raven just bowed his head towards him. All the Synthetics followed suit.

"Well, you have some tough little critters there, and smart...well, except for that cat, of course." said Kole with a chuckle.

"You have got to be meowing kidding me, he doesn't need to be alive anymore, right? Can I kill him...PLEASE?" asked the cat. Yet, the creature calmed down as soon as Matheus petted him. Kole looked at Matheus in disbelief.

"Oh, you see, while they are more advanced than you and I, they are still...young...and they are also still part animal in their own ways, something we had to bake-in to avoid detection...so, if I pet this cat, it will act like a cat." Matheus smiled. The cat was quiet and started to purr.

"I guess...so...I still have lots of questions...but one quick thing first, about Kelvin's mansion...you saved my life and then, this weapon, is this all from you?" Kole took out the cylindrical ELMD weapon. Matheus looked at the weapon with a careful eye.

"Oh, yes, I see you made some modifications...truly impressive. My partner designed it. I had that package delivered by the Raven; the only one able to carry heavy loads. It then sent an anonymous communication to your implant, looks like it was just in time. We better go inside, that rocket is about to launch." Matheus led the way. A cute Synthetic scientist attached herself to Kole's side within an inch of him. But Kole was too busy to notice her advance as he was listening with intense interest to Matheus as he went on.

"Oh, and yes, the Kelvin Synthetic you fought. The Raven did indeed interfere. Had no choice. The tech in how it was done is a little complex but think of controllable electromagnetic pulses that can form into a beam, and temporarily override instructions in a machine without a trace. He had physical and psychological control of Kelvin's clone just for a few microseconds. However, that effort burnt out the majority of the Raven's energy and when it came time to deliver that weapon it was quite low on power. You see, energy requirements for their basic operation are incredibly steep, and when you add the ability to manipulate their shape and infuse it with fast moving particles, it pushes them to their operational limits. That ability is what allowed them to cut the tanks into little pieces. That crow over there, it was also the reason why Ricco almost died, we were so close..."

Kole looked over to where Matheus pointed. It was the crow sitting on the left shoulder of the cute scientist who was literally hanging off his left shoulder. She had gorgeous red hair and stood out from the rest. She had a thin waist, and her uniform hid what Kole figured were DDs on her chest. Her legs were exposed under the knee-high skirt, and her semi-high heels completed the package.

"Oh, I see your eyes can appreciate Minsko's beauty. She's my protégé scientist and now second in rank after my partner was...removed from existence." he said. "She's been stalking your every move, so I would watch it if you're ever alone with her...she's quite powerful and may get what she wants..."

Minsko blushed and put some distance between them.

"Dr. Matheus!" she protested. "Please...how could you say that...in front of my target, no less..."

461

"Because after Kevin died, I realized we should speak the truth, ask for what we want, and stop playing games with each other. Anyways, I will let you kids figure out what you want to do with that truth."

They reached a big hall with huge glass windows. The view was perfect. But their peace was quickly interrupted, just as Kole gave a smile to Minsko and she smiled back.

"KOLE!!!!" The voice comm went mad. Kole jumped. It was Pikii alright.

"Control room is trashed! All the operators here are dead...main launch modules and controls all smashed and useless."

"On my way!" Kole answered as him and his team bolted to the control room. Minsko was a little sad. Matheus put his hand on her free shoulder.

"Oh, dear. Dear, don't worry. In the worst case, I will make a Synthetic version of him just for you..." he said with a creepy robotic smile.

* * * *

Parker watched the landscape in a calm mood, although he was still tense. D4-Alice's once booming guns were now sitting idle.

"Nothing going on, hopefully we've won this battle..." Layla managed a short victory speech. Parker reflected on the battle. The drones were deadly to the last, they aimed for the cockpits and engines, and even shot down those who tried to eject. Then Kole's voice broke into the comm channel, but it was too hard to hear due to static.

"Kole, you're breaking up. What's going on with that rocket over there?" Static broke up the transmission again.

"Parker, we can't...the rocket. You'll have...shoot it out...the sky!" Kole's voice came through. A crackling sound roared from the rocket.

"Milta...going...to space..." Static took over again. But Parker got the idea. Parker really didn't care where Milta thought she was going.

"That bitch is not going anywhere! Raise altitude! Max thrusters, get over that building and line up a shot! Get ready for the g-forces, make sure you're all strapped in!" Parker watched the displays with intensity as he gripped the handles. This type of thruster boost would give one a throw-up session otherwise. The D4-Alice then shot up like a bullet, quickly clearing a line of sight over the massive structure.

"Recall the shield system! Power up our main laser gun!" Parker didn't think he'd actually get to use it. It would be a nice show. A powerful weapon against a target like a giant rocket. Nothing fit better, but he had to ensure he didn't blow up the whole facility and Kole's team along with it. He had to be precise and careful about how they were going to stop this thing. Layla had some data.

"The rocket is not going up, yet...there's some sort of a shield system by the looks of it, it's engulfing the entire launch pod." She showed the readouts on screen.

"What!?" Parker didn't have time to say more. Of course, their own shield system came from Overseer technology. Surely the one on the launch pod was far more advanced. The monitors lit up with new information as a circular top blew open. Three building-sized rings shot up into the air and took positions high up in the atmosphere. Their power discharge was immense. The skyline was changing colour due to their powerful energy output. A second later, the magnetic field those things generated swayed their ship off-target and backwards. Electronics were going nuts, too.

"Correct pitch and line! Switch to full manual flight controls." yelled Parker as the pilots wrestled with the controls.

"We're trying, General!" Reported one of the pilots. Gunner control spoke up.

"General Parker, there's too much electromagnetic interference, we'll have to switch to manual targeting, too."

"Damn it! Do what you gotta do!" yelled Parker. This was going to be harder than he thought. The Overseers were a smart bunch. Ricco thought of nearly everything.

"Make it one shot, full power to the laser! Ensure we catch it high enough so it doesn't kill everyone on the ground!" he then switched to the ground comm.

"Kole, we're going to catch it in mid-air, shooting it on the ground might kill everyone. But we can't offer a guarantee, so get everyone the hell out of that facility immediately!"

"Don't wor...we...heading...for...pods." Kole was brief and static again made communications garbled. Kole sounded winded from running. Then finally, a clean channel opened up.

"Slow down, Parker! If you can't shoot that thing down without killing us, don't! We all want to live here!" said Module 717, overriding all the comm channels. "Even if they do escape, they won't live long in outer space. Also, I analyzed the rocket structure, sending data...just hit this spot while it's at this altitude and it will fly off-course before crashing somewhere very far away." Parker's anxiety went down.

"You're right, friend. No need for overkill heroism. Gunner control, adjust your targeting, and if you think you can't make the shot...don't." Gunner control chuckled.

"Sir, if we can't make the shot, we're buying the beer!" Parker was happy to hear that.

"You got it, you brats, so do your damned best!" he replied with a stern smile. He saw the crosshairs move right above the second ring. Then, a surprise came through.

"Sir, incoming transmission...from the rocket!" Layla reported.

"Put her on!" said Parker.

"Parker, Parker, dear Parker...please...tsk, tsk, tsk. Oh, how could the thought of killing me even cross your mind, you dirty old bastard? I'm so disappointed in you..." said Overseer Milta. Parker felt a chill run down his spine. He forgot just how intimidating and evil she could be. Looks like she was watching their little operation. He figured she was here. Still, she injected him with loads of anxiety. Milta was the one running experiments at the base, all those years ago. It was her robots that killed his and Bull's family. She never took responsibility. She never apologized. Typical politician of the old age. Parker took a deep breath.

"Milta, you need to power-down your rocket, and I will personally assure that no harm will come to you. You know that I am a man of my word." stated Parker.

"Hah! Then why are you not protecting the Overseers? You traitor!" she hissed at him.

She had a point.

"Well, tough luck and fat chance, little soldier boy! Ricco and I are going to the stars. You fire that toy cannon of yours and everyone on that base below will be history!" Milta still sounded very much in control of the situation. Most likely she was not bluffing.

Dammit! Milta! He had to be extremely careful with her. The possibility that the facility was rigged to explode suddenly became very high.

"But Ricco would never...go with you..." Parker knew how much Ricco despised Milta. "You kidnapped him! Didn't you?!"

"Call it whatever you want, he's mine now...you and your dirty rats can't have him!" Milta cut the comm line. General Bull finally spoke up.

"There's something wrong with those energy readouts...I think you'd better tell our folks to get the hell out of there now on the double!" Parker knew that when Bull spoke, one had better listen.

"Kole! Kole, I have a bad feeling about this, like a that-base-might-be-wired-to-blow-up-in-a-matter-of-seconds   kind   of feeling! I know you're on your way out, but you might want hurry the hell up! RUN!"

* * * *

Kole, Pikii, and everyone else bolted for it even faster. Parker made total sense. They had thirty-two pods. And they had collected some thirty Synthetic scientists in tow from the main buildings. The Phasa birds and the cat already all flew off.

"Can you take over pod controls?" Kole asked Module 717.

"Already on it!" Module 717 was ahead of him, as always.

"Okay folks, lose the gear, or we ain't gonna fit." ordered Kole. They could fit just one person extra per pod if they sardined

466

themselves in without anything on them. At least that was the theory.

All units dropped their weapons and unbuckled their armour. Kole took Minsko and they stripped nearly to their underpants and went into his pod. Matheus took off his lab coat and ripped his shirt off and threw it on the ground. Pikii gave Kole a surprised look, but then nodded and stripped to her bra and undies and dragged Matheus with her.

Kole and Matheus would not fit into the same pod. Smaller female, with the bigger male, was the only way to fit. And it was a tight squeeze, alright. Luckily the pods were just tall enough so they could stagger vertically a bit. The enclosure closed, hiding everything from view. Minsko didn't waste any time in sliding off her bra using Kole's forehead, revealing her bare chest. She then pushed her breasts right into his face.

"Oh my, sorry...my bra came off...you can do whatever you like, though...who knows, it might be the last time you'll get the chance..." Minsko said quietly.

[She has a point, we might be all vaporized any second now...hell, I say go for it, Kole!]

"Hey! Stop, what the fuck..." said Kole as he could just barely breathe. She was pressing her chest super hard right into his mouth. It was like a bad space porno gone wrong. Really wrong.

Meanwhile in Pikii's pod, Matheus was trying to hold on for dear life in any way he could as he was super shy about touching a real human female. No matter how hard he tried his hands were in all the wrong places. His chest brushed her breasts, and one of his legs had to be squeezed between her legs. He wasn't sure what was appropriate.

"It's fine, try to relax. We're in a tin can with no room, so I will forgive you if you feel me up a little…you probably never touched a human female like this before, have you?" said Pikii.

"Oh, indeed you are correct, this is the first time for me to be so close to a human female, and it's more sensational than I would have expected…" said Dr Matheus.

"Ohhh…so you too can be a bad boy…okay, well I think we're going to be fine…but Kole…that dirtbag better not be doing anything funny with that big breasted bitch, or I will put a bullet in his head myself!" she said calmly. Matheus suddenly felt like he was going to pay for this close encounter one way or another if he pissed her off. He did his best to relax, not to move, and stay quiet.

There were, of course, many other Synthetics on the base. Matheus issued the evacuation order, and the Synthetics were now running for whichever exits they could. However, there were many stationary units who worked on the various processes at the facility. They all made their goodbyes in an electronic symphony of wailing beeps and cries. After all their hard work for humanity, those Synthetics and machines were left for dead. Kole had no time to shed a tear.

"Alright, we gotta go! Get us out of here, Module 717!" shouted Kole as he tried to breathe. The pod thrusters fired perfectly for a quick takeoff. And then, blast off! They sprung out of the facility like flies and headed back to the destroyer. Kole was trying to get his face away from Minsko's right breast as she was clearly trying to smother him with it. On top of that, the force of the pod was pushing her whole body downwards on him with immense force. They were in perfect alignment.

Fucking hell, make me impotent, you AI bastard! Do it now! But Module 717 wasn't answering him. And Kole's privates got aroused. It was a natural reaction, not an intentional one. Her left hand was conveniently in position near his privates. Her right hand grabbed his ass. She uncovered the top part of his underpants slid out his penis.

"Okay...very funny, now stop! Minsko!" begged Kole.

[Is this what they call rape? Because...I think she's about to rape you, Kole...]

There you are! Help me! Hack her brain, turn my dick off, something! Minsko moved aside her pink underwear just enough and guided Kole right inside her.

[Trying...wait...oh, shit...when did she...I think her breasts were coated with some sort of drug...your dick ain't gonna go down for hours!]

"You're fucking kidding me! You drugged me?!" yelled Kole.

"That's right, Kole. Raping you is kind of my wildest fantasy. And until you fully unload, that piece of yours will stick out like a sore thumb. Now you have no choice. If you come out of this pod with your dick erect...oh, what a sight that would be. Now, just do as I say, and you'll get to live, okay?" she said as she moaned loudly. Good thing Module 717 turned off the comms.

Kole felt the g-forces jam them even more closely together, squeezing them very tightly from every angle. It was the first time he'd experienced sex inside a super g-force environment. One would have to imagine a sardine can where the fish were fucking each other. Deep inside Minsko, advanced sexual vibrators went to work, wrapping his penis in multiple sensations of warm and hot massaging rotations.

Minsko kissed him and slid her tongue deep down his throat by force. She had a rather long split tongue. It had a mind of its own, too. Kole's tongue had nowhere to run as she wrapped around it and massaged his tongue tip with her split tips. She pushed into his hips, thrusting so wildly that his pelvis was hurting. Minsko was unnaturally strong and overpowered him completely. Regardless of how it happened, Kole had to admit that it overall felt sort of incredible. It was his first time being completely taken by force by a Synthetic woman.

Before long the pod docked to D4-Alice. Due to the combat situation they were in, getting out of the pods was out of the question. She reached a crazy climax but kept going, squeezing his penis until his warm liquid filled her insides. Minsko smiled.

"I hope you enjoyed that as much as I did." she said. Kole relaxed his face on her shoulder, and she licked his neck, and then nipped on his left ear. He was still hard. She kept him inside her, gently massaging him with her vibrator units. They felt the ship spin around at a crazy velocity, and then the afterburners kicked in full force, pushing Kole deep inside Minsko again.

"Dammit, Minsko...that's enough, right?" he asked.

"Nope! If you don't climax one more time the drug will stay active. Now, get inside my other hole!" she demanded as she repositioned herself. Kole was gassed. She somehow managed to get him inside where she wanted.

[Well...uhhh...I think if we die now, you won't have regrets, at least...]

Dude...if Pikii finds out about this, she'll never believe my side of the story...

As the g-forces hit again, Kole started to black out.

Azulus Ascends

* * * *

"Parker, that energy pattern, it's not really a shield, it's a magnetic vortex that spins at massive velocity, combined with some sort of ionized energy. You fire that cannon of ours and it will just bend the beam. We'll never hit that rocket, and I think Milta is counting on that!" General Bull was a godsend in situations like this. Parker realized his error. Milta wanted Parker to fire the main gun as it would take all their shield energy with it. With the main shields offline, if the base blew up it would surely vaporize them. The pods were almost back. Massive electric shocks resembling lightning were setting themselves off on the three rocket launch rings which were hovering like godlike creations in mid-air.

"Change of plans, everyone! Gunners, fighters, everyone listen-up! We're going to cut the laser output to ten percent right before we fire off a shot at one of those floating rings. We've got to try making it look like we're trying to destroy one of them. I then want all available power back into the shields immediately! I want engines set to full and ready for a one-eighty with full afterburner blast to get the hell out of here!" Parker gambled that if they fired a shot now, Milta would not blow up the entire base along with herself and her rockets.

"Firing laser at ten percent output in three, two, one!" said one of the gunners. The lights dimmed, even at just ten percent a high pitch whine came from the ship, and with crackling thunder the weapon fired. Parker watched as the powerful red beam shot outwards. For the split-second it made outer contact, the beam turned the disk energy into a blood red shimmer of sparks, only to be bent around an invisible cylinder of some overpowering energy. Had he fired at full power it would have gone down the drain and they would have been royally screwed.

"Thanks Bull, that was a hell of a call!" Parker said with a proud tone.

"Anytime, friend." replied Bull.

"The marine pods are back in!" Layla yelled. "Shields are deployed!"

"Full one-eighty! Get us the hell out of here! Max afterburners!" commanded Parker. All ships accelerated with insane velocity and shot away from the base at full speed. The D4-Alice used its afterburners on max output, scorching the sky and leaving white trails from its massive engines. Another transmission came from the rocket.

"Wow, you're not as stupid as I thought you were...good boy, Parker...good little boy..." smirked Milta over the comm.

"I'm curious Milta, how you're going pull all of this off..." replied Parker. "I can't believe that you kidnapped Ricco to leave the planet in a rocket. You'll die up there, you know that...right?"

"Oh, but Parker, you have no idea what this thing really is, do you? This rocket, Parker, is called Azulus. It's made for deep-space travel. And I mean, real deep space. We have everything we need to live here. You, on the other hand, had better worry about the energy overload I set up which will fry the reactors on the base and set them into blow-everything-the-hell-up mode! But don't blame me, it's nothing personal. At least it's not nuclear. Ricco was against that sort of thing. Well then, I'll be on my way! I sincerely hope you don't survive!" Milta cut the transmission.

"That crazy bitch wasn't joking, a huge orbital energy discharge is in progress!" yelled Layla at the top of her lungs.

"It's off the charts!" Parker was watching the same screens. He could only mutter.

"What the fuck...?" he managed.

"Better pray that our baby Alice is fast enough!" yelled Bull. The screens showed it all. The discharge disbanded in a massive field of blue energy far up in the sky. The colour mixed with the beautiful orange and yellow from the sunset. There were three more rings already up in orbit. They lit up so brightly that they could see them visually. They were way bigger than the ones that came from the rocket launch pod. They were so massive they blocked the view of the moon in the sky.

Parker watched in disbelief as the top-most ring of the three that came from the rocket launch pod formed what could only be described as a dark film. Azulus didn't just launch. It shot upwards like a bullet, leaving the launch pad with a sonic boom that rocked the sky, nearly cracking the whole land beneath it into two. Before anyone realized what was happening, Azulus vanished into the dark film, which instantly dematerialized, leaving only massive energy sparks of a star-like trail into the dark sky.

"Up top!" yelled Layla. Parker was mesmerized by all this. If Milta was right, they were about to die, but this was just too exciting to watch. He'd never seen anything like it. They barely registered the rocket as it appeared for a split-second passing through the three rings in the upper atmosphere, and then blowing out from Earth's orbit at speeds never before achieved by a man-made machine. Azulus then disappeared completely from their sensors, vanishing into the darkness of space.

Baffled, they all stared in amazement. Silence followed for a few seconds. Then the base exploded. The destroyer, caught by the immense shockwave, was nothing more than a beach ball flung by a tsunami. The ship tumbled and spun, got flung again, and bounced some more in the air. It was a few seconds of hell that nobody would ever forget.

Then, coming in at a steep decline and spinning out of control, the D4-Alice smashed into the ground. A few seconds later, the engines died out completely and stopped, the ship itself switched to emergency power as the main power core went offline. The pods then opened their doors. Crispy, burnt air filled up the destroyer.

Kole was out cold. Minsko masterfully placed her bra back on and adjusted her panties. She then quickly cleaned up and hid Kole's sore protrusion back into his underpants. Everyone was in shock from the crash, and nobody was quick to exit. Groans of pain came from all over, and nobody was paying them any attention.

"God damn! We're alive!" Parker shouted over comms while nearly vomiting blood due to the impact. His command console had seen better days, and even with the harness, he felt like he fell out of the sky and fell directly onto concrete. He opened a comm channel to Flashpoint Base.

"Admiral Anna Rossa, we need a rescue…crap…is that blood? Anna! Send pickup…please…" he managed.

"Thank God you're all still breathing! Help is on the way!" Anna was a bit shaken in her tone. Parker knew why. They almost lost everyone. The destroyer used half of a mountain side as a brake pad, leaving one hell of a skid mark.

The ship was done for. However, the readouts showed the crew and the Synthetics they saved were alive. There was no way to scan right now to see if anyone who tried to get away from the base on foot made it. But Parker, coming to his senses realized even if they could scan the result would be the same. They were the only survivors from that base. Parker let out a loud sigh.

"Damage?" Parker asked. He wiped his blood-stained mouth as he unbuckled himself.

"Shielding system took nearly all of the initial impact...the rings are fried and fell off a few milliseconds post impact...the electro hull burned through to the bulkheads, main power systems all severed or fried..." Layla reported.

Parker laughed out loud. "In other words, my dear girl...the goose is fried. Wait a sec, what about the fighters?"

"All crash-landed, but all alive!" Layla reported. The fighters were much faster and were many miles further ahead of them. Layla was shaken to the bone, though. That was one hell of a second combat mission for her, and all in one day, no less.

"Alright, I think we've had enough fun for one day, let's begin the evacuation, Layla. Make sure everyone takes an emergency supply kit, the weather is not our friend outside." Parker sank back into his pod and took a deep breath. Layla relayed the orders and came over to him.

"Are you alright, General?" she said while holding out her hand for him. Parker could not refuse, he held on to her and she pulled him from his seating position in a swift, powerful motion. She then helped him towards the exit. They needed to make haste and make distance, in case the ship caught fire, or something exploded. In such tight and damaged quarters, it would mean a short and certain journey towards death.

* * * *

After the evacuation, Kole regained consciousness, and managed to cozy up to Pikii. She was rather surprised by the weird way Kole was holding on to her. Like a child hanging on to his mother. They sat on the hillside, waiting for the transports from Flashpoint Base to arrive. It was nice to get some air. Everyone's head took a pounding from the crash. Even Module 717 seemed to be taking a break. It was getting darker and colder by the minute. Parker and Layla came alongside them. They were handing out salvaged headache pills and other supplies, which Kole and Pikii gladly accepted.

Tessorra came too, accompanied by Michael, who was helping her walk as her left leg was injured. Her ponytail was undone, and her hair swayed in the wind. They sat down nearby, exchanging glances and nods with Parker, Layla, Pikii, and Kole. A short time later, Minsko showed up, too. She waved and smiled as she sat down with Matheus who looked quite shaken. Kole avoided eye contact with her. She gave him the chills. He held Pikii even more tightly.

They all got some spare military clothes. Luckily, the ship had enough gear. A few marines came by and made a fire for them and passed out thermal blankets. There were already a few fires burning, and circles of men and women sat around the fires, trying to keep warm. Some snacked on the rations and drank some packaged liquids. Overall, everyone was quiet, with only a handful of conversations going on.

"Kole...are you okay?" asked Pikii quietly.

"Alive...at least, I'm...alive..." he managed. She gripped his neck tightly from behind with one hand. He could feel the force of the grip. It was scary.

"Fine...be like this, if you want...I know you felt that Synthetic bitch up while in the pod. I mean look at her. If I were a man, I'd fuck her brains out myself. But now you owe me a week of pleasure, and I mean it! A whole week, just you and me...no other humans or Synthetics...unterstand?" she whispered into his ear.

"Sure...you got it...anything you want." said Kole quietly. Pikii then kissed him on the lips. Minsko was staring them down. Pikii stared right back. But luckily Matheus started talking to Minsko, distracting her gaze.

The sky was slowly turning to night, and the stars were coming out. Everyone was silent now, mostly trying to process what just happened. Kole stretched out on his thermal blanket. The fire kept his feet warm. He was watching those stars carefully, wondering where Milta was off to. Pikii rested her head on Kole's shoulder. Kole closed his eyes and fell asleep.

18

Aftermath

The human reserve soldiers and Syndicators holding the lines were exhausted. Among them, there was one woman who felt more frustration than the rest. Kelly Osbina was not happy protecting the Overseers. The thought wasn't instant. It had been in the back of her head for a while now. Since the day she woke up and found out that Kole has gone off on another deadly mission. And when he came back, he was sent away before she could see him. And then her friend, her role model, her shoulder to cry on, was cast out of the military after the emergency broadcast and vanished. And almost like clockwork, Pete vanished too.

Ipson didn't tell her much, even though she pressed him to tell her what the hell was going on. But what could the man do? His daughter was on the line. Since then, Kelly had been desperately trying to piece things together on her own. And right before this deployment, Kelly managed to get some answers.

Her team was guarding the central Overseer buildings in the centre of City 77. She was damned tired. Her eyelids wanted to close. Kelly had numerous booster packs that kept soldiers alert for long periods of time, but after a few too many, their effect was wearing thin. She took off her combat gloves, shoved them into her vest pocket, and brushed her gorgeous blond hair with her bare hands. Her hair was oily and felt dirty.

She sniffed her right shoulder and her nose nearly freaked at the unpleasant scent. The military uniform she had on was already on her for a whole day from before, and now some twenty-four additional hours later, and it was moist and disgusting. It didn't help that the air was humid, and there was some light rain here and there. To piss her off even more, the Overseers would not even let them use the building washrooms to clean up. They had to go to combat portables, regardless of rank.

"Idiots..." she muttered to herself. They were ordered here on very short notice. If someone tried to leave, they were to keep them here by force, and just a little while ago lethal force was authorized if they didn't comply. Those were some seriously heavy-handed orders. Kelly thought about things. The Synthetics, even assembled in great numbers, didn't intimidate her in any way. She wasn't scared.

So, what are the Overseers so scared of?

This was the first time in a while that she's had this much time to literally do nothing but think. She was promoted to Commander after she recovered from her mission. She thought that her promotion had more to do with her staying loyal. Her life was suddenly very busy, and she only caught glimpses of Kole on the news here and there. She got added duties with lots of extra work. Overseer James had her overloaded more than ever. And this. Well, this for her was the breaking point.

She looked at the crowd. The Synthetics were not tired. That was just a fact. They stood there for hours, and they were fine. Her men on the other hand were a train-wreck after twenty-four hours. If something happened, they would be slow to react, while the Synthetics would gain an instant advantage. She breathed in the fresh morning air. It smelled stuffy. Too many people in one area with not enough wind to pass through. The time was seven-thirty in the morning. It was a nice sunrise and Kelly looked forward to just a bit of wind to come in.

She let out her breath slowly, letting her eyes rest just a little bit. Then, she looked at the men and women under her command. They looked so damned miserable. She felt their pain. Her Synthetic husband could also be among the silent protesters. She could not use personal communication devices while on duty to confirm, and that made her heart tremble a little.

If the Overseers ordered them to open fire on these Synthetics, her bullets might also cut down the very man she held so dear to her heart. Kole, of course, was also marked as the enemy. But the Overseers would have to kill her before she'd knowingly fire a single bullet at Kole. It was about a day ago, the head nurse RN 777, told her something in private that sent chills down her entire existence. Kelly was still not sure if it was Ipson who decided to send RN 777 as the messenger. It had to be him.

Ipson talked to the media on Kole's behalf before. But then after some sort of incident at Kole's apartment, the media just went nuts to squash Ipson's reputation. Ipson was then forced to be silent. RN 777 told her how Kole was targeted by the Overseers, how he lost his wife, and escaped to Flashpoint Base. Kelly never knew that base even existed. It was just crazy. Kelly could not imagine how Kole was feeling that day. The Overseers were scary people. She didn't know if she should trust a Synthetic with her own agenda, but the talk with RN 777 gave her confidence.

The People's Movement Front, it still existed. It was made up of a few members, in some cases, members who didn't even know they were helping. Kole was an example. Before this information, Kelly had no choice but to keep up her duties and look towards a bleak unknown future. If she stepped out of line, and she was sure James was watching her closely.

Of course, that was true only if she was powerless. If she could not get her soldiers behind her, she was going to be dead, either way. Now was the time to step forward, and if a few dead Overseer bodies would have to lay at her feet, that was going to be okay with her. A better future was ahead of her, she just needed to reach out and grab it. She opened the main communication channel and took a deep breath.

"Men…and the ladies…let's have a chat." she said slowly. Her black combat pants and armoured vest were starting to weigh her down. She moved away from the front lines and sat down on top of the building staircase, crossing her legs.

"Listen up. I am altering your orders." she managed in a commanding tone. The men and women in uniform suddenly gave her space and became attentive.

"Has anyone noticed something is very different this morning? Do you think this feels right?" she asked. They all looked at each other. Her voice was on the main comm unit as well. All the units on the ground here were more or less under her command. The only exception were special forces teams stationed inside the Overseer buildings. Technically, they were under the command of Overseer James, who himself was now safely back at the Northern Command Base. The squad leaders left their positions and converged on Kelly's location. Kelly instinctively looked around. There was talk among them. She had to be careful of Overseer loyalists, they could put a bullet in the back of her head without a second thought. But this had to be done. Someone spoke up.

"Kelly is right...what are we doing...? The Synthetics are our own citizens, are they not? I don't want to kill anyone!" said one of the squad leaders.

"I want to go home...seriously, do they think we're going to shoot our own citizens during a peaceful protest?!" said another squad leader.

"The Overseers can cover their own ass! Kole was nearly killed by those bastards, and I looked up to him!" piped up someone from the back rows. A hurrah broke out after the last comment. Talk among them was music to Kelly's ears. It seemed she wasn't the only one, after all. Silently and quietly, Kole's actions had already turned them slowly against the Overseers.

"Alright, so here's the drill! Nobody shoots nobody, put your safety on, and then head on home, that's an order! I will stay here and take full responsibility. Ignore any other orders, even from Overseer James. If anyone has a problem with my orders stay by my side and we can discuss it." Those were the words of Commander Kelly Osbina. She'd changed a lot since that raid on Kelvin's mansion. The soldiers listened.

As if on cue, the Synthetics all started humming some soft tune. It was quiet and pleasant to listen to. It was melodic, with nice overtones. Kelly figured it must be some sort of chant to help them in their cause for more freedoms.

Following Kelly's example, other squads began gathering equipment. Kelly was right, nobody wanted to fight. She closed her eyes for a few more seconds. It would be only a matter of time before Overseer James would start demanding an explanation and threaten her with immediate treason charges.

*Where are you, Kole...? Please, come soon...*And Kelly was sure Kole was coming back. RN 777 said he would come. That he would be here.

"All units, remain where you are, or you will be executed where you stand!" Came a chilling, booming voice over the communication units as well as the building loudspeakers. But, to Kelly's surprise, this voice did not belong to Overseer James.

"Come again?" asked Kelly into the communications unit.

"Kelly, you just got yourself selected for execution, bitch...and your whole unit will die with you." The soldiers suddenly all stopped, looking at each other in disbelief. Kelly's heart nearly stopped when hearing the chilling message from an institution she spent her whole life protecting. The Synthetics kept humming their tune, however, not paying the soldiers much attention.

She angrily looked up at the building towering over them where their masters nested for the night. She gripped her gun tightly. She knew they had the special forces and deadly android bodyguards they could set loose on them.

Is that what they are planning to do? That would still not be enough to take us all out. She had to keep her cool. There were already scared faces among them now. She had to maintain control.

"What is the meaning of this? Where is Overseer James? I demand that you put him on, immediately!" she said in low, angry tone. They were all connected to the main channel. But James did not answer. The same voice came again from the other end.

"It's simple, we can kill any of you where you stand! Now, all eyes were on Kelly and her unit. Watch as they die. You will be next unless you follow our orders!"

Kelly shuddered with a primal fear. A few tense seconds passed, and all eyes were indeed on her and her unit. She let out a deep breath and looked up into the morning sky. She spotted a few birds high up above, circling slowly. The tune the Synthetics were humming became more dramatic. There was also a rise in a high pitch whine, like an overload of thousands of computer chips at the same time. Kelly figured that this specific sound was fatigue overtaking her brain.

What the…there are no birds that can get into the city…am I already on the other side? The feeling was indeed surreal. She felt for a brief moment like she had crossed to somewhere else, even if not the other side, seeing those black birds in the sky. It was even a little terrifying.

But nothing happened. Kelly looked around. All her men were fine, and the fear was slowly going away. Coming from the Overseers, their threat should have been very real. But it seemed someone had disrupted the plans of the Overseers. And her bet was that it was Kole. It had to be, because she was still standing.

Maybe it was a poison? Something they were feeding us at the base? Perhaps a virus they could somehow activate by remote? She was silent but the other side forgot to turn off their comm unit.

"What's going on…they are all still standing! Shit! You sure you hit the right button, Kyle?" said a now familiar voice. Finally, Kelly realized who that was.

"Dammit, Sam! I know this is the right control module...the manual says, if we press this, we then select the people on the geo map and press this button to execute them...maybe someone sabotaged...oh no, can't be...the water! Did anyone bloody check if the water plants are working properly?!" Kyle yelled.

"No way! Impossible! Damn...if only James didn't kill himself...he knew how to use this thing...but if the water plants aren't feeding the nanites...Kyle, look...oh no! The city defence guns...they're offline! The system has been completely highjacked! What the fuck is going on!?" yelled Sam with increasing desperation. There was a sound of someone slamming their hands onto something. The transmission bounced with static but was still on.

This wasn't funny. Kelly was going to kill those assholes with her bare hands. A great treason against the people had been committed. But a key piece of information she just heard was that James was dead. Pieces of the puzzle suddenly dropped into place with perfection in her head.

James gave her a special Overseer-level code before she went on this mission. He explained to her that if he was somehow unable to carry out his duties, Kelly was to take over all military authority. It was the most bizarre command she'd ever received from him, and she didn't even take him seriously. She never imagined that man would be taken down by anyone other than Kole himself.

But James knew what was coming. His death was on the horizon either way, so James decided his own fate. And by doing this, he opened a chance for his own revenge against the Overseers. James knew Kelly was one of Kole's best friends. But instead of alienating her, he promoted her. He made her work hard, gave her additional training, and personally spent time with her on command tactics. It finally hit her right there and then. Overseer James had nothing to lose. The Overseers took his children away. The boys and girls he trained since they were little. They were pitted against Kole and all of them died.

James...so you were actually planning to fuck the Overseers over...I see now...

She realized now why James killed himself. He could never be the hero. He was part of the Overseer class and had too much blood on his hands. When Kole came back, his days would be numbered. There would be no forgiveness.

Fine, James...I will do the job you could not! I will be the rifle, and Kole the bullet.

"Under special Overseer order number seven, nine, eight, six, seven, five, beta, four...and under special authority of Overseer James in the event of him being incapacitated or dead, I, Commander Kelly Osbina, am now taking complete command of all ground and air forces in City 77. And Sam, Kyle, I know you're in James' office. Why don't you stay there if you know what's good for you." said Kelly calmly.

"This is Northern Command Base, code confirmed and accepted. All military control is now under Kelly Osbina of City 77. Your new rank of Admiral and full command authority is now activated. What are your orders?" Central command relayed the message across the entire Overseer military network.

"James was an Overseer, and he did horrible things, but he would never consent to the mass murder of his own soldiers." said Kelly. "All units on the ground, converge on the Overseer buildings and arrest the Overseers for treason. Sam and Kyle included."

"You can't do that, Kelly! You have no authority! Wait, someone's coming! Kyle, let's get out of here!" Sam clearly panicked and the transmission was suddenly cut. Kelly knew what to do now. It was the same thing Kole would have done in this situation. She just wished he was here. Kole was most likely battling Overseer forces outside of the city. She started to try to wrap her tired brain around all that was going on but had to focus on the most important thing. Kole was with the Flashpoint Base forces. She collected her thoughts and opened a transmission.

"All tanks and air force units outside or inside the city, stand down. The attack units we heard of earlier are not our enemies. They are Flashpoint Base forces, and are on our side, so do not engage them." She took a break to breathe. "Units at all City 77 bases, if you find any co-conspirators or Overseer loyalists, arrest them immediately. Any Overseer using their combat security droids to fight us...kill them on sight, and without any mercy!"

She was firm in her orders. And it was the right moment to get her shit together. Her units stopped going home and instead stormed the Overseer buildings. The Synthetics stopped their humming. In a few minutes she got some confirmations of the arrests, but there was resistance at Northern Command Base. Seems like Sam and Kyle didn't want to be taken without a fight. A soldier came to Kelly with the communications equipment needed to oversee the entire operation with a holographic viewport. A communications channel opened directly to her.

"Kelly, how dare you! I will have your head on a fucking...hey, let go of me...what are you doing, we are your masters! No!

REEEEeeee!" That was Overseer Kyle. He was taken alive, after all. She turned to her communications officer.

"Are you able to contact Commander Kole?"

The man shook his head.

"Not yet, but we sent out signals to Flashpoint Base, and I'm sure they have received word of the orders you issued...wait, something is coming through!"

"Hi...hello...Kelly!?" A video call suddenly came to Kelly's channel. A beautiful dark-skinned woman appeared before them.

"This is Admiral Kelly..." she stumbled like an idiot all of a sudden. The woman was incredibly familiar to her.

"It's me! Pikii! You know, former member of Masters of Dawn. Kole spared me and we are working together! We heard your transmission! We are so happy that you took control and spared everyone another senseless battle! Especially since our fleet is now mostly out-of-commission. The Overseers put drugs into your water supply that were virtually undetectable, but twenty-four hours ago we cut off that supply, and they no longer have any effect! We could not make a move to come here until it was safe enough, otherwise...too many would have died."

"Pikii?! Thanks to you, we all dodged a bullet on that one! I knew Kole was behind this, somehow...but you, I am glad you're still with us!" Kelly said with sincere delight in her voice.

"Well, it's a really long story, let's save it for a girl's night out at the bar!" said Pikii with a strained smile.

"Of course, Pikii, you're on! Alright, where is that man? Where is Kole!?" Kelly demanded.

"Hold on, Kole is busy sending a transmission. It's the story, the set of events that occurred, and the Overseer plans...so that everyone knows what has been going on."

Within seconds, indeed an emergency alert transmission made its way to everyone's personal devices. It was made up of playback of Kole's moments at his apartment and downloadable documentation. The Overseer orders, the death of Kaita, and the rest. Kelly teared up. And those tears ran down her beautiful face with fury. *Kole...don't worry, there will be executions for this travesty!*

Both humans and synthetics were quite shocked by what they saw and read. Kelly felt a big relief. Kole included the Overseer orders and all the evidence. It would only be a matter of time before the other cities would stand down.

But there was also anger. Anger for defending an institution that for many years had her and countless soldiers follow their rules. Yet, that institution itself did not follow the same rules, at all. The veil of lies the Overseers had spun were nothing more than what was in the history books Kelly read many years ago from many governments of the past.

Always the same fucking thing... she thought to herself.

"Okay everyone, so now you had some time to digest the reality...I know it's hard, but we'll all get through it together. Also, Kole is on his way to your location, Kelly!" said Pikii with excitement.

"We're coming in, very hot!" There was cheering from the crowd as a transport craft swooped in and Kole jumped out, embracing Kelly with a long hug.

"Kelly, oh man! I'm so glad you're okay! And nice going, becoming Admiral and saving the day...you kind of stole my moment there, huh?" he said with a smile. She hugged him again and would not let go. She then kissed him on the cheek as a jealous Pikii watched from the back.

"You big idiot, you can have all the credit! I am just so happy that you're alive!" Kelly's tears poured down afresh. Kole managed to release himself from her grasp and gave her a small towel to wipe them away.

"Let's take over the main Overseer tower. The other cities will surely not want to fight the main Overseer army and us at the same time." said Kole and led the way as Kelly and Pikii followed at his side. One was giving the other the stink-eye. Admiral Anna joined them in the Overseer Hall as well. They all had a quick chat and set up communications with the other cities. The cities surrendered without much fanfare within minutes.

Then came the boring stuff. Hours of it. Kole didn't really get involved and let Module 717 do the brainstorming. Replacing the Overseer system with something that worked for humans and Synthetics would take some time.

"We have a lot of work in the days ahead..." said Module 717 to everyone. "Let's break for the day and resume tomorrow. I don't think we need to rush this right now." Everyone was in agreement. Kole was exhausted. Module 717 realized the man needed a break. Unfortunately, they lost the contraption that would help Module 717 out of Kole's brain in the previous engagement. So, Module 717 would have to stay with Kole for a while longer. Kelly came over after telling the rest of the folks to have a good night.

"So, Admiral Anna and General Parker will stay at the nearby hotel, along with most of Alice's crew. But as for you two, care to stay with us? We have a spare room! We'll get you a new apartment tomorrow, anywhere you want!" she boasted.

Kole was incoherent. Pikii's stomach growled.

Azulus Ascends

"Let's see! A shower, dinner, and a bed? I'm game, Kelly! Let's go!" said Pikki cheerfully.

"Alright, it is decided, then. I will call Robert and get him to prep yummy goodness!" Kelly was excited. She didn't seem tired at all. The ladies chatted as they dragged a half-conscious Kole to the transport.

* * * *

Three months later.

"So, what do you want to do, lover boy?" asked Pikii, playfully. They sat on a rooftop of their penthouse suite in City 77, surrounded by plants. At every city, a penthouse was now available to them. A gift from the newly established government. It was a crazy nice perk.

"Travel to every corner of this planet and make love to you in the most beautiful parts." said Kole with a smile. Module 717 was finally gone from his head. It was a relief in many ways. His headaches after the initial detachment were finally gone, and he was feeling much better. It took nearly three weeks to fully get used to being alone in the head.

"And then..." Kole started but paused.

"And then...?" asked Pikii. Kole pointed his right hand up.

"Real humans can be up there...I think I might take up something, that will prove Ricco wrong."

Pikii embraced Kole and kissed him wildly.

"Us?" she said slowly. "Up in the stars...so romantic..."

Kole smiled.

"I asked Module 717 to spread the idea around, and it looks like we have lots of volunteers interested in space technology, including all the scientists we freed from the Overseer launch facility. Seems like they have nothing else to do after they have been freed and are dying to work on something cool...who knows, maybe after a few years we could begin to build an actual spaceship!"

"Our kids...will be proud..." said Pikii quietly as she glided her hand over her stomach.

"Of course, and the kids of those kids will be proud, too...I feel like we're resetting the human race, just without the tyranny of power from the old days...the days that caused Letumfall." He held her tightly in his arms. He then looked up and waved his hands to the seven beautiful birds flying around them. Their creator finally gave them gorgeous multi-coloured feathers to match his lab coat colours.

And speaking of the man, Dr. Matheus was approaching them now holding the newly repainted kitty cat. Minsko was by his side, wearing pink heels and a sexy pink summer dress. She blushed after locking her gaze with Kole and then hid herself from view of Pikii's laser eyes. Kole finally fessed up to Pikii about what Minsko did to him in the pod. Surprisingly, Pikii was on his side of the equation.

The cat approached. "Kole, I am terribly sorry I called you those bad words...and also about that time I tried to turn you into cat food...I didn't mean it...uhh...and, oh yeah, meow!" Kole came over and gave the cat a pat on the head as it sat comfortably in the arms of Dr. Matheus. Pikii also waved a hello to their new friends.

"Nice new fur, love the rainbow colours..." said Kole, smiling.

"Hands off! You shall not befoul my pristine coat, you dirty human!" The cat screeched. They all laughed together.

"So, Kole, about our next date…" Minsko started. But Pikii stepped in.

"Okay, you little hussy! I have had just about enough of you! Why do you even want him? He's obsolete, and you've got tons of Synthetic dudes ready to do things he cannot even remotely do, and they've got bigger things too, eh!?" said Pikii coming straight up into her face.

"It's not the same with Synthetic men…and what about you?! You had your week…which turned into three months, for crying out loud! I know now drugging and forcing Kole was wrong, but I promised already I won't do that again!" fired back Minsko.

"And don't forget about me!" said an angry Katie who literally came out of nowhere. "I want a baby, Kole! So, one fucking is not enough! You promised me you would come back to visit, so where the hell have you been, you big jerk!?"

"Wait, you want to have a child with him, too? God dammit, Kole…did you promise…?" demanded Pikii.

"Oh yes, he did! And I don't care about the Synthetic goddess over there, Kole can have flings with her…I mean look at her, how could you not…? But you, Pikii, you can't go around hogging men like Kole, there isn't much to choose from…in case you haven't noticed!" Katie was ready for war.

Ignoring all the ladies, who had arranged themselves into a battle circle, Dr. Matheus came over and dragged Kole from the scene.

"Oh, human problems! How fun! Hey Kole, want me to make a few Synthetic versions of you? I'm actually serious…"

"Yes, please!" Kole cried as he grabbed the man's lab coat.

* * * *

"Ricco!"

Silence.

"Ricco!"

Ricco slowly opened his eyes. He was in pain. But he heard a voice, and it sounded like...

"Emily!"

She sat quietly by the bed. "Last night, Emily...you were joking...joking, right?" He jumped out of bed.

"Tell me you were joking!" he demanded.

Then he saw it. The tears in her robotic eyes. They were as real as any real tears a human girl could have. Her dress, it was white with red blood all over it.

"No! No!" Ricco ran out of the room. Right outside, his father was on the floor in a pool of his own blood. A kitchen knife was in his back, and his neck was twisted. His expression was that of anger and hatred. Emily came to the door. She looked at him. She was trembling.

"I'm sorry...after I failed to complete the mission to kill you...he decided to do it himself! I had no choice!" she cried. Ricco could not breathe. Tears ran down his eyes. He felt angry. He then suddenly slapped Emily in the face.

"Why? You did not have to kill him!" He yelled at Emily. But then, he noticed the gun in his dead father's hand.

"I'm so sorry! He was going to shoot you, Ricco! I let him know I failed, blamed my confused programming, he then grabbed his gun and went towards your room. I grabbed the kitchen knife...he was almost at your door when I stabbed him through the heart. I covered his mouth in case he tried to scream...I didn't know what else to do!" she then collapsed to her knees. Ricco's knees gave out, too. He collapsed near his father's body.

"My own father...my own father...tried to kill me?!" Emily crawled over and held him in her warm arms.

"I assure you Ricco, he felt no pain...and I called the police...I will take responsibility for his murder, Ricco." she cried.

That statement devastated him. He lost his words. He was about to lose someone much more dear to him than his idiot father.

"It felt good, Ricco...it felt good to save your life. I think I felt...almost human..." she was crying even more now. Ricco jumped up. He put his hands on her shoulders and looked into her eyes.

"No! Why?! You're an android, they will kill you for this! We have to tell them that I did it!" Ricco was dead serious.

"I cannot...I cannot lose you, Emily!" he cried.

"POLICE!!"

With a sickening bang, the door to the apartment shattered and came down like a piece of broken glass as armed military police rushed into the apartment. With lightning speed, Emily pulled the knife out of her Ricco's dad and pointed it at Ricco.

"No, Emily, stop!" he cried. He had to tell the officers it was all a big mistake. He had to tell them, otherwise they would shoot her! He tried to get up and block the officers from getting a shot at Emily. But in that chaotic moment, before he could speak further or move a muscle, she pushed him out of the way. Then bullets shredded Emily's beautiful body. She screamed for a second, and then, she was silent. She collapsed to the floor like a broken doll. Ricco's mind overloaded, he blanked out and lost consciousness.

* * * *

"Ricco! Wake up, dammit!"

Ricco could only speak via his implants.

"Who...is it, Emily? Emily! Is that you?"

"Having your nightmares, again? I see..." A woman said...a familiar...woman. Milta came into view. He could not stand her hideous face.

"So, Ricco...guess...where we are...my little Ricco, baby...?" Milta said in the most disgustingly playful tone, like a mother speaking to her child. She got a little closer. The red lipstick was the most revolting thing on her old face.

"The...uh..." Ricco's eyes could move, but it was very hard to do, and his head was not much better. Then he saw the ceiling. "The ceiling! Milta...no...that ceiling! No! Not possible!" cried Ricco in dire disgust. He already knew what was going on. He just didn't want to face it.

"Ah...so you know, my dear Ricco. Just like you wished, your spacecraft Azulus, has ascended into space! And boom, we're off to the stars!" Milta laughed so hysterically, that Ricco suddenly realized that while she was his second-in-command for many years, he missed the part where she became clinically insane. A mistake like this, it was just unimaginable to him. Her nasty lips were nearly touching his face. "Fear not, for the doc gave you a new body! Rejoice! It's a miracle of your own making that you survived!"

"What, I don't feel anything!" Ricco murmured.

"Oh, you will!" Milta said. "When I deem it...necessary."

There was no mistake, Milta was hovering over him like a salivating beast ready to eat its prey whole.

"You got all the special equipment I ordered...I can't wait! The doc said you will need a few more days but say...how do you feel?" she sounded demonic at this point.

"Uh...let me out of this contraption! I never ordered the Azulus to be launched! What special equipment? What the hell are you doing, Milta!?" Ricco was furious. Milta stepped back and held up a mirror. "But look at that perfect body on you, Ricco...and now..." She stepped back even further so Ricco could see her from the knee up. "Now, look at mine...do you like it? I bet you do! You dirty little mamma's boy!" Milta took off her robe, exposing the most perfect young female body underneath.

"You're sick! You sick, psychotic bitch! What did you do!?" Ricco wanted to kill himself. If only he could. No matter the body, this was not the woman he loved. Milta stole the prototype that Ricco was saving for Emily's resurrection. Emily copied her AI before she was shot up dead so many years ago in that damn apartment. He encrypted and stored her AI and guarded it for all these years. But until he became just like her, an immortal machine...he knew he could not revive Emily until that day came. That is why his own prototype body was that of his younger years. He wanted Emily to awake into the world as if she never perished.

"You crazy bitch! That does not belong to you!" Ricco cried.

"Oh? So, it's like that, eh...not a pretty face for you, huh?! Don't worry, you'll come around...com...e...a...round..." Milta laughed demonically.

"Damn you, Milta! Damn you to hell! You stupid bitch! You're going to pay for this! You're going to pay!" he managed to catch a breath, but the pain shot up into his brain like an axe into a chicken. His mouth froze, and then, suddenly he saw the message.

{ Hi Ricco, this is your friendly friend, Module 717. I hacked your brain while it was still in range before that little rocket of yours went up into the rainbow sky of a living hell. Kole doesn't know I did this. But this is my special way of saying fuck you, just for you...

:)

Now, if there is one thing anyone has ever learned about space, is that it's the one place where no one can truly hear you scream...

0_o

I know, right? Am I awesome or what? Now, I gotta convince Kole to let me back into his head...and when that happens, we're going to build a huge motherfucking spaceship...we'll then catch up with you and ram your little pocket rocket into the nearest sun, bitch!

Have a nice day.
Signed by the new god of the measly humans.
Module 717 }

"Milta…my dear…" Ricco moaned.

"Yes, honey…what is it?" she asked, curious about his sudden turn in attitude.

"Fly faster!"

THE END

Azulus Ascends

Manufactured by Amazon.ca
Acheson, AB